Critical Acclaim for Rut
and *All Over Creat*

"[Ozeki] is a gifted storyteller."
—*Los Angeles Times Book Review*

"Ruth Ozeki is bent on taking the novel into corners of American culture no one else has thought to look—but where she finds us in all our transcultural and technological weirdness. With a combination of humor and pathos that is all her own, *All Over Creation* brings the American pastoral forward into the age of agribusiness and genetic engineering. The result is a smart and compelling novel about a world we don't realize we live in."
—Michael Pollan, author of *The Botany of Desire*

"Ozeki joins the constellation of such environmentally aware writers as Barbara Kingsolver, Annie Proulx and Margaret Atwood, bringing her own shrewd and playful humor, luscious sexiness and kinetic pizzazz to the table, as well her keen interest in the interface between food, family, science and corporate greed, and the dynamics of spin . . . Ozeki nimbly switches points of view throughout this busy, darkly humorous and cunningly entertaining novel, weaving canny psychological insights into each twist in her purposeful yet anarchically tinged plot. Moving neatly between the intimate and the environmental, the familial and the global, Ozeki hones each vivid description, witty conversation and surprising occurrence to illuminate the complex dichotomies between love and responsibility, nature and culture, traditional and corporate agriculture, fact and fabrication."
—*Chicago Tribune*

"Ozeki deftly and sensitively folds the variegated topics together, whipping up a savory treat."
—*Entertainment Weekly*

"A triumph that earns its inclusive title. *All Over Creation* naturally and joyfully folds concerns about genetically modified organisms into a powerful family drama set in rural Idaho. . . . Ozeki's skill at weaving these together is extraordinary . . . Ozeki has created a novel at once educational and entertaining, with multidimensional characters and an engaging narrative voice. It will appeal to anyone interested in love or agriculture or politics or family drama or friendship or childhood or the earth. In short, its appeal is as wide as the creation it champions."

—*San Francisco Chronicle*

"*All Over Creation* opens wider with every plot twist as it moves from tenderness to comedy to sobering truth and the whole world in the eye of one family's storm. This is Edward Abbey's *The Monkey Wrench Gang* updated by thirty years, with modern environmental challenges on the map and women in the front seat, driving the story. Hooray—Ruth Ozeki rides again."

—Barbara Kingsolver, author of *The Poisonwood Bible*

"Ruth Ozeki is the Bob Ross of literary fiction, full of quirky glee and a love for purity in her work and the world . . . [Ozeki] is an assured and talented writer, whose filmmaking background gives a cinematic sheen to *All Over Creation* that most PBS shows, not to mention most decent fiction, couldn't hope to pull off. Despite the big-book trappings and Ozeki's skill, though, the author's most notable trait is a generous comedic and natural spirit."

—*Ruminator Review*

"Ozeki's latest takes on the politics of food with even more ferocity and panache. It's a hyperactive farce but also a serious meditation on crossbreeding (people and plants) . . . *All Over Creation* resembles a Robert Altman film, all the characters bustling in their own orbits until they gracefully veer into each other . . . its joviality—the very thing that makes it such a fun read—leaves one feeling like nothing real's at stake, which couldn't be further from the truth."

—*The Village Voice*

"Rare is the book that succeeds as indoctrination or instruction, while at the same time delivering indelible characters, pitch-perfect dialogue, wholly involving plot. Rare is a call to action delivered in supple, enduring prose. Ruth Ozeki's second novel, *All Over Creation*, stands among that elite handful of books that both teach and inspire, chide and appease. . . . This novel is a tour de force—structurally sophisticated, conceptually

sound, well-rooted in a concern for both people and the earth."
—*The Baltimore Sun*

"This winning novel from the author of *My Year of Meats* is a feast of humor and wisdom about family and friendship."
—*Glamour*

"A rare novel whose prose is as solid as its politics."
—*The Philadelphia Inquirer*

"Beautiful . . . vast and lifelike . . . a modern epic"
—*The Boston Globe*

"A multidimensional, timely and entertaining novel."
—*Boston Herald*

"Ozeki handles all this with a winning mixture of wit and tenderness. It's a jungle of a plot, a riot of literary species, sown with strains of deadly satire and heartrending tragedy—winding around kitchen table discussions about family duty and through the international debate on genetically modified food. She's as good with the broad comedy of wacky political protests as she is with the terrifying ramifications of genetic manipulation . . . But even after growing all over creation, Ozeki returns to her roots: the love between parents and children."
—*The Christian Science Monitor*

"In this scampish, rather touching romp of a novel, Ruth Ozeki strikes a tone somewhere between Michael Pollan, Jane Smiley, Amy Tan, and Carl Hiaasen. *All Over Creation* is the best book I've ever read about potatoes, and it's also good on what Saul Bellow called 'potato love'—the kind that thrives in close, unpretentious families."
—*Seattle Weekly*

"This quirky novel is bewitching . . . Ozeki's story splices a bit of Edward Abbey into an Anne Tyler plot. The fruits of this mix are definitely worth tasting." —*Publishers Weekly* (starred review)

"A wise and witty morality tale."
                    —*Seattle Post-Intelligencer*

"*All Over Creation* juggles politics with comedy, family struggles and romance gone awry. Through multiple points of view, Ozeki swirls around hot-button farming issues, circling in search of steady moral ground."
                    —*The Oregonian* (Portland)

"Readers who appreciate strong female Asian American protagonists like those in works by Lois-Ann Yamanaka will find this novel engrossing. Highly recommended."
                    —*Library Journal*

"Ozeki's characters are utterly charming, and she writes with sensitivity and inventiveness about the complexities of love and nature, deftly humanizing the thorny issues raised by biotechnology with humor and panache in a tale rich in suspense and pathos."
                    —*Booklist* (starred review)

"A feast for mind and heart."
                    —*Kirkus Reviews* (starred review)

"Ruth Ozeki is a writer of great passion and purpose. She fearlessly tackles big issues, stirs up revolutions, and unveils truths with keen insight and humor that touches our hearts and opens our minds."
                    —Gail Tsukiyama, author of *The Samurai's Garden*

"*All Over Creation* is a wholly original novel of amazing richness, a tapestry of zany characters who follow their own hearts and passions. With a natural storyteller's ability to communicate both the hilarious and profound, Ozeki writes about love and sex, bioengineering and social responsibility, deftly communicating her uncanny feel for the texture of contemporary American life."
                    —Paula Sharp, author of *Crows Over a Wheatfield*

PENGUIN BOOKS

ALL OVER CREATION

Ruth Ozeki, author of the award-winning novel *My Year of Meats*, worked for more than a decade in television and film. Her documentary and dramatic films have been shown on PBS, at the Sundance Film Festival, and at colleges and universities across the country. She divides her time between New York City and British Columbia.

www.ruthozeki.com

To request Penguin Readers Guides by mail (while supplies last), please call (800) 778-6425 or e-mail reading@us.penguingroup.com. To access Penguin Readers Guides online, visit our Web site at www.penguin.com.

ALL
OVER
CREATION

RUTH OZEKI

PENGUIN BOOKS

PENGUIN BOOKS

Published by the Penguin Group

Penguin Group (USA) Inc., 375 Hudson Street, New York, New York 10014, U.S.A.

Penguin Books Ltd, 80 Strand, London WC2R 0RL, England

Penguin Books Australia Ltd, 250 Camberwell Road, Camberwell, Victoria 3124, Australia

Penguin Books Canada Ltd, 10 Alcorn Avenue, Toronto, Ontario, Canada M4V 3B2

Penguin Books India (P) Ltd, 11 Community Centre, Panchsheel Park,
    New Delhi – 110 017, India

Penguin Books (N.Z.) Ltd, Cnr Rosedale and Airborne Roads, Albany,
    Auckland, New Zealand

Penguin Books (South Africa) (Pty) Ltd, 24 Sturdee Avenue, Rosebank,
    Johannesburg 2196, South Africa

Penguin Books Ltd, Registered Offices:
80 Strand, London WC2R 0RL, England

First published in the United States of America by Viking 2003
Published in Penguin Books 2004

10 9 8 7 6 5 4 3 2

PUBLISHER'S NOTE
This is a work of fiction. Names, characters, places, and incidents either are the product
of the author's imagination or are used fictitiously, and any resemblance to actual persons,
living or dead, business establishments, events, or locales is entirely coincidental.

ISBN 0-670-03091-0 (hc.)
ISBN 0 14 20.0389 1 (pbk.)
CIP data available

Printed in the United States of America
Set in Garamond Light with Phaistos display
Designed by Carla Bolte

for my father,

who was always kind

ALL
OVER
CREATION

first

Esto Perpetua
("May It Be Forever")

—Idaho state motto

in the beginning ℬↄ

It starts with the earth. How can it not? Imagine the planet like a split peach, whose pit forms the core, whose flesh its mantle, and whose fuzzy skin its crust—no, that doesn't do justice to the crust, which is, after all, where all of life takes place. The earth's crust must be more like the rind of the orange, thicker and more durable, quite unlike the thin skin of a bruisable peach. Or is it? Funny, how you never think to wonder.

On one small section of that crust—small, that is, by global or geologic measure—in Power County, Idaho, where the mighty Snake River carved out its valley and where volcanic ash enriched the soil with minerals vital to its tilth, there stretched a vast tract of land known as Fuller Farms.

Vast, by human scale. Vast, relative to other farmers' holdings in the region, like the Quinns' place down the road. And as for the description, "land belonging," well that's a condition measured in human time, too. But for one quick blip in the 5 billion years of life on this earth, that three thousand acres of potato-producing topsoil and debatably the slender cone of the planet that burned below, right down to the rigid center of its core, belonged to my father, Lloyd Fuller.

It used to be the best topsoil around. Used to be feet of it, thick, loamy. There's less of it now. But still, imagine you are a seed—of an apple, or a melon, or even the pit of a peach—spit from the lips of one of Lloyd's crossbred grandchildren, arcing through the air and falling to earth, where you are ground into the soil, under a heel, to rest and overwinter. Months pass, and it is cold and dark. Then slowly, slowly, spring creeps in, the sun tickles the earth awake again, its warmth thaws the soil, and your coat,

3

which has protected you from the winter frosts, now begins to crack. Oh, so tentatively you send a threadlike root to plumb the ground below, while overhead your pale shoot pushes up through the sedentary mineral elements (the silt, the sand, the clay), through the teeming community of microfauna (bacteria and fungi, the algae and the nematodes), past curious macrofauna (blind moles, furry voles, and soft, squirming earthworms). This is life in the Root Zone, nudging your tendril toward the warmth of the sunny sun sun.

And then imagine the triumphant moment when you crack the crumbly crust, poke your wan and wobbling plumule head through the surface and start to unfurl—imagine, from your low and puny perspective, how vast Lloyd Fuller's acreage must look to you now.

Of course, during most of his tenure and the decades that followed, these three thousand acres were given over primarily to the planting of potatoes, which means that you, being a random seedling, a volunteer, an accidental fruit, will most likely be uprooted. Just as you turn your face into the rays and start to respire, maybe even spread out a leaf or two and get down to the business of photosynthesizing—*grrrrrip,* weeded right out of there. Sayonara, baby.

That's what it felt like when I was growing up, like I was a random fruit in a field of genetically identical potatoes. Burbanks—that's what people planted. Centuries of cross-pollination, human migration, plant mutation, and a little bit of backyard luck had resulted in the pride of Idaho, the world's best baker, the Russet Burbank. From one side of the state to the other spread a glorious monoculture of these large, white, long-bodied tubers with rough, reticulated skin, high in solids content with a mealy texture when cooked and a pleasing potatoey flavor.

Honestly, I never liked potatoes much. I preferred rice, a taste I inherited from my mother, Momoko, and which, in a state of spuds, was tantamount to treason. Momoko used to make me rice balls, the size of fingerlings, to take to school in my lunch box. Lloyd called them "Tokyo tubers"—this was his idea of a joke—and when I was a little girl, I thought it was pretty funny, too. I used to look forward to lunchtime, opening my plastic Barbie box, where, nestled next to a slice of meat loaf or ham, I'd find the two little *o-musubi* sitting neatly side by side. They tasted faintly salty, like Momoko's small hands. If the other kids thought my lunch was queer, they didn't say much, because Lloyd Fuller had more acres, and thus more potatoes, than almost any other farmer in Power County, and I was Yummy, his only child.

No one said much either when Lloyd brought my mom home from Japan after the war, at least not to his face. Just that she was the cutest thing they had ever seen, so delicate and fragile looking, like a china doll, and how was she ever going to handle the work of running a farm? But she did. Lloyd had inherited five hundred acres, adjacent to the Quinns' place and up from where the Snake River was dammed, and he and Momoko rolled up their sleeves and went to work. People used to smile, call them Mutt and Jeff, because Lloyd was one of the tallest men in Power County and Momoko bought her work clothes in the little boys' department at Sears. You can imagine the two of them, standing in the fields, side by side, Lloyd as tall as a runner bean stalk and Momoko barely coming up to his buckle. Dressed in jeans turned up at the cuff and hanging from her shoulders by suspenders, she looked like Lloyd's son instead of his wife. The son they never had. After twelve years of trying, they had me instead—named me Yumi, only nobody in Liberty Falls could say it right. *Yummy, yummy, yummy, I got love in my tummy*. People said I was the apple of Lloyd's eye, the pride of his heart, until I went rotten.

As it turned out, Momoko was a born gardener, or, as Cassie Quinn's mom used to put it, "She may be yeller, but her thumb sure is green." Maybe this was meant to be a compliment, and we all took it that way. Over the years Momoko's kitchen garden grew into a vegetative wonder, and she planted varieties of fruits and flowers that no one had ever seen before in Power County. I remember her whispering to her pea vines as they curled their way up her trellises: *"Gambatte ne, tané-chan!"* "Be strong, my little seedling!" People drove for miles to see her Oriental ornamentals and Asian creepers. Their massy inflorescence burst into bloom in the spring and stayed that way throughout summer and deep into the fall. It was truly exotic.

Momoko must have been proud of Fuller Farms, in the early days. Lloyd surely was. In the first years of their marriage, they battled droughts and early freezes, mildews and viruses and parasites, and a host of pests that nobody could imagine why God had even bothered to create:

Seedcorn maggots, leatherjackets, and millipedes.

Thrips and leafhoppers.

False cinch bugs, blister beetles, and two-spotted spider mites.

Hornworms, wireworms, white grubs, and green peach aphids, not to mention corky ringspot . . .

And, most dreadful of all, the rapacious Colorado potato beetle.

All these creatures were dealt with, and thank God for science.

"Insect infestations are one of the greatest threats to the production of high-quality tubers," Lloyd used to say in the introduction to the speech that he gave every year to the Young Potato Growers of Idaho. "It is crucial to plan the applications of pesticides to harmonize with seasonable cultural practices."

"Seasonable cultural practices"—how he liked the sound of that! I remember him practicing the phrase, standing in front of the mirror in the bathroom, and when I stood there and looked at my reflection, I would practice saying it, too. Fuller Farms seemed living proof to us all that with the cooperation of God and science, and the diligent application of seasonable cultural practices, man could work in harmony with nature to create a relationship of perfect symbiotic mutualism. The first five hundred acres had grown to a holding of three thousand by the time I turned fourteen.

That was 1974, the year Nixon resigned, the year Patty Hearst was kidnapped and Evel Knievel attempted his historic leap across the Snake River Canyon on a rocket-powered motorcycle. But most important of all, it was the year of the Nine-Dollar Potato.

Consider the economics. Year after year you teeter along in a stable 'tater market, breaking even at $3.50 per hundred pounds of premium grade. When the price goes up to $4.00, you make a little, when it goes down to $3.00, you lose a little, but generally you fall in the balance and scrape by. Then, out of the blue, nature blesses you by cursing others. She sends an early frost to Maine, too much rain to California—1974 was certainly an odd year for weather, everywhere except Idaho. The failure of the nation's crops, combined with the explosive demand for french fries created by the burgeoning fast-food market, resulted in a potato shortage that sent prices rocketing into the clear blue heavens. Across the country, housewives who paid $1.29 for a ten-pound bag last year were now paying $2.39, and all of this translated into an unheard-of, unbelievable bonanza, the $9.00 per hundredweight that made my father a rich, albeit flabbergasted, farmer.

So there was Lloyd, in his prime, a Depression-born agriculturalist exercising pride in his new capitalist muscle. *And who gives a flying fuck what happened after that?* That's what you would have thought anyway, if you were me, on a predawn winter morning in 1974, stuffing your clothes and diary into your father's army duffel, lifting the keys to his pickup truck from the hook in the kitchen, and creeping down the porch stairs, out into the frigid night, careful not to slam the door behind you.

cass

Every year in November, as Thanksgiving approached, Cass Quinn would find herself wondering about Yummy Fuller. There was a reason for this. When they were growing up, Liberty Falls Elementary School put on a yearly Pilgrims' Pageant. It was supposed to represent a big feast, and every kid had to play a different food in it. Cassie had started out as a pea. Up through the third grade she was content in this role, but by the time she got to fourth, she had gained so much weight they made her a potato. She said it was fine, said really she didn't mind—that's just the kind of girl she was—but inside she minded a lot. You'd think in Idaho playing the potato wouldn't be so bad—in fact, might even be an honor, but it wasn't. Everyone knew that the side dishes were typecast. The carrot was a tall redhead named Rusty. The green beans were a pair of skinny twins. The cherry tomato went to a rosy second-grader with shiny cheeks. The corn was a tawny kid named Kellogg. Face it. What is a potato? A potato is a fat, round, dumpy white thing, wrapped in burlap, rolling around on a dirty stage.

Some kids never had to be vegetables at all. Some kids got to be human beings—Pilgrims or Indians—and eat the rest of the kids for dinner.

Like Yummy Fuller. As Cass recalled it, Yummy was always the Indian princess, even in first grade, when everybody else in their class was still playing gravy.

"Noble Pilgrims," Princess Yummy used to say, "my people and I welcome you to our land. We know that your journey has been a hard one, and we will help you. Pray, take our seeds and plant them—"

It wasn't like they didn't have real Indians in school. They did. But back then even the Shoshone kids didn't seem to mind, or maybe they just knew

7

better than to care. Year after year Yummy's lines stayed the same, while slowly she grew into her role. Tall and slim, wearing love beads, a buckskin miniskirt, and a headband with a jaunty hawk feather stuck in the back— by the time she entered ninth grade, Yummy made a luscious ambassador.

"Pray, take our seeds and plant them—"

From her position, curled on the dusty stage in her burlap sack, Cass listened to Yummy recite her lines and tried not to sneeze.

That year Yummy started wearing peasant blouses to school, and hip-hugging jeans that she'd turned into bell-bottoms with wedges of upholstery fabric. Sometimes she wore a gold dot, the kind you stick on filing folders, in the middle of her forehead. "It's my third eye," she told Cass. "It's called a *bindi*. Indians wear them."

Cass didn't recall any of the Shoshone kids with filing dots on their faces, and she said so. Yummy rolled her eyes. "*Real* Indians. The ones from *India*."

She would lean against the mailboxes at the end of their road, smoking an Old Gold Filter. They used to meet there after dinner when the summer sun lingered at the edge of the fields, low in the sky. Dump their bikes in the dirt at the side of the road and smoke, while the sun's oblique rays stretched their shadows out long. Cass used to love her summer shadow. Even next to Yummy's it was tall and slim, with legs that just went on and on forever.

It was safe there at the crossroads. The fields spread out in all directions, as far as the eye could see, some dark green with potatoes, some light green with wheat. There was nobody around, and if someone did show up, you could see them coming for miles by the dust they raised. Plenty of time to stub out a butt and flick it into the field, unless it was a truckload of Mexican farmhands, in which case you usually didn't bother. Yummy would squint at Cass and offer up the cigarette, filter first, and Cass would take it between her thumb and forefinger, narrow her eyes, and drag deep. Then she'd hand it back the same way. When the sun set, taking her shadow with it, she'd sit on a large chunk of black stone at Yummy's feet. They'd continue to smoke until the tip of the cigarette glowed red against the indigo sky. Yummy would take a foot out of her sneaker—she'd stopped wearing socks that summer—and place it, storklike, against the inside of her thigh. It's a yoga pose, she told Cass. Her bare feet were long and slender. She wore a silver ring on her second toe, where dirt collected.

Cass had a brainload of pictures like that, even now, twenty-five years later.

ℬↃ

"You don't have to keep on with it," Will said. "If it gets too much."

He was sitting at the table with his morning coffee, looking over some specs on seed potatoes for the spring. He put down the pages and watched as she bundled up a few eggs, still warm from the chickens, tucking them in next to a bread loaf.

Cassie shrugged. "Jeez, Will. What *else* do I have to do with my day?" The sarcasm was lost on him.

"There's always plenty to do around a farm—"

Cass straightened her back, rotating her fists into her kidneys. She eyed her husband, the stolid, broad-shouldered bulk of him, and tried to breathe away impatience. Of course there was plenty to do. Too much. There always had been, and ever since she and Will had bought up the last of Fuller's acres, and she'd taken on the old man and his crazy wife, there was more to do than ever.

Cass sighed and went back to her packing, slipping a small jar of preserves in with the loaf. It wasn't worth the breathing for an answer.

Will knew when he'd got something wrong. "I didn't mean to criticize," he said, catching her wrist as she passed. "It's real sweet of you to look after them."

That's right, thought Cass. She looked down at his wide face. His hair was pulled back tight into a blond ponytail and fastened with a rubber band. She gave it a tug, then bent to plant a kiss on the top of his head. I *am* sweet. Why not? You could always count on Will to find the good in things. But if this was comfort, it quickly passed. Because it wasn't just about sweet, although some sweetness did enter into it. Curiosity? Pity? Cass pulled away and went back to her packing. Resignation. Too many years spent as a potato.

"Maybe you should write to that daughter of theirs," Will said. "Tell her she has to come home."

"Sure thing." Never mind that she hadn't heard a word from Yummy in close to twenty-five years, or had any idea where she lived. "That'll make her hop right to." She gave Will a look as she headed out the door. "You don't know Yummy Fuller."

9

"Yummy, yummy, yummy, I got love in my tummy,
And I feel like a-lovin' you. . . ."

It was her theme song. You could almost hear it playing in the corridors at school when she walked by. Pigtails swinging. It stuck in your head. Cass could still catch its boppy little melody on the cold fall wind. She swung her basket onto the passenger's seat of the Suburban and set off down the road.

The screen door at the Fullers' house had slumped off its hinges, and the mesh was clogged. The aluminum was dull and spotted with age. The old Japanese woman shuffled through the kitchen. She peered up through the dirty screen.

"Yes? May I hel-pu you?" After fifty years in Idaho she still spoke with the deliberateness of a foreigner, carefully pronouncing words, lining them up one after another, and launching them tentatively into the air.

"Hi, Momoko. It's me, Cassie. Can I come in?"

The old woman backed away from the door and held it open.

"Yes. Plee-su."

All the lamps in the house were off, and the shades were drawn. Cass set the basket of food on the kitchen table and yanked the cord on the roll-up blinds, letting in the cold, dim light of the morning. The plastic blinds were torn in places and patched with Scotch tape that had turned yellow and brittle. She could hear Momoko saying something in Japanese behind her. She talked to herself, always had.

Cass looked around. "Did you and Lloyd have breakfast?" she asked, hoping to see crumbs on the counter or dishes in the sink, some sign that a meal had been eaten, but the kitchen looked barren, like a dusty exhibit in a wax museum that no one visited anymore. It was the labels. Lloyd had written them out in black marker on index cards and taped them to the furniture and the various appliances. TOASTER, read one. MR. COFFEE, read another. Momoko was forgetting the names of things. Cass went to the REFRIGERATOR and took out a macaroni casserole she'd left a few days before. Some of the cheese had been picked off the top, but mostly it had not been touched. The old woman watched.

"You want to play with Yumi-chan? Maybe she is in her room. I call her."

A bad day for Momoko, Cass thought. The woman was having more and more of them, days that dissolved backward, dragging Cass with her until she could almost believe she was six years old with pigtails and had come over to play. It was the air in the house. Smelled funny. Maybe a gas leak? No, not gas. Something unpleasant. She opened a window.

"Mrs. Fuller, didn't you fix your supper last night?"

Momoko nodded her head. "Oh, yes, thank you very much."

"What did you have?"

She blinked, slid her eyes from side to side behind her glasses, looking for clues. She pointed to the casserole dish in Cassie's hands.

"I make that one. Nice whatchamacallit. Lloyd's favorite." She nodded.

Cass took the lid off the macaroni casserole and showed it to Momoko.

"Yes," Momoko agreed, looking in. "Pot roast. He like it very much. He is meat-and-potatoes kinda guy."

Cass sighed. "Good for you. I'm glad you had a nice supper. Now, how about some breakfast?"

"Okay. I go upstairs to call Yumi."

"I don't think Yummy's here, Mrs. Fuller. Why don't you go up and get Lloyd? See if he wants to come down for breakfast?"

"Okay," said Momoko. "Then you go out and play."

The old woman shuffled from the room. Cass poached up some eggs and heated water for coffee. She sliced the bread, annoyed with herself for forgetting to buy Wonder. The crusts of her home-baked loaves were too hard for Lloyd. She had seen him struggling one day, sucking on the crust to soften it and then mashing it between his gums. She was out of the habit of store-bought since Will had gotten her the bread machine for Christmas several years back, when potato prices were up. What she'd wanted was a new oven. What she'd really wanted was a whole new kitchen, but that was another story.

She heard Momoko upstairs, talking to her husband. He wasn't bedridden, but he liked to take his time getting up. Mornings were difficult. It was hard for him to get downstairs, and he liked it when Cass could give him a hand.

"You're a big, strong girl," he joked. "Momoko's too small. She'll just buckle. Look! I'm afraid I've bent her in half already!"

"Ooooooh, he is so big man!" Momo said, slapping him. "I carry him all the time on my back! How you say? Like on back of piggy? See? He make me crooked all over!"

Sometimes the three of them could share a laugh.

"You so old man!" Momoko would scold him. "How you get so old?" And Lloyd would smile. "How'd you get so pretty?"

Sometimes it wasn't so bad.

"Breakfast is ready!" Cass called. "Lloyd, do you need a hand?"

She walked to the foot of the stairs in the living room and waited. The room was still and close. It was a nice room and had potential, but it would have to be entirely redone. She rubbed the shiny banister. She could still hear Momoko, muttering upstairs.

"Lloyd?" she called again.

The heavy curtains shut out the morning sun, except for a single shaft of light that shot through the gap where the fabric panels didn't quite meet in the middle. The light touched the air, made it substantial, made it come to life with motes and particles, flying things. Maybe it was the tilt of the shaft, but Cass felt the room shift, no longer familiar. She held on to the banister. Probably just hunger, she hadn't had her own breakfast yet. Still, there was a feeling.

The light came to rest on a dusty horsehair love seat. She had a history with that chair. The last time she'd sat there, feeling oversize, was a year ago, when she and Will signed the last of the documents that Duggin had brought over for the closing. Lloyd sat across from them, sunk deep in his ancient recliner. Momoko had brought them all coffee in stained cups, then joined them, sitting on a small, hard-backed chair, her worn flip-flops dangling a few inches from the floor.

"My colon this time," Lloyd told the lawyer. "Cancer. Nipped it in the bud, but they took out close to a foot of the darn thing. Have to wear a contraption now."

He paused, contemplating his breached innards, then continued, with something like pride. "Always thought my heart would kill me. Never expected this—"

He looked around for confirmation, but no one would agree, or even answer. No one would say, *Yes Lloyd, it sure is funny.* Or, *Absolutely right, Lloyd, with a trigger heart like yours.* Will was looking down at his lap. Duggin was aligning the edges of the contract of sale. Cass stroked the upholstery on the arm of the love seat. She found a hard bit lodged in the nap and worried it with her fingernail. The silence was long, until she broke it.

"You're doing great, Lloyd," she said, too late to be quite convincing. She'd had a run-in with cancer herself, so she could sympathize, but while she was doing great, she knew he wasn't. Recently she had taken over helping him with his colon bags, too. His thick, hardened fingers had trouble with the snaps, and Momoko couldn't remember how the appliances got attached.

Lloyd sighed. "Not likely I'll ever be up to running three thousand acres again, eh, Will?"

"No, sir," said Will, looking up. Blunt. Honest. The old man hadn't run three thousand acres for years.

"It's a lot of work—" Duggin said.

"Don't mind the work," Lloyd said. "That's never been the problem. God knows I worked hard when I could, and we surely were rewarded." He looked over at Will. "Ever tell you about that year? 1974, it was. We got nine dollars per hundredweight. . . ." Then all of a sudden his shoulders sagged. "Don't know what we were thinking, eh, Momo? What were we thinking?"

Momoko didn't hear him. She was watching Cass. "You are Yumi's friend?"

Cass nodded. "I used to be."

"She not here, you know."

"I know. Have you heard from her . . . ?"

"She was too-pretty girl," the old woman said. "If she was more ugly, maybe she not get into trouble."

"Momoko!" Lloyd struggled to stand, but the old chair seemed to stick to his buttocks. His skinny knees flapped open and closed and he looked like some long-legged marsh bird caught in a sump pond, throwing his weight forward again and again. Finally, breathless, he sat back. His bony chest heaved. He closed his eyes.

Will coughed. "If this isn't a good time, we can take a break—"

Cass frowned at him. No point in putting it off.

"Good time?" asked Lloyd, voice tight, speaking to no one at all. "There's no good time. There's no time at all."

He opened his eyes and spoke to Will. "My wife and I want it guaranteed that we can go on living here in this house. That is nonnegotiable, Will. And we keep five acres for Momo's seeds." He turned to the lawyer. "We've made quite a nice little business out of the seeds in the past few years. All Momo's doing, really. Haven't been much use, ever since my heart . . ."

"Of course, Lloyd," Duggin said. "The house and five acres are guaranteed. For as long as you like. Or until—"

Lloyd closed his eyes again and let his head fall back against the upholstery. "I'd always hoped . . ." He rolled his head from side to side as though his hopes were a muscle he could loosen. "Don't know who we're going to get to take over our seed stock. We got hundreds of varieties, some of 'em quite rare."

His white hair, fine spun and charged with static from the friction, clung to the nubbly fabric. When he opened his eyes again, the pale blue irises were covered in a greasy film. He blinked, then let his watery gaze roam around the room to the lawyer, then to Will, to Momoko, and finally to Cass. Looking for answers. Cass looked away.

"All right," he said. "Give me a pen, then. Let's get this over with."

"That's right, Lloyd," Duggin said, handing him a ballpoint. "It's the only sensible thing to do."

"Lloyd? Momoko?"

Cass slowly climbed, listening to the groan of the stairs underfoot and Momoko's murmuring from above. As her head came level with the floorboards, the odor she'd noticed downstairs grew stronger. She ran up the remaining stairs.

She knew the house. She'd known it since she was a child, running along the creaky corridors, adding scuff marks to the doors, sliding down the rickety banister and fingering the scratches in the plaster walls. For all its flaws it was a far better house than her parents' ranch-style prefab, where she and Will lived now. She was looking forward to the day when they could move in and start fixing it up. The door to the master bedroom was closed. She knew that the knob was loose, that it wiggled, and its screws were in need of tightening. She knocked, then peeked in. The bed was messy, but no one was there. She hurried down the hallway to the bathroom.

Momoko was perched like a child on the edge of the bathtub, rocking back and forth and talking quietly to herself. Lloyd lay on the floor in front of her, toppled like a giant on the slick tiles in front of the toilet. He had apparently been using it when he fell, because there was dark yellow urine pooled on the tile around him, and his pajama bottoms were wet in front.

His toes, normally pale and waxlike, had turned dark, the color of a bruise. The small nub of his penis stuck out from the slit in the damp flannel.

Cass knelt down and put her hand on the side of his neck, then felt for his pulse. The acrid smell of old man's urine made her gag. She cupped one hand over her nose and the other hand over his mouth. She felt warm breath in the palms of both. She slid open his eye with her thumb.

"When did this happen? When did he fall?"

Momo shrugged her shoulders.

"When did you find him? Was it just now?"

Momoko pointed to her husband's penis. "*O-chin-chin ga dashite iru wa panashi . . .*"

There was a phone in the hallway. Cass dialed for an ambulance. If it gets too much, Will had said. Yes, suddenly it was much too much.

From the bathroom, Momoko cried, "*Damé! Damé! O-shikko tarashite!*"

Cass finished with 911 and ran back to the bathroom. Momoko was squatting down next to Lloyd, slapping his thigh with her tiny, crooked hand.

"Mrs. Fuller! Don't!"

The old woman looked up at Cass, her silver hair hanging down on either side of her face. She shook her head, sternly.

"*Damé!* Very bad. He did *o-shikko* in his pants!"

Then she stood up as straight as she could, which wasn't very straight at all, brought her hands to her eyes, and let out a low, keening wail. She shuffled backward, two baby steps, just far enough to bump the backs of her knees against the edge of the tub, whereupon she sat abruptly on the tub's rim, then kept on going, sliding with her behind first into the smooth porcelain depression. She lay there on the bottom, in a small curl, sobbing quietly.

༄

"It's his heart," Cass explained for the hundredth time to yet another social worker. "He's had a couple of heart attacks, plus a bout with colon cancer. He had a colostomy last year and wears a bag, but he can't change it himself. And she's pretty senile. They really need services."

The social worker nodded. "I agree, but it's just not practical to be sending aides all the way out to the farm several times a day. In a case like this, usually we recommend one of the children or a family member helping out. . . ."

"I'm not a family member," Cass said quickly. "I just live next door."

"Don't they have any children?"

"A daughter. But nobody knows where she is."

"Have you asked them?"

Cass tried, but she knew there was no point. "Lloyd? Can you hear me?"

Momoko shook her head. "He can hear. He don't want talking."

"Wouldn't you like Yummy to come home and take care of you?"

Lloyd lay perfectly still under the thin sheet.

"He don't want nobody," Momoko said.

Cass sighed. "Momoko, do you have any idea where Yummy is?"

"Yumi?" The old lady's eyes turned inward. "Oh, yes. She is at whatchamacallit."

"Where?"

"Where you go for studying."

"You mean, like a school? A college?"

"That's right," she nodded. "You know, too. You go to same one. How come you not go today? You sick or something?"

Lloyd shifted his long legs under the sheet. "She doesn't know anything," he said, keeping his eyes closed. "We haven't heard from her in years."

"I know! I know! You playing hooky!" Momoko screeched with laughter.

ॐ

Will jerked on the sagging screen door to see if he could straighten the hinges.

"Don't bother," Cass said. "We'll have plenty to fix once we take possession." She looked around the kitchen. The air was close and still, and her voice sounded loud. "I'll start in here and then go upstairs. You do the living room. Look for bankbooks, too. Maybe they sent her money."

Will hesitated. "Bankbooks? That's awfully personal . . ."

"What else can we do? Lloyd said they hadn't heard from her in years, but that means they heard from her sometime. I want to know when, and where she was living, and—"

"Maybe she phoned."

Cass tugged at the top drawer. It stuck. "I'll bet she wrote. She was always writing things down." She pulled harder, forced it open.

The contents illustrated the virtue of thrift gone mad. Nothing had been taken out in years, just added to, until each drawer was crammed full of rusting twisties, wads of cling wrap that had lost its cling, twists of tinfoil filled with crumbs, crumbling rubber bands. There were miniature shower caps made of grimy vinyl for popping over leftovers. Dingy sandwich bags that smelled of old onion. Stained paper towels folded and stacked for reuse. Cass longed to discard, to disinfect, but she finished the kitchen quickly and went upstairs.

She searched the master bedroom, then continued down the hall to the bedroom that had once been Yummy's. She remembered the room as it used to be, with shelves of books and a plastic record player and albums in stacks on the floor. Flower Power decals on the walls, the ceiling speckled with constellations that glowed in the dark. The room's only ornament now sat on top of a white wooden dresser. It was a small framed photograph, in black and white, of a solemn Indian princess standing in front of the screen door of the farmhouse, hand in hand with Lloyd. Noble Pilgrim. The tip of her feather barely reached his hipbone.

Cass opened the dresser drawer, expecting to find the good linens or Lloyd's spare winter underwear, but it was filled with Yummy's old clothes. Socks, some underpants, T-shirts and jeans, all neatly folded, but musty. Cass lifted a T-shirt speckled with blue paisleys and held it to her nose. A familiar smell clung to the fibers—a little animal, some sandalwood, a hint of patchouli. A mother would hide things here. Cass dug beneath a pile of underclothes. Sure enough.

It was a small bundle, carefully wrapped in a worn freezer bag and secured with a thick rubber band. Inside, wrapped in yet another plastic bag, was a collection of photographs and letters. Cass set the photos aside and flipped through the envelopes. There weren't many, maybe two dozen or so, all addressed to Momoko in Yummy's wild, loopy handwriting. The earliest was on the bottom, dated April 1976. The most recent was from 1997. Cass slid her fingers under the rest of the clothing but found nothing more. As she leaned on the drawer to close it, the blue paisley again caught her eye. She pulled out the T-shirt and held it up against her. She'd lost so much weight, it might fit her now. She tossed it around her neck like a gym towel and went downstairs.

Will sat at the old rolltop desk. Cass draped her arms over his broad shoulders and laid her face against the plane of his jaw. She waved the letters in front of his face.

"Got 'em."

"Good girl. You find an address?" He was poring over a ledger of old farm reports, handwritten in Lloyd's antique script. "Poor old guy. What happened in '75?"

"'Seventy-five?" Cass started flipping through the letters in her hand.

"The year he leased out over half his acreage to your father."

"I don't know. I was just a kid. Why?" She checked the postmarks: San Francisco, Berkeley, several from Texas—all places that Cass could imagine.

"He was doing so well up until then. Look at this. Those Nine-Dollar Potatoes in '74, and then next season he goes and leases to your father. How come?"

Cass looked up. "That was the year after Yummy ran away. He had a heart attack. His first one."

"Weird. Look at this. Two years later, after he took the acreage back, he was fighting soil contamination more or less constantly. From what he was spraying, he must have had a problem with leafroll."

"He did. I remember Daddy going on about the aphids. Lloyd hired Daddy on to run the operation for him, but they never saw eye to eye. Daddy was a lousy farmer and lost a lot of the crop to net necrosis. He blamed Momoko's peach tree for attracting those aphids. Wanted to chop it down, but Lloyd wouldn't let him. *Momo* means 'peach' in Japanese."

"I'm with your Daddy on this one. That tree's just asking for trouble. Do you think I can take these records? It's helpful to know."

"You mean, do I think it's stealing? I don't care if it is, Will. Anyway, we own the land now. We got a right to it, I should think."

"I asked him to show me these way back in '83 when we started leasing. But he kept putting it off."

"Well, now you know why."

"He's a proud man."

"Daddy said he was a cheat."

"Ornery, maybe. You know he's not a cheat." Will would always give anyone the benefit of the doubt, and he was right to do so.

Cass draped her arms around his neck again and held the stack of letters in front of his nose. "Look," she said, pointing to a postmark. "Where's Pahoa?"

yummy 🐎

Two peas in a pod. You remember how that went?

Lloyd would come in for lunch. He'd be sitting at the kitchen table, and you'd dance up behind him and throw your arms around his neck, still hot from the sun, and there would be dirt in the pores under his collar and the sour smell of fertilizer on his fingertips as he reached up to cup your chin and hold you still—remember what his cheek felt like, pressed against yours? Then Momoko, sitting across, would compare the two of you, her large husband and her eager little daughter. She'd peer, long and slow—the same appraising look she gave to a pair of melons, figuring how much longer until they'd be ripe enough to pick—and your heart would be racing. You were always so anxious. How did you know? That growing up meant you were becoming less of him. That this was something, inevitably, that any daddy would dread. Finally Momoko would press her lips together. "Hmm," she would grunt. "Two peas in a pod." Only she'd pronounce it more like "Tsu pi-su ina pod-do," and then she'd give a little nod that made it for sure. Did he teach her that phrase? She seemed to enjoy saying it, enjoy her role in your ceremony, although with that act of abnegation, she put herself outside the two of you. What did that cost her? At least a small twinge of belonging, because if your heart was any measure, your face must have lit up like the sun, to hear her pronouncement. Did that hurt her, too? It was triumph to you. Flesh of her flesh, turning from her—you would have banished her entirely, had you not needed the power of her affirmation. Oh, yeah, your allegiances were firmly with Daddy.

And Daddy would chuckle. Pat your cheek. He was always as shy with his love as you were ferocious with yours, but even if its expression was tentative, the fact of his love was absolute. Then. *So what the fuck happened?*

It wasn't your fault! you wanted to cry. It was just *life,* filtering into your prattle at the supper table, that so offended him, and how were you to know? You'd always shared what you'd learned in school, playing teacher even then, telling him all about the Pilgrims, for example, or how the telegraph was invented, or the names for the parts of a flower. "Pistil, stamen, stigma . . ." He'd frown with concentration, repeating the names after you,

19

slowly, as though he'd never heard them before. "And what does a stamen do?" he'd prompt, pretending to be confused. And you would proudly teach, "A stamen does this and such," and he would nod and smile at you and say, "My, my, my!" like he just couldn't believe how one little daughter—and his, at that—could be so bright. His love for you was absolute, all right. Until you changed the subject.

It wasn't your fault that the sexual reproduction of flowering plants failed to hold your interest. You were becoming an adolescent, after all. When your conversation veered off like a car out of control, toward shades of frosted lipstick and the boys who smoked Pall Malls in the weeds behind the maintenance shed at school, Lloyd's face froze. He grew surly at the sight of your love beads, recoiled at any mention of rock and roll. The first time you used the word "groovy," he choked on his gravy.

"You are not leaving the house dressed like that," he said, catching you sneaking out the door in your worn jeans with all the holes and patches. "I won't have you parading all over town dressed like a beggar." You turned around to face him. "Your navel is showing," he added, eyeing it with disgust.

If he couldn't even tolerate your navel, then how was he to cope when life kick-started changes inside you that went deeper still?

The next year, in ninth grade, there was a man, a history teacher named Elliot Rhodes, slouching in front of the blackboard in a rumpled flannel shirt, stroking his mustache. When he read out loud in class, he looked right at you. At first you thought it was your imagination, but after a couple of times you knew it was for real, and your stomach heaved so violently you could hardly breathe at all. At first you mistook this passion for vocation—you'd always known you would be a teacher (or an explorer or a poet, you weren't exactly sure which), and now you understood why! The power of his knowledge made you weak in the knees. That fall, he taught you all about the great civilizations of the world. He pressed you to question your beliefs, to think about real ideas. He considered Japan to be spiritual and deep, and he taught you a koan: What is the sound of one hand clapping? You carried it home in your heart and whispered it to yourself every day, stunned at its poetic profundity. When you told it to Momoko, she looked at you like you were nuts.

"But, Mom, it's Japanese. It's Zen."

"Stupid. Make no sense."

"It's not supposed to make sense. It's supposed to help you reach enlightenment."

"Never heard of it. Anyway, why you need enlighten when you got good Methodist church to go to?"

"Oh, Mom." You sighed, glancing at Lloyd before going one step further. "I don't believe in organized religion."

Lloyd looked up and shuddered.

At church there'd been talk. Rhodes had just graduated from some liberal college in California. He was a hippie, a commie, an anarchist, a freak. What did they know? In fact, he was a conscientious objector, and you knew this because he told you, after school, the day you lingered in the classroom once the other kids had gone home. He'd protested the war in Vietnam. He'd marched on Washington. He admired Asian culture. He could never go over there, as a soldier, to kill. You leaned against the edge of his desk. He looked at you with an enormous aching, and for the first time you understood the tragedy that was war. He reached up, traced the slant of your eye with his thumb, told you he had a thing for—

Abruptly he turned away. Tugged at his mustache and sent you home, but even though you had to walk for miles because you missed the bus, you were brimming with such a wild joy it felt like flying. You'd sensed his struggle, the sudden gruffness in his voice, the violence in the muscles of his back as he attacked the blackboard with his eraser. The back of a grown man. The fall sky turned steely, then darkened to dusk. You did a skippy little jig in the gravel. The stars were out by the time you sauntered into the kitchen.

Momoko looked at Lloyd. Lloyd cleared his throat, wiped pie from the corner of his mouth. "You're late."

"I stayed after school." Surfing the edge of a long-suffering sigh.

"You in some kinda trouble?" Momoko asked, bringing a plate of franks and beans that she had kept hot in the oven.

"No." Pricking the rubbery pink lozenges with your tines. "I had to help Mr. Rhodes."

Lloyd hemmed and hawed, and you could feel the slow ache of his thinking. He took a toothpick from his shirt pocket and started excavating his back molars. When he got to the front incisors, he snapped the toothpick in half and placed it on the edge of his plate. Finally he wiped his mouth with his napkin. "I don't trust that man. He has dubious morals."

"He does not! He's an activist. A man of conscience! Just because he won't go fight a war in Asia. That's more than *you* can say!"

Lloyd drew in his breath like he'd been sucker-punched. Put down his fork and napkin and pushed to his feet. His eyes were as cold and bright as the sun on snow in winter. It was as if he could see into the corners of your mind, know thoughts before you had a chance to think them, track the rebel contents of your heart. As a child you were secure in his omniscience, knowing that everything occurring on this earth did so with his blessing, according to his will. Now you looked away.

"What's happened to *your* morals, Yumi?" His voice sounded dead.

You couldn't raise your eyes from your dinner plate. "I believe anything is okay as long as it doesn't hurt anybody."

Cassie's dad would have whipped her for talking back. You got sent to your room, which was where you wanted to be in the first place.

ᗩ

At the Thanksgiving pageant, Mr. Rhodes slumped in the front row, and standing center stage, you felt him watching. The play seemed silly, and you'd long outgrown your role, but even so, the words were never as rich in all the years you'd said them.

"Noble Pilgrims," you recited, voice trembling, "my people and I welcome you to our land. We know that your journey has been a hard one, and we will help you. Pray, take our seeds and plant them. . . ."

You wanted him to know that you welcomed him, understood him, even though there was a petition circulating at church to have him transferred out of the school district. You knew that Lloyd had signed it. Shoot, he'd probably started it.

When you returned for your curtain call, his seat was empty. Your heart sank.

The following day he asked you to stay after school. He paced back and forth in the empty classroom, ranting about historical accuracy. "It's revisionist bullshit! It was genocide—we *stole* their land, and then we exterminated them. And now we call it Thanksgiving?"

He seemed very angry, like he was yelling at you. "Don't you know *anything* about the Shoshone and the Bannock who've lived on this land for thousands of years, before there even was an Idaho?" Staring at him, your eyes burned, and you wanted to cry. Then he stopped and stood in front of you, and before you knew it, he had pinned you in his arms against the desk, and he was kissing you, hard. It was not at all what you'd imagined, involving a lot more bristle, more teeth and tongue than romance, but he whispered, "So lovely . . ." and ran his fingers through your long hair, and that was enough. It was plenty. This is it, you thought, shivering uncontrollably. It's happening, and you tried to pay attention so that you could remember how his hands felt against the skin of your heart and tell it all to Cass.

He had a baby blue Volkswagen Beetle in a town of Fords and Chevys. On Saturday you skipped 4-H and he picked you up behind the school. He was wearing jeans and an old fisherman's sweater. He took you to a tiny clapboard house on the outskirts of town, which he was renting for the school year. He made a big pot of split-pea soup on top of a woodstove. You helped him peel the carrots, and afterward you ate the soup with big hunks torn from a loaf of French bread. The crust was burned. He had no chairs, so you sat on a mattress in the corner of the living room. You put the empty bowls on the floor when you were done. The room filled with steam from the simmering soup, clouding the windows. The sheets were speckled with grit, and the flattened pillow smelled like the scalp of his head. It was the best smell in the world, and you buried your face in it, hugging it, wanting to take it home with you. There was no toilet paper in the bathroom, only a stack of dusty newspapers, and afterward you found yourself wiping his semen from your aching adolescent pussy with the headlines of an old *New York Times:* NIXON RESIGNS.

ॐ

You phoned Cass right after dinner.

"I did it!" you whispered, and she cried, "No way!" and you could almost hear the screen door slam as she came rocketing out of her house, down the road, and up your driveway. You grabbed her wrist, hauled her panting through the kitchen and up the stairs, slipping past Lloyd, who was headed toward the bathroom. Barricading your bedroom door, the two of you sat, legs crossed Indian style, head touching head.

"I can't believe it!" squealed Cass, "You really—!"

You reached over to clamp your hand across her mouth. Lloyd gargled in the bathroom on the other side of the wall. When you could trust her to be quiet, you let your hand drop.

23

"All the way?" she whispered.

You nodded.

"What was it *like*?" Her eyes were glistening.

You savored her awe, lay back on the pillows.

"It was . . . unbelievably romantic," you said. "He made split-pea soup." You smiled dreamily, staring up past a constellation of phosphorescent stars. When you were little, Lloyd had pasted them onto the ceiling for you, following the diagram from a book that he had bought—Orion, Andromeda, and the Dippers. It had been years since you'd really noticed them.

"Split-pea soup?" Cass sounded unimpressed.

"Mmm. I peeled potatoes while he washed peas. He chopped up carrots and—"

"Yummy, I *know* what's in split-pea soup!" she cried, bouncing up and down on the bed. "What happened *after*?"

"I'm getting to that. The room was hot, so we took off our sweaters."

"And he was driven wild with desire?"

"No. He played his guitar."

"Ooooh, how romantic! What did he play?"

"Jefferson Airplane. Some Dylan. 'Lay Lady Lay.' "

"I *love* that! And then did you do it?"

"No. Afterward. First we ate the soup."

"Did it hurt?" she asked.

"Just a little. The first time."

"The *first* time! Oh, my goodness, Yummy! How many . . . ?" Her face was bright pink now as she pressed her fingers to her mouth. Sweet Cassie, you thought, feeling so mature all of a sudden—and that was when time did a weird, elasticky thing, like a cartoon slingshot, sending you zinging way out ahead of her in years.

"I don't know," you answered, from far away. "Three? Maybe four?"

"Did you, you know . . . ?"

"What?"

"You know . . ." She hesitated again. She sounded lonely, left behind like that. "Did it feel good?"

"Mmmm," you said, smug and inscrutable, adding to the distance between you. "It felt great. Totally far out. No . . . it was soulful. . . . I can't explain."

It wasn't really soulful, but you were already rewriting the experience.

The real story, as you dimly recall it, twenty-five years later, was that it didn't feel great at all, and it just went on and on. What you identified as pleasure started in the silence after the sex part was done and the winter afternoon was growing dark. You lay there, staring at the ceiling in dim light, and held a naked man for the first time in your life. For a little while, maybe fifteen minutes or so, you honestly felt that this was what it was like to be all grown up and happy. Then he rolled out of bed and put on his jeans and started looking for his car keys.

Lloyd left the bathroom and stopped outside your closed door. He cleared his throat.

"Aren't you girls supposed to be studying?"

"We *are*." Your tone ripe and condescending. "We're *doing* our *home-work*."

Cass looked alarmed.

Lloyd hesitated. "Sounds like just a lot of chatter to me," he said. "Finish up and go on home, Cass. It's getting late."

You listened as he descended the creaking stairs.

"Lady," Elliot crooned, strumming at the strings of his guitar, *"you keep askin' why he likes you? How come?"*

You knew not to ask questions like that. Still, he teased you:

"Wonder why he wants more if he just had some. . . ."

He told you all about San Francisco, about the brown hills of Berkeley, about the scene. There was no bullshit, he explained. That's what was so great about it. None of the crappy materialism of middle-American capital-ist culture. You looked around the bare room in the small house. There was very little materialism in evidence. He could use some new sheets for his bed. He slept under a military green sleeping bag with a nubbly flan-nel lining, printed with hunters and ducks. He could use a new frying pan.

You had an idea. There was some extra stuff at your parents' house. They were going to give it away to the church fair anyway. You could bring it next time? It was such a good idea, and you were excited and proud to have thought of it, but to your surprise he smiled and shook his head. "No thanks," he said. "I don't need 'stuff.'" And the way he said it made your heart sink, like there was a larger point you were missing completely.

25

He told you about his friends. One was an anarchist sandal maker. One built drums. Another walked through a plate-glass window while tripping on LSD.

"Was he okay?" you asked.

"He died." He was staring up at the ceiling. "He thought he was going to Europe."

You couldn't think of anything to say to that.

"You know," he prompted. "When he walked though the plate-glass window."

You still didn't get it.

He sighed and lit a cigarette. "Larry was tripping, and he wanted to go to Europe. So he walked through the window, as though the physical laws of gravity and, like, *glass,* didn't apply to him anymore. Like he'd transcended all that. But he hadn't. And he fell. And he died."

Wow. You took the cigarette from his fingers and dragged, hoping that this was an adequate response. You worried about other girlfriends. Surely he must have had lovers, way more experienced than you, who would have known how to participate in a conversation like this. Had he ever been in love with them?

"*Made for each other, made in Japan.*'" He crooned the lyrics of Grace Slick's song, grinning as he wound a strand of your long black hair around his finger. When he sang, sometimes it sounded like love, and you imagined it at night, under the glow-in-the-dark stars, where the air was thick with your dreaming. He would look deep into your eyes. "I love you," he would say. "I love you, Yumi." And you would sob and hug your diary, where you were writing it all down, doubled over with a heartache that was the closest thing you knew to a body's pleasure. "Oh, Elliot," you whispered under your father's starry sky. "I love you, too."

"*Woman with a greasy heart,*" he sang.

What was he talking about? Your heart did not feel greasy, but you wished it could be, if that would make the song be about you.

"*Woman with a greasy heart, Au-to-ma-tic Man.*"

You faced each other, naked and cross-legged on the mattress, and he reached out to trace your nipple. He moved his fingertip up the center of your rib cage, like a zipper to your mouth, and you sucked on it like a lollipop to make it wet.

"Mmmmm, Yummy," he murmured, as he drew the finger back down

26

your stomach and slipped it between your legs. "You're so open, I love that about you. . . ."

And there it was. He'd finally said it. He loved you.

You threw your arms around his neck. "Oh, Elliot," you breathed. "I love you, too!" Pressed your cheek against his, feeling the tickle of his mustache, the rasp of his unshaved skin, holding him for a long time. Then, slowly, you realized that something was wrong. That you were the only one doing any holding. That he was not holding at all. In fact, he was merely sitting there, his arms at his sides. You let go of him, sat back, hugged your legs to your chest. If you could have died, you would have done so, gladly.

"Oh, wow," he said.

You had nothing more to add.

"Of course, I love you, too, Yummy," he said. "It's just that there are so many different levels of love, you know. . . ."

You didn't know, but you were finding out.

"What a downer. I don't want to hurt you, Yummy. Maybe we should just—"

"No!" you cried out, too loudly. "I knew that. That's what I meant, too." You pressed your chin into your naked kneecap. You were shivering, so you pulled his sleeping bag up around your shoulders. The metal zipper was ice cold and bit into the skin of your neck as you wrapped yourself tight in the grimy flannel with the hunters and the ducks. The bag was so old that the waterproofing was peeling off the surface fabric. You concentrated on scraping the flaking plastic with your fingernail. It came off like dead skin. He reached over and placed his hand on yours, to stop you fidgeting.

"Yummy?"

You snatched your hand away. "Don't call me that."

He was surprised. "Why not? It's your name. . . ."

"My name is *Yumi*."

"Yummi?"

"No. Not like *gummy*. Like *you*. And *me*."

"You-me."

"Say it quicker."

"Yumi."

"If you can't pronounce it right, don't say it at all."

He laughed. "You're fantastic. This is what's so great about you. You're

27

very mature for your age." He reached for your hands again. "Yumi, Yumi, Yumi. . . . Life can be complex, but you understand that." He played with your fingertips. "I'm glad we can talk about this stuff. It's so important to stay open." He lay back on the pillow, pulling you toward him. *"Don't ever change, lady,"* he sang.

Your heart swelled. You couldn't help it.

"Mmmm," he whispered, nibbling your neck. "You'll always be yummy to me."

lloyd ✍

How do you tell a story, after so many years? How do you peer into other people's hearts, when life is so complex, and your own heart has grown over, close and impervious?

Lloyd's heart, multiply bypassed by now, had once again been jump-started, leaving him in a rehab ward, curtained off from the other beds. He lay there, an old Bible heavy in his hands, its spine digging into his stomach. He struggled to keep it propped up. His stiff hands fumbled with the pages. The skin on his fingertips was so callused he could barely feel the softness of the paper, and as the book slipped once again and he grasped for it, the tissue-thin pages of the psalm tore under the clumsiness of his touch. *My God, my God, why hast thou forsaken me? Why art thou so far from helping me, and from the words of my roaring?*

That was it. He wanted to roar.

Momoko sat next to the wall, in a reclining chair on wheels. Her head lolled back, and her mouth gaped open. Her woolen hat, which she wore indoors even with the heat on, had tipped off and was lying on the floor by her feet, upturned like a beggar's. Her white hair was tamped down. Her cheeks glowed like old wax.

Maybe she will die before me, Lloyd thought, and no sooner had the notion crossed his mind than he reproached himself for the relief it brought. He closed his eyes. He was very tired. *I am poured out like water, and all my bones are out of joint: my heart is like wax; it is melted in the midst of my bowels.*

The nurse snapped back the curtain.

"How you doing there, Lloyd? Hope you're good and hungry!"

She balanced a tray on her palm, slid it onto his bedside table. "Just let me do your fluids," she said, pushing up his sleeve. "Then I've got you a nice piece of Thanksgiving turkey for dinner. You'll enjoy that."

He kept his eyes shut as she tapped the needle of the intravenous tube. *They pierced my hands and my feet. . . .*

She traced the line to the valve and changed the bag. *They part my garments among them, and cast lots upon my vesture.*

"Now, how's about sitting up and tucking in to some turkey. Hold on, here we go." She touched the button that raised the back of the bed.

Lloyd grimaced. "Let us eat and drink," he said, "for tomorrow we die. . . ." His eyes stayed closed. "Is that you, Grace?"

"Yes, Lloyd. You seem a little peaked today. Anything the matter?"

"Well." He sighed. "It's dinnertime. What do you expect?" He still kept his eyes closed. "I can't eat that slop. You can take it away."

"You haven't even looked at it."

"I don't have to. Take it away."

"You have to eat, Lloyd." Her voice contained a warning.

"Let me out of this hospital and I'll eat just fine."

"Can't let you out until we know you're eating."

"I'll eat when I get home and get some real food."

He opened his eyes to stare her down. The nurse leaned a hip against the guardrail of his bed and crossed her arms.

"You don't have anyone at home to take care of you."

"We'll manage. We always have."

"Well, that's just what we don't know. Your wife can't manage. I'm sure you realize that."

He struggled to sit up taller in bed. He looked past her to Momoko, slack jawed and sleeping in the chair.

"Doc says you have a daughter. Maybe she——"

"No," he said. "I have no daughter."

ॐ

"Why you crying?"

"I'm not crying."

"Look like crying to me."

The nurse was gone, and Momoko was awake now. She gripped the

29

guardrail of his bed, raised herself up on tiptoes, and peered into his face. "Mmm. Look like crying. Something wrong?"

"Oh . . ." Defeated. "I can't explain. It's the food. I can't eat it."

"What's wrong with food? Looks like some good food." She picked up the fork and patted the instant potatoes. "Mmm. Here. I gonna feed you."

She brought a bite of boneless turkey to his mouth. He screwed up his face but parted his lips and let her put the fork in. He tried to chew, to swallow, but the turkey tasted like pasteboard.

"Oh!" He shuddered, spitting it into his tissue. "It's horrible! I can't eat that!" He sank back in bed, exhausted.

"You acting like a little kid. How you gonna come on home if you don't eat?"

"Momoko, please!"

She shook her head and frowned. "Shame for good food gonna go to waste. If you don't want, then I eat. Okay?"

Through half-closed eyes he watched as Momoko cut the turkey slices and finished off the vegetable medley. The potatoes stuck to her dentures and made them smack against the roof of her mouth. *The meek shall eat and be satisfied. . . .*

She mopped up the last of the gravy with a soft, white bun, then returned to her chair. She spotted her hat on the floor and picked it up and put it on her head. It had a small brim like the flange of a mushroom. She leaned back and folded her hands across her chest. Within minutes she was snoring softly. Lloyd watched her. His mind drifted to thoughts of their seeds and the future, but he brushed away the worry, for now.

He was just glad that dinner was over.

By the time the nurse returned, Lloyd was drifting off to sleep.

"Well, my goodness gracious!" Grace said. "Will you take a look at that! Good for you, Lloyd!" She stood with her hands on her hips, looking at his empty plate. He was too groggy to correct her.

"Good to the very last drop!" she said, removing the tray and giving the table a wipe-down. She leaned over to adjust his sheet, then lowered his bed. She patted his arm. "I'm proud of you," she said. "You keep eating like that and you'll be out of here in no time."

He managed a smile. "Grace?"

"Yes?"

"Happy Thanksgiving. . . ."

30

pahoa ℬ

PAHOA

Cass typed in the letters, then sat back while the search engine churned. With the new high-speed connection, the download was almost instantaneous. When the hits came back, she scanned them quickly.

Hawaii. Pahoa was a town on the Big Island. She selected a site at random.

PARADISE FOR SALE!
Stunning & productive 20-acre property
with established groves of macadamia nuts & mangoes . . .
Guavas, grapefruits, and avocados!
Spacious home with 6 bedrooms!
Complete solar power throughout!
Twenty acres of Paradise!

Guavas. Macadamia nuts. Mangoes. Made their three thousand acres of Russet Burbanks seem downright dull. She sighed. Cass could not imagine paradise. In Liberty Falls the weather report predicted cloudy skies with a scattering of snow flurries. Patchy fog. Lows in the mid- to lower twenties. The first hard frost had come early this year, and now the wind was picking up. Outside the window the satellite dish rattled in the Quinns' bare front yard. The cottonwood tree, dry and brittle, creaked the way it did only in winter.

The office was insulated beneath the drywall, but the room still felt exposed and cold, a large, boxlike addition sticking off from the kitchen. They'd built the office when they started to increase the size of their operation, and Cass tried to keep things neat, but it was a challenge. Along the back wall, the shelves piled up with farm reports, ledgers, and all the paperwork. FAQ sheets on seed potatoes and some recent issues of *Spudman* magazine lay scattered on the long folding table they used for farm meetings. Another table held a monitor for the DTN, the network subscription service with data on weather and futures prices.

Cass sat at the main computer, which they used for business, accounting, e-mail, and running the global-positioning-system software. In front of her, printouts of GPS maps were tacked to the wall, showing topographical and yield data from previous years' harvests, and beside them hung a USDA Potato Disorder Identification Chart with color photos of every affliction that might befall a spud. The cell phone that Will used when he was out in the field was resting in its charger. There were several land-line phones as well, one with a headset that Will wore during office hours. Cass had bought him the headset when he started getting neckaches. She thought he looked cute with it on.

"Like a receptionist." She sat on his lap and adjusted the mouthpiece, then pulled the rubber band off his ponytail, combing her fingers through his blond hair so it hung loose around his shoulders. "There."

"I feel like a goddamned stockbroker." He dumped her off and ambled back into the kitchen for a refill on his coffee. The wire from the headset dangled over his shoulder. "I didn't become a farmer to sit behind a desk."

Cass checked her watch. Will would be annoyed if he knew she was surfing the Net again. He thought it was a waste of time and couldn't understand why she'd want to spend a minute more in front of the computer than she absolutely had to. At least this was legitimate.

She typed "Yumi Fuller, Hawaii" into the search engine. A list of course offerings came back from various institutions including the University of Hawaii, a continuing-education program, a high-school-equivalency night school, and a local prison. All taught by Yumi Fuller, M.A.

Cass checked the descriptions of some of the classes: Introduction to the Novel, Composition Level I, Japanese Poetry in Translation, Creative Nonfiction. There was no information on how to contact the instructor, but Cass felt she was getting close.

She went back to the search engine and on a whim typed in "Yummy Fuller." The engine transported her to another real estate site.

YUMMY ACRES!
Aloha! I'm Yummy Fuller, licensed Realtor at
Yummy Acres Realty.
Looking for your Hawaiian dream home?
A piece of Paradise to call your own?
Let me show you these listings today!

A list of properties followed, modest quarter-acre lots in a subdivision, built on what looked like the bare rock of a cooled lava flow.

Looking for a fresh start? A place to call home?
Just drop me an e-mail or give me a call!
Let me make your dreams into a reality!

A woman with long dark hair smiled ruefully from the corner of the home page. She was wearing a crown of flowers on her head. Cass stared at the picture, but it was small and indistinct, and she couldn't be sure.

There was a "Contact Me" button, so Cass clicked it and started to type. "I am looking for Yumi (Yummy) Fuller, originally from Liberty Falls, Idaho. Her dad is dying, and her mom needs help. If you are her, could you please contact me at CassQ@Spudnet.com. P.S. I am her old friend and next-door neighbor Cassie Unger."

She sent off this e-mail. Then she addressed an envelope to Professor Yumi Fuller, M.A., at the University of Hawaii.

Dear Professor Fuller,
I am looking for Yumi (Yummy) Fuller of Liberty Falls, Idaho. If this is you, it has been a long time since we have communicated. I am writing to you to tell you some sad news, that your father, Lloyd Fuller, had another heart attack—I think this is his third or fourth one now, but I lost count—and what with the colostomy (they found a bit of cancer there a couple years ago, too), well, the doctor says now his condition isn't very good. Although he has always been lucky and beaten the odds, the doctor thinks he may only have another couple of months or so left to him. Your mother, Momoko, is well, physically speaking, but she seems to have a touch of the dementia. I guess maybe it is Alzheimer's disease or she had a mild stroke, which is what happened to my father, although his stroke was a big one that killed him. (My mother is deceased as well, from breast cancer.)

I tracked you down on the Internet from the letters you sent to your mother and I hope you don't mind that I am writing to you out of the blue. I just thought you should know about your mother and father, and maybe you would like to come home now to say good-bye. I just hope this letter finds you in time.

Sincerely yours,
Your Childhood Friend,
Cass (Unger) Quinn

"I think I found her," Cass whispered, climbing into bed.

"On the Internet?" Will was half asleep.

"I think so. I found two. I just hope one of them is her." She pointed her toes and nudged them between Will's shins. She eased her cold fingers under his armpits.

"Ow," he muttered. "Cold."

"I sent an e-mail and wrote a letter. I didn't say anything about taking care of them. I just said maybe she should come home and say good-bye."

"Mmm. That's good."

"Bet she won't, though. It's been so long." She curled against Will's warm chest. "What do you think?"

"Dunno," Will mumbled, trying to stay awake, to oblige her desire for conversation. "What happened back then anyway?"

"She had an affair with one of our teachers at school. Her daddy found out. She was only fourteen, and you know how Lloyd is. So she ran away. Started a spell of bad luck for Lloyd. For everyone, really. That's all I know."

He nodded, and as he drifted back toward sleep, his hand reached for her like a blind mole, burrowing in the dark. His touch was not deliberate. Just an aimless sort of probing into adjacent soil, down the slope of her hip, up the rib cage. It was this random meandering across her body's terrain that first uncovered the pea-size lump. Now his fingers stiffened when they touched her chest.

"Cass." He sighed. He placed the heel of his palm against the slick twist of scar tissue. His fingers groped for heft, for bulk.

But Cass intercepted him, smoothly capturing his wrist as she counted the days. It was early, but you never knew. She guided his hand to her stomach and released it. He was safe down there, no danger. From there he could find his own way. She relaxed into him now, began to let herself answer. *A little window of life.* She tried to visualize the sperms swarming her egg, picture them coming together. It wasn't always easy, but she knew it was important to keep positive images in your head.

"What's this?"

"You asked me what she was like."

Will took the photos from the freezer bag and flipped through them. There was a picture of Lloyd, holding an infant Yummy in the palm of his hand, making her fly like an airplane. There was an Easter picture of Yummy in front of the church and another holding on to Momoko's hand in front of hedges of honeysuckle and mock orange.

"Cute." He handed them back to Cass "What's that one?" It was a group photo, taken at school after the Thanksgiving pageant.

"Are you in it?" Will asked.

Cass nodded. He narrowed his eyes, held the photo closer.

"Which one is you?"

She pointed to the edge, where she was standing amid the side dishes.

Will laughed. "Well, if you don't make the cutest, plumpest little—"

"Don't," Cass warned.

He walked out to the office, still laughing.

Cass was in two other photos as well. The first had been taken at a birthday party, Yummy's, of course. Yummy was perched on a footstool in the center of the picture, surrounded by balloons and offerings. Cass sat on the horsehair love seat at the edge of the frame, so far over, it seemed like an accident that she'd gotten into the picture at all. The colors had faded. Pale balloons stuck to the wall behind the love seat, held there by static electricity. It had seemed like magic at the time, Cass remembered, but Lloyd had explained it using simple science. Friction. He'd rubbed a balloon against his thigh, and the sound of the taut rubber against the fabric of his trousers made her want to sneeze. The rough upholstery prickled the backs of her thighs. When the photo was snapped, the rest of the children were facing away. Just Cass and Yummy were caught looking toward the flash. Yummy smiled, poised and self-possessed. Cass, to one side, simply looked stricken.

The only other picture with Cass showed the two girls, older and in two-piece bathing suits, slouching splay-legged in aluminum lawn chairs on the Fullers' front yard. Behind them the lawn sprinkler sent jets of water into the air. Blades of wet grass stuck to their legs, and they were eating Popsicles. Yummy glowered at the camera, and again Cass just looked scared.

Cass placed the photos side by side. Lined up like that, you could see the sea change that had transpired in Yummy—from smiling princess to sullen mermaid, hiding behind damp, seaweedy hair. Cass hadn't changed at all. Not yet. Her changes had come later. She stared at the pictures, points in time, and felt the years swell.

Will came from the office, on his way out to the fields. "Looks like fun," he said, peering over her shoulder. "You two were pretty good buddies, huh?"

She nodded. She walked him to the door and watched him cross the yard, bundled against the cold.

She had thought time would just go on, generating more pictures like these: Cass and Yummy, dressed in bathing suits, in prom dresses, as brides and bridesmaids, and then at baby showers. But the images of her friend stopped a year or so after the photo on the lawn. By then it was winter, and Cass was squirming on the love seat again. No one was snapping pictures. There were no balloons or magic, and the electricity in the room was no longer simply static.

$\mathcal{B}$

They were all in the Fullers' living room: Cassie, her mother and father, Lloyd and Momoko. Everyone except for Yummy.

"I don't know about you, Fuller, but I won't abide obstinacy in a child of mine." Her daddy unbuckled his belt. "For the last time, Cassandra, what were you two girls doing in town? And what was that man doing with you?"

"Where's Yumi, Cass?" Lloyd urged.

"Yes, please tell," said Momoko.

But she stayed silent.

"All right," her daddy said. "Have it your way. Get outside and wait for

Her mother reached up and touched his arm. "Carl, not here."

He jerked his arm away like he hadn't heard. "What are you waiting for? I said git."

Lloyd spoke again. "Carl, wait . . ."

"You got a better idea?" It wasn't a question.

"Not in my house."

"Don't you worry. I'm takin' her outside."

"That's not what I meant. It's not right—"

"That's why your girl's gone running off, Fuller. And I'm going to make real sure mine don't do likewise."

Outside, it was cold, and the moon lit the slick, vast stretch of ice-crusted snow. The farmhouse stood all alone in the middle of it, glowing.

Her daddy's breath turned white as it came from his mouth. Maybe the cold just made him madder, because he went on and on, raising the belt and bringing it down, like he was doing it just to keep warm.

After a while Lloyd came out and stood in the lit doorway.

"That's enough, Unger," he called. "I mean it."

But her daddy just kept on going, the leather whistling in the air, and except for the action of his arm and the belt, it was like everything else was frozen and would stay that way forever.

letters ✍

April 1976

Dear Momoko and Lloyd,

I decided to write this letter even though I don't think it will do any good. You probably still think I'm an evil sinner and I'll go to hell for all my wrongdoings, and if that causes you grief, I'm sorry. It's not your fault. I didn't mean for you to find out. It was *my* problem, and I took care of it the only way I knew how.

Maybe you're mad at me for leaving, too. But I had to. I left for reasons of shame—not mine, which is what you probably hope, but yours, Daddy. Do you remember when that ammonia train car derailed over behind the Ungers? And all the stuff went into the air and we all had to evacuate, and how scared we were because the poisonous gas was going everywhere, on every wind, but you couldn't see it? That's what it was going to be like. I could tell that your shame was going to fill every crack in the house, seep into every second of the day, and suck the air right out of me. And when the word got around, there wasn't going to be any room left for me to breathe in the whole of Power County that wasn't taken up with your shame. It wasn't fair. You might think that the poison was in me, Daddy, but you'd be wrong. I was just the derailed train car. The shame was yours, and I knew if I stayed, I'd be poisoned by it. I'd grow up all screwy and bent with the weight of your shame. So I left. It was an evacuation, Daddy.

So, in case you want to know, I am fine now. Last year was pretty harsh. I was living on the street for a while, panhandling and stuff, but I got by. After that I was sort of adopted by some good people here in Berkeley. It's a real Pan-Asian scene out here, some Japanese, some Korean, some mixed like me—sure is different from Idaho! We live in a big house, and they're mostly all college students, so they have good values when it comes to education. They make sure I go to school every day, and they also help me with my homework. One of them took me to see the cherry blossoms in a real Japanese garden. It's called *hana-mi* in Japanese which means "flower gazing." Have you ever heard about this? It reminded me of your garden in the spring, Mom. I'll bet it's still too early for flowers in Idaho, huh?

Don't worry about me. Don't bother writing back unless you want to, but I should warn you that I'm not ever coming back to Liberty Falls. I hope you are fine and that everything on the farm is fine, too.

> Yours truly,
> Yumi

P.S. If you see Cassie Unger around, please tell her to write back.

ℬↃ

July 1976

Dear Mom,

Wow, you actually answered my letter! I didn't expect Daddy would let you. Maybe he didn't. Maybe I shouldn't be writing to you at all, because it will only get you into trouble, but I guess you can handle him. I'm the one who couldn't. Did I always make him so mad? (That's called a rhetorical question, which means you don't have to answer it.)

Anyway, I'm sorry Daddy had a heart attack, but I'm glad it wasn't too serious and he's okay now. I hope he's not still totally angry at me. I guess I feel a little guilty, but deep down I don't think what I did was so bad. I was just a stupid kid, dumb enough to get in trouble, but smart enough to do something about it. I know he would call that sinful, and maybe you think so, too, but that's just your opinion. Honestly, I wouldn't change what I did, but I guess there's no point in even talking about it. I know he won't forgive me, and probably you don't approve either. That's okay. I appreciate you writing back. Do you miss me? I miss you sometimes. If the time ever seems right, please tell him that I love him in spite of everything.

   love, Yumi

P.S. That's too bad about Carl Unger losing his farm, but it's good that he can go and work for Daddy. Do you ever see Cass? I sent her a bunch of letters, but she never writes me back.

July 1979

Dear Mom,
Wow, thanks for the money order. Guess what I'm going to spend it on? My college textbooks! I got into Berkeley. I got a scholarship and everything! I think I'm going to major in Asian Studies, or maybe English. Or both. So I'll need lots of books, and the money will totally come in handy. By the way, where are you getting it from anyway? Does Dad know?

April 1983

Dear Mom,
So how's the seed business going? Are you planting yet, or is it still too cold? I guess with the new greenhouse you can get a jump on the season. I think it's so cool that you made a business out of it, all on your own. I'm so proud of you!

   Thanks again for the money. It's hard at the end of the semester, making ends meet. Anyway, you won't have to worry about me for a while. It looks like I'm getting a prize for a paper I wrote. It's called "The Exiled Self: Fragmentation of Identity in Asian-American Literature." Pretty heavy, huh? And the best thing is, it comes with a check for a thousand dollars! Isn't that cool? I wish you could come to graduation.

   I'm sorry to hear about Mrs. Unger. She was nice, even if her husband was a creep. When you wrote that he died, I was glad because finally she could be free of him, but maybe she just got hooked on all that abuse and couldn't live without it. I'm glad Cassie married a nice man and got out of there. She never did write me, but if you see her, tell her I said hi.

Are you sure you can't come to the graduation? No, I know you can't. But, I'm thinking maybe I should try writing to Daddy myself.

Love, Yumi

ॐ

April 1983

Dear Dad,

I am writing to tell you that I am graduating from the University of California at Berkeley this year, and I would like to invite you and Mom to the graduation, if you would like to come.

We haven't seen each other for just over eight years now. This really makes me sad. I know there is a lot we don't agree upon, but you are my father, and I would like to have a relationship with you again. I know you think what I did was wrong, and I won't ask you to forgive me, but won't you even talk to me?

I'm graduating with honors in English and Asian Studies, and I'm also receiving a prize. I'm not bragging. I was just hoping that maybe you would be happy to know. I'm enclosing two round-trip plane tickets for you and Mommy that I bought with my prize money. I hope you'll come.

I love you, Yumi

ॐ

May 1983

Momoko and Lloyd,
I hate you.

ॐ

November 1983

Dear Mom,

Thanks for your letter. It took awhile for it to catch up with me. I moved out of the Berkeley house and got a job writing grants for a professor in Plant Sciences. He says that normally he never would have hired an English major, but he was surprised at how much I knew about agricultural stuff. He says I must have just absorbed it, growing up on a farm. Anyway, I need the job since I've decided to go to grad school.

Thanks for the money order. I meant those tickets to be a gift to you and Lloyd, but I can use the money for books.

꿩

March 1984

Dear Momoko,
Why do we have such a difficult relationship? Why can't we just love each other like a normal family? I'm trying to understand why I'm so scared of having kids of my own, and I realized it's because I'm afraid of screwing them up. My friend thinks it's important for me to share my feelings about this with you, so that's what I'm doing.

p.s. please give the enclosed letter to Daddy.

꿩

March 1984

Dear Lloyd,
Fuck you.
Yumi

꿩

November 1984

Dear Momoko and Lloyd,
I'm writing to tell you that you have a grandson. His name is Phoenix, and he was born on the first day of November. He weighed 9 lbs. 5 oz. at birth. He is a magical baby, and I am overjoyed.

I hope you will find it in your heart to be glad. I know I never do things the way you want me to, and I suppose the first thing you will want to know is if I am married. I am not. And you should also know that Phoenix's father and I don't intend to get married. Paul is the Plant Sciences professor I've been working for. I've known him since he was a grad student, and we lived in the Berkeley house together. He's the one who got me off the street and off drugs—I never told you much about that year, but it was bad, and I can honestly say that I owe him

41

my life. He's gay, but we decided to have this child together because, well, that's what happened, and this is San Francisco, and it just seemed right. (Paul is Japanese, Mom, a *sansei*. His last name is Yamamoto, and he comes from a long line of gardeners, too.) Anyway, he and I both agree that since normal families are so screwed up and dysfunctional, we might as well try to have an abnormal one. He's smart and kind and handsome. He'll be a wonderful and nonjudgmental father.

December 1985

Dear Momoko,

Thanks for the letter. It finally caught up to me here in Portland. Paul and I decided to get married after all. He got a job at the University of Oregon, and I came here to be with him. I'm back in school, working on my master's and teaching part-time. Rents are a lot cheaper than in Berkeley, but it rains a lot. Phoenix is one now, and he is so beautiful. I wish you could see him.

December 1987

Dear Mom,

You didn't tell me that Lloyd had a second heart attack in '83. Is that why you didn't come to my graduation? You don't have to answer that. It doesn't matter. Anyway, I'm glad that he was okay. He sure is lucky, isn't he? You don't have to answer that either.

Phoenix is doing great. He's three now, and I've got him in preschool, which hopefully will give me a chance to finish my master's thesis. It's called "Fading Blossoms, Falling Leaves: Visions of Transience and Instability in the Literature of the Asian-American Diaspora." Basically, it's about the way images of nature are used as metaphors for cultural dissolution.

Are you still doing the garden and selling seeds? My love of plants is purely poetic, and Paul thinks it's funny the way I kill anything I actually try to grow. His interest is purely scientific, so we balance each other out. He's doing well, by the way. He got a job offer in the plant-breeding program at the U of Texas, so we may have to move to Dallas. Yuck.

ॐ

May 1989

Dear Mom,

Well, it's final. I got my master's, and Paul and I are getting a divorce. I guess I should have seen it coming. The good news is that he's finally getting tenure, so he can pay child support. I'll need it—the pay scale for the kind of adjunct teaching gigs I can get is for shit. Anyway, I'm sick of Texas, and I'm thinking of moving someplace with a larger Asian presence, so Phoenix doesn't have to grow up twisted. I think I may have a chance at a teaching fellowship at the University of Hawaii, where I could work on my Ph.D. Wouldn't that be exotic?

ॐ

August 1992

Dear Momoko and Lloyd,

I'm writing to tell you of the birth of your first granddaughter, Ocean Eugenia, born on June 21—a summer-solstice child. I'm sending you a picture. She has Fuller eyes. I'm living in Honolulu now. Phoenix and I are living with Ocean's father in a great house on the beach. He runs a surf shop. I'm still working on my degree and teaching, but it's more laid back here, and maybe I've got a better attitude. Paul used to say that adjunct teaching was like any economy of scale, and you just have to treat it like farming potatoes—standardize your product, increase your volume, work the margins, and make sure your courses are cosmetically flawless. Whatever. It's really so beautiful here, and as long as the kids are happy, it's okay for now.

      Aloha,
      Yumi

ॐ

February 1997

Dear Momoko and Lloyd,

Well, I haven't heard from you for a really long time, so here's the news:

43

Whether you like it or not, you have a new grandson. If you want to know his name, you can write and ask me.

Yumi

P.S. This is the last one you are going to get.

ᘒ

December 3, 1998

Dear Cassie,

Wow. Is this really you? I got your e-mail and then your letter. Thank you for telling me about Lloyd and Momoko. I've been wondering what's been going on with them, and this explains why she stopped writing. I hope they're still okay?

Anyway, I went back and forth about your suggestion—I have some pretty complex feelings about my parents, as you can imagine—but I've decided I should see them. I can take a month off during winter break, so I'll be arriving in Pocatello before Christmas. I'll e-mail you with the date and times. Do you think you could pick me up at the airport?

It will be interesting to see each other, don't you think? After all these years?

second

And the earth brought forth grass, and herb yielding seed after his kind . . .

—Genesis 1:12

frank ℬ

It was the first of December, and a cold wind blew off Erie. Frank pushed his skateboard into the wind, cursing it dispassionately, almost by rote so that the curses marked the rhythm of his momentum, driving him forward. *Fuckin' wind—, fuckin' wind—,* and on the *fuck* his foot hit the ground, and on the *in'* it kicked off and came back onto the board, and he was able to glide for the duration of the *wind,* sometimes drawing the word out longer when he hit a rare patch of smooth asphalt, clear of potholes and gravel. The frontage road was for shit, but at four-thirty in the morning, riding his skateboard under the hazy orange glow of the road lights, Frank had the whole place to himself, and the wind was freedom.

Over beyond on the highway, the big semis careened past with a whine that sounded like missile fire, and who could blame them for not stopping in this shithole suburb of Ashtabula? Like, how could you even have a suburb of nothing? Even his McDonald's wasn't twenty-four hours.

Mist from the lake dulled the golden arches. Frank ollied up on the curb, then, just for practice, he jumped and ground out against the cement pylon that supported the sign, flipping the board and coming down hard. The board got away from him. He caught it and tried again, making the landing this time. It was going to be a great day. When he rounded the corner to the service entrance, he stopped short, slamming his foot into the ground.

Something was parked way back in the lot, over by the Dumpster. It was centered in the circle of light from the security lamp, but shrouded in mist. Frank skated in closer. It had the unmistakable shape of a Winnebago, boxy and inelegant, but the body of the vehicle was covered with pop-riveted patches of tin and aluminum, like scales, while its roof had been shingled with some sort of dark, rectangular paneling. A conning tower rose from the roof. It looked like a robotic armadillo, a road-warrior tank, a huge armored beetle—it was the most radical thing Frank Perdue had ever seen.

He veered around to the front. The conning tower clocked around to follow him.

"Hey!" he called out, getting ready to fly.

A door on the side of the vehicle creaked opened, and a figure emerged. He was skinny, wearing army-surplus pants and a ragged sweater with a knitted vest on top. His dirty blond hair was matted into finger-thick dreadlocks that hung down the middle of his back. His ears were pierced with a cluster of silver earrings. Frank relaxed. The guy wasn't old. Not a kid. Maybe in his twenties.

"Hey," the guy said. "Peace."

Frank shrugged. Hippie retard.

"You work here?"

Frankie shrugged again.

The guy looked around, stomping his feet to keep them warm and blowing into his cupped hands. His gloves were missing all the fingertips. His breath turned the air into clouds. "I'm Y," he offered.

But Frankie heard "I'm why?" and he couldn't answer that.

"Y," the guy repeated. "Y's my name."

Frankie shoved his hands in his pockets. Why's his name what?

"You know," the guy persisted. "Y. Like the letter. Like the chromosome. What's your name?"

"Frank Perdue." He heard the words of his name come out of his mouth.

"Frank Perdue! You mean like the chicken dude?"

Here we go, Frank thought, gritting his teeth. It usually ended in a fight. But the creep wasn't laughing. "Way cool. You his kid or something?"

"No way," Frank said. "My parents are dead. No relation to the chickens."

Y nodded. "Too bad. That guy's a rich motherfucker." His eyes narrowed, and he seemed about to say something more, but then he stopped. "Sorry about your parents. So you work here or what?"

"I'm the janitor."

"Awesome. We've been waiting for you."

He pounded on the side of the vehicle. The door opened again, and another guy stepped out. He must have just gotten up, because he was digging his fingers around in his eye sockets behind his glasses. The thick lenses bobbed up and down. A woman followed, wrapped in a long printed skirt and bundled like the others in layers of sweaters. She had wavy brown hair and a silver ring through her nose. "Hey," she said, smiling.

"Well?" the guy with the glasses asked. "Have we reached an agreement?"

Y shook his head. The guy looked at Frank. "We want your oil."

"Huh?"

"Your french-fry oil. The old stuff from the deep fryer that you throw away."

"What for?"

"It's our fuel, dude. Biodiesel. We run off it." The guy turned to the vehicle and raised his arm like a used-car salesman in a lot full of cream puffs. "This," he said, beaming, "is the Spudnik!" He lumbered down the steps and stood next to Frank. "It's a common diesel engine, modified to run on vegetable oil. Quite elegant, if I do say so myself. Fuel's free. She gets twenty-one miles to the gallon on the highway, and on the interstates of America you're never too far from a fuel source. Seems to prefer McDonald's to KFC, but she'll run on just about anything, even Dunkin' Donuts. Been across the country twice now."

Frank blew air. "Awesome."

"You said it."

The guy held out his hand. Frankie shook it.

"Name's Geek, by the way. Kind of goes without saying. That's Lilith. You met Y. What's your name?"

"Frank," said Frank.

"Not just Frank," said Y. "Not just any old Frank. This here's Frank *Perdue,* but he's no relation to the chickens."

"Glad to hear it," said Geek. "So, Frank Perdue, how about the oil, then?"

"It doesn't get changed until tomorrow."

Geek looked at Y, who cocked his head toward the door. Lilith banged on the side of the vehicle. *"Char, le rat, s'il tu plaît!"*

A matted head poked out, covered with wild black hair that looked like it had been chopped with a hacksaw. Chunks of it curtained a small, pointed face. Dark brows. Large, animal eyes, liquid and quick. Looked to be about twelve or thirteen years old, Frank figured. Spooky.

49

"This is Char," said Lilith.

The kid peeled open the seal on a plastic freezer bag and pulled out something fur covered and dead.

"*Voilà.*"

It swung back and forth from a stiffened tail. Frank watched it, transfixed. He didn't get it.

"*C'est un rat.*"

"We'll dip it in the oil," said Lilith. "Then you can show your manager. Say you found it in the fryer."

Frank got it. "Is it frozen?"

"Yeah, but you can defrost it in the microwave."

"Where'd you find it?"

"Char sets traps down by the rail yards."

"Hey, that's sick," Frankie said.

The kid smiled shyly.

Frank hesitated now. "We never had a rat in the fryer before."

"Hey," Lilith said. "Rodents happen."

He led them to the service entrance, unlocked the door, and flicked on the overhead fluorescents. The four of them filed in after him, carrying empty metal drums. Illuminated against the white tile, they looked mangy and sly. Frankie eyed them as he stashed his skateboard in the corner. He looked at the mud on the floor, dislodged from the deeply treaded soles of their combat boots, and he wondered if they were going to freak out and rob him and tie him up and stick him in the freezer, and if they did, would the police be able to trace them from the footprints? He'd heard about cults. Even hippie retards could lose it. They headed straight for the kitchen.

"Hey," Frank called after them. "Just give me a minute, will ya?" He kept his jacket on and put on his cap. If he was going to get locked in the freezer, he wanted to be in uniform. By the time he got to the kitchen, they were draining the fryers. They even knew where the fresh oil was kept.

"You just go about your chores there," Geek said. "We'll take care of this."

The entire operation took less than half an hour. Frank held the door as Y and Geek hauled out three drums of old fry oil. Lilith followed, carrying two industrial-size wheels of toilet paper and a couple stacks of coffee filters. Char sidled up to Frank and handed him the rat in a Big Mac container.

"Char's already nuked it for you," said Geek. "Just tell your boss you made an executive decision."

Frank looked down at the oily rodent, curled in the hamburger container.

"Thanks, Frank Perdue." Lilith handed the heavy rolls to Char. She rested her hands on Frank's shoulders, then reached up and kissed him lightly on the mouth. Spinning on her steel-toed combat boot, she waved and floated out the door.

"Sure thing," he said to the empty doorway. He felt the blood, like windburn, redden his face. He heard a noise and spotted Char—the huge, dark eyes watching from behind the curtain of hair, the quizzical smile. Frank scowled and raised his middle finger, flipping the kid the bird, and in response the kid slowly stuck out a slim, red tongue. A silver ball lay on its spongy surface like a shiny offering, then, quick as a wink, the tongue was gone. The kid grinned and slipped out the door, past Geek, who was coming back in.

"You did us a solid, bro," he said. "We'll be over in the Kmart lot. Come by after work. Have a meal. Char's an awesome cook."

Frankie stood in the doorway like a hostess watching the guests leave the party. He sighed and closed the door. You do someone a favor, he thought, surveying the black boot prints marring the linoleum, and what do you get? A rat in a box and the privilege of cleaning up after. But heading back from school that afternoon, he decided to swing by the Kmart after all. Dudes like that didn't just show up every day, and anything was better than going home.

Not that it was a home. He lived with an asshole named Nuland, who injured his back in a factory accident and took in foster kids to supplement his disability. Frankie slept on a stinking couch in the living room, but Nuland kicked him off first thing in the morning so he could lie there all day and fart and watch the tube. It didn't matter. They were just killing time until Frankie was eighteen and out of the system. Nuland had made a pile off him for the last two years, and Frank lived rent free and did whatever he wanted. It was an okay arrangement, but it was not a home.

The Spudnik was different. When the mute kid opened the door for him and let him inside, it felt exactly the way Frankie imagined a home should feel. It smelled like old socks and french fries, young sweat and dander—smells that were familiar and alive, and his penis twitched in response to

51

the burrowlike warmth. There were other smells, too, new and strange. Candles burning. Musty incense. Shampoo. Food. The lights had all been turned down, and candles flickered. Lilith and Y were sitting cross-legged in the corner with their eyes shut. They were meditating, Geek whispered. Frank sat down to watch. A videotape of the ocean was playing over their heads on a monitor set into the transom above the front seats—a long, low, continuous shot of waves lapping gently on a pebbly beach. The watery sounds drowned out the noise of the parking lot and the highway beyond. Frank closed his eyes, too. He had never felt so relaxed in his life.

When they were done meditating, Geek rolled a joint. Char was cooking dinner, stirring a stew pot. The kid's hair was damp, like a hedgehog who'd crawled out from a shrub into the rain. Warm, fragrant steam rose from the pot.

"Smells good," Frank said.

The kid glanced up, then looked away, but not before the quick grin, like the beam from a moving flashlight, flickered through the mat of hair.

"Char's pretty nonverbal," Geek offered. "Awesome cook, but not much of a conversationalist. From Montreal. Been traveling with us for a couple of months now."

"What do you guys do anyway? Just bum around?"

"Not exactly. We're activists."

"What's that?"

"You know. Political activists."

"Oh." Frank thought for a bit. "You mean, like politicians?"

"Oh, shit!" Y laughed, snorting smoke. "That's very amusing."

Frank didn't get it. Or rather, he got it that Y and the others were laughing at him, and ordinarily that would have made him want to bust someone's head open, but now, with the pot and all, it really didn't matter. He figured eventually they would stop laughing, and then someone would explain. Frankie sat back and waited.

"You're not kidding, are you?" Geek said.

Frank shook his head.

"You're perfectly serious."

Frank nodded.

Geek peered into Frankie's face. "Wow." He took off his glasses and wiped the lenses. "Check it out," he said. "We target a range of food-related issues. Right now it's genetic engineering. We drive around the country to communities and engage with the people and do actions. Basic biotech. Consciousness Raising 101. We're the Seeds of Resistance—that's our name. We also publish a 'zine and a Web site. . . ."

"Bio-what?"

"Oh, jeez. Don't you know anything?"

Frank shook his head.

"Biotechnology," Geek said. "Robocrops. Frankenfoods. Fish genes spliced into tomatoes. Bacterial DNA into potatoes. Corn and—"

"Cool! You do all that stuff right in here?"

"What stuff?"

"What you said. Splicing, you know, whatever . . . fish genes and potatoes and—"

"No, Frank," Geek said. "We're *against* that."

"Oh." Frankie was disappointed.

"You have a lot to learn," Geek said.

"Yeah," Frank agreed, taking the joint and inhaling deeply. "You can't learn shit in Ashtabula."

ᗷᗡ

They ate the kid's excellent dinner, and smoked more dube. The kid started collecting dirty dishes, and Frank went to the sink and rolled up his sleeves. He ran some hot water and squirted detergent on a sponge. The kid bumped against him, gently shoving him out of the way.

"Hey, Charlie, dude," Frank said. "I'm a janitor. I wash things."

Char stared at him.

"That's my job," Frank said.

The kid clicked the silver tongue stud against teeth that were small and perfectly white. Frankie stared. He was still feeling the pot.

Y held out his hand to Lilith. "Bedtime," he said, pulling her to her feet. He turned to Frankie. "May as well crash here."

"Maybe Frank's got a home to go to," Lilith said.

Frank shook his head. "No way. I sleep on a guy's couch."

"Then crash out here with Char," Lilith said. She spun in a circle, dropping a kiss on Geek, another on the kid, and then she danced over to Frankie at the sink. The Spudnik rocked as she approached. She draped her arms around his neck.

"Night, Frank Perdue," she sang into his ear, and when he turned to face

53

her, she kissed him for the second time that day. "Mmm," she said, winking at Char. "Finger-lickin' good."

"Night," Frankie stuttered. He stood there staring as Lilith followed Y into the small bedroom at the end of the trailer. When Char flicked him with a towel, he realized he was dribbling suds.

The kid laid out pieces of foam on the floor, around the base of the dinette table, and piled some blankets on top. Frank crawled under one side of the pile.

"Bonne nuit," the kid said.

"Huh?"

"Bonne nuit," Char repeated. "Good night."

"Oh," said Frank. "Yeah." He lay there for a while. "Hey. Thanks for dinner. It was good."

When Char didn't answer, Frank closed his eyes. Just as he was drifting to sleep on the last gentle eddies of pot, he felt something wriggling across his stomach.

"What the—?"

He snatched at the movement in the dark and came up with the kid's wrist in his hand. He couldn't believe it. He twisted, and Char's small, pointy face appeared in front of him. The next moment the kid was kissing him on the mouth.

He was being molested by a juvenile punk with a tongue stud. This could not be happening.

He sat up and backed away, underneath the dinette. "Dude! What the fuck—?"

Char sat up, too, then threw back the blankets and started to peel off sweaters and shirts, in layers, like an animal shedding skins. The streetlight shone through the windshield, creating a silvery glaze that outlined the slight body. Frank recoiled into the far corner of the dining nook. The last piece of clothing was a sleeveless undershirt, and the kid ducked, pulling it off quickly. For a moment the shaggy head was caught in the cloth, but after a brief struggle, it emerged again. The slim body unfurled, then straightened and arched, and Frankie found himself staring at a perfect pair of girl's breasts. Naked, they gleamed in the light—was it the pot or the moonlight now?—and the transformation was complete.

Animal to human. Boy to girl. Girl to fucking goddess.

She took Frankie by the hands.

"Oh, shit," he said. "I think I'm wasted."

"Je m'appelle Charmey," she whispered, leaning forward. *"Pas Charlie. Charmey. Tu comprends?"*

"I don't understand," said Frank. It was such an understatement. It was definitely the pot. Her laughter shattered like glass. She brought her mouth down so that her lips just brushed his. Her lips were soft, and they teased his lips with nibbles until Frank opened his mouth. Quick as a newt, she slipped her tongue inside. He felt her tongue stud click against the back of his teeth. The kiss went on and on.

"What the fuck?" he said at last, when she stopped to catch her breath.

"Pauvre petit Frank," she whispered, pressing him down on his back, onto the blankets. *"Petit Frank, qui est perdu."*

It was Frank's first fuck. Accomplished by a girl with a pierced tongue, who kissed the length of his body from throat to groin, ran the trembling silver ball up and down his penis, used it to tickle him to the brink, then backed off again, over and over again until finally he couldn't stand it anymore. And he came, and then they did it again until he got the hang of it, and together they rocked the Winnebago until morning.

In the dull dawn light, filtering through the mists that rolled off Erie, Frank stroked the girl beside him, taking in her sleeping face, her breasts, running his fingers through the thicket of her hair. She murmured and turned over, and he caught sight of something dark on the nape of her pale neck that took his breath away. He brushed back her hair and stared.

Frank was a suburban kid, and a foster kid to boot. He knew that the world sucked. He listened to hardcore. He'd grown up in malls. He worked as a janitor at McDonald's and would have dropped out of school except he couldn't think of anything more interesting to do. But all of a sudden things were looking up. He'd just lost his virginity to a girl with a pierced tongue, and if that wasn't enough, now he'd stumbled onto a political stance he could wrap his mind around, one that bespoke a whole new world order. He traced his finger across the slim bone at the top of her spine.

What had made his heart turn over with a definitive thump was the delicate, two-inch-long bar code tattooed to the nape of her neck.

This, he told himself, was truly fucking radical.

lucky &

Spudmen are gamblers, Lloyd used to say. It's a hit-or-miss business, beset by the usual fluctuations in weather, bank rates, oil prices, random factors, and acts of God faced by any farmer. Getting the spuds safely in and out of the ground is only the beginning. After that you store them and wait. It's a lot like timing the stock market: If you hit, there's a lot of money to be made, and if you miss, you can lose the farm. As a result, spudmen are notoriously cagey. They keep an eye on their neighbor. They play it close to the vest.

The rapid growth of the fast-food chains was the random factor that helped fuel the potato boom of '74. In the 1980s it was McDonald's introduction of the Supersize Meal. In the nineties it was Wendy's Baked Potato.

That was the fun, Lloyd always said, in growing potatoes. The randomness. The little bit of luck. In fact, the entire agricultural backbone of the state of Idaho rests on a bit of luck that turned up in a truck garden in Massachusetts in 1872. The garden belonged to Lloyd's hero, a man known as the Father of the Modern Potato, Luther Burbank. His was an American success story, and Lloyd loved it. He would settle into his big chair and pull me onto his lap and read me Burbank's own account of how, as a twenty-one-year-old farmer with an elementary school education, he went out to tend his potato patch one day and found a seed ball!

" 'I use an exclamation point,' " Luther wrote. " 'That is because—well, it was what an astronomer would use if he discovered a new solar system.' "

"Imagine!" Lloyd would interject, putting the book down. It was Burbank's autobiography, *The Harvest of the Years,* and Lloyd would look up from the pages, past my head, marveling at Luther's metaphor and sharing his vision—an entire planetary system in a small ball of seeds!

" 'A potato seed-ball was not unheard of,' " Lloyd read, " 'but it was a great rarity, and I couldn't learn of any one who had done anything about the event even when it occurred. I *did* something; I planted the seeds in that ball.' "

And here Lloyd would look at me, to make sure I appreciated the radical nature of Luther's act. Being my father's daughter, of course I did.

You see, spudmen don't propagate potatoes by planting true seeds.

They do it by cloning. It's quick, simple, and reliable, and you can understand its appeal to farmers like my father, who are into total control. First you cut up a potato into small pieces, each containing an eye, and you plant these. The eyes grow into identical replicas of the parent, bearing their bundles of tubers, some of which you eat or sell, others you cut up to clone again. It's pretty foolproof.

The reason you clone rather than plant from seed is because potatoes, like human children, are wildly heterozygous. Lloyd taught me that word when I was eight. It simply means that if you try to propagate a domesticated potato using seed, sexually, chances are it will not grow true to type. Instead it will regress, displaying a haphazard variety of characteristics, reminiscent of its uncultivated potato progenitors—it may prove superior to the parent plant or may be wildly inferior. At eight, gazing up at my father's face, I didn't know which was worse.

After nature offered up her seed ball, Lloyd explained, Luther prepared the ground with great care, then planted each seed about a foot from its neighbor. The seed ball contained twenty-three seeds, so tiny that you could fit ten of them on the head of a pin. All twenty-three seeds produced seedlings, and here is where Luther was twice lucky: Of the twenty-three sprouts from his seed ball, he found two that were superior to the others in yield and size. That was his luck. The rest was history.

"'It was from the potatoes of those two plants,'" Lloyd read, his voice triumphant, "'carefully raised, carefully dug, jealously guarded, and painstakingly planted the next year, that I built the Burbank potato.'" Lloyd set down the book again. "Imagine!" He stared past me, shaking his head. "Building a potato as fine as that!"

In 1874 Burbank sold those precious potatoes to a seedman from Massachusetts, who paid young Luther $150, which he used to relocate to California.

In 1974, exactly one hundred years later, I slept with Elliot Rhodes and split for California, too, and the price of Russet Burbanks soared. There was no correlation between these events, of course. It was entirely coincidental. Nineteen-seventy-four was a year of rotten luck for me, and Elliot was my random factor, but it was a very lucky year for my father, and most farmers in the state, with the exception of our neighbor, Carl Unger. The Nine-Dollar Potato was the random factor that ruined him.

Because it's not just about luck, Lloyd would tell you. Potatoes also took guts. Cassie's daddy was never much of a gambler, and, although greedy, he was a bit of a coward to boot, which was why, early in the year, he thought it safer to contract his entire crop to the processor for a price of $3.25 per hundredweight. It was a sure thing, but where's the fun in it? Not that my father was anyone's idea of a high roller, but he did have a stubborn and independent nature, a suspicion of large corporations, and even something you might call vision. He didn't like to get into bed with anybody for the promise of a safe buck. So he held out, and when the market soared, Lloyd had a mountain of potatoes, free and clear and promised to nobody, piled sixteen feet high, stored at a cool forty-five degrees, in a cellar the size of an airplane hangar. He started to sell.

Carl had his $3.25 contract and a whole lot of envy. He just could not help himself. Nine dollars per hundredweight was a once-in-a-lifetime opportunity, so he reneged on his contract and sold at the open-market price, incurring the wrath of the processor. Then, desperate to make amends, he tried to buy potatoes from Lloyd. Lloyd refused. Carl offered 250 acres of land for 35,000 bags of potatoes. Lloyd accepted.

This deal must have caused a certain rancor to grow in Carl's heart, rancor that had been building over the years in proportion to the increase of my father's acreage. After I ran away and Lloyd had his first heart attack, Carl no doubt felt that it served us right. He went to Lloyd's hospital bed and offered to lease his fields at a rate that was considerably lower than the going rate, but which was nonetheless determined by the Nine-Dollar Potato. Lloyd, in no shape to run his farm, acquiesced to Unger's demands.

Not a bad deal, as it turned out. Because by the following fall, when potato prices plummeted to $4.00 a bag, Lloyd made more money on the lease than he would have had he planted the land. Carl Unger, on the other hand, went bankrupt. He was forced to go to work for Lloyd, and the following years were bad ones for Cassie. She and I were best friends, and I ran away without telling her, and she must have felt like I'd fallen right off the edge of the earth. Then my daddy went and ruined her daddy, so in some way my family was to blame for all the lickings she received since that night in the snow. I figured she might have some mixed feelings about me coming home. I know I did.

reunion ✍

After all these years. Cass couldn't get the phrase out of her head. She stood by the window in the arrivals lounge with her forehead pressed to the glass. The reflection of the red and green Christmas lights that decorated the lounge appeared to be floating against the dark tarmac outside. It was cold, and snow conditions east of the Cascades had delayed the plane. She had driven up from Liberty Falls just after one o'clock, and now it was late afternoon, and the prairie wind was whipping the snow around the tarmac, just mocking the plows.

She went back to the bar to have a cigarette. Not that she was supposed to be smoking. After the operation she'd more or less quit—she didn't smoke at home at all anymore, didn't even keep cigarettes around—but when she'd gotten in the car that morning, she knew she would smoke again for old times' sake, and as soon as she'd passed the Liberty Falls town-limits sign, she pulled into a 7-Eleven and bought a pack of Old Gold Filters. Will would kill her if he found out, but the thought of seeing Yummy made her crave it again. She smoked with the car window open. Her fingers were like ice on the wheel. If Will asked, she could blame the smell on Yummy.

She ordered another coffee, bypassed the sugar, and dumped in two packets of Nutrasweet. She was trying to be healthy, after all these years.

At four she phoned Will on the cell phone.

At five she had a hot dog and a Coors and another cigarette.

Finally, just after six, she heard the announcement for the Seattle flight. A small crowd had gathered by the gate. They were the same bored people she'd seen waiting all day, but now, one by one, their faces lit up as a long-awaited loved one emerged from the plane. Cassie's face felt frozen. Not eager. Not lit. She wondered if Yummy would recognize her. She was certain she would have no trouble recognizing Yummy Fuller.

And she didn't. Yummy hadn't changed at all. No. She *had* changed. She was taller, and older, of course. Her skin had relaxed about the eyes and cheeks, but her face was burnished by the sun. The people around her—dull, soft-bodied, and white—seemed to squint when they caught sight of her, she was just that bright. She wore cropped pants and a long, loose coat made out of linen, outrageously tropical among the massing

Polyfill parkas that eddied around her like lumpy clouds. She scanned the faces, and when her eyes came to rest on Cass, she frowned and cocked her head, combing the jet-black hair away from her forehead with her fingers.

"Cass?" she mouthed. "Is that you?"

Cass managed a nod, and she watched Yummy part the crowd with the ease of Moses. Then, before she knew it, they were standing face-to-face, and Cass found herself stepping back, the way you sometimes do when you walk out into a strong wind.

"Wow," Yummy said. "Cassie Unger."

"Hi," Cass said. Then she added, "It's Quinn now."

Yummy didn't seem to hear. "You grew."

"Yes. I guess. So did you."

"You're almost as tall as me."

"Not really." Cass tried not to slouch. "You're still taller."

"You've lost your baby fat." Yummy grinned and stepped back to appraise her. "Skinny, even."

Cass crossed her arms in front of her chest.

"Hey, no," Yummy said. "You look great. Just surprised me. Like a different person."

"Yes," Cass said. "I am."

"Hmmm . . ." Yummy said, drawing out the sound, as though unclear as to whether she agreed. "I guess we have changed, after all these years."

"Yes," Cass said. "After all these years."

Three children moved in a loose orbit around Yummy, like insects looking for a place to land. They were obviously attached to her, but they did not look much related.

"Are those your kids?" Cass asked.

"All three of 'em. Feels like a lot more. Do you have any?"

Cass shook her head.

"Well, you can have some of mine." She gestured impatiently to a skinny Asian boy with a baby on his hip, who ambled over, pushing an empty stroller. Yummy took the baby and gave the boy a shove toward Cass. "This is Phoenix. Phoenix, this is Cassie Unger. Sorry, Quinn. She lives next door to your *kupuna*."

It was a week before Christmas, and the boy was wearing a T-shirt and baggy shorts that came down to his knees, and his legs stuck out underneath like thin brown sticks. Scuffy sneakers. No socks. His bushy black hair stood up in bristles. Cass held out her hand to shake, but he drew his away and made a fist, leaving the thumb and pinkie standing. This he waggled at her.

"Howzit," he said. "You can call me Nix."

"He's fourteen," Yummy explained, setting the squirming baby down on his bottom, on the floor. "He's in the process of rejecting everything his mother ever gave him. Including his name."

"Oh, Yummy, that's such crap," Phoenix said.

"See what I mean?" Yummy smiled. She lowered her voice and spoke in a stage whisper. "Phoenix, remember what I told you. This is Idaho. Call me Mommy, and stop swearing or the townsfolk will lynch you." Phoenix rolled his eyes while Yummy grabbed another child, a fair-haired girl with sea blue eyes. "This one's Ocean. She's six and a half."

"Ocean has a nickname, too," Phoenix offered.

"Shuddup!" yelled Ocean.

"It's Puddle," Phoenix said with an evil smile.

"It is NOT!"

"And this is Poo," Phoenix offered smoothly, ducking Ocean's fist and capturing the escaping baby by the back of his suspenders. "He's not doing the walking thing yet." The baby sat on the floor and looked up at Cass, flapping his arms a little. His skin was the color of milk chocolate. Curls sprang from his head, each a soft and perfect vortex.

"What's his real name?" Cass asked.

"Just Poo. Mommy was striking out with the names, so she kind of just gave up." He picked the baby up and offered him to Cass. "Here. Wanna hold him?"

Cass took the baby in her arms. He was heavy and warm.

"That's not true, Phoenix," Yummy said. She turned to Cass. "His name is Barnabas, but he has to grow into it. For now Poo suits him just fine."

"Hello, Poo," Cass said. His eyes were liquid black. He gurgled and patted her cheek.

They collected their suitcases, and Cass waited while they opened them and dug out warm clothes; then she led them out to the parking lot. She felt like a ringmaster at a carnival parade. Their bags filled the back of the Suburban.

"It's freezing," Phoenix said, teeth chattering.

"It'll warm up once we get going," Cass told him.

Ocean climbed into the backseat next to her brother. "Yuuuck! This car stinks."

Yummy turned around. "Ocean, shut up."

"But it does!"

"Ocean—" There was a warning in Yummy's voice now.

The little girl subsided. "It smells like *cigarettes*," she whispered to Phoenix.

"So what?"

"I bet the lady smokes *cigarettes*."

"Why don't you ask her?"

Ocean leaned forward. "Excuse me," she said, tapping Cass on the shoulder. Cass glanced into the rearview as she put the car into reverse and backed out of the space.

"Do you smoke *cigarettes?*"

"Sometimes," she answered the child in the mirror. "Not often."

Ocean's face grew severe. "You shouldn't smoke cigarettes," she said. *"Ever."*

"I know."

"But do you know why you shouldn't?"

"Yes. I know."

"Because cigarettes give you cancer, and then you die."

"I know." Cass pulled up to the exit. She unrolled her window and fed the parking ticket into the slot. Felt the machine tug the slip from her fingers. For a split second she always wanted to resist the machine, to see what would happen if she held on tighter, but she never did. She always released, and the candy-striped barrier arm flipped up and let them by.

"So how come you still smoke?" Ocean persisted.

"Because I'm stupid, that's how come."

"Oh." The answer satisfied the child. She sat back next to her brother. "She says she's stupid."

"I *heard*," Phoenix groaned. "You think I'm deaf? *You're* the stupid buggah."

"I am not!"

"She's at that age," Yummy apologized. "Righteous little fascist."

Interstate 86 ran west from the Pocatello airport to Liberty Falls, away

from the foothills, perfectly straight, perfectly flat, cutting through a landscape that lay covered by new snow. The moon broke reluctantly through
receding clouds. It was warm in the car, and after a while the kids got tired
of bickering and fell asleep. Yummy stared out the window at the bright,
icy expanse.

"There's nothing out there," she breathed. "I'd completely forgotten. So
big. So empty. Nothing growing."

"It's just winter. Things start growing in the spring."

"I know. It just seems so dead now. But it's not dead at all. At rest. Deep
in the soil. It's so peaceful. It's never like this in Hawaii. Everything's growing all the time—a regular hotbed of vegetative activity. But here . . ."

"It's quiet, all right. Not much happens in winter. Aside from the storms."

They drove on a bit, staring at the patch of black highway ahead, and
the broken white lines, and the white snow swirling in the headlights.
Then Cass started talking again.

"About your mom and dad . . ."

"Did you tell them I was coming?"

"No. I didn't want to just in case—"

"I didn't show up. Okay. So what about them?"

"Well, your dad, really."

"I know. He's dying."

"Yes, well, it's just that he . . . well, since it didn't look like you were
coming home and nobody knew where to find you, he went and sold his
acreage."

"Oh?"

"Yes. A couple of years ago."

"How many acres were there?"

"Three thousand."

"Wow. What about the house?"

"There's a life-estate clause in the sale contract. They can live in it until . . ."

"Until they die."

"Yes."

"So who bought it?"

"Well, that's just it, Yum. It was me and Will."

"Oh." There was a long pause. Cass glanced over at Yummy, who was
looking out the window again.

"We'd been renting and farming it for years, but I was kind of worried that you might—" She hesitated.

"What?" inquired Yummy. "Be angry? Feel ripped off?"

"Well, yes. That you might have wanted the land after all."

"Oh." Again Yummy paused.

"Especially, well, seeing how you ended up in real estate . . ."

Yummy turned and looked at her. "Were you really worried?"

Cass felt her face grow hot. She kept her own eyes on the white line ahead.

"Because if you were really so worried," Yummy continued, "why didn't you try to find me? Before you bought it out from under me, you know?"

The close warmth of the car was suffocating. No air. Nowhere to go. No choice but to talk without too much thinking. Cass took a deep breath.

"Because I figured you'd run out on your parents and didn't deserve anything from them. Because I'd been taking care of them and was the only one who cared. Because me and Will work hard and had some real tough times and deserve better." Breathing hard, heart racing now, reckless, words tumbling over one another like spuds into a hopper. "Because it's good farmland, and you don't know shit about potatoes."

It was quiet in the car, and then Yummy spoke, softly, staring straight ahead. "Noble Pilgrim, my people and I welcome you to our land. . . ." She shook her head and laughed. "I can't believe I remembered that." She turned to Cass. "Listen. You're right. I don't know shit about potatoes. At least not anymore. And Lloyd probably wouldn't have left me the land in the first place. So I'm glad you have it, all right? Does that make you feel better?"

Cass nodded. She'd been clutching the wheel, shoulders risen up around her ears, and now she dropped them. "Thanks, Yummy. It does."

"Good. We know your journey has been a hard one," Yummy said solemnly. Cass started to laugh.

"I envied you, you know. I was always the potato."

"Oh, poor Cassie!"

"Do you know what it was like, lying there, tied up in that darn burlap bag, trying not to sneeze?"

"Yeah, but look at you now! Like a beanpole. Anyway, all you vegetables got to do the Pageant of the Side Dishes, and I had to sit there and *watch*. There were so many of you it took *forever*."

"It was our moment of glory! Yummy, do you know what it's like to go through life as a side dish?"

"No."

"I don't suppose you do."

yumi 弓

A white index card, meticulously printed in thick black marker, was taped to the refrigerator. It said REFRIGERATOR. Another that said STOVE was taped to the stove. Over the SINK the sign was warped by splashed water. I could stand there all night identifying appliances, and the kids would get up in the morning and find me, still naming.

They had loved it, of course. Ocean in particular. Like it was a neat game made up just for her, and she ran from sign to sign, collecting words like eggs in an Easter basket. "Toaster!" she cried. "Honey! Microwave!"

"Your grandpa made them," Cass explained. "For your grandma. Sometimes she forgets the names for things."

She'd helped me round up bedding before she left, and I'd gotten the kids settled. Phoenix had claimed the attic, with its sloping room and chipped iron bed, but Ocean and Poo lay tangled in blankets in a corral of sofa cushions on the floor of my old bedroom, sleeping under my ceiling of faded stars. Now, downstairs, the CLOCK said it was almost midnight. I wanted a whiskey, but I knew there wouldn't be any, so I heated water for tea instead. A sticky film of amber grease speckled the sides of the kettle. The plywood under the Formica counter by the faucet had swollen, and the laminate was lifting and peeling away. The faucet coughed, spit air, then began to flow, and the plumbing shuddered. As the kettle filled, I looked down and noticed two small patches on the floor where the linoleum had worn through. They were the imprints of Momoko's feet, unlabeled, of course, the by-product of hours and years she must have spent standing there washing dishes. I aligned my large feet with the marks made by my mother's small ones, covering them up. My demented mother, who forgot the names of things.

As the kettle boiled, I opened a drawer or two, then shut each one quickly as the contents, duly labeled, threatened to spring out and over-

65

whelm me. More by-product. Certain objects tickled recognition: the plastic corncob holders, the meat thermometer, the metal skewers used for stitching bread crumbs into a turkey. I rubbed my eyes to rub away the images before they unfurled into memories. I poured boiling water over a dusty tea bag from the drawer and walked into the living room.

I remembered exactly where the switches were located. In an unconscious sequence of automatic gestures, my hand reached toward the wall just as my foot crossed the threshold, resulting in a flood of illumination that startled me—the spatial relationships were familiar, but the details of the room confused me with their sudden clarity. For a moment I wondered where I was.

But not for long. For one thing, there was a sign that read LIVING ROOM, stuck to the opposite wall. Then, gradually, like a photograph developing, the room found its resolution and I began to recognize objects: love seat, Lloyd's desk, couch, Lloyd's recliner, coffee table, TV. I sat on the couch for a while, then moved to the desk. I shuffled through a stack of papers, old bills mostly, some farm reports, some invoices, and a few old catalogs from Fullers' Seeds.

Cass had gone through the correspondence and kept up with the bills, but inquiries and orders for seeds were starting to come in, and she had put these all to one side for me to deal with. A pad of ruled paper sat next to the pile, something Lloyd was working on before his heart attack. The spidery handwriting wobbled across the page—slow loops, trembling with the effort of toeing the lines. Was he really so decrepit? So feeble? I took a recent Fullers' Seeds catalog over to Lloyd's chair and started to read:

FULLERS' SEEDS
M. and L. J. Fuller—Seedsmen
Liberty Falls, Idaho
Vendimus Semina
Since 1984

To Our Customers:
This will be the 15th year that Mrs. Fuller and I have been joyfully trafficking in seeds. We are proud to announce that this year there are 17 new listings, including many new European heirloom varieties, as well as exciting additions to Mrs. Fuller's "Oriental Collection," such as the Momórdica charantia (Chinese Bitter Melon), the showy Bombax mal-

abaricum (Red Silk Cotton Tree) from India, and the venerable "Hindu Datura," important medicinally and religiously in the Old World.

And while we are on the subject of Exotics, there is a idea in circulation that these so-called "aggressive" non native plants are harmful, invasive, and will displace "native" species. How ironic to hear these theories propounded by people of European ancestry in America! Just consider this: Not a single one of the food crops that make the U.S. an agricultural power today is native to North America. Our plants are as immigrant as we are!

Mrs. Fuller and I believe, firstly, that anti-exoticism is Anti-Life: **"God giveth it a body as it hath pleased him, and to every seed his own body"** [1 Corinthians 15:38]. Secondly, we believe anti-exoticism to be explicitly racist, and having fought for Freedom and Democracy against Hitler, I do not intend to promote Third Reich eugenics in our family garden. Finally, we believe anti-exoticism to be propaganda of the very worst kind. I used to farm potatoes, and I have witnessed firsthand the demise of the American family farm. I have seen how large Corporations hold the American Farmer in thrall, prisoners to their chemical tyranny and their buy-outs of politicians and judges. I have come to believe that anti-exotic agendas are being promoted by these same Agribusiness and Chemical Corporations as yet another means of peddling their weed killers.

Mrs. Fuller and I believe the careful introduction of species into new habitats serves to increase biological variety and health. God in His great wisdom has given us this abundance. **"O Lord, how manifold are thy works! In wisdom hast thou made them all: the earth is full of thy riches"** [Psalms 104:24–25].

And one final note: Mrs. Fuller has asked me to remind you to plant her favorite exotic, a living fossil from the Orient, the noble Ginkgo biloba! A relic species, with fossils dating back to 200 million years ago, this hardy tree grows to 120 feet, with handsome fan-shaped leaves that turn a beautiful golden color in the fall. Now, *here* is a tree that is extinct in the wild and owes its survival to dissemination and cultivation by the hand of man! Mrs. Fuller tells me that the seeds are eaten in Japan and China, and that both seeds and leaves are useful for a variety of conditions associated with aging, in particular memory loss. So don't forget! Plant one for your retirement now!

The seed listings that followed were arranged alphabetically into major vegetable families and genera: the *Allium*, the *Brassica*, the *Chenopodium*. I flipped through them quickly, barely seeing, overwhelmed by the orderly force of my father's opinions. Suddenly the room was full of him, and I remembered the way he would come in from the fields, and Momoko and I would be waiting, and the house would shrink and conform around his approbation. It made me queasy to think about. I stood up quickly and replaced the catalog on the pile of unanswered correspondence. I returned to the KITCHEN, rinsed my cup in the SINK, and climbed the stairs to my bedroom.

I used to close myself into this room, so I could think my thoughts alone. Now I lay down on my little bed and stared up at my starry ceiling, listening to my children breathe. Lloyd had raised these heavens for me—they were luminous decals that came in a kit. The Friendly Stars That Glow. The day he applied them, he stood in the middle of the mattress, my tall, rickety father, as I jumped up and down. He was trying to consult his map of the nighttime sky, something he could not do well with all my bouncing. He told me to hold still, so I lay down on my back to watch. He stood on his tiptoes and stretched across the heavens with Polaris balanced on his fingertip. I could feel the mattress tremble beneath his feet. With the North Star correctly affixed, he smiled, then moved south toward the next horizon.

I was excited at first but soon grew tired of the project. Order in the heavens didn't matter much to me—I must have been about six or seven, Ocean's age—and besides, it was still daytime. The stars were pale green and disappeared against the white ceiling, and I couldn't even see them. *Be still*, Lloyd said. *Be patient*. But patience wasn't in my nature. I fidgeted, and when he reprimanded me, I lay there, arms rigid against my sides like a plank, making a big show of being perfectly still, exactly like Ocean would do now. And just like Ocean, I soon got bored with this game, so I bounced my bottom just a little to see if he'd fall down. *Yumi, I said that's enough!* But I already knew that, and I gave one last tremendous bounce off the mattress and ran out the door, leaving him stranded, tall and precarious, wobbling to keep his balance.

But that night, after Momoko had tucked me in and turned off the light, I opened my eyes and looked up to see the night sky come to life. *Daddy!* I cried, and Lloyd must have been waiting outside my door like a kid on Christmas because he was by my side in a heartbeat.

Look, Daddy! It's heaven!

He chuckled with pleasure at my excitement. He sat down next to me, and I followed his finger as he pointed to the Dippers. I remember a deep, celestial bliss, a sense of galactic stability, which pretty well lasted until my nebula spun out of his control and a dark star crossed my firmament, eclipsing him entirely.

poppies 🪢

Lloyd spotted his wife immediately, sitting by herself at a table in the corner of the day room. She looked so small, curled over and concentrating, like a child at a task. On the floor by her feet was a brown paper bag, and she was taking things from it. As the nurse wheeled him closer, he could see they were seedpods, the size of plums with crowns at the top. She was doing Hens and Chicks, the pride of her ornamental poppies. She could no longer remember the names of these seeds, so she would need Lloyd to write the labels, but that would happen later on. For the time being she was intent on her work, poking the woody casing with the point of a pencil, making a hole, then shaking the minuscule seeds from the ovary onto a turquoise cafeteria tray that she was using as a work surface.

"Oidé yo, tané-chan!" she whispered. "Come here, little seeds. . . ."

When the nurse wheeled him over and parked him next to her, she looked up, surprised.

"Well, well!" the nurse said. "You've been busy, sitting here all by your lonesome!" She kicked the brakes into place and peered at Momoko. "What do you have there?"

Momoko smiled politely, then bent her head and rattled a pod. The seeds bounced across the turquoise surface like fleas. She tipped the tray, and hundreds, maybe thousands, of seeds massed and rolled together like something spreading and alive.

"Well," the nurse continued, adjusting Lloyd's collar. "You'll be glad to hear that our boy did real good in physio today. He buttoned up his own pajama tops and walked to the potty all by himself."

Lloyd groaned. "Nurse, please."

"Even had a nice long bath, didn't we?"

"Sheila! Please!"

The nurse made a big, pouty face. "Oooh, you're hurting my feelings. Sheila was yesterday. I'm Shirley."

"I'm sorry," Lloyd said.

"That's okay, I forgive you." She turned to Momoko. "Aren't you even going to say howdy to your honey?"

"Howdy," Momoko said. Lloyd reached out and patted her hand.

"That's more like it," said Shirley. "Now, let's get those meds down."

Momoko stared at Lloyd's hand, with their blunt, bluish-colored nails, then looked up at his face. "You so old man!" she said. "How you get so old?"

Shirley returned with a pitcher of water. "What a thing to say!"

"Shirley, please," said Lloyd. "It's okay. An old joke."

"Oh, well, I guess it's none of *my* business then." She handed Lloyd his pills and a cup. "Drink up," she said, tapping her foot and looking past him toward the TV in the corner of the room. Several patients and their visitors sat around it, watching a rerun of *Rescue 911*. Sirens screamed as the paramedics used the Jaws of Life to pry a family out from the wreckage of a sport-utility vehicle.

A choking sound from Lloyd made her look back down. "Lloyd? Are you all right?"

He didn't answer. He was staring at the doorway of the dayroom where a tall woman stood, anxiously scanning the patients' faces. He shook his head to clear his vision. He was taking digitalis for his heart, which sometimes caused an oily film to form over the world and rainbows to leak from bright objects. The woman looked unbearably bright to him. The cup crumpled in his grip, and water dribbled down his wrist. He closed his eyes, then opened them again, to blink away the rainbows. He gulped for air. He started to gasp.

"Lloyd!" The nurse sounded urgent but far away. "Talk to me! Is it your heart?"

"My pocket . . ." He plucked at the front of his bathrobe with clumsy fingers. "My nitroglycerin . . ."

The nurse pried his hands away. He could feel her fumbling for the small vial in his breast pocket. He felt his mouth gaping open, jaws stretching wide. She dropped a tablet under his tongue. He shut his eyes, trying not to hear their voices. He breathed again.

"Dad?" It was her. She was standing close by now. "Oh, my God. Is he okay?"

The nurse checked his pulse. "He'll be fine. Who are you?"

"I'm his daughter. I didn't mean to shock him. I called ahead. I talked to Sheila. She was supposed to prepare him."

"Oh, well, that's just fine," said Shirley. "She never told me anything. They weren't expecting any relatives."

"Dad?" the woman said.

Lloyd opened his eyes, but he couldn't bring himself to look up. He looked at his wife instead. The expression on her face was distant and per-plexed, but as he watched, it lit up like the hills when the sun broke out from a cloud. She rose to her feet.

"Yumi?"

His wife's voice was unearthly. The dayroom fell silent, except for the odd whoop of an emergency vehicle on the television, as Momoko hurtled forward, into the woman's open arms. Lloyd closed his eyes again.

"Mom?" The word sounded odd, choked and breathless. "Oh, *Mom . . .*" It was a sigh this time.

It was too much. "That's enough," Lloyd whispered. "Take me away."

He felt the nurse hesitate, and then she kicked off the brakes. "A lot of excitement for one morning," she said, wheeling the chair around. "I think we'll feel a whole lot better after a little rest."

"No, wait!" Now the woman was standing in front of his chair. "I want to talk to my father."

He covered his face with his hands. His knuckles were swollen, and his fingers were like plugs. "Let's not make a scene . . ." he pleaded.

"Dad, please don't do this . . ."

He recoiled farther into his chair, but she stood there, blocking his way, and it was like no one would ever move again or say another word. But then Momoko broke the silence.

"Damé!" she said. She picked up the turquoise cafeteria tray as though she were about to head off down a buffet line, but instead she flung it above her head. The air around her filled with a cloud of black seeds. He could feel them, raining down on top of him, like a tickling wind. He watched them bouncing crazily off the tabletops and skittering across the floor.

"My goodness!" the nurse said. "All these seeds!" She started brushing them from the folds of his bathrobe, then dabbing with her finger at the ones on his head.

"Stop it!" he said, jerking away. "Take me out of here!"

Shirley shrugged and gave his head a final swipe. "Too bad," she said, swinging the chair around. "But who knows? Maybe they'll grow."

"Yes!" Momoko clapped her hands. Then, spotting the pitcher of water on the table, she picked it up and marched over to Lloyd.

"Poppy!" she said, peering down at his face. "Same like father. Get it? It is good joke. Ha, ha." Then she poured the water onto the seed-speckled carpet at his feet. "Okay, poppy. Now you grow up!"

She walked behind the chair and elbowed the nurse out of the way. Gripping the handles, she wheeled the chair toward her daughter, stopping as the metal footrests bumped her shins.

"Say howdy," she commanded her husband.

Lloyd groaned.

"Say howdy to her."

Lloyd was defeated. He looked up at the variegated confusion of light that was his daughter and blinked his eyes.

"Howdy," he whispered.

"Howdy," Yumi echoed.

Momoko nodded. "Okeydokey."

idaho winter ᗽ

Children's children are the crown of old men. . . .

Ocean whispered, "Is that him? Is that Tutu Lloyd?"

. . . and the glory of children are their fathers.

"Yes, but call him Grandpa."

Phoenix pulled at my arm. "Forget it, Yummy. I mean, *Mommy*. He's asleep. Let's go."

"No, look. He's waking up."

"Who's there?" He opened his eyes, swimmingly. "Who are these children?"

I wanted to announce it with pride. "These are your grandchildren,

Dad!" But my voice betrayed me, and my declaration sounded more like an apology. "My children," I added unnecessarily.

He blinked. His eyes were the color of an icicle, a cold prong clinging to an eaves trough. He scanned my children's faces. The kids were not used to the Idaho cold, and already they looked faded. Dehydrated by the central heating, Ocean had developed flaking rashes. Poo's snot turned rock hard in his sinuses, and his curls lay flat. Phoenix had the coloring and temperament of moldy bread. They missed the humid clouds, the teeming seas. But this was good for them, I told myself. They needed to know that Mommy was not all about aloha. That she had cold, high desert in her blood.

"This is Phoenix. And this is Ocean. This is Barnabas, but we call him Poo."

He studied their hair, their complexions. Comparing.

"Say hi to your grandpa, kids."

He said gruffly, "What kind of names are those?"

"What do you mean, Dad?" Knowing full well what he was getting at, of course.

"What kind of children have names like that?"

"Well, your grandchildren. Kids, say howdy to your grandpa."

"Howdy?" muttered Phoenix, turning away. "Like, I don't think so."

But intrepid Ocean stepped up to the plate. "We're *good* children," she replied. "That's what kind." What a kid. No one deserves a kid like that.

He blinked at her and stared. She looked right back, met his ice with her sky blue—the color of cornflowers—until he recognized the sweet side of those Fuller eyes and melted a little for real.

"Come here," he barked.

Ocean approached the wheelchair.

"What's your name?"

"Ocean."

"That's not a proper name. An ocean is a thing, not a person."

Ocean didn't answer for a while. "I know what your name is," she said finally. "It's Tutu—I mean, it's Grandpa Lloyd."

"That's right."

"How come it doesn't mean anything?" Ocean asked.

"Because it's a proper name."

"Actually, it does mean something," I said. Lloyd and Ocean both turned to stare, and the resemblance was stunning. The stubborn blue eyes and the broad forehead. The set of the jaw. The same irritation at being interrupted.

"It means 'gray-haired,'" I explained. "In Welsh. Or something." I could see they were waiting for me to finish, but my nerves had turned me garrulous. "I looked it up in one of those baby-name books in the checkout line. At the supermarket. When I was pregnant with Phoenix and looking for a name. Of course, Phoenix wasn't listed. . . ."

Phoenix groaned, and I stopped. Ocean turned back to contemplate her grandfather. "Lloyd is a good name for you," she said.

"It is?" he asked. "Why?"

"Because you're old."

"Am I so old?"

"Yes," Ocean explained. "That's why you're dying."

That's it, I thought. That's the end of it.

But Lloyd was oddly patient. "Is that right?" he said.

"Yes. Mommy said we have to be nice to you because you're dying, but I'm not going to."

"You're not?"

"No. I'm going to be nice to you because I like you instead."

"Oh," he said, narrowing his eyes. "That's good."

"You mean it's good because you like me, too?" She was being coy now, a little too cocky.

"No," he said, and if he registered the child's disappointment, he ignored it. He looked over her head, straight at me. "Good, because despite your mother's godlike authority over matters of life and death, I am most certainly not dying."

ℬ

"Of course he's dying," Cass said. "I don't mean to be harsh, Yum, but that's not even the question here. It's just that it might take awhile, and what are you going to do for him until then?"

"Me?"

"Well, sure. Who else?"

It was a reasonable enough question, but it had never occurred to me. I'd made this odyssey for the children. I thought I owed it to them, to let

74

them meet their grandparents. But Cass was clearly thinking along very different lines, and it filled me with panic.

"There must be health services or—"

"Yummy, I've been taking care of your parents for almost a year now, cooking and cleaning up after them—"

"I know, and they appreciate it. They really do. Mom was telling me how much Lloyd enjoys your pot roast."

"I change his colostomy bag, Yum."

"Oh. He wears one of those?"

"He needs to be changed twice a day."

"Wow." I watched her. She had taken over feeding Poo, and the older kids were eating in the living room. I really wanted a drink. I'd remembered to stop at the liquor store on the way back from the nursing home, but I had been too strung out for the supermarket. I knew there were some cans of soup in the cupboard and a bag of french fries in the freezer, and I figured I could feed the kids that, but when we pulled up to the house, the smell of cooking wafted across the yard from the kitchen. Phoenix and Ocean, sensing a hot meal, perked right up, and they tore across the snow, leaving me lugging the baby. As I approached the house, I had a sudden strong sense of how it used to feel to come home on a wintry night, in from the cold, and smell dinner in the oven.

Cass had a casserole heating. She took one look at my face and held out her arms for Poo, planted him in his high chair, then instructed the kids to take their dinners and eat in front of the TV. They hesitated, but when I didn't object, they scampered off, delighted. I could hear them quarreling about the remote control, but finally they found some show about cops and settled down. Cass spooned macaroni into Poo's mouth while I told her about the tender meeting between Lloyd and his grandchildren, and that's when she'd casually sprung the subject of Lloyd's care.

Now, thoroughly spooked, I poured whiskey for us both. I sat back down at the table, raised my glass, and glanced around the room. It felt so strange, to sit at my parents' kitchen table drinking whiskey, that I had to laugh. Cass got it.

"I feel like we should hide it or something," she said.

"Yeah, like we'll get caught." I took a long sip. It felt good. It could feel even better. "Hey, do me a favor. Smoke a cigarette so I can have a drag?"

"Have one of your own."

75

"Can't." I glanced toward the living room, where a police siren wailed. Phoenix said something, and Ocean's laughter peaked and faded like a whitecap on a wave. "They're worse than parents."

Cass nodded. "In my purse."

The purse was a loaf-shaped thing, something her mother would have carried. I fumbled around, half expecting compacts and hairnets, and found the pack. Old Gold Filters. I lit up and inhaled, and when the nicotine hit, so did the feeling of being twelve or thirteen, getting high on the rush of another small rebellion. I passed the cigarette to Cass, and for a fleeting moment there she was, the girl I grew up with, who knew how a cigarette should be smoked and shared because I'd taught her.

She exhaled and smiled. "It's good to see you, Yummy. Good to have you back."

Hearing her words, though, I felt another wave of panic. "It's good to see you, too, Cass," I said. "I just wish I could stay for longer."

I didn't wish any such thing, and she knew it. She looked at me evenly, as she pulled Poo from his high chair.

"I mean, I've got to get back to teach, and the kids have their school and all. . . ." I took another drag of the cigarette, passed it back to her, and changed the subject. "God, that tastes good. I quit fourteen years ago, when I was pregnant with Phoenix."

"Oh."

"You ever quit?"

"Oh, sure. A bunch of times. Every time I got pregnant, in fact." She had Poo on her lap now, and she was careful to direct the smoke away from his curls, into the air above his head. Her jaw jutted upward, tightening the muscles in her throat. She paused and watched the smoke disperse, as though she were remembering something, and when she spoke again, her voice was quiet.

"I'd get pregnant, quit, miscarry. Then do it all over again." She ground out the cigarette in the saucer, pressing the filter down to extinguish every last spark.

"Oh, Cassie, I'm sorry. Do you know why? I mean, was there a reason, or—"

"Oh, jeez, Yummy." She looked at her watch over the hump of Poo's back. He was on the edge of sleep. There was a finality in her voice, as though she wanted to wrap up the conversation, get to her feet, and leave, but instead she shifted and sighed.

"Could be anything," she said, rocking the baby gently back and forth. "At first we thought nitrates in the groundwater, so we got the well tested and got filters and everything, but it didn't help. Then we thought it might be one of the other inputs—stuff we use around the farm. For a while Will even thought it might be some kind of chemical exposure from overseas or something."

"Overseas?"

"He fought in Vietnam," she said. "And it could be any of these things, or none of them, or maybe even some combination. It's just impossible to know for sure. And even if we could prove it was something we were using, what could we do?"

"Can't you stop using it?"

She looked pityingly at me. "You really don't know shit about potatoes, do you? We got three thousand acres, it's not that easy."

"But if it's poisoning you . . ."

Poo had fallen asleep and started to slump. Now she hauled him higher on her lap. "Banks don't lend money to farmers who don't use inputs. Not sound farming practice."

Poo woke and started to make little mewling noises. Cass bounced him and smiled. "Mind you, we haven't stopped trying. We've still got hope."

The baby butted her with his big, sleepy head, burying his face in her chest.

I held out my arms. "I'm just weaning him," I told her. "He'll go back to sleep. You want me to take him?"

But Cass shook her head. I watched my son's dark, pudgy fingers knead the front of her pink sweatshirt, looking for my breast, her breast, any breast. Not finding—

"He likes you," I said, then I realized what was wrong.

Cass was resting her chin on the crown of Poo's head, watching me. When she saw the look on my face, she nodded. "Both of 'em." She spoke into Poo's soft baby curls. "It's been seven years now and no sign of reoccurrence, so they think they got it all."

"Oh, Cass." The sounds of a car chase seeped in from the living room. I tried to say something else, but I'd run out of words.

"I told you my mom died of it," she said. "I'm the lucky one. As soon as we found the lump, I decided to have them take everything, just in case. The whole shebang." She smiled and looked down at her chest. "Remember how I used to complain about my cup size? All through high school I was saving up for a boob reduction. Guess you gotta watch out what you ask for."

She rocked back and forth, quieting the baby, who smacked his lips, sleeping again. Her chair leg creaked against the linoleum. She tapped another cigarette from the pack and lit it. "The Lord works in mysterious ways," she mused on the exhale.

"Cass, maybe you shouldn't . . ."

She shrugged and handed me the butt. "Must be your bad influence. I don't usually smoke this much. Will won't let me."

The cigarette tasted stale now. I took a drag and put it out.

"It's funny," Cass continued. "Every time I miscarried, I thought of you. Thought of that horrible trip to Pocatello with that teacher—what was his name?"

I felt my heart start to race. She was opening the door to the past, and I was stepping through it. "Elliot," I said. It had been years since I'd spoken his name, and the syllables tasted as stale and acrid as smoke.

"That's right. Mr. Rhodes. He was an okay teacher, but what a creep!"

"Whatever happened to him?" I asked, nudging the door open wider. "Did he keep on teaching or . . . ?"

She looked surprised and shook her head. "I don't know. He disappeared. I figured you guys had it all planned out and lived happily ever after."

"I never saw him again. Not after that night." After that night there was no happily ever after.

Cass nodded. "Maybe they ran him out of town or something. He just kind of disappeared. You know, it wasn't so bad taking a licking for you from Pa over that business, but I never forgave you for leaving without me. I waited for you, but you never even wrote."

"But I did! I wrote as soon as I got there." My mind was racing. I wanted to explain. I was living on the street. I had to steal a pen. I panhandled to buy stamps. "I wrote lots of letters. You're the one who never wrote back!"

Cass shrugged. "My parents must have burned them. I never got a single one."

"I thought you'd turned against me, like everyone else."

"Honestly, Yummy, I did. I started to think it was all your fault. Each time I miscarried and saw the blood, it just brought it all back. I felt like God was punishing me for helping you out. Crazy, huh? But if that's the case, then how come you're here now with three great kids? You know what I mean? It doesn't make sense. If anyone deserved to get punished, it was you, right?"

I felt I'd been punished plenty. I started to answer, then realized she was talking mostly to herself, musing into the top of Poo's head, and when he twitched in his sleep, it occurred to me to wonder how much the infant mind absorbed, and whether this talk of retribution might seep through his thin skull, to haunt me later on. Her voice grew quiet and still.

"My daddy used to say you were a bad seed. You took all the luck away from here, Yummy." Her breath disturbed my baby's silky curls. "All the life and the luck. You didn't leave any behind."

"Cass, that's not true," I started to say, but just then Ocean appeared in the doorway, nose in the air, sniffing.

"Phew," she said, looking straight at Cass. "It stinks in here. Have you been smoking cigarettes again?"

"Ocean, shut up. This is grown-up time. Go away."

But Ocean ignored me and walked right up to Cass, pausing to examine the two butts in the saucer on the way. "Listen," she said, frowning over her baby brother's head. "I don't think you should smoke around us."

"Ocean, I mean it!"

"It's not good for Poo," she persisted.

"Damn it, Ocean—"

"And you're a bad influence on my mother."

"*I* was the one who was smoking."

Ocean turned slowly and stared at me, then looked back at Cass. "See?" she said, shrugging her shoulders. "See what you've done?"

"That's it." I grabbed her under the arm, fed up with her uncontrollable mouth. She cried out, but I dragged her toward the doorway until Cass spoke.

"Ocean, you're absolutely right."

I stopped and looked back.

"She's right, Yummy. I shouldn't smoke around all of you. I shouldn't smoke at all. So how about I quit? Okay? Right now."

She took the pack of cigarettes and held it out to Ocean, who was sniveling and rubbing her armpit. "Here, you take them. Throw them away for me."

Ocean looked up, vindicated but still a bit scared, not quite sure this wasn't some nasty grown-up joke with a punch line waiting to happen to her, but I gave her a little push between the shoulder blades, pitching her forward, and she took the cigarette pack. She looked at it like it contained a great and evil power.

"Where should I throw it?" she asked, voice hushed.

"How about in the garbage?" Cass whispered back.

"Okay." She tiptoed forward, then stopped. "Where's the garbage?"

"Under the sink," I whispered. We were all whispering now.

She carefully opened the cabinet and deposited the cigarette pack in the garbage container, then closed it firmly and whirled around. She leaned her small bottom up against the door, breathless, as though the cigarettes might try to escape again, might pound and scrabble against the inside of the cabinet like wild things. She waited, but all was quiet, so she wiped her hands together with a great sense of closure. Task completed. Job well done.

"There," she said in a normal voice. "I guess that's that." She gave us a great, beaming smile. "I'm so proud of both of you!"

"Oh, God, Ocean! Give it a rest."

"Mommy, you have a bad attitude," she said, frowning at me. She walked over to Cass and examined her face.

"Hey!" she said. "I saved your life!" Then she skipped off to watch some more TV.

"Want them back?" I asked, but Cass was staring toward the living room. "You want your cigarettes back?" I repeated, getting up and walking to the sink.

"No," Cass said. "She's right. I may as well try and quit for good."

"You don't have to, you know."

"Might as well. It won't kill me."

So I sat down, but later, after Cass had left and the kids were asleep, I sneaked back into the kitchen and rummaged through the garbage until I found the pack, a little soggy from a wet coffee filter, but smokable still. I pocketed it and walked outside into the frostbitten landscape. The moon was shining against the ice-covered fields, and the windows of the house glowed yellow. Next to the house, Momoko's garden was nothing but spectral stumps and stalks and mounds of tumular snow, like the site of ancient burials. Skeletal poplars bordered the garden, and beyond, the white fields stretched out forever.

The snow underfoot made a sound like chalk on a blackboard. It had iced over during the day, but that morning it had still been fresh and soft. When Ocean woke, she was enchanted. She ran to the window and announced her immediate intention to go outside and play, but I caught her at the door. She was a tropical child, with no understanding of the bitterness of cold. I took her to the mudroom and stuffed her into an old pink snowsuit I'd found, and she stood there, straining like small sausage. She was whimpering by the time I shoved a knit cap onto her head, pulling it down low to cover her ears. I zipped her up, catching her throat skin in the metal teeth and drawing a speck of blood, which I wiped off with spit on my thumb. I wrapped her neck in a scarf and knotted it, then clipped mittens onto her cuffs. I made her put Baggies on her double-socked feet and step into felt-lined galoshes. I sat back on my heels and looked at her with grim satisfaction. It's amazing, the routines you remember.

"There. Go on outside."

Ocean's face, what I could see of it, twisted in despair. "But I can't mooooooooooove," she wailed.

Go. Play, girl, play. I shoved her, sniffling, out onto the porch, and she descended the steps like an ancient woman, feeble and tentative. When she reached the ground, her rubberized feet flew out from under her and she fell down hard on her well-padded bottom. She lay there pinkly in the snow, face up, immobile. I watched her from inside the door. Phoenix joined me.

"Yummy, she's not moving."

"Mmm."

"Aren't you going to help her?"

"She's all right. She's dressed for the weather."

He sighed and then pushed past me. He was wearing his surfing jams. It was zero degrees out. He ran down the steps, hauled his plug-shaped sister to her feet, and brushed her off. "Come on, Puddle," he said. "Stand up." He was wearing flip-flops and a T-shirt with a skateboard logo.

Now I lit the soggy cigarette in the dark and shivered. When you're seven years old, you think you know everything. When you're fourteen, you're certain you do. When you're pushing forty, if you're honest with

81

yourself, you realize that your omniscience is wearing thin. If I'd had any foreknowledge at all, I would never have come back here. Now that I was back, I was feeling as restless as if I'd never left in the first place.

Fourteen. It seemed impossible that I had ever been so young, or so in love. So sure of everything. I exhaled and the acrid smoke mixed with the frozen air. I'd forgotten about Idaho winters, how long and punishing they could be.

elliot &

It was not just bad luck that led to Elliot's transfer to potatoes. Rather it was an ironic twist of fate, and one he found very unpleasant when his boss pointed it out. The conversation took place in Duncan's office, on the northeast corner of the twenty-third floor of the D&W building. Twenty-three was an auspicious number. The northeast corner balanced Dragon energy with the Tortoise, auguring material wealth.

"Of course we had the offices feng shui–ed," Duncan explained. "Powerful stuff. Do you know there's a feng shui index in the Hong Kong stock market?"

Elliot shook his head. Clear water trickled down a craggy rock face located against the far wall of the room, gurgling as it spilled into a limpid pond. The sound was playful yet serene. A small Japanese lantern sat on the edge of the pond, and fish flickered below the water's surface. A residue of incense hung in the air.

Elliot sat before the black marble expanse of Duncan's desk, watching his boss finger a floret carved from a Japanese radish. Behind him in the distance, through the polarized glass, Elliot could see the ghostly architecture of the nation's capital glimmering in the twilight.

"Sorry to keep you so late," Duncan said, nudging a plate of seaweed across the sleek desk with the lacquered tip of his chopsticks. "You sure you won't join me?"

"No thanks, Duncan." Elliot eyed the mound of dark, twiglike shapes, glistening in a muddy dressing and dotted with seeds. "I'm going out for dinner."

"Gotta watch it in restaurants, Elliot. Never eat in them myself. Not unless I know the owners."

"That's very . . . careful of you."

"Can't be too careful these days. Never know where your food is coming from." He lifted a ruffled leaf of lettuce to his lips. "Food is sacred, Elliot. Food is life."

"Yes, I can see that." Elliot watched his boss chew the leaf for what seemed like a very long time. Duncan was the junior partner in the firm. Wiley, the senior partner, was an old-school PR man. Duncan was the young eccentric, the wild card, the one Wiley counted on to think out of the box.

"Just got back from a raw retreat in Maui," Duncan said when he finally swallowed. "Fantastic. All the food was exquisitely uncooked, but the power locked in those legumes! The purity! The unadulterated energy! It was life altering." He bowed over a slice of avocado, then speared it with his chopsticks. "You really should go. I'll have Sedona send you the contacts."

"That would be just great."

"It clears the head," Duncan added. "Balances the yang. Equilibrium is the key, Elliot. It enables one to accept what the Universe offers."

Elliot was trying to look open and enthusiastic. He didn't quite know how to interpret the general direction the conversation was taking, never mind predict when Duncan would get to the point. The man had two methods, one a smooth shift into a higher gear, the other a sudden, clutchless grind into reverse.

"I've got some rather fortuitous news, Elliot."

Elliot braced while Duncan took a sip of frothy green tea from a ceramic bowl. He watched his employer's tongue flick quickly against the rough-glazed edge. Duncan had a large collection of historically important raku tea bowls, about which Elliot had learned much during his five-year tenure at Duncan & Wiley. Duncan liked to recount the provenance of each bowl, just before dropping a bomb. The most recent had been the merger of D&W with a prominent Japanese public relations firm, but this news Elliot had greeted with genuine enthusiasm. He'd always had a thing for Asia. He started dreaming of a transfer to Tokyo, maybe a meditation pond of his own.

". . . a divisional reorganization," Duncan was saying. "We're beefing up our Cynaco task force in response to all the recent protests. What we had in mind was developing a proactive management strategy geared toward their NuLife Potato line."

Elliot watched as Duncan rotated the tea bowl slowly in his hands, studying its pocks and careful imperfections. He tried to focus on his equilibrium, to quell the panic that was rising in his gut. He had a bad feeling.

"And this is where it gets uncanny, Elliot. We were casting about for the right talent for the job, when someone from Human Resources remembered that you had taught school in Idaho once upon a time. So we had her pull your file, and there it was. Liberty Falls. As I said to the guys from Cynaco, who would have thought that we'd have right here, on staff in D.C., someone who actually hailed from the Idaho heartland! Who'd actually *lived* among the People of the Potatoes. Who'd taught their children."

"Duncan," Elliot interrupted, "I appreciate your thinking of me, but I was only there for a year. . . ."

Duncan held up his hand. "A year? Or two? Or ten? A single minute, even? It's all the same."

"But what about Tokyo . . . ?"

"Tokyo is eternal, Elliot. It survived firebombing. It will always be there. But don't you see? Tokyo is not your here and now." He placed the tea bowl on the desk with the grace of a grand tea master. He rested the backs of his hands on the polished desktop so that his palms faced the heavens. "You've got to stay open, Elliot. Look at the signs. Old life. NuLife. Get it? How propitious that your past should so perfectly align you with this particular present."

"What present?"

"Potatoes. Ironic, isn't it? How the Universe provides. As long as you stay open." He moved his hand over to a folder at the edge of the desk. "Of course, *what* she provides often proves challenging."

He slid the folder across the desk to Elliot. Inside was a copy of the *New York Times Magazine*. Centered on a stark white cover was a demented Mr. Potato Head, with two bolts stuck in its neck and a badly stitched scar on its forehead. Perched on its head was a tin skullcap, attached to an electrical coil that spiraled off the top of the page. Its wonky plastic eyes were looking in opposite directions. The tag line read, "Fried, Mashed, or Zapped with DNA?"

Inside, spread out over two pages like a *Playboy* centerfold, was a long, plump, beautifully reticulated potato. Elliot scanned the article. The journalist had started off small, almost poetically, the tale of a man planting a new type of potatoes in his backyard garden, but the target of his attack soon became clear. The guy talked toxins. He named names.

The contents of the article looked bad enough, Elliot realized, but the title was genius. Printed across the tanned, genetically engineered skin of the centerfold tuber, in a pastel font, were the words "Playing God in the Garden."

With its power to appeal to a broad range demographic, that title was truly dangerous copy. Elliot sighed.

"Marvelous chance to travel!" Duncan was saying. "I can envision you spending time in the field. Stretching your legs. Breathing that fresh Idaho air."

Elliot sighed again.

Duncan frowned. "I'm worried about your vitality, Elliot," he said. "Show me your tongue."

"Excuse me?"

"Come over here." Duncan motioned across the desk. "Open your mouth." He aimed the beam of a halogen desk lamp down Elliot's throat.

"Hmm," Duncan said. "Just as I suspected. Stagnant *chi* energy. Weak liver function. An excess of damp and wind." He flipped the lamp away. "You really should pay more attention to your diet. You are what you eat, you know. Here, have a carrot." Duncan dangled the vegetable out in front of him. It was blunt and smooth and a bloody reddish-orange color. "What you need," he said quietly, "is time in the desert. The dry air will do you good."

mr. potato head ◈

Geek smiled and took a long, slow hit off the bong. Thrifty Foods was not the biggest supermarket in Ashtabula, but the megastores were too hard to infiltrate and control for a basic C-level action. It was all a question of checkout lanes and customer density. Over eight lanes got to be a problem, since you really needed to station an agent in every other one for maximum jamming. As a target, then, Thrifty Foods was practically perfect. It had ten lanes, but with Frank on board they could break out Mr. Potato Head, who was a sure crowd pleaser.

"Dudes," Geek croaked, applying a throat lock to hold down the smoke. "Thrifty Foods' gonna get its consciousness raised."

Frank wasn't sure about this. He knew a lot of the kids who worked at Thrifty Foods—the baggers, stock boys, and cashiers—and he wasn't at all convinced they were ready to have their consciousness raised quite yet. Wages, yes, but consciousness? Frank sort of doubted they had any to begin with. He sat in the dinette nook next to Charmey, who was making a flyer for the action. She held it up. It was a picture of a potato, stamped with a skull and crossbones.

"It looks very scary, no?" she asked. Frankie hesitated, trying to think of something to say. She pouted and showed it to the others.

"Vaguely menacing, perhaps," offered Geek from the opposite corner. "A bit more humorous than hazardous."

She snatched the drawing away and made a face at him. "It is very difficult," she retorted, "to make a potato look *dangereuse*." She bent down over the paper again and started to erase. Frankie leaned forward and brushed the hair from the back of her neck. He blew gently on her bar code. She shrugged her shoulders, but he could see that she was smiling, and he felt his heart race. He looked up and saw Geek watching them. He leaned back into the nook and traced his finger along the curve of Charmey's spine. He waited patiently until bedtime.

ॐ

The Seeds did a reconnaissance of Thrifty Foods the next day, while Frank was in school. They were timing the action for noon on the Saturday before Christmas, when there would be plenty of moms and kids around. Moms were key, Geek explained. Gotta get the moms. Lilith had shanghaied one of the baggers and got the personnel information from him, and that night they reconvened in the bunker for a briefing. The manager, Lilith reported, took a lunch break at noon and usually went off site. Y nodded. He had drawn a big map of the checkout area and was assigning the lanes.

"We're starting with Express Lane One and doing the odds. We want a female in One because it's closest to the entrance, just in case we get some early police action. Lilith is good with Five-O, so I'd prefer her, if that's cool." He looked around the group. No one objected.

"Good. Frank, dude, you're next, Lane Three, so you can keep an eye on the door. You think you're gonna know some of these po-po, right? You can recognize their vehicles?"

"Sure."

"Excellent. Let us know when they're coming, but once they're on top of us, watch Lilith and do exactly what she does. The idea is no conflict. Just go limp and drop. Got it?"

Frankie nodded. He knew how to deal with the police.

Y continued. "I'll take Lane Five and initiate from there. Charmey's on Seven. Once we have it jammed, Geek'll bring in Mr. Potato Head. Everyone clear?"

It was snowing on the morning of D-Day, so they moved into position early. The snow was good. It would get the shoppers into the store, stocking up in case the storm got bad. It might also slow down the police. By 1100 hours, the Spudnik had established a position in a far corner of the Thrifty Foods parking lot. They had cleaned out the vehicle and stashed their dube in Frankie's cleaning closet at McDonald's, in case they got searched.

"Okay, Seedlings, let's roll," said Y. He was dressed in a clean pair of jeans, a button-down shirt, and a tweed jacket. He'd shaved and tied his dreadlocks tightly back, and he looked surprisingly presentable. Lilith stood next to him, wearing a cloth coat and carrying a purse. They gave a thumbs-up and left the Spudnik. Frankie stood to follow, but Charmey held him back.

"*Un moment . . .*" she said.

She was looking more like a kid than ever, in a pair of baggy overalls, a striped wool sweater, and a baseball cap worn backward. Geek was dressed in a pair of green tights and a matching leotard, and for such a large, round-seeming man, he had legs that were surprisingly thin. Over this he wore a burlap contraption, held up by suspenders, which looked like a giant diaper. He checked his watch, then nodded at Charmey.

"*Allons,*" she said, grabbing Frankie's hand.

By 1130 they had infiltrated the target and were pushing shopping carts up and down the aisles, filling them with tomatoes, squash, jars of baby food, canned corn, bottles of canola oil, miscellaneous snack-food products, and ten-pound bags of potatoes. They all had a supply of leaflets in the child's seat of their carts.

At 1207 Lilith asked to see the manager and was told he had just left for lunch.

By 1212 this information was relayed from Aisle 1: Fresh Produce through to Aisle 7: Cleaning Products & Picnicware, and the operatives headed toward the checkout lanes. A quick reconnoiter revealed a healthy target demographic—mothers with infants, preschool toddlers, and some early-elementary-school children, too.

By 1223 all operatives were engaged with the checkout personnel or closing in on the front of their lanes.

Y initiated the action in Lane 5.

"Hey," he said in a friendly voice, squinting down at the name badge on the breast of his cashier. "Shawna?"

"Huh?" she said. She barely lifted her head.

Frank watched from Lane 3. He was worried. The cashier's streaked hair was held off her face by an enormous plastic claw, and her two-toned lips were heavily lined in dark brown pencil. Frank had gone out with Shawna once, back in junior high. He knew for sure that she had no consciousness. On their date she had barely even been conscious.

"Shawna," Y repeated with a smile. "That's a nice name."

She blinked and froze. Her fingernails, laminated with green sparkly polish in keeping with the pre-Christmas season, hung in midair above the conveyor belt of oncoming groceries. Her eyes were blank. Frank shook his head. Shawna was a frigid bitch. Hadn't even let him kiss her. This was not going to work.

But he was wrong. He had underestimated Y's charm. It took a minute, but by 1225 three things had fully dawned on Shawna: that Y was a cute, hip, older guy; that he was probably not from Ashtabula; and that he was attempting to have a conversation with her.

It was like someone had flipped a switch.

"Thanks," she said, smiling and running her tongue under her upper lip to keep it from sticking to her teeth. She tossed her hair. The conveyor belt delivered a ten-pound bag of bakers. As she dragged it across the glass surface of the bar-code reader, Y took her hand.

"Hey, great nails," he said. "Listen, before you ring that up, I wanna ask you something." His voice seemed to be growing deeper and louder.

"Yeah?" she squeaked. She was practically batting her eyelashes at him. Ol' Shawna sure was stoked now, thought Frank.

"Those potatoes, do you know if they are genetically engineered?" Y asked. His voice was really loud, now, booming over the ambient Christmas music being pumped in through the PA system—so loud that the customers in line at the checkout stations looked up to see what was going on.

"Huh?" Shawna didn't know what he was talking about, and his volume was making her nervous.

"These potatoes!" Y held up the bag. "Have they been genetically engineered?"

Shawna looked around. She didn't want to get in trouble. It occurred to her that maybe this guy was a creep. Then, two lanes down, she caught sight of Frank, grinning like a madman. She narrowed her eyes.

"Listen," she said smartly, "like, do you want me to ring this up or not?"

"I don't know. Could you call your manager and maybe I could ask him?"

"Are you, like, *serious?*"

"Yeah, I really want to know." Y turned toward the fit young mother behind him. "Maybe you could tell me," he said, looking apologetic but still very concerned. "Do you happen to know if these are genetically engineered?"

The woman shook her head. "No, I'm sorry. I don't know—"

Y nodded. "That's the problem, isn't it?" He held out his finger to the infant in the shopping cart, making her dribble and coo. "We don't know because they don't tell us! They're genetically engineering poisons into potatoes these days. But they refuse to label it, so how are you supposed to know what you're feeding your baby?"

Meanwhile Shawna was hollering over to the next cashier.

"Hey, Doreen, you hear anything about someone engineering the potatoes?"

The woman next in line tapped the young mother on the shoulder. "Did he say something about bug poison?"

"Poison?" cried Lilith over in Lane 1.

"Poisoned *potatoes?*" echoed Charmey in Lane 7.

And just then a deep, amplified voice boomed out over the PA system. "Attention shoppers! Did somebody say *POTATOES?*"

The loud reggae version of "Here Comes Santa Claus" drowned out the Christmas carols and silenced the crowd. They turned and stared at the apparition dancing toward them.

It was Mr. Potato Head, twirling a candy-striped cane as he pushed a shopping cart bearing an enormous boom box toward the cash registers. Now, Mr. Potato Head was not just any old spud. He was a sweet, sporty potato, friendly and dapper. He had big, googly eyes and lozenge-shaped ears, as pink as Pepto-Bismol. He wore a green leisure suit and a Santa Claus hat perched on the top of his bald, orbicular head. He hung his cane over one arm and did a spudly little soft-shoe on his spindly green legs.

He positioned his cart in a central location in front of Lane 5, then danced along the aisles, distributing paper daisies and leaflets. By now the children, tired of waiting with their moms, were laughing and clapping. They ran to him and tugged on his burlap hide. They jumped up and down.

The Seeds quickly followed suit, passing leaflets to the customers in their lanes. Then they pushed their shopping carts forward, circling Mr. Potato Head's boom box like a wagon train shoring up defenses. Frank started joining the carts together with inconspicuous lengths of precut baling wire. The barricade would not be much of a deterrent to the police, Geek had explained, but it would make their arrest more spectacular. When the cops showed up, the Seeds would close ranks and cordon themselves off in the center. In order to reach them, the cops would have to tear the shopping carts apart or tip them over—a noisy business. Crude and violent. Very impressive.

Charmey, meanwhile, had opened a bag of Idaho bakers and tossed a couple of spuds to Y, who juggled them and threw them to Lilith, who added a squash, and before long, dozens of potatoes, zucchinis, squashes, and even tomatoes were tumbling through the air in precise, intricate arcs. Mr. Potato Head returned to the center of the circle and continued his soft-shoe amid the flying vegetables, and the children started to clap and cheer.

Frank finished securing the carts and stood to one side, scanning the store. He caught sight of Shawna talking to a fat fuck named Phil who had once been Frank's supervisor at Mickey D's. Shawna pointed one long green nail in Frank's direction. Phil narrowed his eyes and headed back toward the glassed-in office area, where Frank saw him pick up the phone. Frank headed toward Y.

"Yo, dude. The manager's back on site, and he's making the call."

Y nodded. Without missing a beat, he walked to the boom box and slowly faded down the volume. On cue the jugglers snatched the vegetables from the air. When the music was quiet, Mr. Potato Head took up a small microphone.

"First we want to thank Thrifty Foods for opening its doors to us," he said. He turned to the kids, wiggling his rosy, discoid ears. "Who wants to play a game with Mr. Potato Head?"

The children had formed a circle around him He pulled out a big red tomato and held it up for them to see.

"What's this?" he asked. "Can anyone tell me?"

"A tomato!" cried a little girl in front.

"Very good!" said Mr. Potato Head. "You think it's a tomato. Now, how many of the rest of you think it's a tomato?"

The others nodded in agreement. It was a tomato, all right.

"Well, what if I told you it *wasn't* a tomato?" Mr. Potato Head pulled out a chiffon scarf and draped it over the tomato.

"What if . . ."

He held the scarf out in front of him for the kids to see.

". . . I told you . . ."

He circled slowly.

". . . it was . . ."

The kids held their breath.

". . . a *flounder!*" And with that he yanked off the scarf to reveal a large, slimy fish. Charmey had defrosted it the night before and daubed it with glycerin to make it drip and glisten. A clamor went up from the circle of kids.

"Yuuuuck!" they cried. "Gross!" They screwed up their noses.

Mr. Potato Head raised his black, sluglike eyebrows. "You said it, kids." He tossed the fish over his shoulder to Charmey, who caught it neatly in a burlap sack.

"Now try this one. What's this?" He held up a potato. This time the children weren't so sure.

"A potato?" asked a little boy.

"Nope." Mr. Potato Head stepped forward. "It's not a potato. . . ." He reached behind the boy's ear and pulled out a candy cane.

"Ooops, it's not a candy cane." He handed it to the boy and tried again. He reached behind the ear of a little girl. This time he pulled out a plastic Christmas tree.

"Oh, dear! It's not a Christmas tree either," he said, handing it to the girl, who gave a little skip and turned around to show her mother.

"No, my miniature friends," he continued, holding up the potato and draping it once again with his scarf. "This potato is not a potato at all." He leaned over the heads of the children and invited a mother to pull off the scarf. "It is . . ."

The woman giggled, then gave a yank.

". . . *bug poison!*"

And sure enough the potato had been transformed in his hand into a large spray can of household insecticide, which he held up for all to see.

"This, my friends, is the perverted magic of biotechnology." Mr. Potato Head's voice grew serious now, as he addressed the mothers over the heads of their offspring. "But genetic engineering is no joke, not when it comes to the food you feed your children. As of 1997 over thirty genetically engineered crops were approved by the U.S. government for sale, including potatoes that are genetically spliced with a bacterial pesticide and tomatoes crossed with fish genes to increase their resistance to the cold. Then there's corn, canola, soybeans, squash. . . ."

He had the mothers' attention.

Frank, meanwhile, was counting. He figured they had about five minutes before the cops showed up. He looked around for Charmey. He tested the strength of his wire.

"Approximately sixty to seventy percent of processed foods now contain some form of genetically modified corn or soy. That means infant formulas, baby foods, pizza, soda, chips. . . ."

The mothers scanned the contents of their carts.

"And it isn't just vegetables either. . . ."

Frank looked out the window and realized he was wrong again. Five-O was pulling into the parking lot. Three squad cars. He alerted Y, then stood close to Charmey in case things got rough. Y passed the word on to Mr. Potato Head, who started speaking faster now.

"Who here drinks milk?" He looked around at the circle of children, then to the mothers behind. There wasn't a woman without a gallon and a child.

The assistant manager ran to the door as the police approached.

"Po-po's here, dudes," Y said. "Hang on. Here we go!"

The Seeds retreated to the center of the circle of carts. Frank secured the opening with the last of the wire, then took Charmey's hand, forming, along with Lilith and Y, a tight line of defense around Mr. Potato Head, who raised his cane and his voice.

"That's right. Even milk! The big corporations have introduced genetically modified food into your supermarkets and therefore into your bodies, without your knowledge or consent. There's been no long-term testing of their safety, but the government doesn't make them put warning labels on these foods. . . ."

The cops approached, six of them, assessing the situation. Frank recognized a couple of faces, but the one he knew best was a sergeant named Meinike who'd busted him and confiscated his board, just for doing nose grinds off the benches by the senior center, a vengeful action seeing as there weren't even any seniors sitting on the benches at the time. He was a mean mother. The other cops held back, but Meinike charged right over.

"All right, punks," he growled. "Party's over."

He grabbed a cart and hauled on it, trying to break through, and looked quite perplexed when it resisted. He began to rattle the carts, trying to pull them apart, but Frank had done a very good job with the wire.

"Without labels, you don't even know what you are buying and feeding your families!" Mr. Potato Head shouted, bug eyes popping, jumping up and down. "It is a violation of your consumer's right to know!"

Meinike was really pissed now, and the other cops closed in. "You're under arrest for trespassing and creating a public disturbance!"

Three of the patrolmen pushed through the crowd of customers and attacked the circle from the other side.

"We're not disturbing the public," Mr. Potato Head said. "We're educating the people." He turned back to the crowd. "Learn about the issues!" he shouted over the clatter of carts. "Your children are at risk! Their futures— the future of *life itself!*"

The Seeds began to chant, "Power to the people!" as the police broke through. The first person they reached was Lilith.

"Police brutality!" she shrieked as soon as the cop touched her. Her body went limp, and she dropped to the floor as though she'd been shot.

"Oh, my God, they're hurting her!" a woman cried. The mothers grabbed their kids. They continued to watch from a safe distance.

One by one the Seeds fell to the ground, until Frank was the only one left standing. His friends lay there, absolutely still and chanting, as the cops tried to haul them to their feet. Meinike approached him.

"Well, the chicken man. What a surprise."

"Shut the fuck up, Meinike."

"Oh, sure, Frankie. Anything you say." He slapped a handcuff on

Frank's wrist. A cop was dragging Charmey up by her armpits. It looked like he was hurting her. Frank pulled away, but Meinike jerked his arm behind his back and attached the second cuff. "Calm down, will you?"

Charmey threw back her head and screamed. Frank twisted, breaking free from Meinike. He lowered his chin, took aim at the cop who was holding Charmey, and put everything he had into a head butt into the officer's rib cage. The man staggered. Charmey dropped to the floor. Meinike spun Frankie around, drew back his fist, and delivered a sucker punch, deep into Frankie's solar plexus.

"What's wrong with you, chicken man?" he said as Frankie crumpled. "I said calm the fuck down."

ᛒᛉ

"The point of the exercise," Geek explained later, when they'd finally gotten back to the Spudnik, "is theatrical." He toweled off his hair, still wet from the snow outside, and watched Charmey wrap an Ace bandage around Frankie's cracked rib. Frankie flinched. "Passive resistance," Geek said. "Nonviolence. You make the police look like brutal oppressors in front of the citizens. You're not supposed to get hurt."

"They were hurting Charmey," Frankie muttered.

"Mais non," Charmey said, securing the bandage. "It was only my acting. You must relax your body totally, *comme ça.*" She stood and fell to the floor of the Spudnik and lay there, grinning up at him. *"Tu comprends?"*

They'd been arrested and taken to jail for a couple of hours, but when complaints started coming in from Thrifty Foods shoppers and even the store management, the police had to let them go. It was sweet, especially when Meinike tried to charge them with shoplifting, and the Seeds pulled out their register slips and demanded their groceries back—four ten-pound bags of Idaho potatoes, two pounds of zucchini, a dozen butternut squashes. One of Meinike's beat cops loaded them back into a paddy wagon. The snow had been falling all afternoon, turning to sleet as it came in off the lake. The cop dumped them at the edge of the Thrifty Foods parking lot and gave them one hour to clear city limits. They howled into the wind as the wagon pulled away, high-fived each other, and chucked icy snowballs at the retreating taillights. They cut through the parking lot. Geek trailed behind, lugging the potato head and tripping on his big burlap diaper.

Miraculously, the cops had left the Spudnik alone. It was covered with a thick hump of snow. Geek had tied in to a power line in the parking lot before the action, and they'd kept the heaters running, so it was snug and warm inside. Charmey peeled off Frankie's wet coat, wrapped him in a blanket, and leaned closer to inspect his rib.

"We got one hour, dude," said Y. "That doesn't give you much time."

Frankie's rib cage spasmed again. "I can go over to Mickey D's," he offered, "and get your stash for you. While you get ready."

"Don't bother," Y said. "We'll stop on the way. We're ready. What about you?"

"Me?"

"Yeah. You need to pick up stuff from home?"

"I don't have a home," Frank said.

"You do now, if you want it."

Frank stared. Y combed the snow out of his dreadlocks with his fingers. "We're heading out west, to California. Lots of supermarkets between here and there."

"You mean I should come?"

"Only if you want to."

Frank nodded, trying to stay cool, but inside he felt like he was going to explode. *Want* to? He'd never wanted anything more in his life. He didn't get half of what they were doing, but they were cool about it. Charmey smiled. She seemed to want him around. Maybe they all did. He sat back, taking in every detail of the Spudnik—the tie-dyed curtains and boxes of flyers, the computers and the cramped kitchenette. Just then the vehicle started to heave. The door burst open with an icy blast, and Geek straggled in. His green tights sagged at the knees, and his burlap diaper was heavy and wet with melting snow. His glasses were completely fogged.

"Dudes," he said, teeth chattering. "I juh . . . just gotta say, sometimes I *hate* being the frig . . . friggin' *potato!*"

nulife ॐ

"The baby's daddy is Hawaiian," Cass said. "A native, which makes sense, 'cause he's pretty dark." Will accepted this information with a grunt as he heaved a fifty-pound sack of chicken scratch off the tailgate and onto his shoulder. Inside the truck bed Cass humped another sack over to the edge. "Yummy said he's a musician—the father, that is. They were living together, but she broke up with him because he can't hold down a job."

Cass hoisted the sack onto his other shoulder and stood. "The little girl's daddy sells surfboards in Waikiki, and the oldest boy's father teaches something about plants. He's Japanese. Yummy said he was still a homosexual when she got pregnant."

The words came out of her mouth in a steamy cloud of white. Will was already walking toward the barn, the heavy sacks making his gait seem lighter somehow. She waited until he returned, vaguely aware that she was pushing it.

"I don't see how that could be, do you? The homosexual part, I mean. They must have had sex, right? Otherwise how did they do it?"

"Cass?" Will stood at the tailgate as she wrestled the last heavy bag over to him.

"I mean, did she seduce him, and then he just converted?" She looked up, panting slightly.

"That's a whole lot more than I need to know."

"Oh, Will." She frowned, squatting in front of him. "You're such a prude."

"How am I gonna look her straight in the eye if you go putting thoughts like that in my head?"

He looked so perturbed she had to laugh. She tipped the deadweight over his back, balanced the two sacks, and gave him a pat on the top of his baseball cap. The cap, from the Spudee Seed Potato Company, was decorated with a cartoon of a cute potato in a diaper. The company's motto was "We handle 'em like babies."

"I'm sorry," she said. "I'll shut up." She removed a work glove and wiped the hair off her forehead with the back of her hand. It was hard to shut up, though. Yummy's life was just so different from any she knew, and she wanted to tell Will all about it. She wanted to talk and puzzle it out. It was a pity he wasn't interested. She jumped from the empty truck and went around to the cab. It wasn't gossip. It was life, and it had been a long time since she'd had a girlfriend to talk to.

"I'll take the truck on back, then," she said.

"I could use some coffee," he called over his shoulder.

She brought up the subject of Yummy again after lunch. "I don't think she's planning on staying. She said she can only take a month off from her job. She's a teacher, you know."

Will was having his coffee and reading the mail. "What's she planning on for Lloyd and Momoko?"

"Leave him in the nursing home, I guess. Find something for her. They would probably have to split them up because of her dementia. I just hate the idea of it."

"Cass . . ." He looked up from the envelope he was opening with a bread knife.

"I know. I know." He was right, of course. Pity aside, the whole point was for her not to take on any more, but she couldn't help saying, "Listen, maybe we should have them over for Christmas. We've got a tree anyhow, and it would be nice for the kids. I can't see Yummy getting around to doing much."

"Won't that be rough? Having all the kids around, I mean."

Cass contemplated this observation—like if he'd said the winter is cold or the sky is blue, it was so timeless and true as to merit little more than a shrug of acknowledgment. Of course it would be rough. It was always rough to see people's beautiful children. Especially rough to see Yummy's. Will knew that. Why was he even bothering to mention it?

"Sure, but Christmas is for kids. I think we should. If you don't mind."

It would be rough for him, too. He wanted children as much as she did.

It had dawned on them slowly. In the first years of their marriage they were busy establishing the farm, and then her parents got sick, but by the time her parents died, it was clear they had a problem. For a while they focused intensively on getting pregnant, timing their lovemaking for months on end, consulting fertility specialists and researching new techniques, but something would always happen, some setback. Usually it was a miscarriage. Sometimes it was a difficult harvest or an onset of blight. Then, when things settled down again, one of them would suggest they try again. Generally it was Cass, because time was running out and she was most aware of it, but sometimes Will brought it up, too, when she got discouraged. They'd even started adoption proceedings, filling out the questionnaires and doing the home visits with the social worker, but just when Cass was starting to let herself get excited, she'd been diagnosed with her cancer. That took the wind right out of their sails.

It had been awhile since either of them had broached the subject.

Now Will took a sip of coffee. He was fingering a potato brochure that had come in the mail. "Here," he said, handing it to her.

The sudden shift caught her off guard. She took the brochure and studied it.

"Cynaco's NuLifes," he said. "It's interesting. They genetically engineer the plant with a natural pesticide built right in. The beetles eat the leaf and die. They say you can reduce the chemical inputs by more than half."

She took a sip of coffee, settling into her role of skeptic, the cautious one, now that she sensed where he was headed. "I don't know. It couldn't be as simple as they make it out. We'd still need some systemics, wouldn't we?"

"Yeah, but not as much."

She ran her eye down the specs. "Expensive."

"No beetles, Cass. And with the NuLife Enhanced, no leaf roll either. Otherwise we'd be doing several sprayings with Monitor, not to mention—"

She handed him back the brochure and went to the sink. "I don't know, Will." She rinsed her cup, then turned, shoulders hunched and arms crisscrossed in front of her chest. She stared at his profile as he studied the specs, scouring them for answers. It was a handsome face, a sturdy, innocent, American sort of face, the kind that ought to live its life and die contented, but instead, now, when he looked up at her, she watched it twist into something more complex than its features were ever built to convey. "How do we know if it's . . ."

"We don't," he said. "But they say it's safer than pesticides." He was trying to reassure but his voice revealed the doubt that had been eating at him, like a root rot, starting with the war and growing deeper with each disaster. "We can start small, do a couple of test fields, say, the ones closest to the house." He spoke quietly. "At least those . . ."

She walked over and hugged him into the curve of her body.

"Cass . . ." He crumpled the paper in his fist and turned his face into her stomach.

She took a deep breath, stroking the long, faded strands of his hair and tucking them behind his ears. "You really want to go through it all again?"

"There's always a chance. We gotta operate on that assumption, right?"

"Right." She released him. "Until we don't." She started to walk away, but he reached out and grabbed her hand.

"But safer is better, right?" he insisted. "No matter what."

"Safer is better," she agreed.

He tugged at her wrist, reeling her back in to the frail comfort of his powerful arms. "We'll turn over a new leaf," he said, nuzzling her.

"A NuLife, you mean." Resisting, but smiling now.

"Exactly." He sat her down so that she straddled his lap. He picked his cap off the table and put it on her head. The visor pointed jauntily to one side. "You game?"

"Oh, sure. Why not?" She leaned so their foreheads and their noses touched. Her eyes crossed, and his face went all crooked. She gave him a peck of a kiss and stood up. "For a NuLife Enhanced, even."

She put his cap back on his head. The little diapered spud smiled at her cutely. *We handle 'em like babies.*

christmas 🎄

The phone rang once in the middle of the night.

"Yumi . . . ?" His voice was as thin as thread, unraveling into the darkness.

"Who is this?" I cupped the receiver, whispering so as not to wake up the kids. It was Christmas Eve, and Ocean was sleeping lightly. "Dad, is that you?"

"Yumi—" His old voice broke, choked on spittle. He coughed and swallowed two, three times, then took a deep breath. "I have made up my mind." Trying to sound firm, resolute. "You must come on home now. Your mother and I have decided . . ."

My heart was pounding. "Dad, I'm here. I am home." There was a long silence. Outside I could hear the wind. The little green hands on the clock at my bedside glowed in the dark. "Dad, are you okay? Do you know what time it is?"

"Why, it's morning." He sounded surprised that I should need to know.

"It's four o'clock in the morning. It's the middle of the night."

"Oh, my!" His resolution crumpled. "Is it?" Thoroughly deflated now.

"But I thought—" Breathing harshly, he tried to understand, but then, "Oh, no—" and his voice broke off. "I must have been dreaming. . . ." His words trailed into a low sob that ended in a hiccup.

"Listen, Dad, we'll talk later, okay? Will you be all right until morning?"

"Oh—" he said, the syllable echoing through all the failing chambers of his heart. "Yes. I . . . I suppose so."

"I'll come by tomorrow. I'll talk to the doctor."

"Yumi, wait!" he cried, rallying.

"What is it?"

"Where's your mother?"

"She's here, Dad. I brought her home. She's with us. She's fine."

"Bring me home, too. Please! Get me out of here!"

"I can't do that. You know I can't. You can't manage on your own, and there's no one here to take care of you."

"But you . . ."

"Dad, this is temporary. I'm only here for a visit. I don't live here, remember?"

"Oh . . ."

"Try to get some sleep."

"Oh, Yumi, I can't sleep! That's the problem. They keep waking me up. All this fussing. No sleep at all . . ."

When I hung up the phone, I heard Ocean calling. "Mommy . . . ?" I scooped her up and carried her into bed with me. "Is it Christmas yet?" she asked.

"Almost, Puddle," I told her.

"Don't call me that."

"Okay. Go back to sleep now." I had stayed up late stuffing their stockings, and the whiskey I'd been drinking tasted thick on my tongue. I closed my eyes and pulled her in close, to calm her with the authority of my own body's exhaustion.

But Ocean was full of sleepy worries. "Mommy, I know who that was on the phone. It was Santa Claus, right?"

I rubbed her forehead. "Ocean, honey. You don't believe in Santa Claus, remember?"

"I know," she said. "But Poo does. It's a good thing Santa found us all the way out here, isn't it? In the middle of nowhere."

"It's not nowhere," I said. "It's Idaho."

"Is he going to get here on time? We're a long way from Pahoa."

"Yes we are. Now go to sleep."

∂

We celebrated Christmas at Cass and Will's house. We unwrapped presents under the tree in the living room, and the kids disappeared into Will's office to try out their new games on his computer. Poo was busy shredding wrapping paper on the floor under the tree, and Momoko was attempting to retrieve some of it before he ruined it all, smoothing it and folding it, to use again in Christmases to come. I was looking at the gift I'd just unwrapped. It was a photo in a frame.

"I found a bunch of them," Cass said. "Momoko had them hidden in your bureau drawer. She wanted to give you that one."

I turned the little picture over in my hand. The frame was made of a light-colored maple, its beveled edges carefully oiled and polished.

"Will made the frame," Cass added. "He's good at carpentry."

Will shrugged, embarrassed.

"It's beautiful," I said. "Thank you."

Inside the small frame, behind the glass, was a faded photograph. Lloyd, as a young man—dressed in a V-neck cotton undershirt and an old pair of khaki trousers that must have been from his army days—standing on the edge of a vast tilled field. Above his head, balanced on the palm of his large hand, was a black-haired baby. Me, of course. He was holding me by the belly, like a model airplane. I was wearing a diaper and nothing else. Maybe I was flapping my pudgy arms and kicking my legs, or making cooing noises, but my face was lit with a bright-eyed infant rapture.

The black-and-white photo had browned over the years, but you could tell that Lloyd's hair would have been paler than the dusty earth and his eyes would have matched the color of the sky, cloudless, above the horizon. Momoko must have taken the picture, and she had timed it well, catching my gaze when I was looking right into the lens of the camera. I looked very Japanese at that age—there was little of Lloyd apparent in my face, but that didn't matter to him. He held me carefully, and it was easy to imagine my delight as he piloted my small body, cutting and banking through the blue, no, the sepia sky. He held the promise of an entire life in the palm of his hand. This was an awesome amount of power, but you could see he felt good with it. Looking at his face, you got the feeling that he was relaxed and happy. Handsome. And, above all, proud.

βЭ

He had fallen asleep in his wheelchair, with a pad of paper on his lap and a pen in his hand. Someone had pinned a sprig of holly, tied with a bit of red-and-green ribbon, to the lapel of his threadbare bathrobe. It hung there, askew. I hesitated in the doorway, hugging the doorjamb.

"Merry Christmas, Dad."

He opened his eyes and looked up at me.

"How are you feeling?"

He shook his head. "I'll be fine. As soon as I get out of here."

A Christmas party was under way in the dayroom. One of the staff was playing an out-of-tune piano, and the patients were singing carols. I'd left the kids and Momoko there eating cookies and drinking sweet punch.

"Ready for the party?"

He groaned and covered his face with his hand. I went to his side to wheel him out, but when I reached down to take the pad and pencil from him, he tightened his grip. Then I caught sight of the words, centered at the top of the page in his spidery handwriting, FULLERS' SEEDS. VENDIMUS SEMINA, and below that, "Mrs. Fuller and I . . ."

My heart sank. I sat down on the edge of the bed. "Dad, I just don't see how you're going to manage."

"Manage what?" He clutched the pad to his chest.

"Anything. Living at home, never mind keeping Fullers' Seeds going."

He turned the pad over. "I don't see how it's any of your business."

"The doctor says you need to be in a nursing home. She says you're not—"

"She's a fool. She doesn't know what she's talking about." He stared at me until I looked down, and then he picked up his pen. "It has nothing to do with you. You can take all those children of yours and go on home now. Go back to your tropical island. You've done your duty. I'm not dying. I'll try to let you know when I am."

The imperious dismissal felt like a slap. "I am leaving," I said. "Believe me. I'm just trying to help you understand, is all. The doctor was real clear.

102

They're not letting you out of here unless you have someone at home to take care of you."

He grew pale hearing that. His voice wavered. "They can't. They have no right. . . ."

"You can barely walk," I said, feeling righteous and calm. "You can't make it up and down the stairs by yourself, or even to the bathroom. And Mom can't cook or clean anymore. She barely even remembers what a stove is."

"Your mother's memory is fine. We have a system. . . ."

"The doctor says it's Alzheimer's. Cass has been bringing you food for months now, even before this last attack."

"Cassie Quinn's a good girl. She was just helping out. Besides, she's a neighbor."

A good girl. I hated him even more for saying that. "She told me you can't even change your *bag* by yourself."

The words punctured his hide. His head dropped and swayed, and he raised his swollen hands from his lap. "My fingers," he said, spreading them in front for me to see. "They're too thick."

"Dad," I said coldly, pressing my advantage, "changing a colostomy bag is more than neighborly. It's what a nurse does."

"Your mother tries to help me," he said. "But she can't remember."

"You live too far out for social services. They can't send health-care workers all the way out to the farm."

He fell silent and thought for a while. "What . . . ?" He couldn't finish the question.

"The doctor suggested a long-term managed-care facility."

"A what?"

"Managed care."

"Sounds like a prison," he said, trying to joke. "Maximum security . . ."

"It's not like that, it's—"

"*No!*" He put every last ounce of strength he had into that word. He closed his eyes, and when he opened them again and searched my face, he saw his future as I saw it, and the vision horrified him. "Please," he begged, so humble now. "I can't go to one of those places. I won't survive. . . ." His words started coming faster, frantic, while his fingers plucked at the folds of his bathrobe. "Everything's going all wrong, Yumi. You don't

103

know what it's like. They won't leave me alone. Always pushing and poking. I can't get a good night's sleep. They keep trying to make me eat. And the food . . . I'll die here, I know I will. I have to get back home. It's my only chance!"

"Oh, Dad! For God's sake!" The exasperation in my voice stopped him short. "What am I supposed to do?"

Tears were pooling in his eyes, and a thin line of spittle leaked from his lower lip down the stubbled chin. He wiped it off. His hand trembled. He hadn't shaved.

"Stay," he said.

"I can't. I've got a job and classes to teach, and the kids have school. . . ."

The fight leaked out of him. He bent his head, and the knob of his spine protruded from the neck of his robe. He stared into his hands, as though the key to his failure lay in the lines of his upturned palms. "Not for me," he said. "For your mother. If I can't take care of her, they'll put her away. She won't have her garden. Her seeds. They're all she remembers, Yumi."

I felt like I'd been punched. I got to my feet.

"All right," I said. "Only long enough to get you out of here. Then you'll have to figure something else out."

He raised his face, but I couldn't see his expression. I was already standing behind him, kicking off the brakes on his wheelchair and shoving him forward.

guru 🪶

FULLERS' SEEDS
M. and L. J. Fuller—Seedsmen
Liberty Falls, Idaho
Vendimus Semina
Since 1984

To Our Customers:
As you know, Mrs. Fuller and I make it a policy only to sell open-pollinated seeds, which we encourage you, our customers, to grow and save and multiply as you choose, in accordance with **God's Plan.**

We have been hearing recently about some very worrisome developments in the world of the Agricultural Sciences, concerning what is called Genetic Engineering, and Mrs. Fuller and I would like to share our thoughts on this troubling new trend.

In the past forty years, scientists have made rapid advances in this field of genetics. They have made many discoveries about DNA, and they have learned how to splice genes from one of God's creatures to another. **They are now able to create novel life forms that have never before existed on God's earth.** Scientists now appear to understand the innermost workings of Life Itself. But do they? Is this something mankind can *ever* know?

Some say that it is entirely appropriate for us to engage in Genetic Engineering. God made Man in **His Own Image,** after all, so it is only natural that we should strive to emulate Him. In fact, say these apologists, it would be an insult to God *not* to use the intelligence He bestowed upon us to its fullest potential. But even up to, and including, the very **Act of Creation?**

We believe this is mere rationalization, one that should sound familiar to all of us, and not just to the pomologists amongst our readers! For, having eaten the apple from the Tree of Knowledge, now mankind knows sorrow and death; and here we must ask: Is our answer to that original transgression, once again, to defy **God's Will** and to set our sights on the **Tree of Life Itself?** Do not forget, the Lord put a flaming sword at the entrance of Eden, to keep Man away, **"lest he put forth his hand, and take also of the Tree of Life, and eat, and live forever"** [Genesis 4:24].

Having eaten from the Tree of Knowledge, we should know the difference between good and evil, but we do not. **We are not gods.** Scientists do not understand Life Itself, and when they meddle in its Creation, they trespass on God's domain. Beware of the ungodly chimera they manufacture in their laboratories!

It is our nature and our sorrow to confuse Man's mortal hubris with **God's Divine Will.** Mrs. Fuller and I hope that there are enough of you out there who share our views, and who will choose to cultivate wisely this Garden that we were given, rather than to turn it into a wasteland.

"Amen," intoned Geek.

He put down the catalog and looked around the group. It was New

Year's Eve, and the Spudnik was parked in a truckstop off I-80, near Ogallala, Nebraska, where they'd stopped to score some fuel before turning south. Luckily, they'd found a Kentucky Fried Chicken that was just about to dump their fryers, so they topped up the tanks, ate dinner, and settled in for the evening. Geek was reading through some material that they'd picked up at an organic-farming collective in Iowa, when he'd come across the catalog.

"Seeds, are you thinking what I'm thinking?"

Y was standing on one foot in the middle of the Spudnik, facing the dashboard, doing Vrikshasana—the Tree pose. His hands were raised over his head, palms pressed together, index fingers aligned and pointed toward the roof. The bare sole of his foot was pressed against the inner thigh of the leg he was balanced on. "I don't know, Geek," he said, keeping his eyes fixed at a spot near the transmission. "What are you thinking?"

Geek held up the catalog again. "L. J. Fuller."

"What about him?"

"He's the one!" Geek looked around the room for support. "You don't think this dude's amazing?"

Frank shrugged. He was holding a skein of yarn looped between his two hands, and Charmey was winding the wool into a ball. Lilith was knitting a sweater. The air smelled of wet wool and incense and sodden fried chicken.

Geek jumped to his feet, rocking the Winnebago. "Seeds, it's time to wake up!" he yelled. "We have found our *guru!*"

Y lost his balance and his foot hit the floor with a thud.

Lilith put down her knitting. "Geek, what are you talking about?

"Our master. Our guru. This is him. The one we've been waiting for! A humble seedsman, but a visionary. A born leader of men."

"Get real."

"No. I mean it. He's perfect."

Y moved into Warrior One—Virabhadrasana, lunging forward on one leg and raising his arms overhead into a V. "Dude's a major Christian. All this God shit is way too heavy for me."

"But that's the whole beauty of it! Don't you see how amazing this is? He's an icon! Totally salt of the earth. The American farmer making a lonely stand, defending his seed against the hubris and rapacious greed of the new multinational life-sciences cartel. In Idaho, no less! It's Mr. Potato Head's cloning ground, his place of origin!"

"So?"

"So I don't know. It's mystical, that's all. Like some sort of friggin' harmonic convergence. Liberty Falls? Power County? Like, can you believe how wild that sounds? What a mind-fuck!"

"What's your point, man?" Y asked, coming into Mountain pose, then sitting down on the floor.

"I just have a feeling, is all. I think we should check this dude out."

"I thought we were going down to someplace warm." Y lowered himself onto his back now for Shavasana—the Corpse pose.

"Trust me," Geek said. His eyes were blazing, his voice hushed and urgent. "We must go west, Seedlings. I have a feeling. We're heading for something dynamite!"

His words hung, twitchy and volatile, in the close air. Suddenly Charmey threw down the ball of yarn and scrambled toward the bathroom. She slammed the thin door behind her, and they listened as she started to retch.

"What's wrong with her?" Geek asked.

"It's the KFC," Lilith said, tossing her knitting onto the table. "The smell kind of kicks off her morning sickness."

third

I have thought often lately that If It had not been the potato it would have been something else, for I was determined before that time to find the vulnerable spot in Nature and make her my co-worker . . .

—Luther Burbank, *The Harvest of the Years*

the promiscuity of squashes 🕉

She called it her "seed money," not knowing that the idiom already existed in English. For Momoko it simply described the small amounts of cash she earned from her mail-order seeds, carefully culled, to send to me over the years.

At first she must have worked alone. As I remember, Lloyd had always been a bit disparaging of my mother's garden. It wasn't that he disapproved of seeds per se, but he was a large-scale potato farmer, a monoculturalist, so you can imagine how nervous all that diversity must have made him. Over the years, as he watched her garden grow, Lloyd thought her frivolous for planting what seemed to him to be a confusion of flowers, fruits, and vegetables.

Of course, it hadn't always been so. In the beginning, when the potato operation was still small and he needed her help in the fields, Momoko grew mostly functional foods, which appeared on the dinner table. This he could understand. He could appreciate a bit of greens or a squash now and then, and he approved of her economy. But after the potato operation grew to a scale where he needed hired help and her labor was no longer necessary, and then I was born, and then I left, somewhere during this time and thereafter, Momoko's garden began to change. She began to branch out, and soon there was an extravagance of blooms, in sizes and colors and shapes Lloyd had never seen. And vegetables whose names he did not know. And fruits with strange pips.

You can imagine his unease, growing denser every year, in tandem with the garden's lush perimeters. Pressed, he could not say why. Of course, no

111

one was pressing him to do or say much of anything, especially not Momoko. Not since the night in February when they woke to the groan of the stair, lay side by side, listening in the dark to the sigh of the porch door closing, complicit in the mounting silence.

"Go," she said. "Bring her back."

But he hadn't.

That night Momoko more or less stopped speaking to him. She moved into my bedroom, where she lived for close to a decade. After his heart attack she took care of him, preparing his meals and bringing them to his bedside and later, when he was better, leaving them on the kitchen table. But she didn't eat with him. She didn't talk to him, more than was absolutely necessary. She closed herself inside my room and whispered and stared up at the stars.

Under his window, her garden grew.

In '77, after bankrupting his neighbor, Lloyd recovered his fields and enough of his health to enable him to farm and prosper for the next several years, until 1980, when prices bottomed out and he took a beating like everyone else. Still, he thought as he struggled along, he was doing better than Unger, who by this time was dead.

But his luck didn't last for long. In 1983, when I was graduating from college, he had a second heart attack, and a bad one. Knifelike, it cut cleanly through his ties to the world. He leased his remaining acreage to Will and gave up on spuds.

The potato habit was a hard one to break, and the transformation happened slowly. One of the things Lloyd loved about potatoes is that they stayed alive. I remember going with him to the cellars at harvest, when the crop was being loaded in, and he swept his arm across the vast tumbling mountain of tubers.

"Look, Yumi! They're alive. Living and breathing." Then he explained how cloning worked and how every potato was capable of creating endless offspring out of chunks of its living flesh, and I felt so proud, like I was a little chunk of his. I can see why he was excited. In a very real sense a potato plant is immortal—the Russet Burbanks that Lloyd, and all of Idaho, grew were literally chips off the old block of Luther's original. There is something divine in this potency, but it needs care and protection. Unlike grain, Lloyd would say dismissively, which can be stored indefinitely, there is an art to storing potatoes. They come out of the ground at about fifty-five degrees and are transported to the cellar, where the temperature is slowly lowered, half a degree a day, until it reaches a careful forty-five. The breathing rate of the potatoes slows. Usually they can stay that way for almost a year before they start to wither and die. Of course, that is the problem with living things— they have a life span that cannot be exceeded.

When compared to the succulent, rollicking poetry of potatoes, the farming of seeds is a dry and persnickety task. For a spudman like Lloyd, seeds are superfluous. But during that first year of his recovery from the second heart attack, as he watched Momoko cultivate her garden, he realized that for her, seeds were the sole objective. She tended her plants, allowing them to ripen, to flower and die—and only then did she get down to business: shaking the seeds from their brittle pockets or teasing them wet from their flesh, drying them and sorting them, measuring and labeling them, and slipping them into envelopes for dissemination by the U.S. Postal Service to destinations around the world. Neither snow nor rain nor heat nor gloom of night. . . . She was more reliable than the birds and the bees, and with a far greater reach.

Her customers wrote her letters. He discovered the correspondence in my old desk, where Momoko conducted her business. Each of the sheets had been carefully read, and the difficult words were underlined and translated into Japanese.

Dear Mrs. Fuller,
This is the second year we've planted your Kyoto Three Feets, and I cannot tell you what pleasure they bring. They've done real well in our Nebraska heat. Our neighbors, who teased us at first for growing such spindly cukes, now are begging for seed after sampling how tender, crisp yet densely fleshed they are. So far we've refused to tell them who our "supplier" is, but this year we've decided to relent. But before we give them your name, we'd like to place our order in case you run out!

Dear Mrs. Fuller,
My wife and I want to thank you for your heroic efforts to preserve the rich diversity of heirloom tomatoes. It was such a thrill to find that you were growing everything from Cherokee Purples to Thai Pinks to Green Zebras. Without people like you, the human race would simply forget what tomatoes ought to taste like. The artifacts sold in supermarkets, that they have the gall to call tomatoes, could just as well be made of

113

wood pulp or cardboard, for all the taste and texture they have. We live in an insipid world. Thank you for making it a little less so.

Dear Mrs. Fuller,

Thank you again for agreeing to take on my grandfather's seeds. He gave them to me on his deathbed and told me that his father had brought them over from Bavaria sometime in the mid-1800s, sewed into his hatband. Grandpa said they were our family's only legacy from the old country, and he begged me to take care of them, but I live in a high-rise apartment building in Chicago! I don't know a thing about gardening! I didn't even know what kind of vegetable the seeds were for! When we got your letter saying that you were naming them Lott's Purple Podded Pole Beans, my mother and I just sat down and cried. Grandpa would be so happy to have a bean named after him. So, I just want to say thank you from him and from our whole family.

They were heartwarming letters, but Lloyd found it disconcerting to realize that his wife had a set of connections and friendships, a whole world, about which he'd known little or nothing.

Bedridden again after the second attack, he watched her, first from the bedroom window and then from the parlor, through the heavy drapes. Later, when the weather warmed up, he shuffled out to the back porch and kept an eye on the top of her straw gardening hat as it moved through the dense foliage. Finally, when his legs got stronger, he followed her into the garden.

At first, afraid of seeming invasive, he kept to the outer edges while she moved up and down her rows. Then, when she didn't appear to mind or to notice, he began to meander around the beds. Even the air here was different—thicker and humid and very much hers. He was careful not to crowd her, observing where she was working so he could stay on the opposite quadrant of the garden plot. He felt like a lesser piece in some large board game—if she was the queen, he was not even a castle. But as he skirted the edges, he noticed she was watching him, too, ducking behind a trellis of peas or turning down a row when he looked her way.

He watched her dig and hoe, weed and whisper to her seedlings. "*Gambatte ne, tané-chan!* Be strong, little seed!" Slowly, as he succumbed to the allure of her plants, watching them play out the range of their diversity in the fullness of nature's cycle, Lloyd got over his attachment to spuds.

He started to carry things for her. Tentative at first, he just picked up after her—a trowel she'd left behind or a pair of pruning shears—depositing the tool on the ground nearby where she was working and backing off again. Then he started trailing along behind her with a rake or dragging a hose, and although she hesitated at first, soon she began to accept his being there. Lloyd even fancied it felt a little like the old days when they worked in the potato fields, silently, side by side.

That first season he got hooked on cucurbits. It is a well-known fact that squashes are among the most promiscuous of garden vegetables, and Momoko, when she finally started talking to him, confessed she was having a hell of a time keeping her Shanghai squash from cross-pollinating with her Mammoth Kings, and her Sweetbush from her Whangaporoas. She had resorted to a fastidious regimen of hand pollination, which Lloyd learned about for the first time when he followed her into the garden at dusk to identify the flowers that would open the next morning. He watched her crouching in the dirt, thinking how it was that during their thirty-five years of marriage he'd had no idea she knew so much.

"Better down here," she said. "Squash very sneaky. Like to hide." She flipped up a fat, hairy leaf to uncover the papery furls of an unopened flower. It was attached to a slim stem. "This one is boy flower. See?"

There was something about these heat-loving vines, twining and tendril bearing, that appealed to Lloyd, and before he knew it, he had folded his long, stiff legs and was down on his knees in the warm dirt beside her.

"Color just starting to come, so tomorrow he gonna be ready." She stroked the pale yellow blush that stained the veins on the underside of the petals. She tore off a short piece of three-quarter-inch masking tape from a roll and wrapped the tape around the tips of the petals, then located another flower. This one grew out of a small striped bulb, and the blossom had just begun to break open. "This one a girl flower," Momoko said. "See? She got little baby squash." She stroked the shiny swollen ovule at the base of the petals, then tore off another piece of tape. "Her flower just start to open, see? But is too soon. She must wait." Deftly she sealed the petal's tips shut. "Bee so quick, maybe he get inside with some other squash's pollen, then baby is no good. You gotta shut her up tight until the right time."

The next morning when the dew had dried, they were back, crawling through the garden. Momoko located one of the taped males and plucked it, severing the stem several inches down the peduncle. Then she carefully unwrapped it, tearing off the crepey petals of the flower to reveal the pollen-saturated anther. She handed it to Lloyd, who held it while she prepared another. Then she chose a taped female flower from a neighboring plant. She looked around.

"You hear bee?" she asked, cocking her head and listening for the hum.

"I don't hear anything."

She shook her head. "Bee is coming. She so fast, so we gotta hurry up. If you see bee, you must go shoo, okay? Make her go away."

Lloyd nodded.

Holding the female flower by the fruit, she removed the tape. Lloyd watched as the flower began to unfurl, a blooming in slow motion, but of course it wasn't slow at all. Just the opposite, because the wrinkled petals, once freed, spread far more eagerly and rapidly than was normal in nature and within minutes had billowed into a raggedy-edged corolla. Inside, revealed, were the plump quadrant lobes of the stigma, sticky and receptive. Lloyd was transfixed. Just then he heard the buzz and felt a slight breeze brush his neck.

"Damé!" Momoko said. "Shoo! Shoo!" She waved her hands at the large bumblebee and plucked the naked, petal-less males from Lloyd's slow fingers. Holding the first one by the stem like a brush, she swabbed its pollen-covered anthers onto each of the glistening lobes of the female's stigma. Then, while Lloyd waved his hands over her head, keeping the bee at bay, she repeated the process with the second.

"It is better using two boy flowers for one girl," she said. "Sometimes three."

As soon as she finished, she drew the female's petals together again, sealing up the fertilized pistil and taping the flower shut. She took the discarded corollas from the males and draped them over the female bud, creating a layered cocoon of wilted petals.

"Bee so hungry, sometimes she chew right through tape."

She marked the pollinated flower with a twistie and a tag of aluminum cut from a soda can, onto which she had scratched the date with the sharp tip of a knife. *"Gambatte kudasai, ne!"* she instructed the blossom. "You try your best for me, *ne!"*

The bee had found a discarded male in the dirt and was straddling its anther.

"Is okay," Momoko said, squatting down beside the next female flower. "She can have leftovers."

∞

The squashes were stored in the root cellar. There weren't many, and the cellar steps were thick with cobwebs. I brought up an armful and let them spill onto the counter next to the stove, where Cass was warming some food for Poo.

"What are these?"

Cass took a long, torpedo-shaped one in her palm, hefting and turning it over, then scored the skin with her fingernail.

"Looks like a zucchini, but the skin's too tough. More squashlike. Maybe it got crossed with an acorn or a butternut. Ask Momoko. She'll know."

Momoko was sitting at Lloyd's desk in the parlor. Phoenix and Ocean were lolling on the rug, watching the television at full volume. It was all they did these days.

"Turn that down," I told them, stepping over their bodies.

"Momoko doesn't like it if we turn it down," Phoenix said.

"Momoko isn't even watching. She's doing something else."

He sighed and turned it down with the remote.

Momoko immediately lifted her head. "More louder, please."

"See?" said Phoenix. "I told you." He turned the volume back up.

The living room belonged to the kids and Momoko now; one by one, its ties to any external, verifiable reality were being severed, and it was developing a demented logic of its own. Phoenix had taken to moving around Lloyd's carefully lettered signs to trip up his grandma. The living room wall now said BEDROOM. The chair had turned into the CEILING. The teapot was a REFRIGERATOR. At first I tried enlisting Ocean's help, turning her against her brother to change the signs back again, but the fun of befuddling Momoko always won out in the end. As a result Momoko was now sitting on the CEILING, at a desk that was a DOORSTOP. I gave my children a foul look, a real Hawaiian stinkeye, which they ignored, and then I restored the signage. I couldn't reach the ceiling without standing on Momoko's chair, so I crumpled that index card and threw it at Phoenix's head.

"Hey," he said. "Chill."

Momoko was poring over an old gas bill.

"Mom, that's old. We paid that already." I dropped two of the large vegetables, one round, the other long, in front of her. "What are these?"

Momoko looked at the large, mutant squashes and shook her head. "I don't know." Then she started to giggle. *"Uri wa iyarashii no yo."*

"What do you mean?"

She picked one up and studied it, turning it over in her crooked hands. "Maybe is a little bit zuke, and little bit Delicata, and little bit . . . whatchamacallit. Sweet Pumpkin." She handed it back and pointed to Ocean and Phoenix, who were fixated on the screen. "Like them. All mixed up."

She bent over the stack of old bills again, moving her finger along the surfaces, as though by touching the numbers and letters she might understand.

$\mathcal{B}$

"What did she say?" Cass asked, guiding Poo's hand carefully toward his mouth with a spoonful of mashed potatoes.

"She said squashes were promiscuous." I sat down and started to roll one of the clumsy vegetables from hand to hand, across the kitchen table. Poo was watching me closely, and he began to kick his legs and bounce in his high chair, slapping his palm on the tray in front. Cass wiped his mouth and took the spoon from his hand.

"Here. Let me see that again."

I rolled the squash over to her, and she examined it. "Too green for a butternut."

She set it down on the tray in front of Poo. With great concentration he placed a pudgy hand on either side, picked it up, and crowed with delight. He held it over his head like a prizefighter raising his trophy, then hurled it to the floor, where it exploded.

We contemplated the pieces, scattered all over the kitchen.

"I wonder why they call it a squash?" I mused. "Why not a smash or a shatter?"

"Well, I guess because it squashes when it's cooked?"

"Right." I started picking up the pieces. "You think the kids will eat it?"

118

He'd knocked her up the very first time they did it. That's what Char told him, counting backward on her fingers, eyes glowing in the darkened Spudnik.

"Forty-one, forty-two, forty-three . . . forty-five days. And now it is already two periods that I have missed! It is certain, Frankie!"

She reached out and grabbed his wrist, then pulled his hand beneath her cotton undershirt to her breast.

"Can you feel?"

Her breast felt great, as awesome as ever. "What?"

"It is bigger, no?" Impatient, she pulled off the undershirt. He watched. There was always this moment, as her arms were stretched above her and her head and shoulders were swaddled in the tube of cloth, when her breasts would just *be* there. He had never forgotten the shock he'd felt when he saw them for the first time, and always, during this moment of her undressing, he felt the same sense of surprise, followed by gratitude. They were the sweetest breasts he had ever seen. Not sweet tasting, like fruit or candy, but sweet like the ache you might feel for a weak thing. He reached out and touched the other breast. He couldn't tell if they were bigger, but she seemed to want them to be, so he nodded.

"Yeah," he said, and she beamed.

"Oh, Frankie. It is happening! Aren't you excited?"

He nodded again. The last couple weeks, driving through the plains, had been hell. She'd been sick and throwing up a lot, and she hadn't wanted to be touched. Frank figured that was it. He'd knocked her up, and she wasn't interested in him anymore. The problem was, he was still very interested in her. Now, as he sat in front of her with his hands on her breasts, he felt quite excited, but he suspected his reasons might be different from hers. He took his hands away, embarrassed. He didn't want to lie to her.

She looked surprised, and then she laughed. *"Pauvre petit Frank,"* she said, mocking him. She caught his hands again and pulled him toward her. He resisted for about half a second.

"You feeling . . . I mean, is it okay?"

She lay back on the nest of bedding and drew him on top. *"Sois gentil,"* she whispered.

Carefully he levered his body like a ramp, tilting on the fulcrum of his knees, but he stopped short, afraid of putting any weight on her. She guided him inside. "It is fine. It doesn't hurt." She arched her back and pressed against him, to get him started, then giggled. "Frank Perdue, you must relax! You are stiff as the board of wood."

He attempted a few tentative thrusts, then froze altogether. "Oh, shit!" he said, looking like he'd just seen a ghost.

"What is wrong?"

"You don't think—"

"What?"

"You don't think that it's, like, *watching* us, do you?" It seemed to him a reasonable fear.

"Watching?"

"You know . . . the *baby*."

Charmey started to laugh. She wrapped her arms around his neck, and before he knew it, she had rolled him over and she was on top, riding him like a child on a hobbyhorse. Her smile turned rapt, abstract, and for a moment she looked like the kid he'd first mistaken her for. Then she leaned over so that the ends of her hair brushed his face and their noses were almost touching.

"Do you know how big is your *bébé* now?" She held her fingers up in front of his eyes. "This big. Like the bean . . . how do you say? Of the leema."

"A lima bean?"

"Oui." She arched her back and took his hands and placed them on her belly. "If our *bébé* is watching we must teach her, no?" She looked down at him sternly. "We must teach our *bébé* not to fuck like a plank, Frank."

That was all fine, Frank thought, and he did his best, but the whole thing seemed unreal. The Seeds seemed to welcome the idea of the baby, so he felt he should, too. The problem was, he had serious doubts. He tried to imagine himself as a father and just drew a blank. He wished Charmey hadn't said that about the lima bean. It only made things more complicated. Now whenever he thought about the baby, all he could picture was succotash.

The following day they reached Salt Lake City. The Spudnik, like a tropical pod swept along by wintry air masses, came to rest in a parking lot of a mall just outside the city limits. It was warm inside. Geek lit up a fat dube of Maui Wowie.

"Frankie, my boy," he said, passing him the joint. "You and me, we're gonna smoke this and then take a long walk, little brother."

Frankie took a toke. "Now?" He choked. The reefer was sweet.

Geek nodded. "Seeds got work to do."

Y was setting up a small video camera on a tripod, straddling the transmission. He knelt on the driver's seat facing into the Winnebago, fiddling with some small clip-on lights attached to a grid overhead. He angled the beam, running it down the glossy length of Lilith's naked torso. Charmey had covered the dinette table with an Indian-print bedspread, and now Lilith sat there in lotus position, against a velvet backdrop, fingering a zucchini. She had a fine golden down, like spun metal all over her naked body, that picked up the light from the spot. Between her breasts hung an Egyptian ankh. Charmey was stirring up a large cauldron of mud that Lilith was going to use in part of her act.

"It's for the Web site," Lilith explained to Frank. "I become a symbol of Earth, begetting life, the primeval Mother. I have to access a really deep part of myself, and it's hard if there are too many people around. You don't mind, do you? It's just for a couple of hours."

Frankie did mind. It was five degrees below zero and raging outdoors. He preferred to stay indoors and watch Lilith cover her naked body in mud, but Charmey made a face at him and handed him his coat. She put on a big pair of headphones and aimed a long microphone at Lilith, who had closed her eyes and had started to chant softly. Y focused the camera and gave a nod to Geek, who took a final hit off the roach.

"Let's go," he said, grinding it out in a saucer.

Frank followed Geek out the door. When he looked back, Charmey wrinkled her nose at him and stuck out her tongue.

"Hey!" Lilith called, opening her eyes. "Shut the door! It's freezing."

Outside, Geek surveyed the sprawling parking lot and the shopping mall beyond. It was a solid embankment of retail, sitting squatly in the haze of snow. "It's a beautiful world, Frankie," Geek said. "A great big beautiful world."

Buzzed, they cut through the staticky blizzard. The parking lot went on and on.

"Where we gonna walk?" Frank shouted into the wind. The frigid air was spoiling his high. He trailed morosely along until they reached a set of large glass doors, which slid open to admit them. Once inside, Geek stopped. His round-rimmed eyeglasses were white with steam. He took them off and wiped the lenses. He linked arms with Frank's. They started to stroll.

"Look at all this," Geek said in a hushed voice, gesturing around him at the endless storefronts, the vaulted arcades, the tiled corridors. "A veritable temple to consumer culture. Aren't you curious, Frankie?"

"About what?"

"About the big picture?"

"Sure." Now the warmth of the mall was thawing Frankie's frozen high, and it hit him like an unexpected wave. He started to giggle. "Shit, dude, I'm really fucked up!"

"Not to worry, little brother. It's just the tetrahydrocannabinol coursing through your veins."

"Yeah?"

"THC," said Geek.

"Right."

They passed a one-hour photo store. There were brides in frames in the shop window. Snapshots of puppies. Babies in diapers.

"What were we talking about?" Frankie asked.

"About the big picture. About the future of life."

"Oh," said Frank. "Hey, Geek, that reminds me . . ."

They passed a corner kiosk selling Gummi bears and roasted nuts. The nuts smelled good, like sweet burned honey, making his penis swell a little and nudge against his jeans.

"Reminds you of what?" Geek asked.

"Nothing," Frank said. "Hey, can we get some nuts?"

Geek waited for him while he bought a bag of honey roasted. "Did you know that the FDA says that peanuts are the most pesticide-saturated food in the American diet?" Geek said.

"No shit," Frankie said. The warm, salty-sweet nut taste exploded in his mouth.

"Do you care?"

"Not really. Want some?" He held out the hot little bag. Geek shook his head. "C'mon, have some. They're good." He dumped a small pile in Geek's palm. Geek picked one up and popped it in his mouth.

"Mmm. I like the taste of toxaphene," he said, eating another.

"Me, too."

"Zesty diazinon. Delicious DDT."

"Want some more?"

"Sure," Geek said. "Thanks." They continued to walk. "Did you know that peanuts are seeds?" Geek said, pausing to toss one into the air and catch it in his mouth. "What do you know about seeds, Frankie?"

"Not much, Geek." They walked past Payless Shoes. They walked past a Bugle Boy and a Blockbuster. The mall was pretty empty on account of the weather, but there was a girl in the Gap who gave Frankie a look that made his penis go hard all the way.

"Do you know anything at all?" Geek asked.

"About seeds?" Frank thought for a moment. "You find 'em in apples? You spit 'em out?" The girl disappeared behind a rack of hooded sweatshirts.

"That's right," said Geek. "What else?" They walked past a booth where you could get your face put on a T-shirt.

"Stuff grows from them?"

"Precisely!" Geek beamed. They sat on a slatted bench in front of Computown U.S.A. As soon as they stopped moving, everything cranked down into slow motion. Geek's voice punched through from very far away.

"Seeds are like language, Frankie."

"Language?" Frank was having trouble hearing.

"Or software, if you like."

"Oh, sure, software." That was better. They had computers in his high school back in Ashtabula. It was the only class he liked. "Why didn't you say so?"

"Excellent," said Geek, sitting back and smiling. Next to him was a huge palm growing in a planter. He fondled a frond. "Now, take a pea, for example."

"A pea?"

"A pea's a program, Frankie, designed to absorb carbon dioxide, minerals, water. You with me so far?"

"Sure, Geek." He leaned forward. It seemed extremely important to concentrate, to understand what Geek was saying now.

"When you plant the pea, it's like downloading software. The pea unstuffs and decompresses into a complex set of instructions powered by the sun. This program allows the plant to create its own food, which makes it grow."

Frankie nodded. The palm frond waved gently above Geek's head.

"In the process the pea gives off oxygen, creating a platform to support the life of other organisms, like bacteria, or us. In a sense we're just byproducts of that program."

"Of the pea?"

"Precisely." Geek nodded. "And all the other plants, too. Each one is a complex software program, and so are we. And the really wild part is, we're all interactive! We can all *learn*, Frankie, and that's the marvel! The pea trains the farmer, and the farmer trains the pea. The pea has learned to taste sweet, so that the farmer will plant more of it. Vegetables are like a genetic map, unfolding through time, tracing the paths that human appetites and desires have taken throughout our evolution. It's the coolest thing. And as their human symbionts, we service their DNA—"

"Symbi-whats?"

"Symbionts. We depend on plants. They depend on us. It's called mutualism. The balance between nature and culture. At least, it used to be. But now the balances are shifting. You see, Frankie, there used to be this line that nature drew in her soil, which we simply weren't allowed to cross. A flounder, she said, cannot fuck a tomato."

"Ha, ha. That's a good one, Geek."

"A bacterium cannot breed with a potato."

"Right!" This, too, was something he could understand.

"Until now."

"Now?"

"Until genetic engineering. Go back to language for a moment, Frankie, and think about this: Genetic engineering is changing the semantics, the meaning of life itself. We're trying to usurp the plant's choice. To force alien words into the plant's poem, but we got a problem. We barely know the root language. Genetic grammar's a mystery, and our engineers are just one click up the evolutionary ladder from a roomful of monkeys, typing random sonnets on a bank of typewriters. We've learned a lot about letters—maybe our ability to read and spell words now sits halfway between accident and design—but our syntax is still haphazard. Scrambled. It's a semiotic nightmare."

Frank sighed and shook his head. "You lost me, Geek. I was never any good at English."

They left the bench and the palm tree and entered the slipstream of the mall's great boulevard, eddying past the vending carts selling crystals and carpet cleaners. Magnetic bracelets. Turquoise jewelry. Sunglasses. They took the elevator down and walked through the Food Court. Frankie was hungry again, and he bought a bag of fries at Burger King. They took the elevator back up and walked for a while longer.

"Wanna fry?"

"No thanks," Geek said. "They look delicious, though." He threw his arm around Frank's shoulder. "Did you know that the Aymara of Peru have hundreds of different kinds of potatoes, and they can tell them apart by taste, and they have *names* for each one?"

"So?" Who needed them? The fries tasted great.

"We only have maybe a dozen kinds left in commercial production here, because engineers have decided that potatoes all have to be the same size. Diversity is inconvenient to mechanized farming. This is what happens when agriculture becomes agribusiness. When engineers replace poets, and corporations gain total domination over all our food and all our poems." Geek cocked his head. "Monoculture," he said. "Has a sad and hollow ring to it, no?"

Frankie listened, but he couldn't discern any ring at all, just the low drone of the filtration system, recirculating the warm mall air.

"I can't hear it, Geek," he said. "And besides, what's the big deal? A potato's a potato, right? As long as you can make it into fries that come with a burger and a Coke for a couple of bucks. I'll tell you, that's a good meal where I come from."

"Right-o," said Geek, removing his arm from Frank's shoulder and clapping him on the back. "I can understand that."

"No offense. I mean, I like all that stuff you were saying about the peas and the software. And the part about corporations and total domination and stuff totally sucks. But you gotta understand, it's the protesting that really turns me on. Doing the actions. And I like you guys, so if you say something's worth fighting, I'll go along with it. But for me, I don't really

125

care what I eat, you know? Like, these fries taste great, and I figure I'm just gonna die anyway. Sooner or later."

"Well, that's true enough."

"Is that lame?"

"No. But I can see why Charmey likes you. She's kind of got a thing about dying young. Did she tell you?"

"No."

"That's why she's so excited about the baby. She always wanted to have one, but she didn't know if she'd get around to it in time."

Frankie stopped walking. "That's totally fucked up!" He shoved his hands deep into his pockets and started kicking at the floor.

"That she wants a kid? Aren't you into it?"

"Oh, sure, but I'm seventeen years old, dude. I'm too young to be a father."

"Charmey is pretty clear about raising it by herself."

They started walking again. "It figures," Frank said. "Just when things were going so great." They arrived at the portals of the mall. Outside, in the parking lot, they could see bundled shoppers bent against the wind.

"No need to change your plans, Frankie," said Geek. "You can still ride with us. Head west. Hang with Charmey. Help her out. She'd appreciate that."

"Geek, man, you don't get it. It's not about the kid. I can get used to that."

"So what's the problem?"

"I *love* Charmey. I don't want to fucking lose her."

poo ⌘

Ever since their conversation about the NuLifes, Cass and Will were making love on schedule again. In the past this had been somewhat of a chore, as the regimen took some of the spontaneity out of it, but this time felt different. Maybe it was just having Yummy next door, but everything felt a little sexier and more alive.

Cass and Will spent the winter months catching up on the paperwork and bookkeeping. This year Will was trying to master the GPS software, and it was driving him crazy. He'd sit at the computer swearing at it, trying to input data and generate readouts and maps. He hated being indoors, and it seemed like the desk work had doubled since they'd installed the satellite system. It had seemed like a good idea. The geographical information about field conditions provided by the GPS promised to allow them pinpoint accuracy in applying fertilizers and other chemical inputs, and the resulting cost reduction in pesticides and herbicides would pay for the system, but precision farming was new, and they had yet to see any savings. Still, there was the health and safety factor. Will was never one to begrudge expense when it came to safety. He wanted the reassurance of knowing he was doing everything possible.

With Will fuming in the office, Cass took to spending part of each day helping out over at the Fullers'. Yummy was also at her wits' end. She was trying to get the house ready for Lloyd, consulting with a social worker to have railings and fixtures installed in the bathroom, along with hand grips and carpets and nonskid surfaces. The old plumbing was failing, so Cass said to go ahead and have that repaired as well. Since she and Will technically owned the house, she felt she ought to participate in the structural decisions. Yummy seemed pleased that she wanted to get involved.

Workmen traipsed in and out. Momoko wandered from room to room, confused, getting in the way. Yummy had enrolled the older kids in school, but there was still Poo to look after, and when Phoenix and Ocean got home, they demanded her attention. Phoenix was already having problems. He was smaller and scrawnier than the Liberty Falls kids, who picked on him for being Asian and for having a weird name. A week after the semester began, Yummy got a call from the principal's office. Her son had broken a classmate's nose with a karate kick.

"It wasn't *karate,*" he told them when they picked him up. "It was Thai boxing."

Yummy narrowed her eyes. "In Hawaii it makes a big difference," she said to Cass. "We differentiate between ethnocultural *styles* of breaking noses."

Yummy was worried about losing her jobs. She had found substitute teachers to take over her classes, but she was trying to run her real estate business by telephone, making long-distance calls to Pahoa at all hours of the day.

"For Christ's sake, Barney," she yelled into the phone, "I only got into this because you said you would help out, remember? You're supposed to be showing lots, not surfing!" She slammed the phone down and saw Cass watching. "Sorry," she said, combing her hair back from her temples. "It's Poo's dad. He makes me crazy, totally *lolo*. We sort of broke up, but we still work together on this real estate thing. It seemed like a good idea at the time. He's a ukulele player when he feels like it, and I really needed to cut back on the teaching."

His name was Barney Kekuku Parker. When the phone rang again, Yummy glared at it. "If it's him, tell him to go fuck himself."

Cass picked up the phone. His voice was tropical, sweet and thick. He started talking before she could even say hello. "Baby, lissen up," he crooned. "I'm takin' care of t'ings, so you settle your daddy nice, den you bring your sweet leilani pure-passion ass back home to me, wahine."

It sounded like music, but she could barely understand what he was saying. "Uh, this is Cass Quinn speaking. I'm Yummy's next-door neighbor—"

"Hey, Cass!" His voice sounded more normal now, less like a song. "Thought you was Yummy. Howzit going?"

"Fine. Everything's just fine."

"How's my Poopoo? Yummy says you've been taking good care of him."

"Poo? He's a wonderful baby."

"You said it. He's laid back—takes after me. Now, you make sure he doesn't get all uptight and haolefied out there in potato country!" He laughed a huge laugh that filled the phone lines from Pocatello straight across the Pacific. "Just kidding. Tell Phoenix the waves are bad. And tell Yummy to chill."

Cass hung up the phone. "That was your daddy," she told Poo. He waved his spoon at her. She tried to imagine what Barney Kekuku Parker looked like. "He said you should chill," she told Yummy, who groaned. "What does howlified mean?"

"Is that what he said? *Haole* means 'white person.' He's afraid your honky influence will rub off on his son."

"Honky?"

"Jeez, Cass! You're kidding, right? Where have you been?"

"Here. In Liberty Falls."

A few days later Cass offered to take Poo out for a couple of hours, to give Yummy some time to herself before the older kids got home. Cass suggested it casually, like it didn't matter to her one way or the other. And it *didn't* matter. Not at first. She was just trying to be helpful. But Yummy seemed so grateful. She packed up extra diapers and a bottle and a change of clothes, handed Cass the bag, and dumped Poo into her arms. He chewed on the edge of his mitten and contemplated the two women.

"You really want to do this?" Yummy asked.

"Sure," Cass said. "If it would help."

"Oh, Cassie! Would it ever. . . ."

Soon it became a regular thing. Back at home Cass would spread out a big blue blanket on the living room floor and place Poo in the center of it, and then she would sit down and play with him for hours. He was a fat, placid baby, who still hadn't quite mastered the trick of walking unassisted, although he was learning to push himself to his feet. He'd start on his belly and lift his bottom up into the air, then sneak one pudgy foot, then the other, around to where they would support his weight. Then he'd push off with his strong little arms and come to an upright position. He'd stand there and wobble for a while, and Cass always held her breath, hoping that he'd walk for her first. But just as he'd start to take that step, he'd lose his balance and topple, coming down hard on his diapered behind. He looked so disgruntled she had to laugh, and that would make him laugh, too. Assisted, he could dangle from her fingers and cruise around as though he were really walking, and he liked that, but he seemed equally content to sit in the middle of his blanket and play patty-cake, or roll a ball to Cass, or bang a spoon on the bottom of a pot.

When he got tired out, she liked to lie down on the floor next to him, resting her head on her arm so that her face was on level with his. He'd look at her with his black eyes and reach out to touch her nose or put his fingers in her mouth so she could nibble them. She started calling him "little bear," because that was what he looked like.

Sometimes she'd take him shopping in Pocatello, put him in the shopping cart and push him around the aisles at Wal-Mart or ShopKo, watching the mothers cast sideways glances at his curly black hair and chocolate skin. If he fussed, which he rarely did, she'd carry him on her hip, holding him to her cheek or sitting him down by the cash register while she wrote out her check. The cashiers watched as he clenched her blond hair in his dark fingers.

Is he yours?

That's what they wanted to ask, but mainly they didn't dare. Most people thought he was from the reservation, and Cass noticed that when she had him along, some people treated her differently, too. It wasn't so much what they did but rather what they didn't do. She grew to recognize the slight hesitation before they spoke to her and the glance, back and forth, between his face and hers. But Poo would stare at them, eyes steady and old seeming, until they glanced away.

When she had him along, the world looked different, and she liked the way she saw things she'd never noticed before. Some were just little things—the way bright candies were displayed down low, close to the ground, on eye level with a baby in a stroller, or the way that certain pebbles, or clods of dirt, or clumps of grass might look delicious to a baby, who was learning to taste the world. But she noticed other things, too—the way she herself felt acutely visible with the baby in her arms, and the way some people's faces lit up when they saw a child. His warm weight was like living ballast, thrumming with energy, giving her substance. Folks were drawn to that.

Cass thought about this afterward, lying on the bed during Poo's nap. She had turned up the space heater, and the baby, dressed only in a fresh diaper, lay warm and heavy against her chest. When she had him along, she could tell a lot about people. She could recognize the mothers immediately from their knowing smiles, and she was surprised at the bond she felt with them. She could tell the women who didn't have children, too, the ones who looked longingly at the softness of Poo's cheeks, imagining what it would be like to finger his supple spine or to feel his little paws grip her sweater, like he was doing now, in his sleep. These women scared her, and she turned from them quickly, as though what they did not have was catching.

It was hot in the bedroom. Gently she tipped Poo over onto Will's place in the bed next to her and took off her sweater. She paused, then took off her shirt, too. She gathered the baby up again and rolled onto her back, holding him securely against her.

"Hey, little bear," she whispered.

He smacked his lips and wiggled his fingers, but soon his long eyelashes were still against his cheek, and his sleep was sound and deep. She could feel his rapid heart beating against hers. She felt his breath tickle her skin. Secretly she believed that his infant proximity, his naked belly pressing against hers, might increase her chances of conceiving. She would never tell Will this—it was a superstition, and she knew it was silly—but it couldn't hurt to hope either.

ℬↄ

A short while later, when Will came in for a cup of coffee, he saw the baby's blanket spread out like a small sea on the living room floor and the baby's toys scattered around it like boats. In the kitchen a few rubbery cubes of carrot littered the sink.

"Cass!" he called, but she didn't answer, so he followed the trail of infant gear up the stairs and into their bedroom. There he found his wife, sound asleep in the middle of their bed, with Yummy's diapered baby lying, bottom up and belly down, on top of her. It was hot in the room. The baby's little brown body almost hid the scars that ran across his wife's pale chest.

Will watched for a while, then walked to the bathroom, shutting the door quietly behind him. He lowered himself on the edge of the bathtub and stared at the faded pink bath mat, waiting for the tears to come. When he finished, he wiped his face with a towel and smoothed back his hair, redoing the rubber band on his ponytail. Then he went downstairs to make a fresh pot of coffee, thinking how Cass would surely like a cup when she woke up.

seeded ℬↄ

One problem with having children is this: You can easily miss the moment when some twist of your fate unfolds. I was doubled over the back of the car seat with my butt in the air, looking for a teething ring, which Poo had thrown to the floor and was now vociferously demanding, when the black-and-white cow approached the Pontiac.

"For God's sake, Poo! Hang on to the damn thing, will you? Now, wait here."

When I turned around, the cow had her big black nose pressed up against the driver's-side window.

"Hello," it said in a masculine voice, knocking on the glass with a front hoof. "Hello . . . ?"

131

"Aaaaagh!" I screamed, which in itself surprised me. I am not usually a screamer.

"Sorry," said the cow. "I didn't mean to scare you."

"Oh, jeez!" My heart was pounding. "What the fuck?"

At the sight of the cow, Poo started to clap his hands and bounce up and down. The cow cleared its throat, and the deep voice climbed a precarious octave toward something approximately female. "My name's Daisy the Dairy Cow, and I'm here to tell you some very interesting facts about the milk your children drink. . . ."

I opened the door hard into Daisy's round stomach.

"Listen, Cow. That's just great, but I'm late picking up my kids, and I have to get my father out of the hospital." Daisy didn't budge, so I tried glaring. The threadbare beast had three goofy flowers growing like sparse hairs out of its large head. I gave up. It was hopeless. "Why am I telling you this? You're a cow. Could you get out of my way please?"

Daisy's voice returned to its normal male pitch. "Sure. But here . . ." He dug around in a woven basket that hung on his foreleg. The basket was filled with crumpled paper flowers and a sheaf of flyers. "Just take this home and read it and if you have any questions, there's an 800 number at the bottom." He handed me a flyer with his hoof. I took it and dropped it on the seat of the car.

"You're not going to read it, are you?"

"No."

Daisy sighed, then leaned over and looked through the back window at Poo. "Moo," he said, knocking on the window and waving a hoof. Poo gurgled and wiggled his fingers like a sea anemone. "Cute kid," Daisy said. Poo hurled his teething ring to the floor again.

Phoenix and Ocean were nowhere to be seen. I had told them to be ready and waiting. I scanned the entrance of the school building. Several young people, ratty and earnest, were darting forward and waylaying mothers. They were dressed in jeans and headbands and tie-dyed scarves and layers of shaggy knit things that looked like matted fur.

"What's wrong?" asked Daisy.

"Nothing. Just the way those kids are dressed." I was feeling homesick. We had a lot of kids like this in Pahoa—hippies, earthmuffins, white rastas, and back-to-the-land types. They came for the cheap real estate and excellent *pakalolo,* and because you won't die of exposure if you happen to smoke too much and pass out on the beach or by the side of a road.

Daisy ducked her head apologetically. "Usually we try to dress a little more straight when we're doing an action, but this was kind of spur of the moment."

"Spontaneous, huh? Far out. You mean, like a happening?"

"No," he said stiffly. "It's more political than that."

"Political? Well, now, we don't get too many of you hippie-agitator types 'round these parts," I drawled, trying to hit the right twang of hostility and suspicion.

Daisy backed off and nodded his large head so mournfully that I felt sorry for him. "Listen, Cow. I'm just kidding around. The dress code reminded me of my misspent youth, acid flashbacks, Berkeley in the sixties or something."

"Oh, right," said Daisy, relaxing. "Hey, cool. I can relate." He cocked his head. "You're too young to have been dropping acid in the sixties."

"You're right," I said. "It was the seventies."

"Oh, man, the seventies sucked," the cow said sadly.

"Sure did." Together we watched the raggedy crew dart around with their pamphlets. Phoenix was talking to a skinny boy wearing a ski cap pulled down low over his eyes and big, baggy pants.

"Phoenix!" I yelled. "Get over here." Phoenix looked up and flapped his hand impatiently. "Who's he talking to?" I asked the cow.

"That's our Frankie. Our Frank Perdue."

"What a name!"

"You said it."

"Poor kid."

"Totally."

"Phoenix!" I hollered again.

"Phoenix," Daisy said. "Now, that's a cool name,"

"Thanks. I like it, too. But he hates it. Prefers to be called Nix."

Ocean emerged from the school building and looked around, then spotted the Pontiac. I waved, and she came running like a good daughter.

"So how come you call him Phoenix?"

"Habit, I guess. Nix sounds so negative."

"Gotta get through the negative to reach the positive."

133

I looked at the cow. "Good point." I took a deep breath. *"Nix!"*

Startled, Phoenix glanced up, then high-fived Frank Perdue and started loping toward the Pontiac. His sister skipped up and tagged the fender, making a big show of getting there first.

"Hi," Ocean said, panting. She looked from mother to cow and back again. "Who's that?"

"Get in. We're in a hurry. We have to pick up your grandpa by three."

"I'm Ocean," said Ocean to Daisy. "Who are you?"

"I'm Daisy the Dairy Cow. Do you like milk?"

"Cows are girls," she said accusingly. "You sound like a boy."

"Well, I'm not really a cow. I'm a man in a cow costume."

"Is that like a wolf in sheep's clothing?" she asked me.

"Ocean, get in the car. We have to go."

"Well, is it?"

"Yes." I got in behind the wheel.

Ocean turned to the cow. "I don't think I'm supposed to talk to you, then." She climbed into the backseat next to Poo, who had fallen asleep.

Phoenix jogged up.

"Nice of you to join us." I reached across the front seat and opened the door for him. "Get in."

Phoenix sighed and rolled his eyes.

I started the car. "Good-bye, Daisy."

"Hey!" Daisy banged on the hood of the car. "Check out that flyer, okay? It's unbelievable."

I pulled away and looked in the rearview mirror. Daisy was watching us go, waving his foreleg.

"Oh, *gross*," Phoenix said, picking up the flyer from the seat. "This is *so disgusting!*"

"What? What's disgusting?" Ocean cried. She undid her seat belt and hung over into the front seat to get a look, but Phoenix held the flyer just out of her reach.

"Ocean, sit back and buckle up. Phoenix, tell her what it is and stop tormenting her."

"It's this stuff called bovine growth hormone, and they shoot up cows with it."

"You mean like drugs?" Ocean asked. "Why do they do that?"

"So the cows'll make more milk, stupid."

134

"What's a 'bovine'?"

Phoenix ignored her and started to read. " 'This overmilking leads to a condition called mastitis, resulting in open sores on the udders of the cows . . .' "

"Ewww yuck!" said Ocean, throwing herself against the backseat. "What's an utter?"

". . . that leak pus and blood into the milk you drink."

"I'm gonna puke," said Ocean.

"You don't even understand what it's about," Phoenix said.

"I do, too! It's about blood and pus in milk. Mom, I'm never gonna drink milk again, okay?"

"No, it's not okay."

I glanced over at my son's profile as he read. "Listen, son, that's all just fine, but you can't believe everything people tell you, especially some guy dressed up in a cow suit."

"Oh, *Yummy!*" he said. He hates it when I call him son. "They're *activists.*" He folded up the flyer and stuck it in his knapsack. Like that explained everything.

I winced. "*Especially* activists, son. Especially activists in cow's clothing." Listening to the words coming from my mouth, I was struck by how easy it was to sound like a parent.

ॐ

My father sat in the passenger's seat, wrapped in a blanket like a mummified cadaver, shrunken and hauled from a crypt. The kids, scared by his extreme fragility, were in the back, lined up, neat and quiet. Lloyd kept his eyes half shut, his gaze fixed on the landscape passing outside the window. I didn't know what he was watching for, but somehow I doubted he was finding it. There was nothing out there. Finally he gave a deep sigh and closed his eyes.

"You okay, Dad?" When he didn't answer, I figured he must be asleep, or maybe he just hadn't heard, but then I caught Phoenix's eye in the rearview mirror, silently asking the real question—*Is he dead?*—and I understood that while he was still alive, this question would accompany his every pause or silence. I tried to smile reassuringly at Phoenix. When we had gone another mile or two, Lloyd spoke, so soft and slow it seemed his answers were part of a conversation happening somewhere else, far away, in a different life or time.

"I'm fine."

And then, "I'm just tired, that's all."

"You can rest when we get home. You'll be in your own room." I was thinking about the room and the work I'd done to get the house ready for him, worried it would not be right.

"Oh," he whispered. "My own room!" His head dropped back onto the padded headrest, and I glanced over to see a tear leaking from his wrinkled eye. "That's exactly what I want . . ."

When I was a little girl, I used to make him presents—ashtrays from plasticine and macaroni paintings. I would wait, so excited, for him to come home from the fields before my clay cracked or my noodles came unstuck. Darting to the window or onto the porch, I'd search the horizon for the cloud of dust that signaled the approach of his pickup. When he finally walked through the door, he would see me waiting and bend down and coax the offering from behind my back.

"My, my, my," he'd say, turning the object over in his hands. "It's exactly what I wanted."

⌘

Cass was waiting for us. She and Will were in the house, and their Suburban was parked in the driveway. Next to it, in the middle of the turnaround, was the most bizarre vehicle I'd ever seen. It was covered with armored plating and looked like something that you might want to take camping in Beirut or Bosnia.

Phoenix exhaled. "Awesome!"

Cass and Will came up as I got out of the car. "What is it?" I asked.

"Used to be a Winnebago, by the looks of it," said Will. "They showed up about an hour ago."

"Who did?"

Cass shrugged. "Some young people. I've never seen them around here before. They said they knew you."

The way she said it made me nervous, as though the apparition were my fault. Phoenix and Ocean edged closer for a better look. Will peered into the Pontiac at my father.

"Hey there, Mr. Fuller. How you feeling?"

Lloyd looked up weakly. "Will Quinn? That you?"

"Sure thing, Mr. Fuller. Here, let me give you a hand getting out." He took Lloyd's elbow. Lloyd tried to sit forward, and you could see how, in his mind, he was swinging his legs toward the ground and lifting his body out of the car the way he'd done all his life, but this time, after jerking his torso a few inches forward, he fell back against the seat and closed his eyes. Cass squeezed my arm. "This isn't going to work," she whispered.

Will looked over at me. "Maybe I should carry him?"

"Could you?" I said.

But Lloyd opened his eyes and held up his hand. "No!" he said, still catching his breath. "Wait." He closed his eyes. We waited.

Just then a noise from the camping car made us all look up as the armored door swung open and a tall man emerged. He had a long, flowing beard and hair matted into dreadlocks that hung below his shoulders. He was draped in a caftan. A second guy followed, clean-shaven and stockier, wearing glasses with thick, round lenses. They took in the scene and sauntered over to the Pontiac.

"Hey," said the bespectacled guy. "Is that your dad?"

I nodded. His deep voice sounded familiar.

"You just getting back from the hospital?"

I nodded again. We watched as the bearded man walked over to the passenger's seat. He bent to look inside. "Hey, dude," he said.

Lloyd opened his eyes, and a strangling noise rose from his throat. He stared at the man, taking in the beard, the dreadlocks, the garb. "Oh," he whispered. "My Lord!"

The man leaned in toward my father and reached out his arms. "Can you put your hands around my neck?" he asked. "It'll make it easier." Then, without an upsy-daisy or another word, he scooped up my father.

For a moment Lloyd looked stricken. Then he raised his arms and encircled the man's head. He closed his eyes, and his lips began to move in prayer.

"Where do you want him?" the man asked.

"Up—" I stammered. "Upstairs."

He carried Lloyd quickly toward the porch, and I stumbled after.

The bespectacled man held the door open and cleared a path through the kitchen. "You don't recognize me, do you?" he said, smiling. "I'm Daisy."

We climbed the stairs. The kids held back, watching. Momoko was nowhere to be seen. She must have been hiding in the seed shed.

I had rented a hospital bed and had it installed in Lloyd's bedroom, and, entering now, I saw that while we'd been in Pocatello, Cass had turned back the covers and found some cut flowers for the nightstand. The bed lamp cast a warm circle of light upon the pillow.

The tall, bearded man entered the light and lowered Lloyd onto the bed. My father's lips were still moving. He opened his eyes.

"Lord," Lloyd whispered, his hands still clasping the bearded man's neck as he searched his face, " 'I am poured out like water. . . .' "

"You take it easy and get some rest now, sir," the man said, disengaging Lloyd's arms, settling him, then pulling up the covers. "You're just all tired out."

I watched the last remaining strength drain from my father's frail limbs as he gazed adoringly at the face of the stranger.

᪥

"Y?" Cass asked.

"Short for Yeats. That's my last name. First name's Melvin."

"Nice to meet you, Melvin," I said. "Have a cup of coffee."

"Just water for me, please. I don't do caffeine."

"Are you Church, Melvin?" Will asked.

The man looked perplexed.

"He means Mormon," I interpreted. "Latter-Day Saints. It's big around here. They don't do caffeine either."

He shook his head. "No. Life is my church. And if you don't mind, I prefer to be called Y."

I put a glass of tap water on the table in front of him, then poured coffee for Will and Cass, who hung back alongside the kitchen counter. Cass had brought over a pot roast for dinner, which was in the oven. I was hungry and wanted to eat, but the children were restless after the somber car ride home and hovered now around the edge of the newcomers' aura, drawn to them. They were strange and exotic in Idaho, but they reminded the kids of Pahoa.

"I hate my name, too," Ocean confided.

"Why?" asked Y. "Ocean's a beautiful name."

"Mom, can I be O?"

"No."

"I want to be O."

"Forget it, Ocean."

Cass and Will sipped their coffees and watched the strangers the way they watched the wind when it turned, bringing weather.

"Yeats is Irish, right?" Will asked. "Like the poet."

"That's right."

"Will Quinn," said Will, holding out his hand, testing the wind's direction.

"Hey," said Y. "Fellow Irish. Right on."

"Where'd you learn to do that?"

"Do what?"

"Pick up the old guy like that. Carry him . . . you know."

Y shrugged. "Used to be a psych nurse."

"A *nurse?*" Phoenix said, disgusted.

"Men can be nurses," said Ocean. "Just like girls can be doctors."

"And men can be cows," the big man with glasses told her pointedly. He came over to help me with the tea.

"Your name isn't Daisy," I said. He had a nice face. Buddha-like, behind his glasses.

"No," he said. "It's Geek."

"I think I prefer Daisy."

"That's cool."

Y was laying his rap on Will and Cass. "Trained as a nurse in the service and worked at a VA hospital back east. Then I met Lilith, and she turned me on to a whole new way of being. Things started to groove, so we just took off. Hooked up with buddy Geek here and went in on the Spudnik. Then Charmey came on board. Then Frankie. Others join us now and then. Life on the road, dig it? One big flow."

I turned to check Cassie's pot roast in the oven. I was looking forward to their flowing right on out of here, but Phoenix's eyes were shining, and Ocean was entranced.

"We came here from Hawaii to meet our grandma and grandpa," Ocean was saying. "How come you came here?"

"Are you gonna stay?" Phoenix asked. "You can eat dinner with us. We got lots of food, and you can camp out in the yard and—"

I spun around. "What the *fuck*, Phoenix!" The words were out of my mouth before I could stop them. Everyone was looking at me now, and in a flash I saw myself as they were seeing me, wearing Momoko's faded,

139

flowered apron and brandishing a wooden spoon. Two months in this house and I'd turned into what I would have become if I'd stayed—a small-town lunatic housewife.

"That's okay," Y said. "We don't eat flesh."

"But," Geek said smoothly, addressing me, "now that you mention it, we would like to camp out here for a while. We came here to learn about the seeds."

"The seeds?" I looked around the room for clarification, but no one seemed prepared to give any. What do you do when a caravan of hippie activists shows up and wants to camp in your driveway? Cass opened her mouth, then closed it again. Will sat back and studied the refrigerator.

"We're called the Seeds of Resistance," Geek said, as though that explained something. "We traveled all this way just to meet you."

"Me?"

"Not you," said Y. He bowed his head. "M. and L. J. Fuller," he intoned. "Seedsmen."

"We're on a pilgrimage," Geek said. His eyes were shining behind his lenses, as though the contemplation of my parents had lifted him into a transcendental state.

"Why on earth . . . ?"

"They're awesome!"

"They are?"

"Totally radical." Geek pulled a worn pamphlet from his pocket and handed it to me. "Look at this!"

It was one of Lloyd's photocopied newsletters. I turned it over. *To Our Customers . . .*

"Have you read it?" Geek asked. "This is like radical shit."

"Yummy . . ." Will glanced over at Cass. "We've been meaning to tell you. Folks around here know about it and make allowances, but Lloyd's been getting a bit carried away recently, and some of the stuff he goes on about is pretty nutty. . . ."

"Nutty?" asked Y, eyes still shut. "That's a sacrilege, man! He's totally profound. M. and L. J. Fuller are like prophets!"

"Prophets?" Will looked bothered, like he'd felt the weather in the room take a sudden turn for the worse.

Y opened his eyes and spread his arms wide, as though offering benediction to the worn tablecloth. "They are prophets of the *Revolution!*"

Momoko had come in from the garden and was hunched over Lloyd's desk in the dark. A single reading light illuminated the desktop and the sheet of paper she was trying to read. Her face hovered inches above the surface. I walked up behind her and laid a hand on her shoulder.

"Lloyd's home, Mom." I fingered the straggling ends of my mother's hair. And your daughter is having a nervous breakdown. And there's a caravan of hippies camping out behind the barn. Oh, and you're a prophet of the Revolution.

At least the labels on the furniture were right.

Momoko looked up and nodded absently but didn't move. I patted her back. Her hair was thin, but pure, pure white.

"Come, have some pot roast."

Momoko held up the sheet of paper and tapped it with the side of her finger. "Did I pay this one? I can't remember."

I took the paper from her. It was the damn gas bill again. I waved it in front of her face.

"This is *old!* I told you. It's three years old. Look at the date!"

She squinted at the tiny print. "What date is today?"

"Oh, Mom! Just get rid of it!" I ripped the bill in half and dropped the pieces in the wastebasket.

"No!" she cried. "Don't throw! Maybe we will need later!" She leaned over and retrieved the pieces from the wastebasket, spreading them out on the desk and smoothing them down. Her movements were slow; it seemed to take forever. I watched, hypnotized by her trembling fingers, by the torn, jaggedy edges that refused to meet, but I was unable to move or to help or to walk away.

"Where is Scotch tape? You see Scotch tape?"

They were like birds now, her hands, as they dipped and hovered over the desktop, trying to find, trying to find . .

Then, with no warning, they fell to her lap. Shot out of the sky.

She looked down at them. "Lloyd is home," she said to her old hands. She sat for a while, thinking deeply, then nodded to herself. "I make him nice pot roast. He is meat-and-potatoes kinda guy." She stood up and shuffled off to the kitchen.

organs ℬ

He was there, the strange man who'd carried him. There when Lloyd woke, leaden, trying to breach the oily surface of sleep; still there when sleep pulled him down again into its cloying depths, closing above his head without a bubble or a sigh. All through the long night, Lloyd could sense the man's silent attendance, and he was glad.

A seed shall serve him; it shall be accounted to the Lord for a generation.

When dawn broke and he opened his eyes and could focus again, he saw the man perched on the straight-backed wooden chair by the bedside, somewhat blurry in the gray morning light filtering in from the window that framed his head. The man was not sitting properly in the chair, Lloyd noticed, but balanced on top of it, cross-legged like an Indian. His eyes were cast down to a distance just short of the bed, staring at the braided rag rug, or perhaps at Lloyd's worn slippers. Sometimes his lips would move. Sometimes his eyes were closed. Praying, Lloyd thought, and so he closed his eyes and prayed, too.

Be not far from me; for trouble is near; for there is none to help.

The door opened quietly. Lloyd kept his eyes shut, pretending to sleep. "How is he?" he heard his daughter whisper.

"He's cool," said the man. "Slept like a baby."

"Is he sleeping now?"

"I think he's awake."

"Dad?"

Lloyd listened to her tentative footsteps approach his bedside, felt her peer down into his face, felt her breath against his skin. He opened his eyes. "What?" he demanded.

She jumped back. "You scared me. I thought you were asleep."

"Then why were you talking to me?"

"Good morning, sir." The man interrupted before she could answer. Lloyd looked at him and saw things now that he hadn't noticed before. The clutter of metal rings that perforated his earlobes. The ratty dress he wore. The matted, fleecelike hair. Lloyd had shorn sheep with shorter pelts. And cleaner.

"Why are you here?" Lloyd asked.

142

"Because you need me," the man answered.

"Get my wife."

"I'll help you, sir."

Lloyd shook his head. He struggled to sit up, then sank back against the pillows. "Get Momoko," he said.

"Dad." Yumi was wheedling him now. "Mom's out in the garden. Y can help you."

"Why? Why what?"

"Because Mom is too weak, Dad. You know she can't—"

The man cleared his throat. " 'Y,' sir. Like the letter. That's my name."

"What kind of name is that?"

"It's short for Yeats," the man said. "But you can call me Melvin."

⌘

"Melvin, why don't you cut off some of that hair?"

Melvin looked up from the operation he was performing upon Lloyd's naked abdomen, swabbing the area around the puckered stoma. "Would you prefer that?"

"I'm just afraid you're going to get it caught in that glue."

He glanced away as Melvin applied the adhesive to his skin and reattached the ring. His skin was like paper, and he feared it would tear, but it never did. He tried to avoid looking at the stoma itself. He looked back again as Melvin slipped the plastic bag over the ring and secured the collar. The apparatus made him feel not quite human, as though he were sprouting some kind of kitchen appliance from the side of his torso. It felt brittle, like the shoot from the eye of a potato. But with or without the bag, his body was strange to him now. It was old, an old man's body, and Lloyd couldn't quite fathom how or when that change had occurred.

"All set, Lloyd," Melvin said. He peeled off the latex gloves and dropped them into the trash, then brushed the thick locks back from his face and readjusted his kerchief.

Lloyd shook his head. "You ever try taking a comb to all that mess?"

"No, sir. That's the point."

"What point?"

"They're dreadlocks. You're not supposed to comb them."

"You mean, you grow 'em out of your head like that on purpose? My goodness. What does your wife think?"

"Lilith isn't my wife."

"You're living in sin."

"That's a matter of opinion, sir."

ॐ

"What's a nostomy?" It was the girl asking. Ocean.

"Colostomy," Melvin said. "It's the operation your grandpa had."

"What kind of operation?"

"They put a little hole in his stomach."

"Why does he need a hole there?"

And now the boy answered. "Because his asshole doesn't work any-more, so they had to drill a new one."

Ocean. Phoenix. Ridiculous names.

"Melvin," Lloyd called out.

"Yes, sir?"

"Nothing."

Why were all these children in his room all the time? They had the whole house to play in.

"How come he can call you Melvin and we can't?" Ocean asked.

"Because he's an elder."

"What's a nelder?"

"*Elder,* dummy," Phoenix said. "It means the same thing as 'Tutu.'"

"Your grandpa's older than us, so he's an elder. We must give him re-spect."

"Just 'cause he's old?"

"Yes. Because he's old. And wise."

With the ancient is wisdom; and in length of days understanding.

ॐ

He grew to tolerate them, Melvin and his friends. He liked the way they gathered in his room, settling around his bed, to listen to him talk about seeds and farming. The air in the room changed when they all trooped in, like someone had opened a window. They smelled of oxygen and peat-moss.

Momoko liked them, too. She sat by his side on a chair they'd brought up from the parlor for her. Melvin's girl, Lilith, usually sat on the end of the bed, and sometimes she'd massage his feet, grown fat with the edema that

144

had turned his toes a purplish gray. Like dusty grapes or stunted spuds. Dead things. He was shocked every time he looked down and saw them, and at first he tried to hide them under the covers, but these kids didn't seem to mind.

"Let me rub them for you," Lilith said. "It's good to keep the circulation going."

She was Ocean's favorite, and the boy liked her, too. Turned red whenever she stood near him. Lilith had started teaching Ocean some kind of dance, and sometimes he'd look out the window and see them leaping and spinning in circles and waving their arms all over, bundled up against the cold. Modern dance, they called it. Expressive. Improvisational.

They reminded him of the Young Potato Growers, the way they watched him as he talked, carefully taking in every word. Young people had such clear eyes. It had been a long time since anyone had listened to him like that. He tried to remember his yearly speech. *Seasonable cultural practices.*

"What else?" they urged.

Protecting your potatoes from pests is important. It is crucial to plan the applications of pesticides to harmonize with seasonable cultural practices.

"Too many P's!" they howled.

Lloyd nodded sheepishly.

"Were the agricultural-chemical corporations paying you?" they wanted to know. "Kickbacks? Sponsorship? Is that why you promoted their products?"

"No," Lloyd said. "They supported our events and the like, but that wasn't it."

"What was it, then?"

He shook his head and looked at them, eyes clear, brows furrowed, trying to understand. He sighed.

"Well, that's how things were back then. We just believed."

"But people *still* believe!"

"No," Lloyd said. "They don't. Not like they used to."

"But they're still using it! You said so yourself. The chemicals, the poisons—"

"It's more complicated than that. Margins are tight. Prices are down. You need higher yields to make a profit, and inputs maximize your yields. A lot of these fellas, they're cash poor. Got their whole lives tied up in their land and one season's harvest. Not a whole lot of room for error. It takes guts to try something new, far as I can see."

"But when you listen to these guys, all they do is say how great the stuff is—"

"That's all it is," said Lloyd. "Just talk. Deep down they know."

"—all the while it's killing them. It's like they're junkies, man!"

"Well, I wouldn't know about that."

"When did you stop believing?"

"Well . . ." Lloyd closed his eyes. He didn't know how to answer.

Any resemblance to the Young Potato Growers stopped with the way they dressed. The Young Potato Growers were a clean-cut bunch, but this lot was a disgrace.

"Are they poor?" he asked his wife. "Are they destitute? Is that why they wear that garb?"

Momoko shook her head. She was wearing a ratty old sweater with holes in the elbows, dotted all over with balls of pilled wool that clung to her like dung to a sheep's bottom. Crusted bits of food and sticks and dirt had become part of the knit. Her trousers had tears in the knees and seat, which she had long since stopped repairing. She took a damp wad of Kleenex from the rolled cuff of her sleeve and blew her nose. The tissue disintegrated in her fingers.

"Momoko," Lloyd said, "why don't you change your clothes? Let Yumi find you something nice to put on."

She shook her head and sniffled, then tucked the wad back into her cuff, but it fell out again. Wherever she went, she left behind a trail of soggy tissues.

"It's the death of the land," he told them. "Soil's dead now. Water's dead, too. You should have seen the birds when I was a boy! Oh, my goodness, the sky would be black with 'em!"

"Oh, man!" they said. "You are so *cool!*"

I am? Lloyd thought.

He is? his daughter wondered.

She would stand at his bedroom door and hover on the threshold or by the ledge of the windowsill, as though to ensure an escape route should she need one. It made Lloyd nervous.

"Don't they drive you nuts?" she asked.

"No. I like them. You drive me nuts."

She looked hurt. "Me? Why?"

"The way you're standing there. Either come all the way in or get out."

She hesitated, then came in and sat down on Melvin's chair. She stared at the same spot on the carpet for a long time, but the effect was not the same as when Melvin sat there. Melvin gave off a sense of calm, which settled around his shoulders as though all the molecules in the air were aligning and coming to rest around him. Yumi's molecules were just twitching and fidgeting all over the place, the way they always had.

"How can you tolerate them?" she asked at last. "You hate hippies."

"Is that what they are?"

"Of course that's what they are! Don't tell me you didn't notice. Look at Melvin's hair!"

"They are respectful," Lloyd said. "They listen."

"They take drugs, Dad. They smoke pot—can't you smell it on them?"

"They smell like the outdoors."

"Fine. Look at the way they dress, then. You would never have let me out of the house dressed like that."

"Didn't seem to stop you. You left anyway."

"I left because you couldn't tolerate my lifestyle," she said.

"You left because you couldn't face your mother and me after what you'd done."

∂ꝺ

She'd been fourteen years old. How can a fourteen-year-old have a lifestyle? But looking at the boy, Phoenix, he saw that one could. The boy skulked around the house wearing a pair of brand-new Carharts, so big they slipped way down around his hipbones, showing a good six inches of his boxer shorts underneath. What was keeping them up? Lloyd wondered. It made him nervous to watch the boy, worrying that he'd lose the whole lot altogether.

"You steal those trousers off of someone's clothesline, boy?" Lloyd asked, trying to make a joke. "Could fit two of you in there, one in each leg."

When the boy still refused to answer, Lloyd gave up. "Get a belt," he said curtly.

The girl was different. She was still just a little thing and dressed in whatever it was that her mother put on her. She was more interested in what was going on inside a person's body than what the person wore on it. She stuck by Melvin like a burr whenever he was changing Lloyd's ostomy bag. The operation continued to bother her, and she bothered Melvin, asking questions incessantly:

"What's a nintestine?"

"Do I have a bowel?"

"How does it get to my butthole?"

Finally Melvin called Lilith, who took the girl into the bathroom. Down the hallway Lloyd could hear them, talking and giggling.

"That *tickles!*" Ocean squealed from time to time, and then their voices dropped down again to a murmur.

He had drifted off to sleep when the door to his bedroom flew open and Ocean burst in, buck naked, covered with paint.

"Tutu Lloyd!" she cried. "Look! I've got *organs!*"

She twirled around as though to show off a party dress, so he could see what had been painted on her skin: great sulfur-colored lungs on either side of a purplish liver; a large, bean-shaped stomach; a loopy mass of gray, serpentine intestine; a pair of small, podlike ovaries.

"I've got two," she explained happily as she traced the fallopian tubes that sprouted from the pods like tentacles. "Phoenix and Poo don't have any, because they're boys." She bent over to inspect her belly. "Don't they look like flowers?"

Lloyd averted his eyes. "Put some clothes on," he said. His voice came out sounding harsh and cruel, and instantly he regretted it.

Ocean froze. Her arms dropped to her sides, but just as quickly they rose again to hug her chest, smudging the greasepaint and smearing the carefully drawn twists of her viscera. Desperate and naked, she looked at Lilith, who stood in the doorway holding a paintbrush.

Lloyd panicked, tried to think of something to say. His mouth opened and closed, but no sound came out.

"Why don't you show him your heart?" Lilith suggested.

Lloyd looked at her gratefully. "Yes," he said. "Show me your heart."

It was bright red and plump and purple veined, tucked beneath her rib cage.

"Can you feel it beating?" she whispered.

"My goodness," Lloyd said.

"I can feel yours, too."

Her small hand on his bare chest was warm and light. When she scampered from the room to show her organs to her mother, Lloyd laid his hand on the spot she'd touched, as though to hold in the warmth, and when he removed it, he noticed the stain on his skin. He turned over his palm. It was smeared with the bloodred paint from her greasy heart.

zesties 𝄇

"Waffle Fries."

"Dinner Browns."

"Simply Shreds."

"Potato Zesties."

"What are we going to tell them?" Lilith asked, peeling off a sticky orange label and applying it to the side of the box of frozen Zesties.

"Depends on what we decide to do," said Y.

"I'm for staying," Geek said. "I want to learn more about their seed operation."

Y closed the freezer door and moved on to the next one. "What about our work?"

"This is our work, and what better place to do it? This is the heart of potato country. Awesome place for actions."

"Criss Cross Fries."

"Twice Baked Potatoes, three different flavors."

Y studied the stacks of newly labeled boxes and shook his head. "So we say like, 'Hey, dudes, I know we just met and all, but do you mind if we live in your driveway?' "

"No," said Geek. "We offer to pitch in and help." He held out his hand to Frankie for another sheet. The labels were bright safety orange, each carrying Charmey's illustration of a spud overlaid with the skull and crossbones. Underneath the graphic read a warning: DANGER! BIOHAZARD! THESE POTATOES **MAY** CONTAIN A GENETICALLY ENGINEERED PESTICIDE! He stepped back and squinted at the freezer shelves. "Hey, these new labels show up great! They pass the squint test."

"Golden Crinkles."

"Curley QQQ's."

"Lloyd won't mind," Lilith said. "He acts crusty, but he's really sweet inside. Did you hear what he was saying about the death of the land? That blew me away. I want to use that on the Web site."

"What about the old lady?" asked Frankie. He was acting as lookout, scanning the aisles for stock boys and supermarket management.

Geek rubbed his hands to warm them up. "She's cool. She showed me the greenhouse and the seed shed. What a collection! It's like a gold mine in there."

"So who's the problem?"

"Yummy," said Lilith, making a face.

"*Yumi,*" Geek corrected. "You pronounce it 'Yumi.' She's not so bad. She's just got a lot going on with her parents and her kids."

"Whatever. She's very uncool. You checked out her Web site. *Yummy Acres?*"

"I agree that's dumb, but I like her. She's a teacher."

Lilith snorted. "Geek, she's also a real estate agent. She supports the private ownership of land!"

"Tater Tots."

"Tater Babies."

"Fast Food Fries." Y was finishing the last stack. "Can you believe they would name something 'Fast Food Fries'? Like that's a selling point?"

"I bet they taste great," said Frankie wistfully.

"I bet all this shit tastes great," said Y, closing the freezer. "Okay, Seeds. That's all twenty-seven different varieties of frozen processed potato products, not including all the flavor variations."

"Wow."

They stood back and admired their work. All the boxes and bags of potatoes, stacked on the freezer-section shelves, now carried safety-orange biohazard labels, permanently and prominently displayed on their sides, facing the consumer.

"Excellent work," Y declared, clapping Frankie on the shoulder. "What the government won't provide, the citizens must. Stop-N-Save shoppers deserve to know what puts the zest in their Zesties and the curl in their QQQ's, eh, Frankie? How we doing? You think it's safe to hit the dairy section?"

Frankie shook his head. "One of the stock boys is looking at us funny. I think we should split."

"Hey," said Lilith, glancing around. "Where's Charmey with my produce?"

ॐ

They found her in the Fresh Foods section, pushing a shopping cart and digging through a heap of waxy cucumbers. *"Quel dommage,"* she said, wrinkling her nose. "Not one organic vegetable in all of Power Country."

"I can't perform with nonorganic," Lilith complained, picking up a cucumber and looking at it in disgust.

"Can't be helped," said Y. "Just wash it real well and say it's organic."

"I'm not putting that toxic shit inside my body!" she cried. "And anyway, I can't believe you're saying this! Talk about a total sellout! Isn't it?"

Lilith looked around the group for support. Geek studied a squash. Charmey moved on to the bell peppers. Several shoppers stopped to stare.

"Keep your voice down," Y said. "It's not like you're telling people to *buy* nonorganic. Your message still has integrity. Consider it advertising."

"Is that what you think I'm doing? Advertising? This work is sacred to me!" Eyes blazing, she hurled the cucumber at Y's head. He fielded it expertly, plucking it out of the air like a football, which seemed to make Lilith madder. She stormed down the produce aisle toward the checkout and the exit.

"I'll talk to her," said Y. "Go ahead and buy the stuff. She'll use it." He tossed the cuke to Charmey, who put it in the shopping cart along with the other vegetables.

"What's up with this act of hers anyway?" Frankie asked.

Geek sighed. "It's complex. C'mon. Let's finish up and get out of here."

They followed Charmey past the salad greens, toward the root vegetables, and paused while she inspected the turnips.

"You know we have the Web site, right?" Geek said. "Mostly to promote our political agenda, but there's also a part that Lilith runs. It was her idea. The Internet is so full of porno for men, she wanted to create an erotic site for women."

"Wow," Frankie said. "Cool. Why?"

"She envisioned a women-only space where sex could be both fun and sacred. Where women could log on and look at empowering images and exchange stories and get turned on. She wanted the gateway to be nonthreatening, so she chose food production as a theme, because traditionally that's been woman's work and as such is a good platform for social critique."

Geek picked up a parsnip and tossed the turnip into Charmey's cart. "The food/sex thing's been done before, but Lilith does it quite literally. The site is called 'The Garden of Earthly Delights.' I set it up for her. Lilith does her routines, and we videotape them and upload the material from Internet cafés or public libraries, wherever we can find some decent thruput. Then we invite women to respond—"

There were several shoppers nearby. Geek lowered his voice. "I don't know. We get a lot of hits, but I don't know how many are from women."

From across the aisle, by the onions, Charmey made a snorting sound.

"What do you mean?" Frank asked.

Geek coughed, then wiped his glasses on his sweater. "It's the e-mail. Maybe it's because I'm a guy and I recognize the diction, but 'Oh, yeah, I dig your melons' or 'I'm gonna ram my fat yam up your pressure cooker, baby' does not seem like a feminist sentiment."

"Oh," Frankie said. "Right."

Charmey spun on her heel and took off toward the checkout aisles. They followed, standing in line behind her, but she ignored them. She picked up a folded leaflet from a display at the register and read it with her back turned to them.

"Lilith doesn't seem to get it," Geek continued. "She says I'm sexist. Says it's just healthy role play and that the e-mails prove that women are responding to the site by getting in touch with their machisma." He shrugged. "Maybe. This year we added the Secret Garden. It's a membership site. We take Visa, MasterCard, American Express. It's pretty unbelievable. We're raking in the dough."

Charmey turned on him. "*Comme tu est bête!* Of course Lilith gets it! She is not stupid. Except somebody must work and make the money, no?" She thrust the leaflet at Frankie and left them standing there.

The checkout girl was waiting. Geek started to unload the produce onto the conveyor belt. "Charmey's right, of course. The site pays for our traveling and actions and helps with legal expenses."

Frankie looked down at the paper he was holding. It was an information sheet put out by the Idaho Potato Promotions Council. "Fun Facts About Potatoes." He stuck it in his pocket.

"I don't get it," he said. "That's a good thing, right? I mean, Lilith is doing something she wants to do anyway, plus it pays the bills? What's the problem?"

Geek nodded. "No problem," he said, pulling out his wallet. "Sometimes it makes the rest of us feel a little scummy, is all."

a growing season ✍

"Be careful!" Lloyd said. "You'll spill all over the bedspread."

I held my breath and stared at the hole in his stomach that formed the egress of his intestine. It was bright red and shiny, an angry nub. The skin surrounding it was fragile and my hands unsure. I daubed too hard.

"Don't wipe so hard! Oh, now look what you've done!" It was only the tiniest bit of blood, but it horrified us both. "Where's Melvin?"

I turned away, still holding my breath, and hauled open the window. The cold, fresh air cut the stench from his bowel. I stood there, breathing, while the nub dried, and he lay against the pillows with his eyes closed, recovering from the indignity of depending on his blundering daughter. Looking out his bedroom window I could see all the way from the driveway over to the garden and the greenhouse to the fields beyond. My face burned and the chill air felt good.

"I'm cold," Lloyd said. "Shut that window and come finish what you started."

A teal-colored pickup truck with the Sheriff's Department insignia on the door panel turned into the driveway.

"Who's that?" Lloyd asked, struggling to sit up. "Is someone here? Is it Melvin? Tell Melvin to come up here. I need him."

"It's not Melvin." I closed the window and stepped away. Two cops climbed down from the truck, scanned the property, then strolled toward the house. The gait was unmistakable, the slow roll of a holstered hip, like they had all the sweet time in the world. Farm bred and big, they were pig-faced motherfuckers—but I was trying not to say this kind of thing out

153

loud anymore. I put my hand to my mouth and bit my knuckle. The children were with Cass, looking at some newly hatched chicks, which is to say they were as safe as they could be and still be on this earth. Poo was napping in my bedroom, still too little to be in trouble with the law.

"Who is it?" asked Lloyd. "Where's Momoko? Aren't you going to go downstairs and see who it is?"

"I can see."

I turned back to the bed and secured the flange on his apparatus. I snapped the bag on tight.

"Ouch," he said. "Who is it?"

I tossed a bathrobe at him and headed for the door. "It's the police. Maybe they've come to arrest your hippie friends."

I have a runaway's fear of the cops. The sight of a uniform triggers a cloaking response—recoil like a mollusk, shrink back against a wall. Cops can smell a runaway, and as soon as they catch a whiff, they start looking. If you let them lock eyes with you, you're toast. I've tried hard to overcome this response. I don't want my kids growing up cowed by the authority of the state. But no matter how often I assert my own authority—that of a parent, a professor, an abandoned Ph.D.—the time I spent on the street overshadows it all. Fear is catching. When Phoenix was little, I saw his face grow cloudy at the approach of a patrol car, and even Ocean, who is afraid of nothing, fidgets in the presence of an officer of the law.

Then again, perhaps this is not about being a runaway at all. Maybe it's perfectly normal—a healthy response, even, to the sight of a man with a club and a gun.

When the knock came, it was surprisingly gentle. I expected the house to shake and the shutters to fall to the ground. I went to the door. The flimsy mesh of the screen obscured the details of their faces but offered me little in the way of real protection; it was as insubstantial as a San Francisco fog.

"Miz Fuller?"

Now, who would that be? I glanced over my shoulder, hoping Miz Fuller would stride forth, drying her hands on her apron, and deal with these thugs.

"Yummy Fuller, ain't it?" said the older of the two. "Mind if we have a word?"

I backed away from the door and let them open it. They followed me into the kitchen. I saw them look around at the stove labeled BREADBOX and the clock labeled MR. COFFEE—the place looked like a nuthouse. Damn Phoenix, I thought, even as the sign reminded me.

"Coffee?" I asked, and was relieved to hear that I sounded almost normal.

They looked at each other. "Yes, ma'am," said the younger. "If it's no trouble."

I got two mugs from the cupboard, trying to keep my hand from shaking as I poured the milk into the pitcher.

"What can I do for you, Officers?" Setting the mugs in front of them. Steady. Remembering to give them spoons.

I glanced at their faces as they loaded up their coffees. They could be brothers or cousins or clones, one a bit older, the other still damp. The two of them stirred their coffees in unison. I watched their spoons going 'round and 'round. They were solid-looking men. Pleasant. Respectable. Nice Jack Mormons, sneaking a cup of oversweetened hot caffeine. The older one wore a badge, identifying him as the sheriff. I put him in his mid-forties, balding and thick around what had once been a waist. He had the fair skin of a blond, ravaged by the sun and the wind and a lousy diet. His face was spread with a fine network of exploded capillaries. He cleared his throat.

"Sorry to bother you, Miz Fuller. With your daddy being so sick and all."

I nodded graciously. Of course. They were here to deliver their condolences. On behalf of the entire department.

"I got nothing but respect for Lloyd Fuller," the sheriff continued.

As it should be.

"Course, some folks had a problem with him over the years on account of those crazy ideas of his, but it ain't him we come about."

It ain't?

"It's them other people. The ones you been allowing to stay on your daddy's property here. That gang of hippies."

He said the word "hippies" like he was hawking up a ball of phlegm and blowing it out his lips. I looked at his face again and saw that it was not pleasant anymore, but stupid and cruel. He caught my eye.

"What about them?" I could feel the tremor in my voice, a jaggedy rise in pitch caused by the constriction in my throat, as the whole script unrolled before me: the Spudnik, busted for the narcotics that those hippies were most certainly carrying; me, convicted of harboring drug dealers and being an accessory to the crime; my kids, sent into foster care on some brutal farm, while I served time in the Power County penitentiary. *Oh, please, God, get me out of Idaho, and I promise I'll never set foot here again.*

"Well, we're just keeping an eye on them. They were involved in a ruckus at the potato-processing plant over in Pocatello the other day, and yesterday some property got defaced in the Stop-N-Save. We got complaints about them disturbing the peace at the school, too. Maybe you heard about that?"

You could look at it that way. Daisy had disturbed my peace with his basket of flyers, never mind the entire gang moving into my parents' driveway.

"You could talk to them," I said. "I don't know where they are, but I'm sure they'll be back soon."

"Oh, we know where they are," the sheriff said. "They're over at the public library. Right now it's you we want to talk to. The reason we're here, Miz Fuller, is we wanted to know what your connection is. We figured you must know them, since you're letting 'em stay here."

This was easy. "There's no connection," I said confidently. "Absolutely none. I don't know them at all. It's my father and mother they came here to see. They're interested in the seeds."

The sheriff was watching me closely. He didn't say anything.

"You know. Fullers' Seeds." I was anxious to clear up this confusion, to get the answer right, but I was speaking too quickly. "My parents' business? Of course, it's not much of a business, more like a hobby, really. They're retired. It keeps them busy. . . ."

"Well, Miz Fuller," he said, "we don't have a problem with your parents' business either. My ma buys kales and lettuces off them, and she gets a good crop of greens, if you like that sort of thing. It's these other folks we're concerned with." The sheriff grinned then, and I thought I saw a flicker of malice kindle in his pale blue gaze. Like he knew me. Like all of a sudden this was personal. "We thought that what with your *background* and all, you mighta had some previous acquaintance. . . ."

I heard my children in the yard, and the screen door slammed. My heart stopped. I wanted to jump up and scream, *No! Don't come here. Fly away! Fly away!* but I couldn't move. The kids, well trained about cops, braked at the threshold. Their voices fell silent, replaced by the tiny, insistent peeping of a baby chick. Phoenix couldn't keep his lip from curling. Ocean had her hands cupped in front of her heart, and the peeping was coming from there.

"Billy Odell?"

It was Cass. She had come up behind the kids and now stepped between them and into the kitchen. She held out her hand to the sheriff, who got to his feet.

"Hey, Cassie. Long time no see."

"What are you doing here, Billy?" She helped herself to Mr. Coffee. "Dropping by to say hi to Lloyd?"

"Yeah, well, partly." He turned to me. The malice was gone now, and his eyes were just plain dull blue. "How's your daddy doing anyhow?"

"He's fine," I said automatically. "He's dying. Want to see him?"

"Oh, Yummy," Cass said. "Lloyd isn't going anywhere for a good while yet."

"I didn't say he was going anywhere. Why should he? He's exactly where he wants to be."

Cass exchanged a look with Sheriff Billy Odell. The name sounded familiar. I wanted to smoke a cigarette. I got up and dug around in the junk drawer for the pack I'd hidden. Ocean eyed me from the threshold, cupping the chick in her hands, but she didn't say a word.

"Go find a box for that bird before you suffocate it," I told her, but neither she nor Phoenix moved. I lit up and inhaled and felt better immediately. "The sheriff was asking about the Seeds," I said to Cass. "There was some kind of trouble at the Stop-N-Save."

"What kind of trouble?" Cass asked.

Sheriff Odell hesitated. "Some jokers went and put a bunch of stickers all over the potato products in the frozen-food section."

"Stickers?"

"With a skull and crossbones," the younger officer said. "Like they was poison. A couple of the employees said they saw some hippie-looking kids hanging around. Fits the description."

"What do they have against potatoes?" I was feeling conversational all of a sudden, but no one answered. Cass just frowned at me, and Odell shrugged.

"Couple days ago we got a heads-up from Pocatello. This same gang was demonstrating illegally at the plant over there and harassing the workers when they come off shift with some kind of communist propaganda."

"Oh, well," said Cass. "I know about that, and it's a lot of baloney. My cousin works at the plant, and I heard what happened."

"What happened?" I asked.

"Exactly nothing. One of them got dressed up like a Mr. Potato Head toy, and the rest of them passed out some brochures, is all." She turned back to the younger cop. "Aren't you the Patterson boy?" she asked.

"Yes, ma'am."

"How's your ma? She still in chemo?"

"No, ma'am. She's all done with that. Doc says she came through just fine."

"I'm glad to hear it. You tell her Cassie Quinn said hi."

Cass really knew how to deal with law enforcement. I was impressed.

"For goodness sakes, Yummy!" she said when she had seen the sheriff to the door. "That was Billy Odell. You used to go out with him. How could you not remember?"

Phoenix, hearing this, gave me the stinkeye and left the room, but I could tell he was sticking nearby. Sometimes he treats me like I'm the one who needs looking after. When he was little, he used to crawl up onto my lap and play patty-cake with my cheeks, holding my face between his small palms. "Calm down, Mommy," he'd say, looking deep into my eyes. "I love you."

Now he just wants to reject me.

"I never *went* with Billy Odell," I called, loud enough so that Phoenix would hear.

Technically it was true, even though Cass's words had brought to mind the image of Billy Odell putting his hand inside my top and pawing my breast, what little of it there was at the time. We were thirteen, and it was his birthday party, and we were down in his parents' cellar. I remembered the splintery wood digging through the thin fabric of my dress, and the cobwebs, and the row of canning jars filled with pickled vegetables trembling on the shelf as he knocked me against it. We used to call it dry humping, and there was never any question of letting him go further. He got so mad at me for not wanting to put my hand on the hot, upholstered lump that was his penis, he almost started to cry. He called me a cock tease. He moaned and told me his balls would turn blue and fall off and it would all be my fault. Lousy birthday. Should I have jerked him off? I didn't think so at the time, but who knew he'd become sheriff?

"I can't believe you forgot," Cass said. She turned her back to Ocean, who was still hanging around the doorway. "You let him go to second base," she mouthed in my direction.

How did Cass remember things like this? From upstairs I heard Lloyd calling. He must have heard the sheriff's truck drive away. Cass was holding up two fingers. "Billy used to make a peace sign like this and say 'Hay! Farm out!' It was his quote in the yearbook, remember?"

"Okay, stop. Enough. I remember." I glared at Ocean, who was cupping the chick against her chest in one hand and raising the two fingers of the other. "Don't," I told her. "Go upstairs and tell your grandpa that everything's fine, then find a box for that poor bird before you crush it."

"I can't," Ocean said importantly. "Chicken Little is imprinting on me. That's her name. Wanna see?" She approached and parted her thumbs. A tiny beak poked out from the opening, and I could see the chick's bright, beady eye. "Okay, that's enough," Ocean said, sealing up the small cave of her hands. "I don't want her to imprint on *you*."

"Gee, thanks." It was heartwarming, the confidence my kids had in me.

"Cass said I could keep her if you said okay. Okay?"

"Okay."

She skipped off to join her brother in the living room. We heard her bellow, "Hay! Farm out!" followed by the sound of Phoenix, groaning like he'd been bludgeoned. I waited until I heard my daughter's small feet pattering up the stairs and into Lloyd's bedroom, then I lit another cigarette.

"How do you remember this stuff?" I asked Cass.

"You know what it's like here. It's not as if a whole lot happens. Good thing you're back—"

"Glad to oblige."

"—with a brood of fatherless children and a gang of dirty commie hippies in tow. No wonder Billy is nervous."

"For your information, all my children have fathers. And I didn't bring the hippies. They just appeared. And if they're in trouble with the police, they'll just have to *dis*appear." As soon as I said the words, I regretted them, because Phoenix materialized in the doorway, followed by Ocean. I reached for the ashtray.

"It's okay, Mom," Ocean said philosophically, eyeing the cigarette. "You can't help that you're an addict."

"You can't make them go," Phoenix said.

"Why not?"

"Because they're our friends."

"No they're not, Phoenix," I said. "I know the type. They're parasites and freeloaders."

"No they're not. They're—"

Cass interrupted. "Phoenix, you promised to help your sister set up a box and a broody light for that chick, remember?"

Phoenix gave me an evil look, then stomped out the door. Ocean followed, rattling down the steps, crying out, "The sky is falling! The sky is falling!" Just then we heard the sound of an RV lumbering into the driveway. From the window I could see my children running to meet it. The armored door opened and the Spudnik sucked them up inside like an alien vessel.

I turned to Cass. "I'm telling you, if the cops are nosing around now, it's only a matter of time before they come back with a warrant, and I guarantee that Winnebago has enough stuff in it to get us all thrown in jail."

"What do you mean, stuff?" Cass asked.

"Drugs. Pot. *Pakalolo*. Illegal substances."

"Oh." Cass frowned and took a sip of her coffee. "You think so?"

"Believe me." I got up and cleared the mugs off the table, still half filled with thick, sweet coffee. I dumped them in the sink and squirted detergent inside, running scalding water into them until the suds started to spill over the rim. "I know the scene."

Cass still looked dubious. "They seem okay," she said. "The French girl's going to have a baby."

"Oh, God. That's just what we need."

Lloyd called from upstairs. "Is anybody there? I need some help!"

I groaned and clutched the edge of the sink.

Cass shook her head. "Face it, Yum. It's too much for you to manage on your own. And once planting starts, I'm not going to have a minute free—"

From outside came the sound of feet marching up the porch steps and voices singing, " 'With a chick chick here, and a chick chick there. Here a chick, there a chick. Everywhere a chick chick. . . .' "

The screen door burst open, and the parade trooped into the kitchen. Y led them, dressed in his caftan and a down vest. Lilith, draped in tie-dye, beads, and tinkling bells, walked with Ocean, who now carried the chick in an upside-down crocheted hat. Frankie and Charmey followed, side by side. Geek guided Momoko carefully by the arm, and Phoenix brought up the rear, slouching, but looking smug.

"Oh, great," I said. "A convention." My mother was wearing a ratty knitted shawl with crazy rainbow stripes and long beaded fringes. "What's she doing with you? I thought she was in the greenhouse."

Y held up his palms in a position of surrender.

"Whoa, Yummy, dude, stay chill. We just took her for a little drive into town. She was helping us get a library card."

"Melvin!" Lloyd's plaintive voice drifted down from the second floor.

I looked at Y. "Melvin, he wants you."

"My name's Y."

"My name's Yumi."

Y headed for the stairs. "I'll go see what he needs. Then let's meet in the parlor. It's less smoky in there."

$\mathcal{B}$

"What we'd like to propose," Geek said, "is that you let us stay here through a growing season."

They had me surrounded and immobilized, sunk in my father's old checkered recliner. Cass sat at Lloyd's desk, looking on. Momoko was perched on the love seat, with Geek at her feet. The rest of them sat crosslegged on the fraying rug.

"It's March now," he continued. "That would mean until September."

I frowned. "And why should we let you do that?"

"Well, for one thing we can help with the seeds, right, Momoko?"

He tapped her knee. Momoko blinked, then nodded. Geek shook his head. "It's amazing! I've never seen anything like it."

"Like what?" Cass asked.

"Their operation. The greenhouse. The warehouse." Geek paused, inclining toward Ocean and Phoenix. "It's like a vault," he breathed, infusing his voice with an undercurrent of awe that worked like magic, pulling them in. "A vault, full of treasures—"

"Treasures!" Ocean echoed. I watched her warily.

"Or more like an ancient, dusty library, maybe. Shelf upon shelf filled with rare and valuable books. . . ." He paused to contemplate the effect of this metaphor.

"What do you mean?" Phoenix, too, was riveted. He didn't even like books.

Geek paused to let the image ripen, but I interrupted.

161

"And how exactly does all that pertain to us?"

He sighed and gave me a rueful smile. "You teach literature, right? So what you are sitting on here at Fullers' Seeds is a library containing the genetic information of hundreds, maybe *thousands* of seeds—rare fruits and flowers and vegetables, heritage breeds many of them, and lots of exotics. These seeds embody the fruitful collaboration between nature and humankind, the history of our race and our migrations. Talk about narrative!"

"Here?"

"Yeah. In the shed." He gestured out back. "And the greenhouse and the fields. I don't know whether you care or not, but some of these seeds could be the last specimens of their kind left on the planet! Momoko has been collecting them for almost half a century. She and Lloyd have been planting them out, year after year, to keep them viable."

He turned to the children.

"Kids," he exclaimed. "Your grandparents are planetary *heroes!*" The light from the late-afternoon sun, slanting though the window, glinted off the thick lenses of his glasses.

"Heroes?" Phoenix asked.

"They're saving these plants from extinction. It's such crucial work! We've got to help them stop the genetic erosion of the earth's ecosystem. We've got to act *now!*"

"And why is that?" Casting my parents as planetary heroes was the last straw. I thought they were merely prophets of the Revolution.

Geek lowered his voice and glanced up at Momoko. She was dozing. Her eyes were closed and her mouth was open.

"Their storage system is a mess," he said softly. "They've got thousands of different kinds of seeds in shoe boxes and envelopes and canning jars. A lot of them are unmarked. It's an archival nightmare." He paused as my mother let out a soft snore.

"So?"

He looked at me, and I was startled by the seriousness of his expression. Maybe I had read him wrong. Maybe this wasn't just rhetoric.

"She's forgetting the names," he said. "If no one knows what they are, and if no one plants them, the seeds and their stories will die."

"But what about Lloyd?" Cass asked. "Can't he remember?"

Y spoke up then. "Well, that's the drag, you see. Lloyd's mind is okay"—

he glanced up toward the stairs—"it's his body. Between his colon and his heart, I don't think he'll last out the growing season."

So I capitulated, with the provision that the Seeds divest themselves of illegal substances while on the property and refrain from political agitation within the county line. The children were happy, and, watching them, I started to feel an overwhelming sense of relief as well. Charmey said she would help with the cooking. Y and Lilith would see to Lloyd's needs. Geek and Frankie would work with Momoko in the garden, first cataloging, then planting, and finally with the harvest. It seemed too good to be true. My mind slid over the inevitable, and I focused on short-term possibilities. If this worked out, maybe I could leave, take the kids back to Hawaii, as long as I came back at the end, to wrap things up. After dinner I lit a cigarette and walked outside into the garden.

It was a clear night and cold. On the far edge of the field the greenhouse glowed like a large, faceted lantern. I wandered over, thinking that maybe Momoko had left the lights on. Instead I found Geek, inspecting an elaborate web of narrow hoses. He looked up when he heard me.

"Come in," he said. "Close the door."

It was warm inside, and the humid air and scent of peat hit me full on. "Oh! It feels like Hawaii!"

"You've never been inside here?"

"No. I thought it was all closed up and everything was dead."

I walked down the aisle between the benches. Plants lined the shelves, their branches, leaves, flowers, and tendrils all spilling and twining, green and lively. I reached out and stroked a fern. It had been months since I'd seen anything grow.

"It's nice here," Geek said, unclogging a miniature tap and blowing air through it. "You think anyone would mind if I brought a hammock and slept out here?"

"Ask Momoko. I don't mind."

"It gets kind of crowded in the Spudnik, with two couples."

"It's wet in here, though." A drop of condensation formed and fell from the glass pane onto my head. "You could make a tent out of a tarp."

"A tent and a hammock," he said. "And a corner bar that serves small blue drinks with little umbrellas. You could join me in the afternoon for tropical cocktails."

It sounded nice. "The kids miss Hawaii."

"You do, too."

"Yup. I hate it here." I walked along the rows of seedlings, running my finger across their feathery tops. He didn't say anything and the quiet made me want to talk. "I ran away when I was fourteen. This is my first time back."

He lowered the hoses to the workbench. "But you've seen your parents in the interim?"

I shook my head. "No."

"That's pretty intense." He picked up a plastic connector and fitted it back into the end of a hose. "I won't ask why you left. But why come back?"

"Beats me. I guess I felt the kids should meet their grandparents. They've all got different fathers, and I wanted them to know they shared something other than just me. But mainly I was curious. I'm thirty-nine. You get that way."

"Great," he said. "That gives me something to look forward to."

"What, like in the next decade?"

"Yeah." He shrugged. "More or less."

I watched him work, cleaning out the valves with a sharp piece of wire. I felt old and cranky. "So are you guys really planning to stick around here and help with the seeds, or was that little speech of yours more or less bullshit?"

He looked up quizzically. "Why do you doubt us?"

"Hey. Life on the road, man. Just one big flow, right? All I want to know is, are you going to flow on out of here or can I count on you?"

"Sure," he said. He pushed his glasses up with the back of his hand. "Listen, I'll make a deal with you. We'll stick around as long as you do."

"Great." It was not exactly what I wanted to hear. "You better set up that bar and get those blue drinks coming quick. I'm going to need them."

He held up the web of hosing and grinned. "I'm working on it."

wireworm 🐛

"You have two choices for accommodations," Jillie said. "The Liberty Motel or the Falls Motel."

Elliot looked up from the computer. Jillian was perched on the edge of his desk, balancing a legal pad on her knee and showing thigh beyond it. "Huh?"

"Pay attention, Elliot," she said, tugging down her skirt. "I don't have to do this, you know. I'm not your secretary. I'm just trying to help so we can get out of here and get some food. I'm starving."

He sighed. "Sorry."

"Which will it be?"

"Which is better?"

"They both have telephones."

"Oh. Super."

"The Liberty allows pets—"

"The Falls," he said.

It was going to be a long night. Elliot took a sip of cold coffee as he watched Jillie on the phone. If he leaned back in his chair, pushing the limits of its hydraulic tilt feature, he could almost see up into the dark triangular grotto formed by her crossed thighs. He tried to calculate if he'd have time to grab a bite to eat with her, take her home, fuck her, come back to the office, and finish his press release by deadline. Not likely. Something would have to go.

Food.

No, she'd already expressed her feelings about that. Maybe they could fuck now, or in the cab on the way to a restaurant. Maybe they could get takeout and go to her place. He sighed. He could see he was going to have to forgo the fucking. It was always the fucking. Hardly seemed fair.

He looked back at the screen and reread the lead:

Political Activists or Just Plain Old Pests?

Whatever you call them, their politics are familiar: anticorporate, antigovernment, antiglobalization. And most offensive of all, anti-American. These so-called radical environmentalists represent the latest fad in the protest movement that traces its roots to the sixties. And, like their progenitors in the political proscenium, the target of their opposition is progress.

Ugh. Too many P's. Where did they get these speechwriters?

"What's that all about?" Jillian was standing next to him now, peering over his shoulder and butting him with her pudendum.

He sighed. "Potatoes."

165

"Huh?"

"It's a speech I have to give to a bunch of farmers. No big deal. Listen, Jillie, I gotta come back here tonight. You wanna just get takeout and catch a cab and . . . ?"

"Forget it, Elliot. I need real food. Meat and, yes, potatoes. Come on!" Elliot sighed and got to his feet.

"I don't get the connection," she continued in the elevator, taking Elliot's hand out from under her skirt. "Radical environmentalists don't like spuds?"

"You're not making this easy, Jillie."

"It's not supposed to be easy, Elliot. If it were easy, you wouldn't want it."

The digital voice chip in the elevator, programmed to a feminine tonality, announced their arrival in the lobby. Elliot grimaced. "I don't like her," he complained as the elevator door slid open. "What happened to the ding? I liked the ding."

"I've noticed that you're a bit of a Luddite, Elliot." Jillie's heels clicked across the marble lobby of the D&W building. Elliot lagged behind, admiring the tautness of her calves. He felt terribly sad. Why was he such a horny old bastard? Why was Jillian so excruciatingly young and lovely just now?

"No, I'm not," he said. "I'm all for progress. I just miss the good old ding."

"Yeah, well, you and your ding. How did that go?"

Out on the street Elliot held his hand up for a taxi.

"'My ding-a-ling, my ding-a-ling . . .'" Jillie had a nice singing voice.

He held the door open for her and climbed in after. She stopped singing long enough to give the driver the name of a steak house. Elliot stared at his hands, lying on his thighs. They looked like dead animals. Roadkill. Run over and lifeless.

"You're right, Jillie. I shouldn't have mauled you in the elevator. I should appreciate you for your mind."

"That's okay. I forgive you. Now, tell me, it's got a great ring to it, but why Liberty Falls?"

"I'm giving that speech at a big Potato Promotions Council meeting in Pocatello, and I—"

"You're meeting to promote big potatoes?"

"Right." He could tell she was just trying to keep him talking.

"And these potato-hating radical environmentalists are . . . ?"

He sighed. She didn't really care. "It's biotech they hate. Genetically engineered food. Potatoes, in particular. They mobilize all over the country and dress up in costumes and do actions—"

"That's adorable! What do you mean, actions?"

"You know. Political actions. They're activists."

"Like what you used to do in the old days? In Frisco? Sit-ins and happenings and stuff, with your fists in the air?"

Oh, God, she was so young.

" 'Power to the People' and all that?"

"All that," he said. "And boycotts and teach-ins and street theater—"

"Street theater? Oh, God, not those awful *puppets?*"

She was cracking up. He watched her patiently. An idea was beginning to dawn on him. "Listen, are you interested in this?"

"Not really."

"Because it's a good story." If he could get her interested, maybe she could sell it to her editor. "It's not all just puppets and unwashed kids. Some of these groups are engaging in heavy-duty terrorist tactics—arson, blowing up labs and research facilities. Last year they tore up a bunch of transgenic-crop test sites around the country. They're linked to large international groups with lots of media clout in Europe, and we think they may be planning something. A protest against potatoes or—"

"No!" exclaimed Jillian. "Possibly planning a protest against potatoes?"

He grimaced but soldiered on. "Things are heating up after all the WTO fuss in Europe. You interested? You think Wurtz would run something on this?"

"No, Elliot. I'm just probing the workings of your slimy PR mind."

"Hey," he said. "I used to be a journalist, too, you know."

"Before your fall. So what's in it for you?"

He smiled. "Purely the pleasure of passing on helpful information to you," he said, placing his hand on her knee. "It's what I do. It's why you like me. Why you deign to slum around with me and tolerate my advances. I'm a useful guy."

"*Used* to be," she said, pushing him away. "Back when you were still doing big tobacco. People were interested. Plus it was sort of a thrill, dating someone truly on the side of evil. I used to get a lot of points for that."

"Tobacco is old, Jillie. Biotech is cutting edge. It's just a matter of finding the right angle. You'll see."

"And yours is . . . ?"

"The human angle, Jillie." His voice was husky. "C'mon, I'm looking for a little grassroots support, here."

"I get it," she said, slapping his hand as it crept up the inside of her thigh. "Let me guess. You're going to some podunk potato town to pimp some poor farmer's wife—"

"Cute. Too many P's."

"—for the heartbreaking story of harassment by the Luddite left."

"Always looking for an attractive victim. You think Wurtz would be interested?"

"Nope. Wurtz isn't interested in potatoes. No one is interested in potatoes. Didn't you used to live in Idaho?"

"Oh, please."

"Teaching high school or something?"

" 'In my salad days—' "

"Dodging the draft?"

" 'When I was young and green of judgment—' "

"Elliot, I said it was okay that you tried to maul me in the elevator because I felt sorry for you. It is not okay in a taxi."

"Can't help it. I'm an activist, babe. Just looking for a little action."

fourth

◈

O, Mr. Burbank, won't you try
    and do some things for me?
A wizard clever as you are
    can do them easily.
A man who turns a cactus plant
    into a feather bed
Should have no trouble putting brains
    into a cabbage head.

—Anonymous, quoted in
A Gardener Touched with Genius: The Life of Luther Burbank

spring 🐝

Every seed has a story, Geek says, encrypted in a narrative line that stretches back for thousands of years. And if you trace that story, traveling with that little seed backward in time, you might find yourself tucked into an immigrant's hatband or sewn into the hem of a young wife's dress as she smuggles you from the old country into the New World. Or you might be clinging to the belly wool of a yak as you travel across the steppes of Mongolia. Or perhaps you are eaten by an albatross and pooped out on some rocky outcropping, where you and your offspring will put down roots to colonize that foreign shore. Seeds tell the story of migrations and drifts, so if you learn to read them, they are very much like books—with one big difference.

"What's that?" Ocean asks at this point in the story. She loves stories. Laps at their shorelines, licking them up like an incoming tide.

The difference is this: Book information is relevant only to human beings. It's expendable, really. As someone who has to teach for a living, I shouldn't be saying this, but the planet can do quite well without books. However, the information contained in a seed is a different story, entirely vital, pertaining to life itself. Why? Because seeds contain the information necessary to perform the most essential of all alchemies, something that we cannot do: They know how to transform sunlight into food and oxygen so the rest of us can survive.

Of course, this is what planting is all about—the ancient human impulse to harness that miracle and to make it perform for our benefit. To emulate the divine author and tease forth a new crop of stories from the earth.

Spring comes late to Liberty Falls, but by March the farmers are already chafing at the bit, surveying the fields and mapping spring rotations, checking over equipment and inspecting their seed. They scan the skies where the clouds meet the horizon, as though by looking hard enough they could stave off the cold air masses that flow down from Canada. They stare at their fields, kicking at the frozen sod as though by the force of wishing they could make the earth thaw. They wonder what luck, good or bad, God has in store for them, but mostly they are filled with a wild, irrational hope. They are ready to resurrect the year.

I was tired of winter, too, and making plans to transplant my little seedlings. If we went home soon, I might still be able to teach the remainder of the semester, but if I stayed away any longer, this school year was lost, and with it all pretense of an academic career. Adjunct teachers are the professorial equivalent of the migrant Mexican farm laborers hired during harvest. If you can score a good contract at the same farm every year, where the farmer pays on time and doesn't cheat or abuse you, then it's in your best interest to show up consistently from year to year. Neither job gives you health insurance or benefits. Harvesting potatoes might pay slightly better in the short run, but teaching gives you the warm satisfaction of nurturing young minds, at least inside the classroom. The minute you step outside, however, this satisfaction is undermined by the college administration. The nontenured faculty form a downtrodden, transient underclass, inferior in every way to the landed professorial gentry.

I knew I had to get back, but as the days passed, I couldn't seem to make the decision to leave. When you're caretaking someone who is sick or waiting to die, you get hung up in a morbid limbo, waiting for something to happen, to release you back into your life. Not that I was doing much caretaking. Y and Lilith were looking after Lloyd. Not that Lloyd was showing any signs of dying.

"Where's Melvin?" he said. "Just get me downstairs. I can move about fine once I'm down the stairs."

"Dad, you're supposed to be taking it easy."

"The year doesn't wait. We have to get going on those transplants."

"It's early. It's still freezing outside."

He waved his hand in my direction, like I was an annoying fly to shoo away. "Gotta start the leeks."

172

Geek was helping Momoko with the starts, and Ocean was pitching in. From time to time the boy Frankie would show up, which meant Phoenix would deign to join them. They'd stand around the potting table in the greenhouse, making exotic mixtures of peat, sand, grit, lime, and leaf mold. Geek was planning to concentrate on the soybeans, planting out all of the forty-odd varieties in my parents' collection, to make sure that the seed was still viable and to build up the stock.

"They're pretty!" Ocean said. She had been making little paper pots out of old newspaper and filling them with soil, and now Geek gave her a sack of soybeans, labeled JEWEL. She took out a bean. It was shiny yellow with a black saddle. She poked her finger into the soil and made a hole, dropped in the bean, and patted the hole closed.

Geek watched approvingly. "Kids, did you know that more than half of the soybeans planted in America are genetically engineered? And a third of the corn, too."

"So?" Phoenix asked.

"So? That's over sixty million acres! Nature's own varieties are slowly dying out. Soon all we'll have are genetically modified mutants."

"Mutants," said Phoenix. "Cool." He high-fived Frankie. There was only three years difference between them, and Phoenix thought Frankie was just about perfect.

While the rest of them planted, I drifted in and out, sniffing into the corners of the house and the outbuildings. It felt so strange, being back in this place where I'd abandoned my childhood. What did I expect to find now? A little-girl-shaped shadow, perhaps, covered in cobwebs at the back of some forgotten closet. But she hadn't left a trace. The storage room where the seeds were kept was dark and cold. There were rows of shelves covered with old boxes of all different kinds: shoe boxes, kitchen appliance boxes, but mostly old Kleenex boxes—my parents really went through the Kleenex. The boxes were filled with reused envelopes, in turn filled with seeds. The envelopes were ancient, too, with canceled postmarks and the addresses crossed out. They must have saved every envelope they'd ever received, because there were thousands, each one carefully slit across one end, filled with seeds, then taped shut and labeled. Or at least some were labeled. Many were not.

In the dim light Momoko crept around the shelves, shifting boxes from side to side, pulling out envelopes, and tipping out the seeds. "Dr. Wyche's Kentucky Wonders?" she muttered. "Large Mottled Lazy Housewifes? Gollie Hares?"

"*Phaseolus vulgaris.*" Geek nodded. "She's doing the bush beans."

He followed Momoko around with a video camera, filming an inventory of the seeds and plants, trying to help her identify them. Sometimes she'd get the names right, and sometimes she wouldn't. She got very upset when she forgot. One day she sat down on the floor of the storage room and started banging her head with a muddy fist.

"What is *name?* What is *name?*" Over and over. It was just some damn pea, but she couldn't remember, and she just sat there in all that dirt, smacking herself until I grabbed her wrists and held them.

"Mom," I said. "Stop. It's okay."

She looked at me with tears in her eyes. Her white hair was smeared with mud.

"What is *your* name?" she said.

"Cut it out, Mom." I thought she was joking.

Geek helped me get her upstairs to Lloyd's room, and he talked her down, but after that, Y brought Lloyd downstairs every day and sat him in a wheelchair in a warm corner of the greenhouse so he could help out for a few hours. She was a lot calmer then. Lloyd sat there triumphantly with a plank on his lap and a marker and a pile of labels, carefully writing down the names of things. His hand was so shaky you could barely read the letters.

One day Geek sent Phoenix to the storage room to locate some soybeans—Amish Greens or Beijing Blacks or Agates. Momoko was in there with a miner's light attached to her forehead, and even though she was pretty deaf, she must have heard Phoenix come in. She raised her face, and the beam from the lamp cast shadows on her sunken cheekbones, illuminating her ghostly white hair. She scared the shit out of him. He stepped back, knocking over a shelf of lettuces or something, and she started cackling like it was the funniest thing she'd ever seen. After that, whenever she saw him, she yelled "Boo!" But he'd get her back, pretending to talk without making any sound, just moving his lips. "What?" she'd say, cupping her hand to her deaf ear and shaking her head in frustration. "More louder, please!"

Mostly we all tried to keep her out of the storage house. She seemed happier poking around in the dirt, planting things, and nobody wanted her to start that head-banging business again. Every day was different for her. We tried to give her more good days than bad.

Geek set up his hammock in the corner of the greenhouse, and I took to hanging out with him in the evenings, after the kids and my parents had gone to bed. I'd lie there in the humid warmth, strung between two posts, watching him plant things. He had rigged up some drip-irrigation tubing to connect with an old glass beaker, which he suspended above the hammock and filled with ice cubes and a powerful blue drink made with rum and pineapple and curaçao. The system worked on gravity feed, and I'd swing in the hammock and sip the cerulean liquid from the tip of a miniature hose, controlling the rate of its flow with a nozzle. He had downloaded some old Hawaiian music off the Internet: "Sweet Leilani," "Blue Hawaiian Moon." The tropical lyrics tugged at my heart. The twang and wow of the slack-key guitar, the gentle sway of the hammock, the humid air—intoxicated by these, I could almost forget I was in Idaho. But never for long. Something always happened to bring me back.

ॐ

She was in the living room with a handful of index-card labels and a roll of tape. She was looking around at the furniture, as if a secret were hidden under a cushion or in the upholstery. I watched from the doorway as she wavered, trying to decide. Then she darted toward the TV and labeled it RUG. My heart sank. She put CHAIR on the sofa. She had TABLE in her hand as she headed for the floor lamp.

I was thinking, So what if she's losing her words? What do they matter? The names of things are arbitrary constructs, mere social conventions, as easily changed as the rules of a child's game, and why should one encryption of reality, mine, be more valid than hers? But even as I thought this, even as my heart was aching with dismay and sadness, I couldn't help but make the correction.

"That's the lamp, Mom," I said. "Not the table. The table's over here." I peeled the index card off the shade, but she dashed over and snatched it away from me.

"*Damé!*" she said. "No!" Her voice was hushed. She pressed it back onto the dusty fabric surface until it stuck. She stepped back and looked at it, once again satisfied. The lamp was a table. All was well.

I took a deep breath, trying to realign myself to this new groundless-ness.

She gave a dark little chuckle. "I gonna teach him lesson," she said.

"What?"

Her voice was low, conspiratorial now. "You know that Nix? He is very bad boy. He play some tricks on me, moving all the labels. So now I trick him back. I move them first, then she think he did it."

"She? Who is she?"

"His mommy. When she catch him, boy, oh, boy, she get plenty mad!"

Dumbstruck, I stared at her. She flipped through the remaining labels in her hand, studying them, then looked up at my face, as though seeing me for the first time.

"Who are you?" she asked blankly.

She wasn't joking.

I left her there and walked out to the porch. The coast was clear of chil-dren. I lit a cigarette and smoked for a while, then crossed over to the greenhouse. When I got closer to the building, I heard Ocean's high-pitched chatter, interspersed with Geek's voice, explaining something. They both looked up at me from the hammock where they were rocking. Chicken Little was cheeping on the ground below, scruffy and preadoles-cent, her first pinfeathers poking through her baby down.

"Come in," Geek said. "Join the party. You look like you need a drink."

"I was looking for one. Is the bar open?"

"It can be." Geek vacated his place in the hammock for me. I climbed in next to Ocean. She sniffed the cigarette smell on my clothes but decided not to say anything, and I was grateful. She snuggled in next to me, happy to have me there.

"Hello, my sweet Puddle," I said.

"Hi, Yummy Mommy." At least she knew who I was.

Geek handed me an end of narrow hose. "I've improved the system," he said. "I've added a splitter, so two people can sip simultaneously." He sat down in a beat-up lawn chair next to the hammock and rested his feet on the edge, rocking us gently and sipping his branch of the hose. Ocean clamored for a taste, so I let her have a small one.

"I was just reading to Ocean about a hero of mine," Geek said. He held up an ancient-looking book. "Luther Burbank, the inventor of the Russet Burbank potato. This is his autobiography."

"Oh, him," I said, vaguely recognizing the book. "He was a plant breeder or something, wasn't he?"

Ocean frowned. "He was a wizard," she said, correcting me.

"That's right," said Geek. "The Wizard of Horticulture. He was brilliant."

"Like Geek," Ocean said, always the little flatterer.

"No. I'm just an amateur. Burbank was the real thing. He invented hundreds of plants. The Shasta daisy. The spineless cactus."

"What's the point of that?" I asked. Geek's delivery system was like an IV tap, and the rum was entering my blood. "A cactus is supposed to have spines."

"He thought the pads would make good cattle fodder in the desert. He reported that he had to pull thousands of cactus spines out of the cactus pads with pliers, but in the end he succeeded. It took him years."

"Ow!" Ocean cringed. "What's a fodder?"

"Food," Geek said. "Parmahansa Yogananda told this story about Burbank in *Autobiography of a Yogi*. He said Burbank would talk to the cacti to create what he called 'a vibration of love.' He would tell them that they had nothing to fear, that they didn't need their thorns because he would protect them. Apparently it worked."

"Wait!" cried Ocean. "That means he lied! He pulled out all the spines and told the poor cactus he'd protect it, and when the cactus finally believed him, he went and fed it to a cow!"

"You're teaching my daughter to lie to plants?" I asked, holding out my hand. "Give me that book. Where'd you find it?"

Geek passed it to me. "On your father's bookshelf."

It was a dusty old tome with a green cloth cover. *The Harvest of the Years.* I opened it to the first yellowed page and read the opening paragraph aloud.

" 'Back of every plant, every shellfish, every burrowing rodent or ravaging animal, and back of every human being, there stretches an illimitable and mysterious heredity. . . .' "

The words were familiar. Ocean was studying my face, listening intently, so I read on. " '. . . The newborn child has a heritage of tendencies and inclinations which furnish the foundation or groundwork from which he must build his house of Life.' "

I closed the book.

"I don't get it," Ocean said. "There's too many big words."

"It just means that you'll probably be like your mom in some ways," Geek said.

"Oh, goodie." She snuggled in closer to me.

She did not inherit her good heart from me. Or her sunny nature. I tipped her pretty little daisy face up to mine and gave her a huge kiss, then I handed the book back to Geek.

"Phoenix's dad is a plant breeder," I said. "Maybe it's my tendency to end up with guys who prefer vegetables."

"If so," Geek said, handing it back, "you should keep the book. Maybe you can learn something about your heritage and inclinations."

"You want to know what my heritage has taught me? If you're a cactus, you'd better hang on to your spines."

"I believe that," Geek said, looking at me closely. "But Burbank said that the secret of improved plant breeding is love." He started making the hammock rock in a wider arc, then dropped his voice like a mesmerist and started to speak in a thick German accent. "You haf nussing to fear," he murmured. "You vill no longer need your defensive thorns. I vill protect you." He looked deep into my eyes. Ocean giggled.

"Right," I said, looking down at the heavy book in my lap. "Like it's ever that easy."

pests ℬ

"Check this out," Lilith said, draping herself along the curve of Y's spine as she read over his shoulder from the computer screen. " 'Political Pests—A Proactive Defense.' "

"Perfect," said Y. "Sounds like an invitation."

"I don't know," Geek said. He was surfing at the next computer. There were only two in the Liberty Falls public library, but at least they had high-speed access. "We promised Yumi we'd lay off the actions, remember?"

"Screw that," Lilith said. "That was only within Power County. This conference is in Pocatello."

Frank was sitting with Charmey on the floor behind the computers. Hearing talk of an action, he looked up.

"This is major," said Y. "All the industry heavies are going to be there.

And check it out, the dude giving the keynote? His name is Elliot Rhodes. E. Rhodes. Is that perfect or what?"

"Erodes!" Lilith said, drumming on Y's back. "I say we pie the fucker."

The librarian frowned from across the room. Geek typed in the URL for the Potato Promotions Council and pulled up the schedule for the conference. He whistled. "Check out the dude's bio. He's doing NuLife for D&W."

"What's D&W?" Frank asked. It had been months since they'd done a good action, and all this planting was for shit.

"Duncan & Wiley," Geek said. "PR firm that spins for Cynaco. They specialize in damage control and crisis management, only they call it 'solution imaging' and 'media intervention' and 'constituency building.' Obfuscating crap. These days it's all about building fake grassroots organizations as fronts for the corporations and participating in stuff like this Potato Promotions Council. They've spun for everyone from big tobacco to the petrochemical conglomerates, and now it's the gene giants. Basically they suck."

"We going?"

Geek shrugged. "Don't see how we can pass it up, do you?"

This suited Frankie just fine. When he had first signed on to travel with the Seeds, he felt like he'd been tapped by an elite squadron of resistance fighters. Now he found himself living in a trailer with a pregnant girlfriend, parked in someone's driveway. Taking care of old people. And if Ashtabula was bad, Liberty Falls was the pits. There were almost no paved roads to skate on, and the ones that weren't dirt had been surfaced with some kind of crushed gravel, like out of the fucking *Flintstones*. Everything around the farm was dirt and dust, fields and fields of it. At least in Ashtabula there were parking lots.

Charmey seemed happy, though. Every morning she would stand on the Spudnik's step looking out at the bare fields where the tractors were working and rub her hands over her hardening belly and breathe deeply. She said the country air smelled crisp and fresh, but the dust got in Frank's throat and made him cough and spit. They should just pave the place, he thought. Keep the damn dust down. Watching her trundle up to the house to fix breakfast for the old man, Frankie felt his heart sink. He could just picture them, years from now, stuck here with a pack of squalling kids and laundry flapping on a line. His third foster home had been like that. It was a bad scene. That foster mother had been doing way too many drugs, and her boyfriend finally beat her up so bad that Frankie's social worker couldn't ignore it any longer. They took him away, and her real kids, too. He felt bad for her kids, entering the system, but he was glad to be out of there.

Charmey was curled up on the floor of the library next to him, flipping through maternity magazines. Now she yawned and gathered up a stack of books and handed them to Frankie. "Who has the library card?"

Frankie looked down at the books in his arms. *Home Birthing. What to Expect When You're Expecting. Introduction to Midwifery.* It was too much. He'd gotten used to the idea of making love to her, even with the baby growing inside. What he couldn't quite wrap his mind around was the fact that now the baby was going to have to come out. Charmey and Lilith spent hours on the Internet studying images of women giving birth. They tried to get Frankie to watch.

"See?" Charmey said, squeezing his hand. "It is not so bad."

Frankie gulped and nodded, but his mind was screaming. Not *bad?* It was fucking *gruesome.* The women were huge, panting and heaving like dogs, their eyes bugging out over these gigantic stomachs while bright red babies inched out from between their legs. Aside from the blood, there was mucus and tissue and slime. Charmey leaned in close to the screen, her face rapt and glowing, studying every detail, like this was a beautiful thing. He looked away. He couldn't bear to imagine her like a flayed animal, bucking and screaming in pain. He wanted to protect her from this, not participate in its coming.

"*C'est magnifique!*" Charmey sat back and looked at Frank. "*Ooh la la!* Look at this face!" She took his hand and ran it across her belly. He tried not to flinch.

"What's important, Frankie, for you as the coach, is to stay calm," Lilith said, scrolling to yet another birth site and double-clicking.

He'd heard this before. Stay calm. Keep your sense of humor.

Time her contractions. Offer her encouragement, reassurance, support.

Distract her. Take her mind off the pain. Help her stay focused.

Massage her, unless she doesn't want to be touched.

In which case don't touch her.

Breathe.

He would never remember all this, and it was depressing to know in advance that he was going to blow it. This was a feeling he had grown up with. He figured he'd be lucky just to make it through without throwing up.

He carried Charmey's books to the front desk and dropped them in front of the librarian. The librarian read the titles, raised her eyebrows, and gave him a long look.

"Are these for you?"

Frankie hesitated. Charmey had disappeared into the stacks again. "They're for my girlfriend."

"Congratulations," the librarian said. Frankie looked up, surprised. The librarian was smiling and her voice was friendly. "At least I assume you're the happy father-to-be?"

"Yeah," he said, watching as she ran the bar-code reader across the books' spines. "I guess so."

At that moment Charmey came up beside him. "Oh, yes!" she said. "We are so happy." She gripped his arm, and her eyes were blazing.

garden of earthly delights 🐍

There was no mistaking that Mr. Potato Head. The same demented, walleyed stare, the tin skullcap, the screwy electrical coil spiraling crookedly out from the top of his head. It was the potato from the cover of the magazine section come to life in the main conference room of the Sheraton in Pocatello. It was shouting antibiotech slogans and forcing its way in, just as Elliot was taking the stage to deliver the keynote.

Elliot seized the microphone. "You see," he said smoothly, gesturing to the blundering spud and his cadres as they were hustled away by hotel security. "This is *precisely* why your industry needs our help with pest control."

He couldn't have done better if he'd planted the potato himself. With a warm-up act like that, "Political Pests—A Proactive Defense" was a resounding success. The presence of the enemy seemed to galvanize the growers, underscoring the subtext of Elliot's message: that their industry was under attack, and they needed D&W's crisis-management services. He made a note to suggest to Duncan that they start paying protesters to show up at events like these. If he could find out who they were, some members of this group might even be recruited. There was nothing like a good confrontation to get the blood pumping.

Maybe Duncan was right, he thought. Maybe his *chi* was stagnating in

D.C. When the conference ended the following afternoon, he checked out of the Sheraton and rented a car. Filled with a sense of adventure, he headed west. On the outskirts of the city the lights of the fertilizer plant twinkled against the backdrop of a late-afternoon sky, and the tall stacks belched their plumes of ocher smoke. There was a bleak appeal in the stretch of interstate leading out of Pocatello, a tickle of promise, of things hidden, as though his presence here, long ago, had imbued it with a singular and unique significance. He would spend the night, he decided, then drive around the next day and check out the school where he had taught. The landscape seemed alive with memories, lying just below the shimmering surface of asphalt and the surrounding fields.

At the first sign for Liberty Falls his heart started to beat faster. When he spotted the orb of the water tower, looming over the horizon like a moon on stilts, he pulled onto the exit ramp and spiraled down. The town spread out below him, anchored at one end by the courthouse and the top of Main. From there the broad street descended past the four churches at the intersection of Church and, a block farther south, the four banks at the intersection of Commerce, marking the boundaries of what had been a bustling downtown. He drove slowly. Many of the old storefronts were boarded, and a sign on the grocery store that used to be called Earl's read, WE GIVE UP. A few new businesses—Satellite & Cellular Services, Video Rentals—had taken over some of the storefronts. The camera shop had survived, and so had the Farmer's New World Life Insurance. From there Main took a dive, bottoming out at Union and the railroad tracks. The grain elevators rose above this lower part of town, looking out over the Snake River, flooded on account of the dam. Beyond lay the fields, still dead looking and bedraggled from the long winter.

In the prairie twilight the town was ghostly and still. He got out of the car and stood by the railroad tracks, bracing himself against a punishing wind. A tumbleweed skittered across the wide street. He hadn't recalled there being tumbleweed.

He turned away from the wind to face the empty tracks, stretching on forever. The towering grain elevators, branded with the town's name, provided some vertical relief, rising up off the desert floor to challenge the lowering sky. Liberty Falls—a flattened and relentlessly two-dimensional western prairie enclave. Had he really ever lived here? How could he have forgotten? Or, more cogently, why did he want to remember? It was growing dark. He got back into the car and turned the heater to high, then drove to the Falls Motel, stopping for a flattened hamburger and a bag of greasy fries at a local drive-thru. In Liberty Falls not even the fast food was franchised.

Holed up in his motel room with a six-pack of beer, Elliot was certain this detour was a tedious mistake. He thought about checking out and going back to Pocatello, but it would be stupid to have come all this way and not see the school. He turned on the television, then turned it off again. He took out his laptop and the thick folder provided by the Potato Promotions Council. It was filled with the usual state boosterism. He flipped through the information sheets of yields and profit margins, tossing the charts into the wastebasket. He read the Fun Facts About Potatoes, then checked his watch and phoned Jillie.

"Do you know that the average American eats a hundred and sixty-five pounds of potatoes in a year?"

Over the phone line he heard Jillie sigh.

"That's how much I weigh," he added.

"I don't eat your body weight in potatoes in a year," she said. "And I doubt you do either."

"Well, that's just it. Someone's eating our share."

"Oh, gee. Unfair."

"Do you know that it takes three hundred ninety-three million, seven hundred seventy-nine thousand, five hundred forty-nine four-inch french-fried potatoes to go end to end around the earth's equator?"

"And?"

"You can get thirty-six fries to a potato."

"What's your point, Elliot?"

"No point." He dropped Fun Facts into the wastepaper basket. Underneath was a photocopied sheet of orange paper, unlike the rest of the glossy presentation materials. At the top was a crude drawing of a potato, with a skull and crossbones through it. The caption read:

CONSUMER ALERT
When Is a POTATO not a POTATO?
*When it is a U.S. Government Certified **PESTICIDE!!!***

"Oh, fuck," he said.

"We can't," Jillie pointed out. "You're in Idaho, remember?"

"No . . ." He scanned the rest of the page. At the bottom was the address for a Web site.

Jillie was saying, "Unless you want to have phone sex . . ." Her voice was husky. Lately he'd noticed that she was far more likely to come on to him when there was no danger of actually following through. Now he cut her off.

"Jillie? Listen, I gotta go. I'll call you later, okay?" He heard her whine as he hung up, but he was already hauling out his laptop and jacking into the phone line. While the computer dialed up, he read the flyer more carefully.

Why does the U.S. government classify CYNACO'S NuLife® potato not as a food but as a pesticide?

Cynaco's NuLife® potato has the DNA of a bacterial toxin spliced into its genes. The result? The potato manufactures the poison in every one of its cells. This toxin is effective against the Colorado potato beetle. Any unsuspecting beetle who takes a nibble from the leaf of a NuLife® will keel over and die.

Convenient? Yes. Safe? We don't know. Despite studies suggesting possible hazards to both human health and ecological safety, the NuLife® has never been poison-tested by the EPA.

But poison testing *is* being carried out at our dinner tables every day. Our government and the Biotech Industry are conducting a massive experiment on unsuspecting, uninformed human subjects—You. And me. *We Are Their Guinea Pigs!*

Visit our Web site at Seeds-of-Resistance.com for more information on biotechnology and food safety. Food is life. You are what you eat. **Demand accurate and responsible labeling on all genetically modified foods! It's your right to know!**

Elliot crumpled up the sheet. How the hell did they manage to slip it into the promotional material? He logged on to the Web site and cursed the crappy motel phone line. It was taking forever to download, and Elliot was used to thruput. Finally the images materialized on his screen, and his eye grazed the captions.

SEEDS OF RESISTANCE. Scrolling past the short mission statement, he came to a map of America. The group was traveling across the country, doing actions along the way. They had posted photographs and descriptions of several supermarket interventions, an arrest in Ashtabula, and a little "night gardening" at a test site in Iowa, where they'd ripped up genetically engineered corn by flashlight. Most recent was a demonstration at a potato processing plant in Pocatello and a labeling campaign in a local Stop-N-Save. That was good, Elliot thought. They must have a base nearby.

He perused the site quickly. They had sections on the history of the WTO, how to convert engines to run off biodiesel, and strategies for mounting safe and effective street actions. There were links at the end, and he followed a couple. The Seeds were plugged into the usual web of anarchists and radical environmentalists, but one link, tucked to one side, stood out from the rest: Lilith's Garden of Earthly Delights. He clicked it and entered the portal.

Earth Is Life! Love Your Mother!

It was laid out like a comic book or a storyboard from a dirty movie, with stills of a woman, naked and caked in mud.

Get Down and Dirty!

He had to laugh. The pictures were clumsy, and the video clips even more so. The woman had a decent body, but the content was ludicrous. Still, as he clicked his way through the pages, something else, more organic than electronic, started to seep through the glowing digital field and leach into his skin. What was it? A sense, as keen as the primary five, but more abstract. A feeling that flowed through his body, tickling his genitals and quickening his pulse. It ran from him like a dormant taproot, newly awakened, starved and probing deep. He opened a beer and lingered in the Garden, and then it hit him.

It wasn't lust. It was nostalgia.

He stared at the pictures of Lilith as Mother Earth. Her body was unenhanced, full and natural, which seemed like an erotic novelty. Naked, she reminded him of the earnest hippie girls who'd danced topless in grassy fields in Berkeley during the Summer of Love. He remembered the patterns and textures: the cheap Indian print, the crushed and balding velvets. In a thumbnail video Lilith's long body was encased in a sheath of leathery clay, and then, like an insect shedding its skin, she broke free into a glorious new instar. Mudwoman in molt. Earth begetting life. It was primal and primeval. Tinny sitar music played from the laptop speakers, and her voice was thin.

"In the beginning," she intoned, *"the Goddess gave birth and form to Herself."*

There were candles surrounding her. An Egyptian ankh hung around her neck, nestling in between her tumular breasts. Each breast was crowned with a sproutlike nipple that broke free from the earth. He could almost smell the incense.

"We honor her fecundity, the spontaneous regeneration of her procreative force, the spark of her being."

. . . In those days there had always been a girl like this Lilith in his life. Dovelike girls. Unlike Jillie, who had more of a sneer than a coo.

He leaned his head back and closed his eyes. He felt a little like he was tripping again, as though entering the Garden had triggered a wellspring of dormant lysergic acid. The pixels lingered on his retina, creating a glimmer like sunlight on water. An icon of a zucchini offered a hotlink to something called the Secret Garden. In the name of research he entered, but before he could find out what Lilith was going to do with the vegetable, the download overwhelmed the puny capacity of the phone lines at the Falls Motel, crashing his computer.

He reached for the beer and realized the can was empty. He went to the window, where the six-pack was stashed. Popping another, he looked out over the highway at the desiccated fields under the streetlights, stretching off into the distance. He remembered the first time he'd laid eyes on this landscape. It looked bleaker now.

Overall, the world was a harder place these days. Maybe the soft, dovelike, pigeon-toed girls of his youth just couldn't survive.

Like that one. Here. In Liberty Falls.

Yummy.

He said it out loud.

"Yummy?"

He had thought that was her name, but now, saying it, he began to question his recall. How could it be? The more he repeated it, the more improbable it sounded, until he could barely connect the sound with any memory of her at all. Instead, the whine of that song kept running through his head: "Yummy, yummy, yummy . . ."

AM radio crap.

He used to drive a Volkswagen beetle. Baby blue. In the dim winter twilight after school, she would sit next to him and twirl the radio dial.

"I got love in my tummy. . . ."

No. That could not have been it.

He closed the curtains and checked his watch. The NuLife task force was keeping late hours during Potato Promotions Week. He dialed the office.

"Hey," he said. "Listen, didn't Cynaco have a Pinkerton operating around here on grain-patent infringements? E-mail me his name, will you? We've got a pest control problem. It's time to get proactive."

He had trippy dreams that night of walking through a plate-glass window, and he woke each time he was about to fall. He didn't sleep well. When the sky grew light, he went in search of the school. It wasn't hard to find. In his sleep-deprived state he drove automatically, allowing his hand to signal the turns, his foot to tell him when to brake, and before he knew it, he was pulling his rental car up to the curb. He turned off the engine and stared at the squat façade. The mild sense of anticipation he'd felt en route now faded. He watched the kids hitching up their backpacks as they moved toward the entrance. They seemed familiar, but he couldn't imagine knowing any of them, certainly couldn't imagine standing up in front of a classroomful of them and having anything to say. And yet he had. The school was called Liberty Falls Elementary, but it went through the ninth grade. He watched a group of the older girls cross the street in front of him. They looked so young, their faces vacant and impervious.

The teasing nostalgia from the night before had vanished completely. He watched through the window as the last of the kids straggled by, and then he took out his cell phone. The private investigator was easy to locate. Elliot gave him a rundown on the Seeds, the address of their Web site, and a brief sketch of their activities in Idaho.

"They're smart," Elliot said. "I'd love to know how they hijacked that promotional material at the conference."

"Shouldn't be hard to find out."

"They cover ground. You'll see from the Web site—"

"Don't worry, Mr. Rhodes. We'll find them."

Elliot pocketed the phone and went in search of breakfast. There was a cozy local restaurant he remembered, with excellent eggs, padded vinyl booths, tabletop jukeboxes, and waitresses who'd worked there for years. Only now he saw that it was called Gringo's. He went in anyway. The counters were the same dull Formica edged in nicked aluminum, but it was staffed by a Mexican teenager in a stained peasant blouse, and the two-egg breakfast special had been replaced by huevos rancheros. A couple of locals looked up from the counter, an older man and a middle-aged woman, maybe father and daughter, maybe husband and wife. It was hard to tell. They watched him for a while, then looked away.

He ordered the huevos and coffee and picked up a copy of the local paper that was lying by the register. Potato farmers were being sued by a local Indian tribe demanding compensation for groundwater contamination from agricultural runoff. Shoshone, he remembered. He ripped out the article. He'd been pressing Cynaco to support InterTribal Agricultural Councils. Maybe he could even get a Shoshone spokesperson to endorse the NuLife—fewer pesticides mean clean water for our people, that sort of thing. Wisdom. Heritage. Indians always made for positive imaging.

He tossed the paper aside as the waitress approached his table. The eggs looked good, but he needed more coffee creamers. When he looked up to call the girl back, he saw the two come in.

They were not from Liberty Falls. He could see that from the reaction of the locals, who had been talking and now stopped and stared.

At first he couldn't tell exactly what they were. Young and disheveled, but beyond that? They wore their badly fitting clothes the way that only teenagers could, with a seeming disdain for superficial appearances. Their pale faces were androgynous, sullen and bruised, the kind you see advertising underwear on billboards in the city.

They had come in to use the bathroom, and when the smaller one came back without the jacket covering her overalls, he saw that she was a girl, pregnant, and starting to show. She looked a bit unsteady. The other one, clearly a boy, made her sit down on a stool. She leaned her forehead against his stomach and hooked her fingers in the waistband of his jeans. She rested there for a while, fiddling with the buttons on his fly, while he kneaded her shoulders. It was quite a sexy little picture. As he watched them, Elliot felt a peculiar stabbing sensation, located in his solar plexus, which he identified as regret. It took him by surprise. At first he mistook it for the normal regret any man would feel at the sight of a beautiful babe

188

with another guy. But these two were just kids, and this particular regret went deeper, triggered by that burgeoning lump in her belly. He stared at it. He'd seen lots of pregnant women. Most of his friends in the city had had pregnant wives at one point or another. What was it about this girl, here in Liberty Falls?

There. He felt it again. A fluttering sensation in his chest. Not quite a pain. Was it his heart? He started to panic.

Just then the boy looked in Elliot's direction, and, catching him gawking at his girlfriend's stomach, he stiffened. To Elliot's surprise, instead of rising to the challenge and staring the boy down, he found himself dropping his gaze to the plate of huevos in front of him, which were swimming in a puddle of puce-colored beans. The grated cheese had hardened on top like a melted plastic lid. He frowned. The fluttering subsided. He wasn't used to rolling over like this, so he looked back up again, ready to assert himself unblinkingly, but the two were already standing, the boy sheltering the girl with his arm as he ushered her out the door.

Elliot gave up on breakfast. He took a last sip of coffee, then went to the cash register to pay. He looked out the window at the two kids cutting across the parking lot. From the back, at a distance, they looked familiar.

"What's their story?" he asked the waitress. "They don't look like they're from around here."

The waitress took his twenty and punched the keys on the ancient cash register. The drawer made a dinging sound when it slid open. He accepted his change and handed her a five-dollar tip for a four-dollar meal.

She slipped it in her pocket. "Heard someone talking about a gang of hippies staying out at someone's farm."

"Oh, yeah?" He sorted slowly through his bills. "You get a lot of people like that passing through?"

"Nah. Not so many. Just the ones who come in the summer for the recreational activities."

Elliot could not remember any recreational activities. The girl eyed his wallet. "The reservoir," she added. "They go there for water sports and stuff."

Elliot took out another five-dollar bill. "Do you know where these hippies are staying?"

"Nah." She shook her head and started wiping down the Formica as Elliot replaced the bill in his wallet.

The local woman at the counter spoke up. "Heard that Fuller girl's been harboring them down at her daddy's place."

"Really?" Elliot said.

The old man added, "They was at the potato plant a couple of weeks ago, handing out papers. Funny-looking lot."

"You don't say?" Elliot was moving in slow motion now, buying time.

"They were over at the school, too," the woman said. "Trying to brain-wash the kids."

Elliot put on his jacket and carefully zipped it up. He tucked in his scarf.

"It's a free country," the old man asserted, but his words sounded re-mote. Elliot drew the keys out of his pocket and studied them. You would not want this man defending your freedoms.

The woman snorted. "Peddling drugs, if you ask me. It's just like her to waltz back into town and let her friends live like animals out there on her daddy's farm."

"Who's that?" Elliot asked, as casually as he could, but the old man was already talking and didn't hear him.

"That's Fuller's business. It's got nothing to do with the rest of us."

The woman sniffed. "It most surely does if they're endangering our kids and our community."

The old man took a long, defeated sip of Coke through a straw, ending the conversation. There was no way to pursue the subject, Elliot thought, without sounding persistent, but at least he had a last name. Then the old man shook his head.

"It's a shame," he said. "Lloyd Fuller was always a strange one, but it's a damn shame he ain't got no one except that daughter to depend on. She's a bad seed if there ever was one."

The woman nodded. The two of them fell silent. Ice rattled at the bot-tom of the old man's glass.

Elliot leaned forward. His heart was pounding hard now, sending blood into his ears, and again he had the dreamlike feeling of falling. He pressed his fingertips hard against the edge of the counter to steady himself.

"You okay?" the waitress asked.

"I'm fine," Elliot said. "You don't happen to have a phone book, do you?"

a man in a suit 🕮

The first time Charmey showed up on her doorstep Cass hadn't known what to think. She had taken Poo for the afternoon, and they'd just gotten back from town when the doorbell rang. She swung the baby up off the kitchen floor and went to answer it.

"I saw your car." The girl spoke with a French accent, slightly out of breath. "I have the lunch for him." She offered up a paper sack. "Steamed tofu and vegetables and banana muffins. Whole wheat. The food she gives him is for *sheet.*"

She was dressed in a baggy pair of overalls, wrapped in layers of sweaters and badly knitted things. She looked up from the stoop, and her face was shining. The flicker of recognition in her eye gave Cass the happy sense of visibility she often felt with Poo. She saw herself from the girl's perspective, hip cocked, baby lodged upon it, hazy behind the screen door. She smiled and nudged open the door, holding out her hand for the bag.

"It is mostly organic," the girl said. "As much as I find. Here, I will help you."

She walked past Cass into the kitchen, and by the time Cass had caught up, the girl was emptying the tofu into a small bowl. She looked over at the container of processed pineapple cottage cheese that Yummy had packed for Poo and made a face. "She knows it is *sheet.* For the grown-up, perhaps it is not so bad, but for *le petit! Ooh la la!* You are a farmer, no? So then you know, too. *La dioxine, les hormones.* Especially in the dairy, no? Poisoning into his little body, just as he makes all the cells of his brain."

She reached for Poo, and Cass relinquished him, though she couldn't say exactly why. The girl shrugged off a layer of her knitted coverings, and Cass could see how delicate she was. She was about four or five months pregnant, which somehow gave her the authority to settle Poo in a chair and oversee the shuttling of tofu cubes and carrots from the bowl to his mouth. Cass hung back and watched. The girl was good. She held Poo's attention, keeping him focused on the task, catching a chunk of flying zucchini or providing a bite of banana muffin when he got bored. When he finished, she wiped his face and fingers with a damp towel and handed him back.

191

"*Voilà,*" she said. "*Pardon.* I am Charmey."

"I'm Cass."

Charmey nodded as though she already knew this, knew Cass's name, knew all about her. When their eyes met over the baby's head, Cass caught another look of recognition in the girl's eyes, but this time it was mixed with such sadness that Cass felt hollowed—wordless, childless—and then the look was gone. Maybe she'd imagined it, because Charmey was wrapping herself up again as though nothing had happened, tucking the fabric firmly about her rounding belly as she moved toward the door. She gave Cass a friendly smile and tickled Poo in the soft folds under his chin.

"*À bientôt!*" She turned and lumbered off down the drive.

Charmey dropped by again soon after that. They sat at Cass's kitchen table and drank herbal infusions, while Poo crawled around on the floor at their feet playing with ants. Outside, the spring wind was still gusting hard, keeping the farmers out of their fields and holding up the start of planting. Cass thought the girl's idea to do home birthing in the trailer was the most dangerous thing she'd ever heard. "It's not even a home, it's a Winnebago," she said. "You've got to have proper medical care."

But the girl was adamant. "Oh, no, no!" she said. "We do not believe in hospitals or the paternalistic power structures of Western medicine. Lilith and I will do the birthing together. Like the pioneer women on the Oregon Trail. We are studying how on the Internet."

Cass reached down and hauled Poo onto her lap. She took the ant he offered her and crushed it between her fingers.

The next time Charmey brought maternity magazines that she'd borrowed from the public library, and they looked at them together. Charmey made fun of the fashions and the recipes while Cass pored over each page, hungry for every word and glossy image. Cass rarely let herself go this far. At the Stop-N-Save she occasionally flipped through the maternity magazines like a furtive adolescent with a *Playboy* before returning them to the rack. Only once, years before, had she bought one. She had been on her way home from the obstetrician's after getting a positive test and had stopped off to pick up a carton of ice cream to celebrate. The cover featured a story about "Celebrity Moms," but she'd bought the magazine for an article called "Things You Should Know When You're Pregnant Over 35." The miscarriage happened that night, while she was reading the magazine in the bathtub. Will had rushed her to the hospital, but there was no help for it. When they came home later, she'd found the magazine on the bathroom floor in a puddle of water.

But this time everything felt so different. Before, it had just been her and Will. Momoko and Lloyd lived down the road, but they were old and ebbing. Now, with Yummy and the kids, and Poo and pregnant Charmey and the rest of the Seeds, the Fullers' place was churning with a life force that eddied and caught Cass up in its currents. She missed a first period. And then another, and for the first time in so long Cass found herself facing down her own desire, throwing open her arms to welcome it in all its wildness. Desire was vital, she reasoned now. Wild desire, and ferocity of faith.

Still, she decided she would wait to tell anyone until she'd gotten a positive test. Until life was safely moored inside her, with enough momentum and substance to sustain itself beyond her fears and superstitions. At nap time she curled her body around sleeping Poo and let herself daydream. The first person she would tell would be Yummy—after Will, of course. She extended her finger and gently touched the baby's nose, his chin, his cheek. She felt a rush of courage. She could hardly wait.

ॐ

She woke from her nap when Poo started pawing at her shoulder, surprised to see that it was nearly four o'clock. She got the baby dressed and gave him some milk, then put him in his stroller and headed next door. The stroller bounced over the rough dirt road, and the wind was blowing up the sand from the adjacent fields. She leaned down and draped a blanket over the stroller to keep the grit out of Poo's face, but he started to protest. He squinted into the wind. Dirt didn't bother him. He liked the wind. He liked to see where he was going.

On the way up the drive she saw Ocean and Phoenix, wind whipped and all bundled. They were racing back from the greenhouse. Breathless, they ran up next to her.

"Yo, *brah*," Phoenix said, slapping his brother's little palm. Poo bounced up and down in his seat. Ocean danced along beside Cass, tugging at the baby bag.

"There's a man!" she gasped. "A man!"

"Oh?" said Cass.

"In a suit!" Her fine blond hair was blowing wildly, into her mouth, her eyes. The wind was snatching her words.

"A man in a suit?" Cass asked, frowning. "Who is it?"

Phoenix shoved his hands into his pockets. It was a noisy wind, so he spoke loudly. "Some creeped-out buggah. They knew each other. Yummy sent us out to help Geek and Grandma in the greenhouse, but they're in town, and anyway that was just to get rid of us. She wanted to be *alone* with him."

"Is he from the sheriff's?"

Phoenix shook his head. "He's a newspaper reporter or something. Slick motherfucker."

They were right by the door. "Shhh," Ocean said. "Don't call him dirty names. He'll hear you."

"Oooh, ex*cuse* me!" Phoenix said, lowering his voice, mocking her. He tiptoed up the steps like a cat burglar, holding the door open for Cass. "Shhh," he said, puffing air into Poo's face as Cass carried him by. Poo blinked his eyes. Ocean punched her older brother's arm, and together they crossed the porch.

And stopped. Because there in the kitchen, on the bare patch of linoleum by the sink, stood Yummy, wrapped in the arms of the man in the suit. Only it wasn't really a suit, just a tweedy-looking jacket and khaki pants. They were standing there frozen, as still as a statue, and for a long moment all Cass could hear was the noise of the wind rattling the shutters and the creaking of the house.

"Oh, no," Phoenix groaned softly. "Not again."

Cass's first thought was to turn away. Instead she opened the screen door, and the children slipped in.

"Mommy?" Ocean said.

The two broke apart quickly. Yummy looked dazed, like she had just been woken up.

"Whoops," she said. "Sorry."

The pattern of tweed was pressed into her reddened cheek, as though she had been sleeping against this man's shoulder for a long, long time. He seemed familiar, handsome, like men on TV commercials for nice cars or life insurance. He had an easy confidence that was way too big for Momoko's kitchen. They stood next to each other, Yummy and this sure-looking man, bodies inclined, like two trees with shallow roots, tipped by the wind so that their upper branches touched, and this entire scene looked both so familiar and so wrong. And then Cass got it.

"Oh, no," she breathed as her heart sank like a stone. "Not again."

bad seed ∂

"Yummy?"

His intonation was questioning, but my response was as to a command. Wordless, I opened the screen door, and when he stepped across my parents' threshold the foundation of their house seemed to shudder. It was like being on drugs again, and even while a dim part of my mind resisted, my arms betrayed me. If I held on to him tightly, it was just to keep from falling. If God himself had bust through the ceiling, I wouldn't have been surprised.

"Yummy Fuller," he said, breathing my name into the top of my skull, as though the act of labeling me brought a long-sought relief. He let go and stepped away, and if ever I needed the house to anchor me, it was then. Weak-kneed and shaking, I backed away and leaned against the counter, aligning my feet in my mother's footsteps by the sink, as though they would support me. He looked around, taking in the signs.

"What luck," he said. "I happened to be in town doing some research for a story. Found myself driving by and thought what the hell, so I turned in. I didn't expect—"

"I don't live here," I heard myself say. "I'm just here for a visit."

"Even more of a coincidence, then."

"I live in Hawaii now." I could not believe the inanities issuing from my mouth.

"And I live in D.C." He smiled. "I can't believe this. You look great."

"What brings you back?" Trying to regain some formality now. I could hear the kids in the living room, or rather I couldn't hear them, so I knew they were listening. "Oh, that's right. You're researching . . ."

"An article," he said. "For a newspaper."

"What's D.C.?" It was Ocean, standing resolutely next to the refrigerator.

"Washington, D.C.," I told her. "You know, our nation's capital. Ocean, this is Elliot. Elliot, my daughter, Ocean." I raised my voice. "Phoenix, come in here." I wanted to get this all over with.

My son slunk through the door. "This is Phoenix. He's my oldest."

Elliot opened his mouth to speak, then closed it again. Phoenix grunted something on his way through the kitchen. Ocean wanted to hang around, but I shooed her out the door after her brother, to find Geek, to help Momoko, whatever. Smart kids. They knew when they weren't wanted. Ocean was marching and stomping her feet and singing, "Nobody likes me, everybody hates me. . . ." Her voice got farther and farther away. "I'm going to the garden to eat worms, yum, yum, yum. . . ."

When I turned around, Elliot was staring at me.

"Phoenix?" he asked. His voice was thin and hushed now.

"Risen from the ashes." I couldn't look at him.

He reached out and put his hands on my shoulders. "I'm so sorry," he said, holding on to me. I let him, for old times' sake. He wasn't stupid. He got it. He knew why I named my firstborn Phoenix, and why I was shaking so hard.

♌

There are some things you never forget. Some things that transport you like a bad acid trip so that, in a flash, it is 1974, the floor in the backseat of the Volkswagen Beetle is covered with sodden newspapers, and no one is saying much as the little car heads east. Grace Slick croons on the eight-track. The sky looms gray, and the interstate goes on and on. You hold Cass's hand and stare out the window at the ice-covered horizon. Grace sings, *"You are the crown of creation, and you got no place to go. . . ."*

Cass leans forward between the seats.

"Uh, Mr. Rhodes . . . can you play something else?"

He ejects the tape. The AM radio comes on. You roll your eyes at Cass, pretending that Elliot is a very square old man.

He's a very bad driver. You snicker every time the car lurches forward or comes to a less than graceful stop, and soon Cass is giggling, too. He tells you both to shut up, which of course makes you laugh harder. He's looking for an address that he wrote on the back of a Mr. Donuts napkin. You don't stop snickering until he pulls up on a side street that parallels the railroad tracks. The buildings are decrepit. Suddenly it's not so funny.

196

The three of you just sit there in the little Beetle, staring at the dingy doorway.

Cass knows you are scared. She squeezes your hand and whispers, "You don't have to—"

But you shake your head. Elliot turns around and looks at you over the back of the seat. "Ready?" he asks. You look away and blink.

"Wait," Cass says, and for the first time ever, she's stronger than you, stronger even than Elliot, and she glares at him. "Just give her a minute, will you?" Then she says, "You just take your time," and pats your arm, like she's learned how to comfort a person from the ladies at church. The patting annoys you, and you shake her off.

"God! What's the big fucking deal. Come on!" You shove the seat back forward into Elliot's face and kick open the door.

"Atta girl," says Elliot. You give him the finger.

The wooden door leading into the building slumps and hangs ajar, scraping against the broken concrete of the stoop. The hallway stairs are dark with ancient varnish, and the walls are the color of mold on curdled cream. The banister is sticky with grime. You climb the stairs single file—first Elliot, then you, then Cassie behind. Elliot wears his hiking boots open at the top, with the laces wrapped around the ankles, making his jeans bunch up at the cuffs. The sight is comforting somehow, like you're following him up a mountain trail. The treads of the old wooden stairs sink against the risers, under his weight. You feel their sogginess under your feet, too, and if you close your eyes and ignore the stench of stale sweat and cabbage, it might just as well be soft earth, or moss, or even a forest floor.

But of course it isn't. You reach a door. Elliot knocks. Someone opens it a crack and you can see the sliver of a face behind the security chain, a wary eye, a nose. Elliot says something ludicrous and prearranged, and the door closes, then opens again, wider this time. The three of you push in like stooges.

The room is brown, furnished with a dingy sofa and a couple of beat-up metal folding chairs. The dirt-streaked windows face a railway spur, leading to the switching yards. You can hear the trains heave along the rails, feel their locomotion through the floorboards, vibrating against the soles of your feet, up your knees to your tummy. A tired-looking woman

197

with wire-rimmed glasses looks at you and then at Cass. She has lank blond hair, held back with a rubber band.

"Which one?" she asks. You feel Cass shrink, and you step forward bravely.

"Me."

The woman eyes you, then speaks to Elliot. "It's legal now, you know. You can take her to a clinic."

Elliot shakes his head. "Not here. Not without her parents' knowing."

"Take her out of state, then."

Elliot hesitates. "She's a minor."

The woman looks at him like she wants to spit in his face, but then she drops it and sighs. "I swore I'd never do another one of these," she says. She turns to you. "Ready?"

She tells you to use the bathroom, and when you come out, she is wearing stained green scrubs over her T-shirt. Elliot and Cass are seated on the sagging couch, side by side. They watch you follow the green scrubs into a small adjoining bedroom. At the last minute you turn and give them a silly little wave. They wave back, and the way Elliot looks at you, the way he hesitates, then leans forward as though to stand, makes you think for a moment that he's going to put a stop to all this, and your heart gives a leap, but he doesn't. The woman closes the door.

An ancient gynecological examining table stands at the far end, its stirrups pointing toward the railway yard and the grimy amber daylight that filters in through the window. There's a lit candle and a stick of incense in a flowerpot on the windowsill. The woman tells you to get undressed from the waist down, so you peel off your jeans and hop up on the table. Feet in the stirrups. You wonder if you should have taken off your socks. The woman makes you lift your bottom so she can slip a plastic tarp beneath. She covers your knees with a sheet, but the plastic makes you shiver.

"Cold?" she asks.

"Yeah." Your teeth are chattering.

She pulls a small electric heater closer to the table, then throws an army-surplus blanket over the sheet. "Better?"

You nod. The woman looks kind, and you relax a little. She takes your hand. "You sure you want to do this? He didn't pressure you?"

You shake your head.

198

"Then tell me."

"Tell you what?"

"Tell me it's your choice. Tell me you don't want this baby."

"I don't want this baby?" you say, but it comes out sounding like a question.

"Do you really want this abortion?"

"Yeah." You shrug. "Sure."

"Say it."

You roll your eyes. "I really, really, really want this abortion."

She looks at you hard, then pats your arm. "All right. Hang on tight. Here we go." And she walks toward your feet and ducks behind the blanket.

You can see the window beyond the horizon of coarse, olive-drab wool that stretches between your knees, which are spread wide open to the world. Off in the marshaling yard you can hear the trains being built, their brakes grinding and squealing, metal against metal. Instead of dissonance, however, this creates a harmonic accident—eerie overtones, not of this earth. You want it to go on and on, infinitely resonating, but it terminates in the heavy clank of two-ton cars coupling.

You cringe at the insertion of cold metal.

The pain is like no other.

After it's over, you lie there on the table while the woman cleans up. The door opens, and Cassie comes in. She chokes at the sight of the blood, but she recovers. She rubs your clammy forehead, pulls your long hair up off your neck, and blows gently against your skin, and this time her comforting works because you start to cry. She kisses your brow.

"You okay?" she whispers, and you nod.

"Let's get milk shakes," you whisper back, because you know she likes milk shakes, and she hugs you and helps you get dressed. The lady gives you a big sanitary pad, which you shove between your legs. You pull up your jeans. Then Elliot comes in, and he wants to carry you out in his arms.

Over the threshold, like a bride in reverse.

He puts his arms gently around you and you feel the last of your strength drain from your legs. You push him away.

"For chrissakes, Elliot," you say, gripping the sticky banister and descending all on your own. "I'm not a fucking baby."

199

After the milk shakes he drives you home. Cassie gets out at the end of the road by the mailboxes, but as you're about to follow, he holds on to your arm. He needs to talk to you. Not for long. Ten minutes. Please. He drives down the road a way and pulls off to the side, next to a snow-covered potato field belonging to Lloyd. It's cold in the Volkswagen, even with the engine running and the heater on.

"Yummy?" He tries to look into your eyes, but you keep your face turned away. "You okay, kid?"

It's like having period cramps, only worse.

"You were really brave back there. You going to be all right?"

You don't answer. You know this is not what he wants to talk about.

"Listen . . ." He looks away, too, staring straight ahead though the foggy windshield. "I know it's bad timing, but I've got a friend. Coming to visit. From San Francisco."

"So what?" You don't understand what this has to do with timing.

"What I mean is, while she's here, I can't, you know . . ."

You don't want to hear any more. You want to stick your fingers in your ears and hum, but more words follow, faster now.

"Actually, I think it's probably better this way, don't you? If we take a break . . ."

You're afraid you'll start to cry if you say anything at all.

"For a while anyway." He has the courtesy to face you then. "I'm sorry about all this. I didn't mean for this to happen." He exhales and engages the clutch. "I know you'll understand." He pulls on the wheel and makes a U-turn, leaving dark tracks in the snow.

At the mailboxes he reaches for your arm, but you slam the door in his face. It's snowing again, and you listen to the sound of his small engine chugging away into the night. From the road you see the porch light shining through the poplars, and that's when you hear it, a whimpering sound—*noooo, nooooo*—like a wounded animal makes, and the sound of a belt whistling through the air. You see Lloyd come out and stand in the lit doorway, and Momoko behind him.

You start to run toward the light.

They're out by the woodpile—Carl Unger, his arm raised, belt in hand, and Cassie, just a shadowy black lump in the cold blanket of white. You hear your footsteps crunching, your voice yelling "Stop! You're hurting her!" and then you're on top of him, pounding at him with your fists.

200

He throws you off his back, and you land in the snow. He raises the belt against you, and that's when Lloyd comes rattling down the steps. He grabs Unger's arm, and for a moment they freeze, two cutouts in the moonlight, blowing big steam clouds at each other. But Lloyd is taller, and Carl's knees start to buckle, and Lloyd keeps on pushing him down into the snowdrift like he's planting him there. When Carl is on the ground, Lloyd lets go and turns to you.

"Where have you been?"

Cass speaks up then. "I didn't tell them, Yummy! I didn't say."

"Shut your mouth, Cassandra." Her daddy struggles to his feet and raises the belt.

"Leave her alone," you say. "She didn't do anything."

"You were in Pocatello with that man," Lloyd says. "You were seen there. I demand to know what you were doing."

You get up slowly, brush off the snow, and look your father in the eye. "We were having milk shakes," you say, which must have squared with his information, because for a minute, knowing that much to be true, everyone relaxes a little, wanting to believe that's all there is to it, and now they can all go home.

"To celebrate my abortion." You look from Lloyd to Cassie's daddy, shrug at the two of them, and turn toward the porch.

Carl spits into the snow. "She's a bad seed, Fuller. First thing in the morning I'm calling the sheriff. We'll run that bastard out of town."

But Lloyd says nothing, doesn't even hear. He moves, catching up with you on the bottom step. Then he grabs your shoulder and spins you around, bringing his hand down hard across the side of your face. The blow snaps your head back. You hit the newel post and crumple. You fall at his feet. Staring up at him, you experience a great surge that feels like triumph at first, but it quickly subsides, and then it's like life on earth as you know it has ended right there, and you've woken up dead or on Mars. When Lloyd finally speaks, his voice is shaking with rage.

"What gives you the right?" he asks. "What gives you the authority to take an innocent life?"

"It's *legal* now!" you cry.

"That's not a law, that's a license to commit murder!" He squats down and grips you by the arms. His chest is heaving. "It's a sin against God, Yumi! Don't you see?"

You cringe and pull away from him. There's blood coming from your nose, dripping onto the snow, and it is just too much blood for one day. "It's not a sin," you say, gulping for air. "It's *my* body. It's *my* fucking life. . . ."

He looks at you, and you see his revulsion. He stands. Steps over you and climbs. He has to hold on tight to the railing. At the top he turns, and his eyes are like ice, so cold and bright his gaze would have frozen the landscape if the winter hadn't already. You're scared then, truly, because you know you've gone too far, and so has he.

"God creates life," he says. "Only He can choose to end it." The screen door slams behind him.

Carl Unger snorts. He turns to Cass. "Your little friend here is gonna burn in hell. You going with her?"

Cass draws away and shakes her head.

Unger nods. "Thought so. Now, get on home. I'll get your mother. I'm not done with you yet."

You lie on the bloodstained steps.

"Yummy?" Cass whispers.

Her daddy lurches forward, belt in hand, half raised. "I said get! Now! I don't want you speaking another word to this little whore."

"Yummy?" She takes a baby step backward. Then another. Away from her daddy. From you. Away from your glowing house. You lift your face.

"Go, Cass." Your voice is hoarse and old sounding, not like you at all.

Cass turns and runs into the darkness.

double-click &

Careful not to wake him, to depress the mattress or tug on the sheet, Cass inched her weight over to her side of the bed and lowered her feet to the floor. Felt for her slippers and her robe. There were spots in the old floorboards that groaned underfoot, but she knew exactly where they were. She'd known them as a child, when she slept down the hallway, keeping an ear out for the creaks and grunts that escaped from her parents' bedroom, and she knew them now, as an adult, ever since she and Will had moved into the master bedroom. Knowing them so well, it was easy to avoid them.

She wrapped the old robe tightly around her. She placed her weight carefully, timing her steps to Will's breathing. Once in the hallway she could navigate more quickly. Once in the kitchen she could walk normally again. The bedroom was in the far corner of the house; she couldn't bang pots, but she could relax and let Will slip from her mind. Poor man, she thought in passing. He worked so hard. She put on a kettle of water for tea.

Warm tea. Made from herbs. Like mint to soothe the stomach. Nettle to cleanse the liver. Sage to satisfy the soul. She carried her steaming cup to the office and logged on to the computer.

She typed in the URL, bypassed the home page, and went straight to the photo listings. She was working her way through Eastern Europe and had made it halfway through the Bulgarians. She'd done Africa and Asia already. She was saving Russia for last. She quickly scanned the list: *Boris, Georgi, Ignat, Mitko, Vasil*. These were the boys, and she would start with them, because Will needed a son to help out on the farm. But then she would move on to the girls: *Ana, Donka, Kamelia, Nadka, Veselinka*. She would be overjoyed with any child, but in her heart of hearts she wanted a daughter.

Kamelia. What a pretty name. You wouldn't even need to do much, just change a few letters. But Donka! The kids at school would have a field day with that. Donka would need an American name for sure. Cass double-clicked on Donka, to take a quick peek. The description was disappointingly brief, but the thumbnail photograph showed a delicate girl, with black eyes that seemed to get bigger and deeper the longer Cass looked at her. She bookmarked the child and added her to the favorites folder.

This precious little girl—the descriptions all began like that: *this charming toddler, this lovable baby boy*—followed by a few notes describing the particular child's condition: *Donka was born a bit prematurely. She is able to form a few words, and she can sing to herself, but her speech is not perfectly clear. She has no other apparent disabilities. She enjoys watching TV.*

Many of the children were disabled, and there was even a space in the search request form where you could specify the degree of disability you could tolerate in your adopted child: none, mild, moderate, severe. But regardless of the cleft palates, the anomalous spines, the limps and stutters and damaged brains, all the descriptions ended like Donka's: *This child is searching for a loving home.*

What words can she form? Cass wondered as she gazed into Donka's dark, pixelated eyes. If you were an orphaned Bulgarian baby, what would you want to communicate to the world? It didn't matter if Donka couldn't speak so clearly. Words were overrated anyway. Certainly Will didn't have much use for them. He'd be a good daddy to a wordless child, and it was nice that the girl liked to sing. They could all sing and watch TV together. They could call her Donna.

Will had once expressed interest in a Vietnamese child, but when they'd looked at a site together and he'd seen the birth defects and the land-mine injuries, he shook his head and turned away.

"I can't," he said. "I'd want to take them all."

Later that night he had a nightmare. She woke him and held him as he rocked back and forth. "Oh, God, Cass," he said. "It's like we defoliated all the babies, too."

Now, thinking about Will, she felt guilty. He hated what she was doing—window shopping for children, he called it—and he saved articles from the newspaper for her about people with Internet addictions. He didn't come out and say it was like pornography, but she knew that's what he thought. It was unwholesome, a sad fantasy, and she always felt lousy and hungover the next morning. It was useless, too, since even if she and Will made the decision to adopt, by the time the paperwork was done and the home studies were concluded, these particular kids would be gone or grown. But even knowing this, she still couldn't resist her folder of favorites, poring over their pictures in the middle of the night. From time to time she was tempted to delete the lot of them, but that felt wrong, too. Having chosen them, she could not simply drag them into the trash.

Double-click and the child is yours. Double-click and the baby is aborted. But it wasn't so easy. For Yummy, perhaps, but not for Cass. It wasn't easy and it wasn't fair.

She was sick of watching the haphazard way Yummy parented her children, hauling them around, the way she talked to them and the language she used. It was so clear they were unhappy. Phoenix was still getting bullied in school. The kids were calling him names—*Jap, faggot*—although after the Thai-boxing incident they kept their distance. Yummy just shrugged and told him to work it out.

"You're in Idaho, Phoenix. What do you expect?"

Ocean had come home every day for an entire week in tears because a classmate was calling her a love child.

"Love child!" Yummy said. "How sweet!" She grabbed Ocean and gave her a loud, smacking kiss, then cuddled her roughly. "Ooh, my love child. My little love puddle."

Cass looked down at her lap. It was embarrassing to watch.

Ocean wrenched herself away from her mother's embrace. "Stop it!" she yelled. "Don't call me that! It means I don't have any father!"

Yummy sat back, pulling her long hair off her face and letting it fall. "Well, you tell your friend that's a biological impossibility," she said. There was an edge to her voice now. "Come on. Say it. 'Biological impossibility.'"

"I can't!" Ocean cried.

"Say it!"

"Bilogi—"

"Bi-o-logical."

"Bilological . . ."

And now Elliot Rhodes goes and shows up, and there was Yummy, acting like a complete idiot around him, like she was ready to jump right back into bed with him. They'd already been up to something when she and the kids had walked in on them. They'd stepped apart, and he had looked at her coolly.

"You're—" he said, then waited for someone to help him out, and of course Yummy obliged. Cass would have been perfectly happy to let him wait forever.

"Cass," Yummy said. "Cass Unger."

"Quinn," Cass said, but nobody heard her.

"Of course," Elliot said. "Yummy's friend." He smiled at her, like a parent trying to be gracious. His eyes were flicking back and forth between Poo's dark little face and hers, comparing.

"Cute baby," he said. "Is he—"

"He's mine," Yummy said.

Elliot raised his eyebrows and glanced past Cass at Phoenix and Ocean, who were standing half hidden, as though he were expecting more children to pop out.

"Just the three," Yummy said. "That's it. No more."

Cass felt her face redden with shame, but even that didn't belong to her

205

entirely. Yummy's babies, Yummy's shame. She felt Ocean beside her, clutching her pant leg. Poo squirmed in her arms. Behind her, Phoenix slammed the door and headed back out into the wind. Something small and hot burst inside her chest. Poo sensed it and started to cry. Yummy held her arms out for him, and he went to her gladly.

Elliot was putting on his coat. "So," he was saying to Yummy. "Are you free for lunch? Tomorrow?"

Yummy nodded.

Stripped of the baby, her reason for being there, Cass turned and walked toward the door.

But it wasn't over. Not quite. Not yet.

"Cass?" Yummy said. "Could you take Poo again tomorrow afternoon?"

Cass couldn't bear it. "Will wants to start planting as soon as this wind lets up." Her brain felt squeezed and useless.

"Just for a few hours . . ."

Old habit won out. "All right."

Outside, Phoenix was throwing stones against the side of the barn, but he was far enough away so that the wind carried off the sound of impact. Silent rock against old wood. He looked so small under the towering poplars bending stiffly in the wind. Beyond him stretched the empty fields, overhung with a pale cloud of swirling dust.

Cass headed toward home. Halfway there she realized she was holding on to her stomach. Just thinking of Yummy together with Rhodes made her sick, as though the sight itself carried a taint. For the rest of the evening she tried to keep the images from her mind, but it was too late. That night she dreamed about the horrible brown room at the top of the stairs, and the train yard beyond, and the mournful, eerie overtones of steel straining against steel. Waking, she realized it was just the wind creaking in the poplars, and she relaxed. A few minutes later the cramps started.

It didn't take long. It never did. In the grim yellow light of the bathroom, she washed away the traces that smeared the insides of her thighs. It wasn't fair, she thought, bitterly. But it was a damn good thing that she hadn't told Will after all.

$\mathcal{B}$

"Cassie?"

Will stood next to her, hand on her shoulder. He reached over for the mouse and closed her files, then shut down the computer. The server had logged her off already. She'd fallen asleep.

"What time is it?"

"Time to get up," Will said. It was still dark outside, but he was dressed. He was ready for his coffee and breakfast. She followed him into the kitchen.

"Will?" She was groggy, but she needed to talk to him. To explain what had been going through her mind.

But he was in a hurry. "What?" he asked as he put the coffee on, annoyed that he had to. He wanted to be in the fields before dawn. It was the start of planting.

So she kept it simple. "I want to think about adopting again."

He couldn't keep a grimace from rippling across the plane of his face, but he controlled it. "Cass," he said, evenly, "can't we talk about this once the crop is in?"

He hated the social workers and all the forms and home visits. Home invasions, he called them.

"Fine," she said. "I'm sorry." She meant it. She hoped he would remember the conversation later and understand.

He put his hand on her arm as she reached the refrigerator door. "Honey, I know how you feel."

She elbowed him aside. No, she thought. You don't. She broke the eggs one by one into a bowl, beat them, and lit a fire under the skillet. That was the problem. He didn't know how she felt at all.

rocket-powered motorcycle 🏍

The jagged sound of my father's breathing filtered into my bedroom through a baby monitor, which Melvin had installed in case Lloyd needed help in the night.

"I don't want people spying on me in my own house!" Lloyd had said, eyeing the plastic transmitter on his bedside table. It was shiny white with pink and blue buttons and softly molded edges.

"It's not people," Melvin said. "It's your daughter."

"What earthly good would she be?" He plucked at the sheets in frustration. "Put that eavesdropping contraption in your camping car and maybe I'd see the point."

"Out of range," Melvin said.

"Listen," I said, "I don't like it any more than you do, Dad. It's just in case."

He stared at me, then closed his eyes and let his head fall back against the pillow. "In case of what?" he said. "In case I decide to run away?"

Now, in the gaps between Lloyd's exhalations, I could hear Ocean and Poo breathing softly in their corner and the creaks of the settling house. At night the house sounds were palpable, pressing against my skin. I tried to be still. I stood in front of the mirror and undressed slowly, examining my body in the green glow of the night-light, *nude!* as Cassie used to squeal. How prudish she was. I hugged myself to keep my limbs from twitching. I wanted to stomp and shatter the silence.

Instead I slipped on my robe and tied it tightly around my waist. It was the same mirror I'd had as a child, and I'd grown up in front of it, turning and craning my neck, searching for clues to the future. The mirror was the same, but the girl was gone, leaving only phantom limbs and a flicker of her excitements. The particular collection of cells that comprised her, the ones that Elliot had stroked and fucked, had long ago been sloughed off and replaced by new ones. Cellular turnover occurred in seven-year intervals, didn't it?

Cell by cell you slip away, then resurrect.

And now? Elliot was back, and I could feel my cells quivering, all set to betray me again. He was still a handsome man, slightly thicker, not the whip-thin hippie I'd loved as a child, but to sleep with him now would make me somehow complicit, wouldn't it? A molester of my own childhood?

Phoenix could tell what was going on the minute he saw us in the kitchen. Fourteen is an unforgiving age, and he still wasn't talking to me. But it wasn't just Phoenix. They all knew. Cass, and Ocean, too. Later, in my starry bedroom, in my arms, Ocean confessed to me in a whisper,

"Mommy, when I see people kiss, it makes my little butt hurt."

What does *that* mean? She was small and warm in her flannel pajamas, squirming in her mommy's arms. Sweet cheeks. Tangled hair.

Good night, Puddle.

In the weeks before Elliot arrived, I'd been flirting with Geek in the greenhouse. It was a desultory flirtation, killing time. We'd lie crosswise in the hammock, side by side, and rock to "Blue Hawaiian Moon."

"Are you trying to seduce me?" I asked him once, sipping indigo nectar from the overhead feed, watching it travel through the loops of clear tubing.

"Can I?" he asked. We were sharing the tube.

"No. I'm too old for you," I said. "A whole different generation."

"Don't be ridiculous," he said, twirling the ends of my hair. "Age is relative, and anyway I'm a product of the Summer of Love. Love is in my nature."

I was tempted. It was easy to forget I was ten years older than this person who swayed beside me playing with my hair.

Just as Elliot had been ten years older than me.

But of course it was different. Geek wasn't a child. A child can't be held responsible, can she? No matter how much she might have felt she was to blame? But even as I tried to absolve myself, I knew that in my awkward, childish way, I had seduced Elliot, hanging around the classroom after school, loitering by his desk at dusk. Of course I was complicit. And if so, if together Elliot and I had miscarried my childhood, maybe now, together, we could bring that girl back, to comfort and even to forgive. After all, he said he was sorry. The minute I heard those words, I knew I wanted to sleep with him again.

I lay in bed and stared at the peeling stars. I turned down the volume on the baby monitor and reduced my father's breathing to a faint static interference. Pretending his breaths were waves on the beach, I drifted off to sleep.

$$\mathcal{B}\mathcal{D}$$

In the clarity of the day, as I bundled up Poo to take him next door, the anticipation of the night before turned leaden. Cass was no help. She had on a frilly apron over her sweatshirt and would barely meet my eye as she lifted the baby from my arms. She didn't approve, and I felt a temptation to linger, to ask her for a cup of coffee and a word of absolution. I wanted to explain to her, carefully, all that I was thinking and feeling, and maybe it would take the better part of the afternoon, but that was all right, too. My date with Elliot felt like a sentence, compared to the safety and the comfort of Cassie's bright, sunny kitchen. But she blocked the door. It was the first day of planting, she told me. Will had left early for the fields, and she was busy. She'd be feeding the workers lunch today, as well as covering the office.

"Gosh, Cass," I said, "I didn't realize . . ." But just as I was reaching out my arms to take Poo back, the phone rang and she pulled a cordless handset from her apron pocket and withdrew into the house with my baby.

I sat for a while in the Pontiac, smoking a cigarette and trying to rekindle some excitement, but the feeling eluded me. I headed into town. I hadn't been able to think of a restaurant, so he suggested meeting at his motel. Already things were different. For one thing I could now drive myself to get fucked.

I looked for his car in the lot, a baby blue Beetle, but of course it wasn't there.

I knocked, and for a moment I panicked, almost turning to go, but it was too late. Mr. Rhodes opened the door. I couldn't look at him. Instead I looked past him into the room.

Things were different.

There were sheets on the bed. There was no soup on the stove. The windows were curtained, not clouded with steam.

He reached for my hands. Speechless, I allowed him that. He shook his head and held on to my fingertips. "You haven't changed," he said.

Glancing up at him then, I felt young and suddenly reckless. I took a step forward and placed my hand on his cheek. He closed his eyes, mute now, turning his mouth into my palm. The naked arch of his neck bent to my gaze, and I felt my confusion abate beneath a wave of tenderness and power. His breath, warm against my palm, made my skin tingle all over, and then I remembered—*This* is what it feels like to be fourteen and thrilling at the edge of sex when it is still brand new, testing the waters where his desire laps your shore, sticking in a toe, and not understanding the swiftness of the current—

Enough. This is enough. Stop here—

But the pull of the past was stronger than I was. It caught me up. He slipped a DO NOT DISTURB sign around the doorknob. There had been too many locked motel doors, and it was happening too fast. Always too fast. But once locked in, I had to go through the motions.

He scanned my face, then drew me in close. With my face pressed into his neck, I could see the coarsened pores of his skin. I thought about his cells as I tentatively kissed them. I breathed and tried to recall his scent, the one I vaguely remembered from the flannel of an old sleeping bag, but it wasn't there. Something else. Blackboards and chalk. The smell of felt erasers. No . . .

Cologne.

Expensive, but still I choked on it. I pushed him away. He caught my hair, wrapped it around his fist and tugged.

Oh, he said. I remember your hair.

He buried his face in it. I shut my eyes. If he would only tell me more about who I'd been, I would tolerate the cologne and maybe even grow to love it. His hand was on the small of my back. His fist never loosened its grip on my hair as he backed me across the dull beige carpet. The sway-backed mattress sagged under our weight—the springs had too much give, too soft for the hips and the heels to find purchase, to push him away. I placed my hands against his chest. I wanted to explain. Maybe I could make a joke of it—*I don't like sex that bounces, Elliot*—I could give a little laugh—*I don't like to wallow*. But it seemed awkward to demur on the grounds of an insufficient mattress. He removed some of my clothing, then some of his. The mustard-colored bedspread felt like spun plastic, cold where it touched my skin. I lay there, passive, staring up at the stained and perforated ceiling as he traveled over my body, touching my breasts, humming his discoveries wordlessly into my thighs.

Talk to me! I begged him silently. *How have I changed? What do you remember—*

He arched his back and spread my legs, and just then a memory surfaced, a quick flash to the very first time he pushed inside, how unexpected it was and how much it had hurt and how, to stifle a cry, I'd bitten my lip until it tasted sweet and I was bleeding from two places at once. And when finally he'd pulled out at the end and seen the blood and recoiled in shock from the stain of my virginity—*You didn't tell me!*—I had lied and told him I was having my period.

It wasn't much of a memory, but it was enough for now. As he eased his body against mine, I locked my ankles around his waist, and before he could start the bed bouncing, I shifted and rolled until I was sitting on top. Then the heat returned. He opened his eyes, surprised, but I could see he didn't mind the way the heels of my hands pressed his shoulders into the spongy mattress, nor did he resist the rhythm I imposed upon his groin. It was not a thrusting so much as a stern undulation that rocked and built, locking our hips in a conjunction that existed solely in the present, so that when we both came, unfettered by any memory at all, I could throw back my head and let my throat open in a cry of reprieve. It mingled with his, then continued along on its own.

$$\mathscr{B}$$

"You are amazing." He lay on his side, reaching out to trace the line of my jaw with his finger. I turned my head away. On the road, outside the thin walls of the motel, I could hear the sounds of large engines as heavy farm equipment rumbled by. Armies on the move. The harrowers were squaring off against the undulating fields. The smell of dust and diesel and acrid fertilizer filtered in through the drywall and hung in the air. Planting had started, and it was spring, and these were sounds and smells that I remembered.

"I have to go."

"Stay." He held on to my arm. "Just a while longer. I mean, don't you think this is amazing? After all these years?"

"I guess so." I studied a water stain on the ceiling. It was shaped like a kidney. Its edges were brown. He wanted to talk now, to reminisce, but now I didn't want to hear any more. It was over. I had to go pick up my kids.

He sighed. "You always were so orgasmic."

I could feel my face flush. This was the danger of nostalgia—once exposed, it became vulnerable to correction. "Elliot," I said, addressing the stain, "I never came."

"What?"

"I never came." I pushed up on my elbows and looked at him. "I was fourteen years old, for God's sake. A fourteen-year-old kid getting screwed by her history teacher is way too uptight to have orgasms."

"You're joking."

"No. If you remember me coming, either you're remembering it wrong or I faked it. Probably I faked it. Now that I think about it, I used to worry about whether faking counted as a lie and a sin, so that shows you exactly how young I was.

"You were only fourteen?"

"What did you think? I was in ninth grade. You were my teacher."

"But . . ."

212

In all honesty I'd probably lied about my age, too, but the fact was, he didn't remember. I could see the doubt and confusion shifting across his naked face as he searched for an explanation. I knew what he wanted to say—*But I was young, too!* And it was true—twenty-three or -four at most.

But I was so much younger.

Nineteen seventy-four. I remember that summer before school started, before I fell in love with Elliot, because it was the last summer of my childhood. The high point in Liberty Falls was Evel Knievel's historic attempt to leap across the Snake River Canyon. There were posters up in all the storefront windows—Evel dressed in skintight white leathers, dripping with fringe, standing next to his star-spangled, rocket-powered motorcycle.

All the kids were going, and I wanted to go, too, but Lloyd said no. He didn't actually come out and say that it was cheap, low-class entertainment—after all, Cassie's daddy was going, and he was taking her, and it wasn't right to criticize your neighbor. Instead Lloyd said it wasn't safe. He didn't approve of thrill seeking. Life was dangerous enough, and it was disrespectful of God to promote jeopardy, never mind profit by so doing.

Later I couldn't help but identify when Cass told me that Evel's safety parachute had opened prematurely, cutting short his flight and sending him and his motorcycle on a slow drift downward, to the bottom of Snake River Canyon. Similarly tethered, I thought I understood what it must have felt like, getting jerked out of the trajectory of one's life like that. I felt a desperate need to cut the cords, to give my own little throttle an extra squeeze and torque and sail out from a cloud of spitting gravel into the clear, empty air. In my mind's eye I could see the ground rising up to meet my wheels, safely, on the far side of the canyon.

What the mind's eye couldn't see, at the age of fourteen, was clear to me now: the real possibility of free fall, sans parachute, sans safety net at all. I sat up in bed and contemplated Elliot, who was trying hard to understand what he barely remembered.

"I can't believe it," he was saying, dumbfounded. "How could I have been sleeping with a fourteen-year-old?"

Not a fourteen-year-old. Not any old fourteen-year-old. Me.

He was my great leap forward, and I had loved him, and he had fallen short, landing me smack in the gulch. I'd been crawling out ever since, had even reached the far side of stability, until now, when life's restless cycling delivered him back to me again.

"Generally guys get sent to jail for what you did," I informed him. "You were a child molester, Elliot."

Watching his face sink as he grappled with this new crisis of conscience, I realized I didn't care. I just wanted to ride his discomfort, hard, until it caught up with mine. I wanted to feel him again, between my legs, my rocket-powered motorcycle, once turbocharged.

I wanted to choke him hard.

I wanted to hear him splutter.

little bear 🐻

She had come by late to collect Poo. Face flushed. Eyes hard and wild and shining. It was a look Cass recognized from a long time ago, and she didn't need to ask where it came from. Poo, sensing his mother's fever, struggled in Cass's arms. He wanted to be near the source, to press against that radiating energy, and who could blame him? She handed him over, and he bounced up and down in Yummy's arms, gurgling and paddling her cheeks with his fat pink palms as she covered his face with kisses. Cass collected the last of Poo's things into a sack and opened the door. Only then, with Yummy standing safely outside, did she ask through the screen, "Are you going to see him again?"

Yummy turned around on the stoop. "I know it's crazy. I know I should just tell him to fuck off, but part of me . . ." She shrugged. "He said he's sorry. I don't know. He's leaving on Sunday. I guess I'll see him one more time. . . ."

"I'll take Poo," Cass said. "It's fine."

🐻

Double-click and bring up the atlas of North America. Zoom into the map of the western states. There were border crossings into Saskatchewan due north, all along the edge of Montana. Portal, Poplar, Climax. Tiny one-man outposts where they never searched luggage or checked the trunks of cars. It would be easy. Cass smiled. Climax. What a place to cross over. She'd always liked Saskatchewan because of the names: Moose Jaw, Lucky Lake, Success. Any place with towns like that had to be optimistic and upbeat.

214

Cass didn't have much experience with optimistic and upbeat, but suddenly she wanted to try.

Will was planting and wouldn't get back until after dark. As soon as he left for the fields the next morning, she went out to the shed, just to see if the suitcases were still there. It took her awhile to dig them out, and when she did finally pull them free, she found them flattened from years of crushing. The fabric was festooned with cobwebs and dangling bits of insects—brittle cricket legs, powdery moth wings. They needed to be cleaned anyway, so she brought them inside and took the vacuum to the sides and corners.

Packing was no trouble. It wouldn't be wise to cause suspicion by having too much luggage, and she could easily fit everything she'd need into the smaller suitcase. The larger one could be lined with pillows. She took a utility knife and made a number of small, inconspicuous slits in the fabric, then widened them, just to be sure. The plaid pattern on the fabric helped hide the openings. She didn't have a passport, but she could enter with her driver's license, especially at a rural crossing. She'd need food, so she packed some in a cardboard box. When she was done, she took the Suburban to the gas station at the entrance to the freeway and filled the tank, then drove home again and waited.

Yummy arrived just after lunch, casually dressed but with a sheen on her that Cass hadn't seen since she'd watched her take her bows at curtain call after the Thanksgiving pageant. She smelled of cigarettes and aromatherapy. Cass had a sheen on her, too, but of course Yummy didn't notice.

"Thanks," Yummy said. "You have time for a cup of coffee?"

Cass thought quickly. "I've got errands in Pocatello."

"Oh." Yummy lingered in the doorway holding the baby.

"Anyway, you have a date," Cass said.

"Yeah. I guess. I don't know." She gave Poo a kiss and cuddled him like she didn't want to let him go. Cass waited. Finally Yummy sighed and handed him over.

Cass forced herself to smile. "Have a good time."

Yummy nodded. "I guess." She reached out and squeezed Poo's foot and backed away down the steps.

"Hey," Cass called. "Stick Poo's car seat in the Suburban, will you?" She watched Yummy wrestle with the plastic seat. It was bulky but sturdy, and Cass wanted Poo to be comfortable. Comfortable, but more than that, she wanted him to be safe. As soon as she saw the Pontiac's taillights turn the corner, Cass headed for her car. Poo whimpered. It was cold in the Suburban. He had just come from outside and wanted to stay inside now. She strapped him into the car seat and went back in for the suitcases. By the time she returned, he had started to cry.

"Please, Poo," she whispered, rubbing his hands. "Please, little bear—"

But he wouldn't stop. All the way down the dirt road he cried, gaining in volume as she cut across town and turned onto the highway. She tried singing for a while, all the songs that normally quieted him, but he just cried louder. She switched on the radio, but in the rearview mirror she could still see the tears squeezing from his eyes and his small body shaking with sobs. She drove for a whole hour and part of the next, until she couldn't stand it anymore. She pulled into a rest area just south of the Montana state line. As soon as the car stopped, his sobbing quieted and he started to hiccup. She thought about the brandy she'd packed in her purse to put in his milk just before they crossed the border. She checked her watch. The border was still eight hours away. She climbed into the backseat and took Poo from the car seat onto her lap. Together they watched the big trucks hurtle by. She gave him his bottle of milk but left the brandy where it was.

He started to doze off as soon as she turned the car around. By the time they were home, he was fast asleep. He was a good little sleeper. She got him out of his parka without waking him and put him down in the middle of her bed. "I'm sorry, little bear," she whispered, then closed the door behind her.

In the living room she retrieved her purse, unscrewed the cap on the brandy bottle, and took a long drink. It tasted terrible, treacly and sweet, but she liked the warmth it brought to her body. She took another big sip, then capped it. She looked around. Barely three hours had passed since she'd driven away, but everything seemed different.

At least she had tried. Even if it was a stupid idea and nothing had come of it, she felt proud of herself for that. She went out to the Suburban and brought the suitcases back into the house and unpacked them. Then she put them away in the storage shed, in the very back, and covered them up with boxes. She thought of how she might explain to Will about the air holes, then realized she probably wouldn't have to. The only time they'd used the suitcases was on their honeymoon, when they'd rented a cabin in the woods for a week. They often talked about taking another trip like that, but with one thing and another . . .

It was after dark by the time Yummy came for Poo. Cass had called over to the house and spoken to Charmey, who said she would get the older kids fed. Cass was keeping Will's dinner hot in the oven, waiting for him to get in from the fields.

"Oh, God," Yummy said as she came through the door. "I'm sorry I'm so late!" She smelled of whiskey and tobacco smoke and faintly of cologne. "Where's my Poo-bear?"

From the playpen in the kitchen Poo could hear his mother's voice, and he started to screech. Yummy crossed the living room. "Hey," she said. "Do you have a beer? I'm dying for a drink."

"In the refrigerator," Cass said. She picked up a few of Poo's toys and followed Yummy into the kitchen. Yummy was standing in front of the open refrigerator popping the top off the beer. She took a long swig.

"Close the door," Cass said. "You're wasting electricity."

Yummy looked at her. "Want one?"

Cass shook her head. Yummy closed the door. A calendar from the local feed store hung there from a magnet, and she started flipping back through the pages. "I've been here over three months! No wonder I'm going crazy." She let the calendar pages fall and started walking restlessly around the kitchen.

Cass sat down at the table, folded her hands, and waited. Yummy bent over the edge of the playpen and let her hair fall in a curtain around her son. Poo reached up and grabbed it and pulled.

"Ouch. Cut it out, baby." She untangled her hair from his fingers and looked up at Cass. "How was he today? Did you have fun?"

"Sure."

"Did you get your errands done?"

"Sure," Cass said. "We got a lot done."

They heard Will's pickup truck pull into the drive.

Yummy sighed. "I better get going." She reached into the playpen and hauled Poo up over the side. Will came in just as she finished getting the baby's coat on.

"Hey," he said. "You coming or going?"

217

"She's leaving," said Cass. Will looked tired. She reached up and patted his cheek. "I've got your dinner in the oven, hon. Wash your hands and you can sit right down."

He gave Cass a kiss on the head, then turned back to Yummy. "Stay for dinner?"

"She has to go home," Cass said. "Her kids are waiting." She followed Yummy to the front door and opened it. "Drive carefully," she said. "You've been drinking."

Yummy paused and looked out at the yard. In the moonlight they could see the cars and the rusting skeletons of farm equipment and the rickety old swing set they'd played on as kids. "It's hardly changed at all," Yummy said. "It looks just like it did when we were little." She turned back to Cass. "Do people change?"

"No," Cass said. "No they don't." Even though she didn't quite believe it anymore.

Yummy nodded. She shifted Poo onto her other hip and walked down the path to the car. Cass closed the door behind her and stood there for a moment, pressing her head to the doorjamb, until she heard the car drive off. The wind had picked up again. They were in for some more weather.

massacre rocks 🐛

"Problem is, we're not seeing the bigger picture. I was looking at the marketing reports on the Internet last night, and what we got now is low interest rates, low inflation, and a strong international dollar. The opposite of '74."

Elliot looked up from a row of souvenir mugs at the men standing in line in front of him, waiting to pay for gas. He was surprised. It was not the kind of conversation he would have expected to hear. There were three of them, farmers, wearing caps with company logos and coveralls stiff with dirt. Just in from the fields. The big blond guy with a ponytail and a Spudee Seed Potato cap was talking, but now his friend in the FMC Fertilizer cap cut him off.

"I'm seeing the bigger picture all right," Fertilizer grumbled. "The bigger picture is this damn weather. If the wind don't let up, I ain't gonna have any crop. The market ain't gonna hurt me if I can't keep the seed on the ground."

"Can't do anything about the weather," Spudee said doggedly. "But we can change our farm policy. With this kind of economy, it all comes down to whether we ought to be market driven or depending on government."

The third man, in an Acme Metal Fab cap, spoke up. "I say the government *should* pay. They're the ones that go and make dumb-ass decisions like NAFTA, letting in all them Canuck spuds to drive the price down. I still got last year's crop in the cellars that I can't sell. Cheaper to dump it."

Fertilizer paid for his gas. "And now with the Europeans boycotting the GMO crops . . . What did you decide about the NuLifes, Will? You planting them?"

Spudee stepped up to the cash register and laid down his quart of milk. He hesitated, eyeing the gum display, then extracted a beaten wallet from the back pocket of his coveralls, took out a twenty, and handed it over to the cashier. While he waited for her to make change, he massaged his knuckles.

"I don't know," he said slowly. "There was a time I laid down my life for my government and was glad to do so." He took off his cap and raked his fingers over his head, combing back the loose hair from his face. He looked exhausted, and even though most farmers looked tired at this time of year, it struck Elliot that there was something else, as if his worn face were at war with his basic good nature. Even his ponytail looked dispirited.

"In Vietnam, the government said spray and we sprayed. Never gave it another thought. Now I got this numbness in my arms that the doc says may be Agent Orange, only he can't tell for sure because of the exposure factor on the farm. It bugs me. Cynaco made Agent Orange for the army. They make GroundUp and now the NuLifes, too."

He held out his hand and accepted his change. His brow was furrowed, giving him a faintly puzzled look, as though he didn't know where all these words were coming from, but he just couldn't stop them.

"The wife's had a bout with cancer," he said. "Mother-in-law died of it. Old Fuller down the road had part of his colon removed." He put the bills into his wallet and then stared at the coins in his palm. He shook his head. "Maybe it's related. Maybe it ain't. And maybe if I was a scientist I could give you a better answer. But I'm just a farmer, so I can't say. What it boils down to is we're sick of chemical inputs, and they say with the NuLifes you can cut back. But you ask where I stand? Damned if I know. So what the hell? We're gonna try a few acres. See what happens."

He turned back to the register, selected a pack of spearmint gum and slapped the change on the counter to pay for it. He unwrapped the pack and offered it around, then the three walked out the door toward their pickups. Elliot watched them go, bending into the wind, then he placed his six-pack on the counter.

Duncan had been right, he thought. There was nothing like a little research in the field. He made a mental note to tell this story at the task force meeting on Monday. Maybe even pass it on to the client. He'd been stressing the environmental safety angle, and this was anecdotal support. It wasn't exactly a glowing endorsement of the NuLife, but at least the man was buying. He carried his beer to the rental car. He had just one more task to accomplish in Idaho.

☙

The Pinkerton's name was Rodney Skeele. Ex-military, in his early sixties. Korean War perhaps. The kind who could sniff out Elliot's student deferment like a dog trained to hunt down land mines. Elliot spotted him sitting in a corner booth with his back to the wall, hunkered over a cup of coffee. He knew that the man had sighted him, too. He could feel Rodney's trained eye as he crossed the room with his tray, taking in the Gore-Tex hiking boots, the Patagonia fleece sweater, the leather-trimmed oilskin Australian hunting jacket. When the data had been duly recorded, Elliot thought he detected a faint sneer, like a shadow, crossing the big man's spongy features.

"Hello there," said Elliot. "You must be Rodney."

Rodney grunted.

"Don't get up." Elliot sat down across from him and held out his hand. "Thanks for taking this on such short notice." He dumped his Supersized Fries into a large heap in the middle of his tray and rubbed his hands together. "Cold out there. Help yourself. Should be extra delicious, don't you think? This being Idaho and all . . ."

Rodney looked at him like he'd dropped off the moon.

Good, Elliot thought. He didn't need the man to like him. "So," he said, inserting a bundle of fries into his mouth, "tell me about the work you do for Cynaco."

Rodney did a quick scan of their immediate vicinity. There was a family sitting at the next booth. A mother with three enormous offspring, each facing off with a Supersized Happy Meal. He lowered his voice.

"Field testing mostly," he said. "Corn. Some canola. Expect more this year, but can't really do anything until the crops are up."

"I don't get out into the fields much. How does that work?"

Rodney shrugged. "Cynaco puts a marker gene in the plant, so you take samples, and the lab tests for that. You got a list of who's signed tech agreements, so if you find that gene in anyone else's field, it's infringement."

"What happens then?"

"Confront 'em. Get a warrant and subpoena their receipts and invoices and look for discrepancies. Cynaco's got lawyers and a CPA who handles that end."

"You ever catch anyone?"

"Bunch of minor cease and desists."

"How come we don't press further?"

"We do." Rodney sighed. "But most farmers settle. Guys around here operate on pretty tight margins. Can't afford to go up against a corporation like Cynaco, and they're not worth suing, not for damages anyway—they're so far in debt a court case would bankrupt them. The idea is to slap 'em back down but keep 'em in business. It's just maintenance."

Elliot nodded and inspected a fry. "Never think to eat these in the city," he said, twirling it and popping it into his mouth. "So basically you know who's planting what?"

"Pretty much. Why? You expecting trouble?"

"Could be. What did you find out?"

"They're hanging out on a farm about twenty miles northeast of Liberty Falls."

"You learn whose farm?"

"Belongs to an old guy named Fuller. Used to farm spuds, but then he quit. Folks around town think he's pretty much of a crackpot these days. Married to a Jap lady he brought back from the war. Both been pretty sick. They got one kid, a daughter. She's back home taking care of them. Sheriff's been out to see her already, thinks maybe she's got connections with this gang of yours."

"Good work," said Elliot. "I'm already in contact with the daughter."

Rodney gave him a long, cool stare. "So why'd you call me?"

"I wasn't at the time. But now that I am . . ."

"You don't need me."

"On the contrary. These kids tore up a couple of fields back east that got major media coverage. If they stick around, these waving fields of genetically modified organisms might be too much for them to resist."

"You want me to run them out of town?"

"No. Just keep an eye on them." Elliot paused. "You a churchgoing man?"

"I'm not LDS, but I know people, if that's what you mean."

"That'll do. You take a look at that Web site of theirs? Good stuff, huh?"

Rodney gave him another man-in-the-moon look. "You want to know what I think? These people are filthy scum."

"Great. Down the line perhaps some of your more devout neighbors might be interested in that, too." He finished off the last of the fries. "Well, that just hit the spot!"

"They put sugar in those," Rodney said.

"Yeah?"

"And beef flavoring. Never used to let my kids eat that crap. But my grandkids, forget about it."

⌒

"I ate at a McDonald's today," Elliot said.

"Oh, my." Jillie was not impressed.

"They put sugar and beef flavoring in the fries."

"So?"

He was lying on his bed at the motel staring up at the ceiling, holding the phone as far away from his face as possible. The receiver smelled of onions and a floral-scent deodorizer.

"Elliot, I can barely hear you."

"Sorry. This phone stinks. It's romantic, you know. Listening to your voice while inhaling a bouquet of aromatic hydrocarbons."

"For God's sake, Elliot, you are mutating into some kind of hideous rube. When are you coming back here?"

"Do you miss me?"

"Desperately." Her voice sounded far away.

"I bought you a present at the gas station today." She didn't answer. "Don't you want to know what it is?"

"What is it?"

"A John Deere tractor mug."

There was more silence. Outside, the wind howled, whistling through the open corridor of the motel.

"I'll be back on Sunday," he said. "Can I come over?"

"No. I've got yoga class."

"Oh."

There was a knock on the door. Elliot sat up. "Whoops, sorry Jillie, gotta run. Room service is here."

"Room service? At the Falls Motel . . . ?"

But he'd hung up already and was at the door, and she was standing in front of him, and everything else dropped away. Her body was torqued at an awkward angle he remembered from an empty classroom at dusk—one leg forward, the other back, as though she were getting ready to shift her weight and run as fast as she could in the opposite direction. He reached out and took her elbow before she could dart away.

"You came."

She resisted, leaned against the doorjamb. "I almost didn't." She fidgeted with the zipper on her jacket, shifting from one foot to the other. "I mean, what's the point?"

"Does there have to be a point?"

She thought about it. "I guess not. There never was."

"No? Wasn't the point just that we liked each other and wanted to be together? Isn't that the point now?"

"I don't know. Is it?"

"Sure," he said, but his answer sounded lame. She was watching him closely, and he felt as though she were looking for something that she wanted, that she had misplaced perhaps, that had been hers to begin with and now she needed back. But then she seemed to give up.

"I hate motel rooms," she said. "Let's go for a drive. I'll show you the ruts."

They took her Pontiac, and she headed west to Massacre Rocks. The late-afternoon sun hung low in the sky. Here and there he could see tractors out in the large field blocks, looking like tiny toys stirring up huge contrails of light-drenched dust. They pulled into the highway rest area and got out of the car. She led him a short distance into the dried weeds and the roadside litter and pointed to the ground.

"There."

At his feet, in the pale, compacted earth, were several deep, parallel indentations. "What are they?"

"You don't know? You're the history teacher. They're wagon-wheel ruts. From the Oregon Trail."

"Oh." What else could he say? They were far from prepossessing.

"I thought you'd like them," she said. "But I guess you're not interested in history anymore. Come on. Let's walk to the river."

They scrambled down through the boulders. She pointed out the landforms: Massacre Rocks, Devil's Gate, Gate of Death.

"Great place for an ambush," Elliot said, looking up at the rocks.

Here and there, traces of the ruts were still visible. Volcanic evidence abounded. Devil's Gate Pass was an extinct crater, she told him. The huge boulders surrounding them had been rolled and polished by a prehistoric flood, which had covered the entire landscape. The second largest in the geologic history of the world.

"What was the largest?"

She shrugged. "Noah's, I suppose."

"How do you know all this?"

"I guess my father taught me."

"My father never taught me anything," Elliot said.

The river itself was shrunken and disappointing. They walked around the edges of the mud flats, then climbed back up and sat on the boulders, looking down the valley. She took a pint of whiskey from the pocket of her jacket and drank from it, then passed it to him. She lit a cigarette and exhaled.

"Tell me about your father," she said.

"He ran out on my mom when I was just a kid. He was a salesman. Office furnishings, water coolers, stuff like that. He was a real womanizer—God, that word sounds dated. Do people even use it now?"

"Nowadays I think we just say slut."

"For a man, too?"

"Why not?"

"My dad was a lousy role model," he said sadly. "He's probably the reason I never settled down."

"Fear of commitment?"

"I don't trust myself not to hurt people."

She nodded, extinguishing the cigarette under her heel. "Elliot?"

He took another drink and braced himself. When women used his name like that, launching it into the air and leaving it dangling, it usually meant trouble. "Yes?"

"Did you miss me?"

"Sure," he said. He had to laugh. "I thought about you all night."

She shook her head impatiently. "No. I mean back then. After I left. Did you ever wonder about me, or worry, or think about coming to find me?"

"I didn't even know you'd gone." This was tricky. It was old history, and what she'd said was true. He wasn't all that interested anymore. "It's not like anyone was telling me much about you," he said. "And I left Liberty Falls myself soon after."

"Oh." She played with her shoelaces. "Nobody came. Not you, not Lloyd . . ."

"Is that why you ran away? So someone would come after you?"

"Not really. I just had to get out of here."

"And now you're back."

"Yeah . . ." She looked out over the vast river valley and brushed the hair away from her temples. He watched her profile, silhouetted against the rocks and outlined sharply in gold by the setting sun.

"You look like an Indian princess," he said.

She looked startled, and then she laughed. "I can't believe you're saying that. You were so offended that I used to play the Indian princess when there were Shoshone kids in the class. Called it revisionist history, do you remember?"

"No," he said. "That was back in the old days. When I was naïve enough to think that history mattered."

"It doesn't?"

"Not on this earth."

"What happened to you?"

He laughed and held his hand out for the bottle. "Here, you better give me some more of that." He took a long swig, and she watched him.

"I'm serious," she said. "You were a good teacher. Different. You really made us think about things. What happened?"

"I never wanted to teach. I just stayed on in school for the deferment.

After I left here I went to D.C. and worked as a reporter. It was post-Watergate, and I wanted to be Woodward and Bernstein, with contacts inside the government and Deep Throat and all that."

"And were you?"

"It was different than I thought. Like I said, I was naïve."

"Why do you say history doesn't matter?"

"Because it doesn't exist. Not in the way your history teacher taught you it does. What you think of as history is just someone's spin of a set of events. It's only a matter of who's more skillful at getting his version on the public record."

"But you're still a reporter?"

"Sort of."

"How can you be sort of a reporter?"

"I write stories. Most reporters approach history retroactively. My approach is more preemptive."

"Oh," she said, but he sensed that she wasn't really listening anymore. The sun was just slipping over the horizon, turning the sky pink and taking the last warmth with it. She looked very small and cold sitting on the rock. He put his arm around her and rubbed her arm.

"What do you do?" he asked.

"Teach a few English classes. Raise kids. Sell a little real estate on the side." She drank back the last of the whiskey. "Funny I should have become the teacher, huh?" She stood up, and, teetering slightly on the edge of the rock, she drew back her arm and hurled the empty bottle into the rocky gorge, toward the river. They waited for the high sound of glass breaking, but it never came.

"You know what I like?" she said, looking out over the rimrock to the endless plains. "I like the feeling that this is just the thinnest of crusts, covering the earth."

She linked her arm through his in a friendly way. "In Hawaii, near where I live, there's a place where you can walk right out onto an active lava flow. You're not supposed to, but you can. It's flowing right down from a volcano, and the crust is so hot you can feel it burning through the rubber of your soles. If you go at night and look down, you can see cracks in the black crust and the red-hot molten lava flowing underneath, just inches from your feet. And you know that if you take a wrong step where the crust is too thin, your foot will go right through and that'll be the end of it. Burn your foot to a crisp, just like that." She snapped her fingers. "A charred stump. That's all you'd be left with. Maybe I'll take you there sometime."

She turned to him and wrapped her arms around his neck and let her weight lean into him. She lifted her face for a kiss, and her mouth tasted like whiskey and cigarettes and fresh air. She pulled away and handed him the car keys.

"I think I'm drunk," she said. "You better drive."

"Where are we going?"

"Back to the motel." She broke away and clambered up the rock, then turned to look down at him. "Better hurry. I don't have much time."

They made love, and it was wordless. He lay on the bed with his arms stretched over his head and his wrists crossed as though bound. He watched her unbutton his shirt and pull it back from his chest, realizing that by not reaching, not touching, he was turning her on, and that to make a move in her direction was to break the flow of her concentration. Her black hair fell forward, curtaining off the ugly room. She watched him, steadily, even as she dipped down to caress him until he felt he couldn't stand the scrutiny, and he closed his eyes, but still he felt her gaze. Not accusing. Just looking for something. And when he opened his eyes again later on, he felt the sudden conviction that at one point he had possessed it—this thing she was looking for—he'd had it, and squandered it, and now he couldn't give it back.

But he could try. That's what he vowed after they were done and she lay resting beside him. He could try to take care. Try not to take too much more from her. This was not a thought he was used to having after sex. He'd made similar resolutions once a relationship had grown tiresome, and he'd wanted out, but not right at the beginning, when things were still so full of promise. She stirred, and he ran his finger down the side of her jaw.

"Hi," he said.

Of course it wasn't really the beginning at all. They'd played out one part already, and this was act two, the curtain had just swung open, and he'd stumbled into the center of the stage. He stood there, full of brave in tentions.

"You're beautiful," he whispered.

She caught his finger in her hand, then curled onto her side, and he could see the worry gather in her face. He felt a fierce sense of caring. Where did this come from? He placed his forefinger between her eyebrows and held it there until the furrow eased under his touch and her eyelids closed. Having failed to do so once before, this time he was determined to protect her. She drew his fingertip against her lips as though it might stop her from speaking, but it didn't.

"Did you finish your research? Will you come back?"

His heart sank. "I want to." A nonanswer. "Yes, I'll try." That was better, but still . . . She released his finger. He felt her drifting. Then he had an idea.

"Listen," he said, rolling over. "Tell me about those kids hanging out at your place. The Seeds of Resistance."

She gave him a strange look. "How'd you know about them?"

He thought quickly. "I overheard some people talking. At Gringo's."

She nodded. "People around here are always talking. It's hell."

"So who are they?" he asked. "What do they do?"

She shrugged. "They just showed up one day. They drive around and stage demonstrations against genetic engineering. I don't know much about it. Why?"

"I think I've heard about them. They were protesting in Pocatello last week."

"Last week?" She sounded surprised.

"At a potato growers' convention. I was covering it as part of my research." He sat up and rubbed his hands together. "You know, I may have figured out a way of getting back here. This story I'm doing is about the American farming crisis, but maybe I could do a side piece on these kids. Follow them around a little, cover their protests. Genetic engineering is a hot issue. You think they'd be into it?"

It was brilliant. With a legitimate inside contact to a known activist group, he could justify another trip to Duncan, and she could keep tabs on them in the meantime. So many birds with one stone. But she seemed less enthusiastic.

"They'd be into anything to help their cause."

"Great. Do you know if they're planning anything? Another protest or . . ."

"They'd better not be," she said grimly. "That was the deal. They're here to learn about my parents' seed business, and in exchange they help out. I really depend on them." She looked upset. "Are you sure it was them in Pocatello?"

"Well, no," he said. "It could have been some other group of radical environmental activists." How had this happened? He hadn't meant to upset her. He just couldn't seem to help himself. He thought about the Pinkerton and felt a major twinge of guilt. He reached for her hands and changed the subject. "I just want to come back here as soon as I can." His voice sounded wistful and kind of lame.

She looked at him, startled, then laughed.

"What's so funny?"

"You don't mean that," she said.

"Why?"

"You can't. Nobody wants to come back to Liberty Falls."

Relieved, he took a deep breath. "It's not about Liberty Falls. It's about you."

He watched her face cloud over with doubt. "Yummy, I'm not going to apologize again for what happened between us, because it isn't over yet. I've never forgotten you." It felt like the truth. "I don't want to lose you this time."

He watched the frown gather once more in that wide-open space between her brows, but this time he didn't touch it or try to smooth it out. He couldn't protect her from himself, he realized, without giving her up entirely, and although he wasn't sure, he suspected that might have been his big mistake in the first place.

The following day, on the flight out of Pocatello, he watched the relentless geometries of the agricultural landscape recede below. It was beautiful, in a bleak, flattened sort of way. The farmers had been worried about the winds, but that didn't concern him. Weather was an act of God, whose crisis management was outside his jurisdiction. He pulled out his laptop. The report on the Promotions Council was easy, but the rest of the week was looking pretty thin. He wrote up a brief history of the Seeds of Resistance and described the in-depth interrogations of their landlady that took place at the Falls Motel, noting that Ms. Fuller had agreed to supply intelligence regarding the Seeds' movements and activities. He read over the report. It sounded okay, but he realized he was going to have to come up with something better if he wanted to get back to Idaho anytime soon.

hoormunger &

The letter came in the mail a few weeks after Elliot left. It was addressed in crude, childish block letters to THE FULLERS, with no return address. Ocean opened it. She had collected the mail from the box and had asked permission first. Of course I said yes. I thought it was from one of her school friends. I was washing dishes at the sink when she asked,

"What's a hoormunger?"

"What?"

She sounded it out. "That's what it says. Har-lits and hoor-mungers."

Phoenix was looking for milk in the refrigerator. He closed the door and snatched the letter away from her.

"Phoenix, give me that!" I said, grabbing for it with soapy hands, but he twisted away, and, keeping just out of reach, he continued to read. His ears turned dark red. He looked up. There was such hate in his eyes.

"It's for you." He thrust the letter at me, pushing roughly past as he headed out the door. His feet clattered down the porch steps.

I read the letter. *Harlots and Whoremongers, Thus saith the Lord God . . .*

"Let me see it!" Ocean whined. "I want to read it, too."

I ripped it in half and then in half again.

"I wasn't finished!"

"You don't need to see it. It's filth." *Because thy filthiness was poured out and thy nakedness discovered. . . .*

She was furious. She jumped up and down, stamped her feet, then tore out of the house after Phoenix. Poor Ocean. She hated being left out of anything.

There were pockets of air where I thought there had been earth. There were vacuums and sudden inversions. I threw the letter in the garbage, then sat down at the kitchen table. My hands were shaking and felt unclean. I got up to wash them, holding them under the scalding water until the skin turned red and I couldn't stand it anymore. I poured a shot of whiskey to keep from being sick, then fished the bits of letter out of the garbage and went after the kids. Geek, I thought. *I shall bring up a company against thee.* . . .

I cut across the garden to the greenhouse. He was inside working on transplants, but he stopped as soon as I came in.

"Where's Phoenix?"

Geek shook his head. "Not here." He watched me as I scanned the greenhouse, looking into the corners. "No one's here, Yumi. What's wrong?"

I walked over to the potting table and laid out the pieces of the letter on the gritty surface. Geek scanned it quickly.

"The kids read it," I said. "They're freaked out. So am I. *'Stone thee with stones? Thrust thee through with swords? Burn thine houses with fire?'* It's horrible. Who would send something like this?"

"What makes you think it's directed at you?"

" *'And I will cause thee to cease from playing the harlot.* . . .' Who else could it be?"

"Could be someone else. Or no one . . ."

"Phoenix didn't think so. He handed it right to me." My voice tightened. "He's furious. I thought he'd calm down after Elliot left, but this letter just set him off again. Maybe it's someone from Lloyd's church. Someone who knew . . ."

Geek brushed the flecks of dirt from his hands. "What's with you and this guy Elliot?"

"He's an old friend. I knew him when I was a kid. He's a reporter."

"An old boyfriend?"

He'd been standoffish ever since Elliot showed up and I'd stopped hanging out in the greenhouse. I hadn't told him much, but now I sensed he knew more than he was letting on. "Phoenix said something, right?"

Geek didn't answer.

"Well, Phoenix doesn't know everything. Elliot taught history at my school. He was a conscientious objector during the Vietnam War."

Geek choked. "A conscientious objector? You're joking, right?"

"Well, that's what he told us back then. Of course, I didn't know him all that well . . ."

I heard a noise and looked up. Phoenix was standing outside the doorway. Ocean crouched behind him.

"Bullshit," Phoenix muttered, kicking the earth.

I raised my voice. "If you're going to swear at me, Phoenix, speak up."

"Bullshit!" he yelled into the greenhouse. He turned to Geek. "She knew him real well. Five minutes after he got here, he had his tongue down her throat."

"Phoenix," I said, "this is so none of your business."

"Yeah? Well what about Barney?"

"Who's Barney?" Geek asked.

"This guy I was seeing back in Hawaii," I said. "It wasn't serious."

"He's Poo's dad," Phoenix said. "He lives with us."

"He was staying with us. It's temporary."

The look in my son's eye was cool and bitter. "That's what you say about all of our fathers." He gave the dirt one last vicious kick, then gripped Ocean's hand and jerked her away.

"Phoenix!" I followed him to the doorway. "That's not fair!"

They kept going, cutting through the garden, skirting the freshly dug beds. Ocean twisted around to look back, but Phoenix kept tight hold of her, and she had to turn and trot to keep up. Bobbing and stumbling. I didn't go after them. I didn't know what to say. I just stood in the empty doorway.

"Damn." I didn't want to cry, not in front of Geek, but he had come up behind me, and now he saw the tears and touched my face. Specks of soil still clung to his fingers, and I could feel the grit on his fingertips.

"Come here," he said, leading me back inside. He wrapped his arms around me, pressing my head against his chest and stroking my hair. I could feel his heart thump under his rib cage.

"Nothing I do is right," I said. "I try . . ."

"You try," he echoed. "You do your best."

"No," I said. "I knew better. Elliot was always bad news. But I've got such lousy luck with men."

"He's a creep," he agreed. "All men are creeps."

"Yeah," I said, then laughed. "I'm glad you're here."

He didn't reply, which seemed okay at first. We stood there while he kneaded the tension out of my neck, but something was hanging in the thick greenhouse air.

"Yumi," he said finally. "I know this is bad timing. . . ."

I felt my spine stiffen. "What?"

"Well, it's just that we're thinking of heading down to San Francisco for a bit."

I pushed him away. "Why? You promised to stay!"

"It's complicated," he said. "It's just for a little while." His arms hung by his sides. "I think it's better this way."

"Oh, really?" I said, feeling nasty now. "And why is that?"

Geek examined the edge of the potting table. "That letter. It isn't about you. It's about us."

I stared at him, not understanding. "You're the harlot?"

"Actually, I think Lilith is the harlot. I'm more of the whoremonger type. Listen, you better sit down."

I leaned against the potting table, and he started to explain about the Web site and Lilith's acts, how it financed their operations. "It's not pornography, really," he said. "It's really kind of sweet and funny what she does, but I can see how some people might find it offensive. . . ."

I dug around in my pockets for a cigarette. I found a crushed pack and lit up. Geek didn't like me smoking in the greenhouse, but he didn't say anything this time. I took a deep drag and exhaled. Nicotine always provided an answer of sorts. I was calm now, conversational even.

"And you've been running this little peep show from here? From my parents' house?"

"Well, no. I mean we did some taping here, but we were doing the uploads from the public library."

"And you think someone in town found out."

"That's what we figure. We got a couple of these letters, too. The postmarks are all local. We thought it might be a good idea to split for a while and kind of let things cool down."

"So this whole business is about you." I glanced down. There was a flyer sitting on the potting table, some treatise on global seed politics. "I heard about the action you did in Pocatello last week."

He didn't ask me how I knew. He just nodded. "Sorry about that."

"So why San Francisco?"

He paused. Maybe he was trying to decide how much more to tell me. "There's a big protest going down, and a man's going to get pied. We got called on to help."

"Pied?"

"Pie in the face. It's the CEO of a biotech corporation. He's speaking at a forum on the future of the world." Geek took off his glasses and wiped his lenses on his T-shirt. "I know it sounds kind of silly. . . ."

I thought about Elliot. I wondered if he'd be interested in pies.

"They're going to use tofu crème," Geek added.

"Tofu crème?"

"For the pie. You know, tofu? From genetically modified soybeans?"

"Oh." It was ridiculous. Suddenly I was furious. "Well, this is just fucking great! You break all your promises, run a porno racket from our driveway, and get us targeted by some religious freak, and now you split to go throw pies?"

"Yumi, we don't want to get you and the kids involved—"

"We *are* involved! I was counting on you. How the hell am I going to take care of Lloyd and Momoko and the kids, never mind all this?" I looked around at the benches that surrounded us, covered with flats of sprouting seedlings. My anger drained, and now I just felt exhausted.

Geek took a deep breath. "You'll be fine." He removed the cigarette from my hand and stepped on it, then led me toward the flats. The seedlings were organized into families: the Legumes, the Cucurbits, and the Umbelliferae. Some were no more than a green gauzy haze, like algae dusting the earth. Others were more robust, an inch or two in height. "They have to be watched," Geek said. "But Momoko's fine with stuff like this."

"I should have left weeks ago, when I had the chance."

"We'll be back," he said. "After things cool down a little."

I wandered down the row and lingered at the back. I fingered the feathery top of a small Peruvian carrot. "Maybe you better not."

"Okay." He looked crestfallen, standing by a tray of buttercup squash, next to the bitter melons. "Listen," he said. "I'm really sorry. . . ."

"Yeah, well, I'm sorry, too," I said, picking up a flat. The little transplants had their first true leaves. "I'm sorry you had to flake out on me. Are these ready to go?"

Geek nodded.

I looked down at the spindly shoots, grown from Momoko's seed. *Cucurbita pepo*. Warted gourds. I carried them out into the sun to harden.

one damn thing after another 🔊

With Yummy, Cass recalled, it was always something. After Elliot left for D.C., she thought things at the Fullers' might settle down, but then out of the blue the threatening letters started, then the Seeds took off for San Francisco leaving Yummy in charge, and now Cass was beginning to regret ever sending for her in the first place. Life was a lot easier when all she had was Momoko and Lloyd to worry about.

She would be in the office trying to catch up on the bookkeeping or work out a bug in the software, and the phone would ring.

"It's me," Yummy would say breathlessly, like she was the only person in the world and Cass ought to know it. "Do you have a minute? I need your help." Cass could usually hear the baby crying in the background.

"Of course it's never just a minute," she complained to Will. "Whatever Yummy wants winds up taking all day. The worst was the Seeds up and leaving like that. She's hopeless without them."

Will didn't say anything. He was just as glad they were gone. Cass had told him about the Web site, and he didn't approve. Hadn't even wanted to take a look. He was out in the fields when Charmey came to say good-bye, and Cass had asked her about it. They logged on and sat side by side while Charmey scrolled through the site.

"It is the people who write those letters who have evil minds," Charmey said. She pointed to a picture of Lilith, buck naked and cradling a large muskmelon between her legs. "This is not dirty. This is life!"

The pictures were a little silly, Cass thought, but not really offensive. She glanced over at Charmey, who had one hand on the mouse and the other resting on top of her own melonlike belly. She was going to miss the girl, she realized. She'd been looking forward to the birth of the baby.

The next phone call from Yummy came a couple of days later, when Cass was fixing Will's lunch.

"It's me," she said. "Can you take Poo? I have to go into town."

There was an urgency in her tone that made Cass stop what she was doing. "Is it Lloyd?"

"It's Phoenix. He's been arrested. I have to go to the police station. They put him in jail, Cass!" Her voice careened out of control. Poo cried in the background.

"Calm down," Cass said. "Tell me what happened."

"I don't know! It was Billy Odell. He called. He said something about Phoenix pulling a knife on someone at school. He doesn't have a knife, Cass. He couldn't have done that!"

"Get Poo ready," Cass said. "I'll pick you up."

She hung up the phone and turned off the stove. She called Will on the CB. "Do you mind fixing your own lunch? I think I ought to drive her in."

"Why can't she drive herself?" He was in the John Deere. She could hear the powerful engine rumbling in the background behind the crackle of the radio.

"She's pretty upset, and besides, Billy isn't that keen on her."

"Odell? What's he got against her?"

"Trust me, Will. You don't want to know."

The police station was a cinder-block building, halfway between town and the freeway entrance. Phoenix was in a holding cell at the back, but Odell wouldn't open the door. He just kept spinning his keys around his forefinger. Phoenix sat on a bench, his eyes fixed on the wall. He refused to look up when Yummy came in. She was carrying Poo on her hip, and she moved toward the cell in a trance. She stood at the bars and stared at her son.

"Phoenix, are you okay?"

He wouldn't answer. Poo grasped the bars and tried to shake them.

"What's he charged with?" Cass asked Odell.

"Well, carrying a concealed weapon for starters. Assault with a deadly weapon. Attempted murder."

"Murder?" Yummy closed her eyes.

"What deadly weapon?" Cass asked.

Odell reached into a desk and pulled out a plastic bag containing a small paring knife. "He had this strapped to his leg with masking tape."

"It's our kitchen knife," Yummy said. She sounded bewildered.

"Good," said Odell. He turned to Cass. "You witnessed that. The perpetrator's mother positively identified the weapon."

For the first time, Phoenix spoke. "Way to go, *Mommy*." Yummy just stood there clutching Poo, who started to whimper. Cass took him, and Yummy held on to the bars as though she might bend them and step on through, to save her son or to strangle him.

"Billy," Cass said, "what really happened?"

Odell sighed. "He pulled the knife out after school and threatened one of the kids with it."

"But he didn't use it. He didn't actually hurt anyone."

"No, but the principal called us. They're reporting all weapons offenses. You know how it is these days. So far we've been lucky here in Liberty Falls. Haven't had any real trouble. We aim to keep it that way." He glared at Phoenix.

Phoenix's eyes narrowed, and he started to say something, then appeared to change his mind. He slumped back against the wall.

"You can't keep him jail," Yummy said. "He's only fourteen."

Phoenix groaned and made a face.

"There's kids a lot younger than that in jail, believe me," Odell said.

"But nobody's pressed charges, right?" Cass asked.

"No. But they don't want him in school. He's suspended until the end of the year. As for next—"

Yummy broke in. "Don't worry about next year. We'll be gone by then."

Odell cocked his head. "That a promise? If it is, then I'll release him into your custody, but if I so much as catch him spitting, I'll nail him, you hear?" He unlocked the cage. "You hear me, boy?"

Phoenix slipped past him like a small, quick fish.

Out on the street he walked silently between them like a prisoner. He climbed into the backseat of the Suburban, next to Poo's car seat. No one spoke until the car had pulled away from the station. Then Yummy turned around and faced him.

"Okay. Let's have it. What's going on?"

It wasn't a question. Cass glanced in the rearview mirror. Phoenix was staring out the side of the car.

"Same stupid shit," he said. "It's this whole thing they're into. They want to clean up the school—"

"Clean it up how?"

"You know. Get rid of everybody. Niggers, Japs, queers, wetbacks, hippie scum, whatever. Anyway, this one kid brought in a handgun and was showing it around—"

"What!"

"He's a fucker. Said he was going to blow me away."

Yummy shook her head. "Wait a minute. Are you sure it was real?"

"His father's the sheriff, isn't he?"

237

Yummy looked over at Cass.

"It was Odell's boy?" Cass asked.

"Yeah," Phoenix said. "Him and his crew. They're like total paramilitary assholes. They were waiting for me after school and dragged me behind the maintenance shed. They stuck it in my mouth and said they were going to blow my brains out. It was such bullshit."

Cass felt Yummy's hand reaching over to clutch her sleeve. "What happened?"

"Nothing. They just sort of tied me up and left me. They said they were gonna get Ocean and bring her back and do us both, but I got loose and tracked her down. She was fine. After that I just stuck close to her."

"When was this?" Yummy asked. "When did this happen?"

He shrugged. "I don't know. Couple weeks ago. Everything seemed cool, but then you got that letter, so I started carrying the knife, just in case."

"The kids knew about the letter?"

"No. But it sounded like the same old shit they were saying." He paused.

"What?" Yummy said.

Cass could barely hear the boy's voice over the car engine. "How you're a whore," he said. "And me and Ocean and Poo are proof of it."

"Oh," Yummy said. "I see." Then she asked, "What about Ocean? Does she get picked on, too?"

Phoenix shook his head. "The kids in her class pretty much all like her."

"What about these older kids? You think she's safe from them?"

"Yeah," he said, then added, "She's blond."

"Right." Yummy faced front again and stared out the window. Finally she turned to Cass. "What should I do?" she asked. "Should I talk to Odell?"

Cass shook her head. "It's just Phoenix's word."

"But that son of his . . ."

"I'll talk to him. No, I'll get Will to. You should talk to Ocean's teacher. It's only a couple more weeks of school, but have her keep an eye out just in case."

She nodded, then turned back to face Phoenix once more. "Why didn't you tell me about this earlier?" she asked. "When Odell's kid brought the gun in to school?"

"Oh, Yummy," he said. "Figure it out."

"Figure what out?"

"*He* was here. You weren't exactly available."

238

grown-ups 🔊

Cass brought Will back over after dinner that night, and we all sat at the kitchen table and listened to Phoenix's story again. When he was done, Will spoke.

"I believe you, son," he said. "I'll talk to Odell in the morning. You did right by not using that knife, but you should never have felt the need to bring it to school in the first place. The thing to remember is, when you have a problem, you tell a grown-up immediately. Got that? Tell your mother, or me, or Cass. Don't keep it to yourself until it blows up into something like this."

Phoenix nodded. He didn't seem to mind Will's calling him son. He couldn't quite look the older man in the face, but I could tell he wanted to. He couldn't bear to look at me at all.

"Tell your sister, too," Will said. "Make sure she understands."

Phoenix went up to bed, and I followed him, saying I needed to check on Ocean and Poo, but hoping for a word from him. Just one word. I hesitated at the steps leading up to his attic and listened, but there was only silence, as though he'd vanished. It was creepy. I went up after him. He was lying on the small iron bed on top of the covers. His eyes were closed. He was fully dressed. Ready.

"Phoenix?"

He didn't answer.

"Don't you want to get undressed, honey? Get ready for bed?"

He must have heard the fear in my voice, because he looked at me then, and his eyes were dark with a terrible kind of pity.

"Don't worry," he said. "I'm not going anywhere."

I couldn't help it. I knew I shouldn't cry in front of him, that I should be the strong one so he could cry and tell me all about his terrors and pains, but that had never been our relationship. The tears just came, and there was no stopping them.

"I'm sorry, Phoenix," I said. "I'm so sorry."

He nodded like he already knew this. After a while he pulled himself up and made room for me on the mattress. I went over and sat down next to him. He draped an arm around my shoulders, the way you might comfort a pal. "Calm down, Mom," he said with a sigh. "I love you."

239

By the time I got back to the kitchen, Will had left, but Cass was still there, so I brought out the whiskey. I sat down and raised my tumbler.

"Here's to our right to bear arms." I drank, then let my head drop to the table. I rested like that for a bit. Crazy thoughts were running through my mind.

"You okay?" Cass asked.

"We used to smoke behind that maintenance shed, remember?" My hands were shaking. I could see my son kneeling in the knapweed and thistle with a gun muzzle in his mouth. "You know what Will said, about how if Phoenix had a problem he should tell a grown-up? That really got me. Poor kid. He hasn't had many grown-ups around."

"Don't be silly," said Cass. "You're grown up."

"No." I lit a cigarette and got up to find an ashtray. "Will is. He handled that well. He made Phoenix feel safe and looked after."

"He's good with kids," Cass said, shrugging off the compliment, but I could tell she was pleased.

"I've never been able to make them feel safe," I said. "Maybe that's what happens when you run away from home. You get older, but you never grow up." I held out the cigarette to prove my point. "See? I come back to this house, and it's like I'm a teenager again. Smoking. Sneaking out to sleep with Elliot. It's like time just folded and my whole life between then and now never happened."

"How can you say that?" Cass asked, waving her hand in front of her face to dispel the smoke. "For goodness' sake, Yummy. You teach college. You've got three kids. You don't know how lucky you are."

"I dropped out of grad school. I can barely pay for health insurance. If my kids grow up into intact adults, it'll be a miracle."

"Don't be ridiculous. They're growing up just fine."

Thinking about them, I softened, or maybe it was the whiskey. "They are great kids, aren't they? And you'd think it would make Lloyd happy. Three wonderful grandchildren ought to more than make up for one lousy abortion, but no . . ."

"Oh, Yummy," Cass said, exasperated now. "He's put all that behind him."

"Bullshit! He's never forgiven me."

"He's an old man. It's hard for him. Keep your voice down."

"Don't make excuses for him!" I emptied the tumbler and poured another large shot. "It's fine. I haven't forgiven him either. You know what I don't understand? He never wrote to me. All those years. Not once. Momoko wrote. Not a lot, but she wrote, and she sent money when she could. But not Lloyd. You'd think he could have cut me some slack, even if I was a sinner. Wouldn't you, if you had a daughter?"

"I wouldn't know," Cass said, scraping at a speck of food that had hardened onto the tablecloth. "Anyway, it was different for that generation. They didn't have any interpersonal skills. My daddy thought love was something you did with a belt." She stood and went to the sink. "I'm going to make a pot of coffee. You want some?"

"No thanks. I'm fine with this." I tapped the whiskey bottle. "He's a righteous old bastard. Prideful, you know?"

"Uh-huh." Cass measured the grounds into Mr. Coffee's filter. She filled the water reservoir and pushed the button. She turned and leaned against the counter and looked at me. "And you're his daughter."

"What's that supposed to mean?"

"Nothing." The water in Mr. Coffee made a muffled sound that built as it came to a boil. It sounded like an engine approaching from far away.

Cass spoke again. "You know, that's something I never could understand. Why *did* you run away?"

The question took me aback. "You know. You were there. I got knocked up by Elliot. I had the abortion. Lloyd hit me. . . ."

Cass shook her head. "My daddy did worse to me. There were times when I hated him at least as much, but I never left. I just put up with it."

Something she said wasn't right, but I couldn't put my finger on it. "It wasn't only that he hit me. It started way before. It was like I had this wildness inside that was driving me, and I was looking for an excuse. If it hadn't been Elliot, it would have been someone else. Billy Odell . . ." I shuddered and made a horrible face.

Cass smiled. "Too bad. You could have been the sheriff's wife."

"Or whore."

"Don't say that."

"It's the truth. Sex was a big part of it. The wildness that was pushing me. I don't know why." Dark coffee started to trickle into the pot. I heard the words, then corrected myself. "No, that's not true. I do know why. It

241

was a way of getting back at Lloyd. Punishing him, you know? The only way I had."

"But why did you hate him so much?"

"I didn't hate him, Cass. I *loved* him!"

And there it was: the unbearable truth, popping out of my own damn mouth. Slowly, I put it all together. "I ran away because I loved him. I ran away because he used to love me, and then somewhere along the line, when he couldn't control me anymore, he just stopped, you know?" Bewildered, I looked up at Cass. "I couldn't stand that."

I blame the whiskey. Straight whiskey, soaking a desiccated heart until it swelled like an old sponge. The salt and pepper shakers jumped when I pounded the table. Clenched my jaw until it ached, but the tears just kept coming. Again. Twice in a night. What a loser.

"Shhhh . . ." said Cass.

"Oh, God, Cass! I loved him so much. . . ."

fifth

Man alone of all Nature's children thinks of himself as the center about which his world, little or large, revolves, but if he persists in this hallucination he is certain to receive a shock that will waken him or else he will come to grief in the end.

—Luther Burbank, *The Harvest of the Years*

lava ✍

The irrigators walk the earth in summer. Like huge aluminum insects, they inch across the contours of the land, sucking water into their segmented bodies from underground aquifers to rain back onto the desert. Rainbirds, they're called. Robotic and prehistoric, mechanical yet seeming so alive, they span the fields and stretch to the horizon. Emitters, regularly spaced along the length of their bodies, spray a mix of water and chemicals into the air, which catch the light and create row upon row of prismatic iridescence, like an assembly line of rainbows. The spitting hiss of the impulse taps is as incessant as a chorus of cicadas. *Tss, tss, tss*—This is the sound I remember from summer.

If you stoop down and examine the sandy soil, taking up a handful and letting it run through your fingers, you'd wonder why anyone would ever try to grow anything here. The wind sculpts a newly planted field into small, rippled dunes, which the rainbirds pass over, trying to saturate the sand before it all blows away. Bunchgrass and bitterbrush lurk at the edges, waiting to reclaim the land.

They say intense igneous activity occurs in zones of high stress, and believe me, Idaho is one of those. It's a fairly modern landscape, formed by volcanic eruptions occurring as recently as 10 to 20 million years ago, when expanding molten rock squeezed up through crustal fractures, to vent and reconfigure the surface of the earth. Imagine all the infernal popping and spluttering, the oozing and seeping, as the magma welled and the lava flowed! From cones and fissures it spread, filling up the Columbia Plateau, where it pooled, and when the fire left the rock, it hardened into the lava plain that you see today, high and youthful, with rich deposits of volcanic ash that proved to be ideally suited to the growing of potatoes—in particular, the Russet Burbank.

The Burbank is a finicky potato and requires enormous precision on the part of its farmers. It has notoriously poor disease resistance and must be coddled with fertilizers and fungicides and other pharmaceuticals like an overbred poodle. But because of its ability to produce a whopping ten-ounce tuber with excellent fry color, from which the three-inch golden french fry standard evolved, the Burbank quickly became the industry's prima donna of potatoes. And once the industry calibrated itself around the Burbank, no other spud could compete. And that's why, in any Idaho summer, the rainbirds shower their mixtures of water and chemistry onto uniform fields of Luther's progeny. Hissing and spitting. Leaching through the porous volcanic rock back down into the aquifer.

Who says I don't know shit about potatoes?

The summer I was ten, I found a lava tube. I stumbled across it one day when Lloyd had taken me and Cassie with him to a farm auction, just north of Idaho Falls. Nowadays auctions are a depressingly frequent event, and every growing season seems to end with a spate of them as the smaller farms go under, but back then auctions were fun. After the initial carnival excitement of the caller and the crowds wore off, Cass and I began to wander, threading our way among the tractors and balers and pickers and cultivators for sale, toward the perimeter of the farmyard and out into the sage. For a long while we just walked, talking about nothing really, while the caller's voice grew faint, then faded beneath the chirp of the birds and the buzzing hum of the insects. We stood on a slight rise under the baking sun. Way off in the distance we could see the windbreak of poplars surrounding the farmhouse. The in-between air shimmered.

"We ought to go back," Cassie said.

I was kicking at rocks with the toe of my sneaker. "We can be explorers," I said. "Maybe we can find something. Some bones or fossils . . ."

"There's no fossils here."

"Artifacts. From an ancient civilization."

The parched earth crunched beneath our feet. The ground was blackened here, and littered with lava bombs and other erupted materials: smooth, ropy coils of *pahoehoe,* and the rough, shattered, crusty *a'a*—the Hawaiian names that only vulcanologists used, or real estate brokers selling cheap lots on the lava flows of the Big Island. When I was ten, though, rocks were rocks. The ground was the ground.

"Arrowheads," I said. "Fishhooks."

"Are you nuts? There's no fish around here. There's no water anywhere. I'm thirsty. I want to go back."

There were sodas at the auction. Hot dogs and potato salad, too.

"No, Cassandra. We must push on." I was an archaeologist. An adventurer. We were studying these things in school. The stiff sagebrush scratched our shins.

There was a dip in the contour of the ground in front of us. I followed it down, clambering over a pile of boulders, then froze. "Cassie! Come here!"

Cass scrambled down and stood next to me.

"Can you feel it?" It was a coolness, circulating around our ankles.

"It's like a wind or something," Cass said.

"It's not a wind. It's like a refrigerator when you open the door." I dropped to my knees and crawled across the rocks, running my hand over them. "Here!" I pressed my cheek to an opening. "It's coming from here."

A small, dark crack, an orifice, the mouth of the earth. It exhaled cool, damp air. I took hold of a rock and started to pull. "C'mon, Cass. Help me!"

Cass joined, and together we dislodged one so that it rolled out of the way, enlarging the hole.

"Don't put your hand in there!" Cass cried, grabbing me as my arm disappeared inside. There were critters who lived in holes. Bull snakes and rattlers.

"It's a cave!" I pressed my cheek against the rock, up to my armpit in the hole. "I'm sure of it. It opens way up inside."

Cass shivered. "It's creepy."

I withdrew my hand. "Come on," I said, pushing at another rock. "We can move more of these."

We shifted a few more small boulders, and then I wriggled, headfirst, through the crevice. Cass had always been chunky. She couldn't have followed even if she had wanted to. I heard her call out, "Yummy? Are you all right?"

"Either come in or go out," I told her from inside. "You're blocking all the light."

It was cool and humid, even though outside it was the hottest day of the

247

summer. I curled up in a ball, just beyond the reach of the light that streamed in from the opening like a shining pillar. I hugged my knees and pressed against the damp rock. It felt good through my T-shirt. The cave wall smelled delicious. I turned my head and sniffed, then stuck out my tongue and gave it a lick. It tasted metallic and cool. I was pleased. It was important for explorers to be observant.

"Yummy," I heard Cass holler. "Answer me!" Her voice sounded muted from above. Inside I could hear the faint sound of bats, twitching and chattering. I stayed very still. I wasn't scared of the bats, because I knew what they were. Lloyd had showed me a colony hanging in the eaves of our house before he poisoned them.

"If you don't answer me this second, I'm going back!"

She sounded scared, and I knew I should call out and reassure her but I couldn't bring myself to disturb the womblike quiet of the cave. It would be wrong somehow. Plus, I liked the power that not answering gave. I hoped the bats wouldn't start to fly.

The interior of the cave stretched on into darkness, but as my eyes adjusted, I could start to see the shape of the wall, the rubble that lay on the floor, the vaulting arch of the ceiling. Near my feet there was a pile of pale, white, sticklike shapes. I poked at one of them, and it broke free, so I picked it up. It was a bone. A clean bone. From a heap of bones. I wondered if I ought to be scared. It was obviously the remains of a meal—suggesting what? A fox's den? A cougar's lair? But these bones were old and dry, so I decided to relax. I couldn't wait to tell Lloyd I'd found a tomb of sorts. I fingered a jawbone. I pocketed a tooth.

"I'm going back now! I'm going to get your daddy!"

I didn't want him worrying, so I decided to reply, and that's when the bats took off. They spread their leather wings and dropped, a huge black cloud, swooping through the stream of sunlight and out into the day. The light from the hole flickered like crazy as they flew past. I heard Cass scream, muffled and far away. There were still more bats hanging there, twitching and chirring, and I was afraid to climb toward the opening, because it might trigger another flight, and the last thing I wanted was to be swarmed in the narrow passage, so I sat there, shaking, for a long, long time.

When Lloyd finally arrived, pried away a few more rocks, and dropped into the hole, my legs were stiff with terror and cold. He called my name, and fear made his voice sound hollow. Or was it the echo of the cave? I saw the beam of his flashlight playing wildly across the stone walls, and I tried to answer—*Daddy*—but my voice shriveled. Still, he located me in the dark with the radar of a father, as sure and keen as any bat's, and he crouched down, took me in his arms, and held me away from the cold rock until I thawed against the heat of his chest. His heart was pounding hard and strong. He didn't raise his voice or say a word. Just held me while I shivered. After a while I pointed to the bones.

"Something got eaten." My voice came out in a whisper.

"Looks that way," he whispered back. "Little bones. A fox maybe. Or a rabbit. Happened some time ago."

"That's what I thought, too," I said, my voice stronger now as I bragged a little. "That's why I wasn't scared."

"Good for you," he said. He turned the beam of his flashlight into the darkness. "It's a fine cave you've discovered. A lava tube, and a mighty big one. Want to go a bit farther in?"

With Lloyd by my side I was afraid of nothing! I jumped to my feet and walked behind him, clutching his hand. We followed the beam of light as it danced across the wet rock walls, pausing to examine a stalactite that hung from the knobby ceiling. The tube went on and on, but eventually he turned back. Secretly I was glad.

"I guess we've seen enough for today," he said.

I nodded and followed him around the twists and bends, toward the small opening of light.

squash patch ✏

The words of the Proverbs ran through his mind: *It is better to dwell in the corner of the housetop, than with a brawling woman, and in a wide house.* But the house was not wide enough, Lloyd thought, and Yumi's vexation ran through it like the persistent hum of an out-of-kilter appliance. It was there in the slam of the cupboard and the clatter of cookware baking sheets and mixing bowls, pots and—

"Where is that damn pan?"

"Which damn pan, Mom?"

"The damn no-stick frying pan."

"The damn no-stick frying pan is in the cupboard under the counter."

"What's it doing there?"

"That's its home. That's where it lives."

"Don't be cute, Phoenix."

"I'm not cute, Yummy. I'm never cute."

Lloyd looked toward the window, trying to judge the condition of the day by the light that leaked in past the drawn shade. Mornings used to be a peaceful time, and breakfasts were delicious when the French girl was cooking. Melvin would come in quietly and raise the shades, then take him to the bathroom, where they'd change the bag and have a sponge bath, while that girlfriend of his tidied up the bedroom so that the bed would be nice and fresh, ready for Lloyd to crawl back into and have some of that good breakfast.

Now the days started with commotion.

"What are you making?" he heard the boy say.

"Eggs."

The girl piped up. "Grandpa's not supposed to have eggs. It's too much cholesti . . . you know."

"Cholesterol. He can have an egg now and then. Where's the butter?"

"You shouldn't fry it. He's not supposed to have fried foods."

"For God's sake, Ocean. Just shut up and eat your granola. Where's the salt?"

"Grandpa's not supposed to have salt. He's on a low-sodium diet."

"Shit! Now you tell me?"

The boy had gotten into trouble at school and had to stay home. He spent all of his time in front of the television set playing some infernal game his mother had bought him to keep him amused. Lloyd sat in his chair in the living room and watched, but the whole thing moved too darn fast to get a fix on. His heart leaped at the sudden noises, and all the flashes and careening made his stomach upset and gave him a headache. At least the girl knew how to play by herself out of doors. She had joined the 4-H and was raising a chick, which followed her around even into the garden. When the damn bird started eating the pea sprouts, Momoko chased it out with a rake.

The problem was, their mother just couldn't handle things. The house was a mess. She could hardly get three meals on the table in a day. Often Cass Quinn would come over with a casserole, and the two of them talked and smoked cigarettes at the kitchen table. He could smell it from upstairs. Occasionally late at night, he could hear her on the phone. She kept her voice low, but sometimes she'd laugh, and the sound always startled him. He wondered who she could be talking to at that hour. Couldn't be anyone in Liberty Falls—people here had to work and didn't stay up late. It had to be long distance, and he fretted about the phone bill. He felt sorry for her, sorry to be such a nuisance, sorry to have disrupted her nice life in Hawaii. He felt sorry for everyone. He wished he could just hurry up and get well so she could leave, but with Melvin gone, the past few weeks had been trying, and he felt weaker than ever.

He heard her harried footsteps coming up the stairs. She kicked the door open with her heel and backed into the room, carrying a tray with a plate and a glass of milk.

She looked around the cluttered room. "Now, where am I going to put this?" Lloyd struggled to sit up in bed. She put the tray on the chair. She had her coat on, ready to leave.

"I . . ." He paused, unable to go on.

"What?" She pushed the button to raise the back of the bed. "Dad, what is it? Is it your bag?"

He shook his head. "The bag is fine."

She shoved the pillow down behind him and deposited the tray on his lap. "Good. I'll help you change it when I get back. I have to take Ocean to school. She missed the damn bus again."

"Wait, I . . . I have to urinate."

"Oh, Dad! Why didn't you tell me before I got you settled?"

She removed the tray. He swung his legs over the edge of the bed until they touched the floor. He tried to push himself up to a standing position, but he couldn't shift his weight off the bed.

"I need help," he said.

"But you could do it yesterday! Here, take your walker."

"It'll be quicker if you help."

Together they inched down the corridor. Her fingers clenched his arm so hard he thought the bones there would snap. When she released him, he closed the bathroom door behind him, but he could feel her fretting outside. He unbuttoned his pajama bottoms and let them drop. He sat down on the toilet like a woman, hanging his head and covering his face with his hands.

"Yumi," he said through his fingers.

"You ready to come out?"

"No." He took a deep breath. "Bring my walker. Leave it outside the door. I'll get myself back to bed."

It took all his strength just to talk. He could get the boy to help. If worse came to worst, he could sit there on the toilet until she got back.

"You sure?" He could hear the relief in her voice as she headed down the corridor toward the bedroom and then came back again. "Okay, the walker's right here. Eat your breakfast before it gets cold. I'm going into town for groceries after I drop Ocean off. I'll be back in a couple of hours. I'll help you with the bag then."

"Yumi . . ."

"What?"

"Is the boy going with you?"

"His name is Phoenix, Dad. Yes. I promised him a new videogame."

"Oh."

She hesitated. "You going to be okay?"

"Yes . . . Yumi?"

"What?"

"I'd like to go to the garden. . . ."

"Oh, Dad!" she said as if he'd asked to go to the moon. "You'll have to wait until I get back. Or phone Cass. Maybe she or Will can come over and help you."

He listened to her clatter down the stairs yelling to the kids. When the car pulled out of the drive and the noise of the tires on the gravel grew faint, he started to urinate. Somehow he made it back to his bedroom.

The plate of eggs was sitting on the small bedside table. They were hard as rubber, swimming in congealing butter. He bounced the back of his spoon on the yolk. He drank the milk and wished he had another glassful.

He managed to change into his clothes. His bag was almost full, but it would have to wait. He knew better than to try to change it on his own. He put his shirt on carefully over it.

He used his walker to get as far as the window. Outside he could see Momoko, kneeling in the dirt, roguing a bed of transplants. He couldn't see what she was working on, though. Lettuces probably. It was high time for lettuces. He knocked on the windowpane with his knuckle, then tried to open it. The sash was stuck, the wood swollen. He gave another rap. She was bending over, inspecting the plants, pulling out the off-type shoots. Finally she looked up. He waved, and she waved back, then returned to her culling. The broad brim of her straw hat covered her face.

He rapped the glass again, harder this time, and when she looked up, he waved his arms wildly. *Come here! Come up!* She put down her trowel and got to her feet. He met her at the top of the stairs.

He made her stand behind him on the landing.

"Look!" he said as he held on to the banister and pushed the aluminum walker over the edge. They watched it clatter down the stairs, tumbling to the bottom, where it came to a stop with its feet in the air. Momoko clapped her hands. Certain kinds of chaos thrilled her. Lloyd sat on the top step.

"Now, you come down after me. Hold on tight in case I slip."

She sat on the step above him and gripped the frayed collar of his coat with both hands, like she was trying to rein in a mule. Holding on to the balusters, he inched himself forward to the edge of the step and then over, down to the next, landing hard on his hindquarters each time. Step by step. Stopping to rest.

"How you get so old?" he heard her whisper when they hit the bottom. He looked up.

"I don't know, Momo," he said, but his answer seemed to confuse her.

"No," she said, shaking him by the collar. "How you get so old?"

He smiled. "Well, how'd you get so pretty?"

She chuckled. She righted his walker and helped him to his feet. He followed her slowly out the back door and into the garden.

He was sitting on a bench by the peach tree, in a small patch of sunlight, when the Pontiac pulled up the drive. He heard the car door slam, and then the trunk. He stood up. He wanted to tell Yumi where he was, to show her what he'd accomplished with Momoko's help, but mainly he didn't want her to be mad. He took a few steps, then realized he was starting to sweat. He took the pillbox from his coat pocket and shook a nitroglycerin tablet from it. His fingers were trembling. The little white pill fell onto the dark earth. It lay there like a seed.

He turned and looked for Momoko. He thought he saw her hat among

253

the snap-pea vines on the opposite side of the garden, but he couldn't be sure. He squared off his walker and started toward the house. He could make it, if he just took it slow. But the next minute he felt the rubber-tipped aluminum legs sink into the soil, pitching him forward off the garden path and into the squashes. He lay there. The smell of the soil tickled his nose and felt cool against his forehead. It was his soil, built up carefully with generous rotations of nitrogen-fixing crops, year after year. Recycling nutrients. Never taking out more than you gave back. So different from the way they farmed potatoes now. This soil still had life, Lloyd thought, and with his face down in it, he took a handful in his fist and squeezed it tight and waited for his daughter to find him.

⨍

"It was the bats, Dad."

He opened his eyes.

"When you found me in the lava tube, remember? I was afraid of the bats."

She hadn't said a word when she discovered him in the squash patch, just helped him to his feet and back upstairs, and now he was sitting on the edge of his bed holding up his shirt while the angry nub of his stoma dried. She was standing by the window looking out at the fields, and she smiled. "You never asked, and I was grateful."

He smiled, too. "You were mighty scared, all right. Shaking like a leaf."

"Then we went inside, remember?"

"Saw that big old stalactite. That was quite some cavern. Went on for about three miles."

"Someone explored the whole thing?"

"The farmer who was selling off his farm that day, he realized that old tube was on his property, so he held on to that bit and developed it into one of those roadside attractions. Opened it that same summer when the crazy fellow tried to jump over the canyon on his motorcycle. Made a bundle off all the thrill seekers who came to watch."

"You're kidding?"

"Nope. Turned it into their retirement plan." Lloyd raised his eyebrow. "Guess they owe you."

"I had a talent for real estate even back then, huh?"

For a moment he just nodded, but in the end he couldn't let it pass. He shook his head. "Can't say I hold much store with real estate developers," he said. "Buying up all the good farmland, turning it into malls and parking lots. Next crookedest thing to lawyers, if you ask me."

But she hadn't asked, and now she turned her back on him and stared out the window while he waited, wishing he'd kept quiet after all.

"I think it's dry enough," he said finally. "Let's finish up."

She came back over and squatted in front of him, lining up the new flange around the stoma. She applied the adhesive and pressed it to his skin. She was wearing latex gloves, and when he looked down, he realized that her hands were trembling. Her head was bent, and she wouldn't look at him.

"How come we never talk about what happened?" she asked.

"What happened when?"

"When I left. When I ran away."

He held his breath as she eased the new bag onto the flange, working from bottom to top. When she was done and the bag was in place, he breathed again.

"Oh, Yumi," he said, "I just don't recall. It was so long ago." He gave the bag a tug, to make sure it was on tight and wouldn't slip off. "Where's Melvin anyway? When are they coming back?"

She peeled off the latex gloves with a snap and dropped them in the trash. "They're not coming back," she said. "You're stuck with me."

frisco &

Frisco was fucking awesome.

Frank had never seen anything like it. They crashed at an anarchist house in Oakland, a bad-ass scene with people cruising by and hanging out in the kitchen and camping on the floor. The Seeds knew everyone, and all these people were their friends. Frank was wary at first—he knew about group homes—but within minutes he felt welcome.

He was happy to be away from the fucking farm and hungry to check out the skate scene in the city, but just as he was about to take off, Geek handed him a spade and a garbage bag full of composted manure, and the next thing he knew, he was toting the shovel and the shit and a five-foot peach sapling through the dusky streets of Oakland. He followed the crew, dressed all in black, to a median strip in the middle of a busy road. They scoped the area for signs of the Man, and then the leader gave the word to dig. Frankie had gotten pretty good at digging and generally hated it, but this was different. Here, in the twilight, under the streetlights, with traffic moving by him in both directions, it was exciting. Quickly he broke the sod in a neat circle and excavated a three-foot hole, then gently lowered his peach tree into the center. He filled in the hole with soil and the compost he'd been packing, tamped it down, and mulched it. The leader looked at his work and nodded. "Right on, dude. You know your shit."

Down the strip the rest of the crew was planting other trees: a pear, a persimmon, some nut trees, and a couple of figs. In a few years they'd be bearing fruit. Food for the people, the leader explained. They were liberating traffic strips and other public land sites across the city. As long as they were neat, the city workers never noticed. Mostly they just mowed right around the trees.

When the eight saplings were planted, the crew shouldered their shovels, and the timing was unreal, because a moment later the automated irrigation system on the median strip kicked in, and it was like a welcome-to-the-neighborhood party for the new transplants. The crew high-fived, then slipped into the shadows.

"We're hacking the landscape, dude," they told Frankie. "Bringing back the commons. We are politically opposed to lawns."

They had torn up the lawn in front of their house and planted a vegetable garden. They kept bees in the backyard. They reclaimed straw bales from the racetrack to use as mulch and ran bicycle posses across the city to tend the vegetable gardens they'd planted in the yards of elderly neighbors.

They did puppet shows for kids. Planted butterfly gardens.

They hacked the plumbing of the house, rerouting the runoff from the showers and the sink into filtration ponds in the garden. They grew water lilies and bulrushes. Willows and water chestnuts. They wanted to farm edible catfish one of these days, but for now they were raising huge ornamental carp for the Chinese market.

Golden Luckies.

Two-toned Prosperities.

They made seed bombs to lob over barbed-wire fences onto the tightly

256

cropped lawns of military installations and corporate headquarters. Packed with the seeds of native flowers, the bombs would take root and grow. Little clumps of vegetative anarchy.

This was agriculture that Frankie could get his head around. Guerrilla gardening. Defiance farming. Radical acts of cultivation. "Dudes," Frankie said, pacing up and down the Spudnik one night, "this shit is awesome! How come you're not part of this scene?"

Y smiled. "We are. We started this house."

Frankie stopped short. "So how come you left, then?"

"Time to move on," Geek said, rubbing his glasses. "We're a network of cells, Frankie. We're part of the underground. There are houses like this in cities and towns all across the country. The Spudnik's one of the links, keeping people connected, you know? Keeping information and energy flowing, but most of all working on outreach. It's all about dissemination, Frankie."

"Dissemination?"

"We're like a seed bomb, dude."

∞

It wasn't Geek who threw the tofu crème pie at the CEO of Cynaco. Geek and Y both had police records, having been busted on a number of occasions for disorderly conduct, demonstrating without a permit, and various degrees of assault. It was more trouble than it was worth, getting them out of jail in Frisco, so they'd retired and now just ran backup.

"I propose the honor go to Frankie," said Geek. "He's from out of town, and he's got a clean record here. Plus he's still a juvenile."

The commander in charge of the pie operation looked skeptical. "He's a novice," she pointed out. "You think he's experienced enough to pull it off?"

"Totally," said Y. "He's cool and fearless. We've done some gnarly actions with him before."

They were sitting in the kitchen of the Oakland house. The commander was cutting butter into a large bowl of pastry crust. She pushed the hair off her forehead with the back of her hand, leaving behind a dusting of flour on her eyebrow. Next to her, Charmey was mashing silken tofu.

"Et tu, Charmey?" the commander asked. "Qu'est-ce que tu penses? Il est très jeune, n'est-ce pas?"

257

"Oui, d'accord," Charmey said. "He is young maybe, but his timing is *superbe.*"

So Frankie was elected to be one of three pie bearers, each belonging to a faction of the Pastry Platoon, which was a detachment of Operation Dessert Storm, launched by the International Food Liberation Army. On the day of the action he was dressed in the bottom half of Mr. Potato Head's heavy burlap costume, hiding behind a large potted palm in the hotel lobby. The top half of Mr. Potato Head was on the floor by his feet. Charmey and Lilith, acting as field agents, were standing by with a walkie-talkie, the pies, and Frankie's skateboard.

The walkie-talkie crackled out the intelligence from the commander: The keynote had ended; the target was on the move. Charmey stepped forward to initiate the action. She was dressed in pink maternity clothes and was pushing a baby stroller, all of which they'd bought at the Salvation Army earlier that week. In the stroller was a backup pie. She headed in a wide arc around the perimeter of the lobby, circling the oncoming CEO, who was crossing the marble foyer surrounded by his posse of bodyguards and underlings.

A flanking guard of hecklers, mingling with journalists and the press, closed in from the direction of the elevators. The hecklers initiated destabilization tactics.

"Sir! How do you justify your claims that genetically altered crops do not need labels because they are safe, when there's no research or evidence to support this?"

"Could you comment on the revolving-door relationship between Cynaco and the FDA, and the fact that so many of your former lobbyists have ended up in key positions in government regulatory agencies?"

"Is it Cynaco's long-term policy to mine Third World genetic resources, engage in globalized biopiracy, and rob developing countries of their ability to produce food independently and sustainably?"

The walkie-talkie crackled again. Lilith dropped the skateboard and helped Frankie flip on the top half of Mr. Potato Head and fasten it down with Velcro. Mr. Potato Head had undergone some further modifications since the Pocatello action: He now had two bolts stuck in his neck and a badly stitched scar on his forehead. Lilith adjusted his tin skullcap and looked at her handiwork with satisfaction.

"Break a leg," she whispered, and handed Frankie the pie.

His legs felt strangely naked in the green tights, but his feet were sure on the board. The marble under his wheels was as smooth as glass, and he pushed off and started to fly. He crouched low and headed straight for Charmey, who was facing him now, having rounded the target to make her approach from the opposite side. When she looked up and saw Frankie coming, she clutched her bulging stomach and let out a piercing cry.

"Ooooooh! *Mon bébé!* He is coming!"

Slowly she sank to the ground.

All heads turned toward her and away from Frankie. As the crowd swayed closer to check her out, a gap opened up, and he took it. He sailed in, staying low and light on his board, ducking and weaving. By the time the CEO saw him coming, Mr. Potato Head had achieved what was later judged to be perfect pie proximity. Frankie drew back his arm and let the pie fly. It achieved maximum impact, neither too high nor too low, hitting the CEO smack on the nose. The consistency of the tofu crème achieved maximum coverage, too, being neither too thick nor too runny. A volley of backup pies from splinter factions started to fly, including Charmey's, just before security closed in and rounded them up, hustling them quickly from the lobby.

Outside on the street a lively demonstration was under way. A parade of mutant vegetables was dancing up and down the sidewalk. Copies of a recent exposé on Cynaco, published in Britain, were being distributed.

From sympathizer copy shops and Internet cafés throughout the city, the commander and her staff faxed and e-mailed press releases out to the international wire services and local networks. When their photographers straggled in, digital images and video clips were uploaded and disseminated, too.

A lawyer was standing by to meet Frankie and the other field agents at the police station. They were charged with misdemeanor battery, but Geek showed up with bail, so they were released and told to appear in court the following week. It was a major party scene when they reconvened that evening at the house, and Frankie was hailed as a conquering hero.

"Way to go, man!"

"Did you see the look on the dude's face?"

"Couldn't, dude. There was too much fucking pie on it!"

"What an arm!"

Geek was online, monitoring the congratulatory e-mail and the updates on press coverage that were coming in from all over the world. The commander was reading over his shoulder.

"The Brits were planning to pie him next week in London," she yelled. "We got him first this time!"

"They're getting us major coverage in the London dailies!"

"Hey! We scored a back page in New Delhi!"

Clippings from the evening papers had been blown up to poster size and hung up on the wall. TV monitors and VCRs were stacked in a corner, taping the news coverage from the networks and cable stations. The Future of the World Forum had been a well-covered event, and who can resist a pie in the face? It was pure eye candy.

"*Tu est magnifique*, Frankie," Charmey whispered that night when they finally returned to the Spudnik and crawled into their blankets.

Frankie was thoroughly jazzed, and he just couldn't come down. "This is *it!*" he said, punching the pillow. "I can't explain it, but I know. This is the kind of shit I gotta do. I was born for it."

Charmey curled up against him and yawned. He draped his arm over her belly and let it hang there, absently rubbing, as he went over the day in his mind. Sometimes when he skated, when his feet hit the board and the wheels started to spin, there'd be this moment when time would stop and the world stopped with it—all movement, all sound—and he'd be the only one, soaring alone through the silence. Everything would be so clear and beautiful he just wanted to howl. That was what it had felt like as he floated across that hotel lobby, only even more intense. He sighed. It was good to find your passion.

When Geek and Y told him they were heading back to Liberty Falls, Frankie went ballistic. Geek worked to reassure him. "Don't worry, little brother. We're planning something big."

pied ✌

In the thick, humid days of an early D.C. summer, Elliot missed the dry air of Idaho, even in the air-conditioned comfort of his office.

"So fuck D.C.," Jillie said, loosening his tie. "Fuck PR! Go farm potatoes."

She looked at him critically. "You're such a hick, Elliot. I can see you being quite good at it."

"A propensity for potatoes?" he suggested, weighing her breast.

"A talent for tubers," she rejoined, dropping her hand to his crotch. "A soft spot for spuds."

But his heart wasn't in it. He'd lost his sparkle, the keen edge of his enthusiasm for her, which, sadly, seemed only to sharpen Jillie's appetite for him. Ever polite, he never failed to rally, but even as he slipped his hands down the small of her back and around the curve of her buttocks, lifting her onto his desk, he was aware of a thinness to their interaction. Together they had a slick veneer. What they lacked was history. So when his phone rang just as he was leaning her back onto his blotter and parting her legs, he hesitated first, but he reached across the desk and picked it up.

"Pied?" he said.

He stepped back and studied Jillie's scowling face as he listened, then sat down heavily in his chair and started to swivel. She leaned on her elbows and watched him go 'round and 'round. He hung up and groaned.

"Who was it?" Jillie asked.

He raised his face from his hands. "A guy dressed like Mr. Potato Head threw a pie at the CEO of Cynaco."

"Ah, yes. Pied."

He dropped his hands and stared at her. "You *knew* about this?"

"Actually," she said, sitting all the way up now, "I had heard, yes. They sent out quite a detailed press release."

"You *heard* and you didn't tell me?"

"I figured you already knew."

"I didn't. Why should I know?"

"Maybe because it's your job? I thought Mr. Potato Head was your beat. Those kids you were tracking. The Seeds of Resistance . . ."

"They're in Idaho," he said. "Besides, they don't pie. Unless of course it's an alliance. With that other group, you know, the corporate crime police."

"The ones who pied Bill Gates."

"Yeah." He looked over at her, reclining splay-legged on his desk. "Wait a minute. Wurtz isn't running this story, is he?"

"Well, yes."

"And you're writing it?"

"Mmm."

"Why didn't you *tell* me?"

"I thought we could have sex *first* and *then* talk about it."

He groaned and covered his face again. "I can't, Jillie. My heart's not in it."

"Since when has your heart had anything to do with it?"

When she didn't get an answer, she brought her legs together and tugged down her skirt.

"So," she said, trying again, "I gather they nailed their target?"

"Smack in the face," he said through his hands. His voice was muffled.

"Tofu crème, huh?"

He just continued to swivel.

"Well," she said, hopping off the desk, "this conversation certainly isn't going anywhere. I'm going to get something to eat." She grabbed her purse and paused at the door. "Maybe you *should* consider potato farming, Elliot," she said. "Because you're kind of losing what it takes for a career in public relations."

He sat there peering at her through his spread fingers, watching the way her tight butt twitched as she walked away. You're telling me, he thought, and then he groaned. Duncan was going to kill him if it came out in the press that the Seeds of Resistance had anything to do with this.

"Jillie!" he called, jumping up. He needed to ask her what was in her story, but the only response he got was the computerized voice of the elevator as the doors closed behind her: "Going down."

Elliot went back to his office and picked up the phone. Duncan was away on a spiritual retreat in New Mexico, which bought him a little time. He couldn't do anything to kill the story, but at least he could find out why the fuck he hadn't been informed. He dialèd the Pinkerton's number. Rodney picked up. He sounded quite miffed at Elliot's question.

"Sure I knew they'd taken off," he said.

"You were supposed to be watching them! What happened?"

There was a long silence. When Rodney finally spoke, his voice sounded distant. "Word got out about that pornography Web site of theirs. Folks here don't think much of that kind of thing, if you know what I mean, and let 'em know. They left town shortly after."

"I specifically said *not* to run them out of town. Why didn't you tell me they were going to San Francisco?"

"Well, now, Mr. Rhodes, I didn't know where they were going, did I? Besides, San Francisco is outside of my jurisdiction."

Elliot hung up, then dialed again. "Can I talk to your mom?" he said.

"Yummy!" he heard Ocean cry. "It's for you. It's the man in the suit. The one from the nation's capital."

Yummy picked up an extension and yelled at her daughter to hang up, but Ocean had wandered off. Elliot could hear her singing her song in the background. "Going to the garden to eat worms, yum, yum, yum. . . ."

"Why didn't you tell me the Seeds had left?" he asked. "Did you know about this action in San Francisco?"

"You mean the one with the pies?"

Apparently everyone had known about this except him. "Why didn't you tell me?"

"I thought you wanted to know what they were doing here. In Idaho. So that you could come back and see me. I thought that was the point."

"It was. It is. But I'll need more than just that for an article, you know."

"Oh. Well, I didn't think you'd be interested in pies. It seemed silly."

"Pies are never silly."

"They're not?"

"No. I mean, yes. Silly is what makes them so insidious. Pies are like stealth bombs on the battleground of public opinion. Media Molotov cocktails that can home in on a CEO and do more damage to that corporation's image in one televised instant than half a dozen articles in the *Times*."

"Oh." She didn't sound at all impressed.

"It's terrorism," he said. "It's assault and battery. It's breaking the law."

"Elliot, whose side are you on, anyway?"

"I'm not on anyone's side. I'm a journalist. I'm impartial."

"Well, I'm sorry. Things got a little out of control here after you left, and they split, but now they want to come back. They just called from San Francisco. They have some crazy idea they want Lloyd's help with. I don't know . . ."

Elliot sat up. "That's good," he said, leaning forward. "You need their help, too, right? It's too much for you to handle alone. Do you know when they'll be coming back?"

There was a long silence on the other end of the phone. "I was going to tell them to forget it," she said. "I don't trust them."

263

He sat back and swiveled around in his chair. He took a deep breath. "Sure," he said. "I can see that." He paused. "Too bad, though. I'd like to hear what they're up to. It might be interesting, and of course it would be great to see you. . . ."

terminator 🐍

On the morning of the Seeds' return, I woke to the smell of baking muffins and the sound of Charmey in the kitchen.

"—mostly fried," Ocean was telling her. "In butter."

I sat up in bed. From the bathroom I heard the sound of water running. I got up and stood outside the closed door. The sweet, humid smell of steam and bath soap wafted from under the door. "Oh . . ." I heard Lloyd sigh. "That feels real good. Haven't had a proper bath since you left."

"Well, you just lie back and enjoy while I go help Lilith change your sheets."

"Melvin?"

"Yes, sir?"

"Don't you go running off like that again, you hear?"

"I'll try not to, sir."

I made it back to my bedroom before Melvin saw me in the hall. I turned up the volume on the baby monitor, and from Lloyd's bedroom I heard Lilith whispering, "This place is a *mess*. . . ."

I went to the window and looked out. Below me was the graceless shape of the Spudnik. Beyond, in the garden, Geek was following Momoko down the rows, nodding as she pointed to the beanstalks climbing vigorously up their poles toward the sky. I had meant to spend more time with her, maybe help her weed a little, but I hadn't gotten around to it.

The Spudnik door slammed and Phoenix came tearing out, wearing a T-shirt I'd never seen before. I heard him take the porch steps in twos.

"Hey!" he yelled. "Look what Frankie got me in Frisco!"

"What's Thrasher?" Ocean asked.

"Skate 'zine. Totally rad."

I heard the oven door open, then close. "Oh, wow! Awesome muffins!"

I sat on the edge of the bed trying to decide whether I felt hurt or relieved. Then I heard my son say proudly, through a mouthful of muffin, "Hey, Char, guess what? I was just telling Frankie. After you guys left? I got arrested and put in the slammer!"

I lay back down and pulled up the covers.

ℬ⌇

A week or so later they called a council meeting on the porch. Melvin helped Lloyd into an old rocking chair, and Momoko sat beside him. It was a warm summer evening. Sprinklers dotted the lawn, and the rainbirds spanned the green fields of potatoes and wheat, as far as the eye could see, pumping pixels of water into the air. A fine spray hung over the earth, catching the last deep angles of light.

Carefully, Geek prepared us. He outlined the political and social agenda of the Seeds. He gave a brief recap of the hazards of biotech, then he explained the idea behind the Fourth of July action.

"We envision something like the Boston Tea Party," he said. "They threw tea into Boston Harbor to protest taxation without representation. We're digging up potatoes to protest genetic engineering without our consent. It'll be an educational event, like a teach-in, to wake people up to the magnitude of this hazardous corporate agenda that is being implemented behind our backs. We'll call it the Idaho Potato Party."

"Cool," Phoenix said, "I'll help."

"Wait a minute," I said. "Whose potatoes, exactly, are you planning to dig up?"

"Well, that's still to be decided," Geek said. "We've closed the Garden of Earthly Delights part of the Web site, by the way . . ."

"Good."

". . . and we're planning to open a Potato Party site with real-time links, so that people can participate online."

Lloyd broke in. "What do you want from us?"

"We were hoping you'd support the idea, sir," Geek said. "Enough to let us hold the event here on your property."

"*Here!*"

Geek ignored me and continued to address Lloyd. "It's the perfect place. A small, family-run seed operation. We thought maybe you and Momoko could teach people about seed-saving techniques. . . ."

Lloyd frowned. "We tell folks about our seeds all the time. They see the

265

sign on the roadside and drive right on in. Get a lot of new customers that way. And as for that other stuff, I've made my opinions about big corporations known in this community and never needed a party to do so. A lot of the spud farmers think I'm nuts, but a lot of them don't, I'll tell you."

"Excellent! You can be a spokesperson."

"Can't say I'm much of a speaker," Lloyd said, but his eyes were glittering, and he rocked a little faster. "What would I have to say?"

"Well, you could talk about the butterflies for starters."

"Butterflies?" Lloyd looked bewildered. "Well, we have a nice assortment of seeds for starting a butterfly garden. Buddleias and—"

"Actually, I was thinking about this," Geek said. He had a folder in front of him, and now he took out a news clipping. "This is from the *New York Times.* 'Pollen From Genetically Altered Corn Threatens Monarch Butterfly.'"

Geek handed the article to Lloyd. Lloyd squinted and rubbed his eyes. He was on a new medication that blurred his vision and made his thinking foggy, but slowly, as he read, the meaning penetrated. "Oh, no!" he said. "Not the *butterflies!*"

Geek pulled out another clipping. "Here's one about the new Terminator technologies."

"Terminator?" Lloyd shook his head.

"It's like a death gene, sir. A self-destruct mechanism. They splice it into the DNA of a plant and trigger it. The plant kills its own embryo."

"But that's madness! Why on earth . . . ?"

"To protect the corporation's intellectual property rights over the plant. To keep farmers from saving and replanting seeds. To force them to buy new seed every year."

"But to develop a trait like that? On purpose?"

Geek nodded. "Crosses the line between genius and insanity. Think what could happen if that gene escapes."

Lloyd closed his eyes. I watched him with a growing sense of foreboding. His elbows were braced against the chair arms, and now he laced his fingers and let his forehead drop to his hands as though praying. For a while the only sounds we could hear were the creak of Lloyd's rocker and the hissing of the sprinkler jets. Then Lloyd spoke.

"Not a lot of time before the Fourth," he said. "What do you need from us?"

"You're not actually going along with this?" I said.

"Damn right I am. Never heard of anything more frightening in my life."

It was like popping a cork. "A party!" Ocean yelled. "We're having a party!"

Lilith ran over to Lloyd and hugged him. Phoenix held up his palm to high-five his grandfather, who fumbled, then shook it instead. Momoko started clapping, although she didn't seem to know what for.

I couldn't believe it. "This is insane! You don't know what you're getting into, Dad. We can't have lots of people swarming all over the place. You're supposed to be getting rest."

"I get plenty of rest. Now is the time to act, right Momoko?"

Momoko blinked, then nodded.

I turned on Geek. "You've brainwashed my father! You're turning him into a goddamned poster boy for your politics—"

"He's doing no such thing," Lloyd said. "This is not about politics. This is about life!"

My face was burning. "Oh, for God's sake, Dad. It's just plants."

Geek said, "Plants have a right to life, too."

And then I lost it. I looked at Geek, and then at Lloyd, and then back again. The two of them—the young radical environmentalist and the old fundamentalist farmer—made a ridiculous alliance, and I started to laugh. "Oh, wow! That's the kind of pro-life bullshit that drove me out of here in the first place!"

Lloyd brought his fist down on the arm of the chair. "A *life* is a *life!*" he said. His eyes were bloodshot, and he could barely choke out the words. "It is God's gift! How can you be so careless?"

It wasn't funny any longer. You can't argue with fanatics. I turned and walked away. Certainly no one thought to stop me. I felt them watching as I crossed the yard.

"Oh, buggah," I heard Phoenix whisper to his sister. "She's plenty *huhu* now!"

A full moon was rising over the barn, still low in the sky and so bright it stretched my shadow out long. I walked to the end of the dirt road where the cluster of mailboxes stood, silhouetted in the moonlight like crooked sentries guarding the adjacent potato field. I sat on a rock nearby and smoked a cigarette, watching the smoke dissipate into the silvery air.

After a while I heard footsteps behind me, but I didn't turn around. Then I heard Geek's voice. He spoke quietly.

"Sorry about all that."

I didn't answer. I heard him shuffling his feet in the dirt. I thought he was going to leave, but instead he sat down by the side of the road, just at the edge of my line of vision. He started scooping up handfuls of sand that had blown out of the field and letting the grains trickle through his fingers.

"Look at this," he said. "Amazing that anything can grow here at all." He looked out over the neat rows of potatoes, row after parallel row, that went on until you got dizzy from the sheer geometry of it. The sprinklers were off for the night, but drops of water glistened on the plants' dark leaves. Geek started to talk.

"The wondrous thing about nature, her gift to us, is her wanton promiscuity. She reproduces herself with abandon, with teeming, infinite generosity. The first knuckle-dragging humanoid to realize this became the world's first farmer, and all the farmers who came after for thousands of years knew this, too. They saved seeds from their harvest, planted them, harvested them, and so it went, on and on, in a perfect, perpetually interconnected wheel of life. Until now."

"Now?" He was making me nervous.

"Now." His voice was tight and his face haggard. He turned, and the moonlight reflected off his round lenses. He looked like a madman with wild, bouncing eyes. "Now it's too late."

I shivered. "You really believe that, don't you? That these are the end times? That basically we're fucked and it's too late to save the world?"

He looked away and shook his head. "Can't afford to believe that. Despair is not a morally acceptable choice." He smiled, and the madman was gone. "I'm not a religious fanatic, and I am pro-choice, you know."

"Listen," I said, "I can't stop you from doing this action, and God knows I can't stop Lloyd, but please understand that he takes this right-to-life stuff seriously. A lot of people around here do. Don't get him all riled up about it. It's not a joke."

"Believe me, I know it's not a joke." He sat there tossing pebbles from the road into the field.

"Why did I let you come back here? You were planning this whole thing from the very start, weren't you?"

He didn't answer, just stood up and offered me his hand. He was whistling "Sweet Leilani."

I ignored his hand and got to my feet. "I should just pack up the kids and take them back to Pahoa, before any more trouble starts." I started walking back toward the farmhouse. Geek walked beside me.

"Hmm," he said with a quizzical smile. "It must be nice to live in paradise."

bugs &

Cass and Will sat on either side of Geek in front of the monitor, watching his fingers fly across the keyboard. Cass had taken typing in high school, so she was fairly fast, but the commands were a challenge. Will was even slower—he still pecked. He had resisted when Cass suggested they ask Geek for help. He prided himself on being able to figure things out. But she said it wasn't every farm that had a computer whiz living next door, and in the end he relented, muttering all the while that it was a sad day when you had to have a Ph.D. from MIT to farm potatoes. And although Geek laughed and reassured them that he was a dropout, his expertise was obvious. He typed something and sat back while the printer whirred. Will just shook his head.

"That should take care of it," Geek said, retrieving the printout and looking it over. "Appears you have a slight dip in elevation at the edge of this field that led to the drainage problem."

"Already knew that," Will said. "So what was wrong with the computer?"

"Bug," Geek said, shrugging his shoulders. "In the software. Thought it might be a virus at first, and I ran a bunch of diagnostics. Then the guy at tech support had me download a patch that seems to take care of the problem. It's a cool program. You can do all kinds of stuff."

Will shook his head again. "I'm still trying to master the basics. Managed to pull up some soil analysis and yield information last year, but I loaded in the data wrong, so my results came up all screwy." He pulled out a couple of maps and showed Geek.

"Wow," Geek said, studying them. "That GPS generates some really detailed information."

"Sure, but all the computer data in the world won't hold back an early frost. It still comes down to weather. And acts of God."

Geek nodded and looked closer at the edge of the map, where Will had scribbled some planting notes. He frowned. "Which field is this?"

"Fuller West Four," Will said. "The one just behind Fuller's greenhouse. Right across the road there."

"Are you planting NuLifes there?"

Will nodded. "Got 'em in the fields closest to both houses. We're trying them out this year for the first time, but we're optimistic. Seem to be doing pretty well so far."

"Do they do what they're supposed to do?"

"Seem to. We're seeing the first of the adult beetles now, and I'm keeping my fingers crossed."

"Do you mind if I take a look?"

Will shrugged. "Sure. We can go over right now if you want."

Cass went with them. She felt uneasy. The sun was high over the potato field in question, one of two separating the Quinns' house from the Fullers'. They walked along the dirt road. The sunlight was shimmering on the glossy surfaces of the leaves. The solstice had come and gone, and now it was the end of June and the rows were closing, forming a single unbroken expanse of green speckled with clusters of pinkish flowers. They followed Will off the hard-packed road.

"There's one," said Will. "Watch." He pointed down to the deep green leaf of the NuLife. A mature Colorado potato beetle had just cruised in for a landing on the leaf's shiny surface. The beetle had a humped yellow carapace, striped and sporty. It ambled to the edge of the leaf and took a nibble. Nothing happened.

"Just wait," said Will.

They waited. The beetle wandered around for a bit.

"Here," Geek said. He pointed to another beetle, staggering drunkenly across the surface of a leaf. He reached out to pick it up, but it tumbled and fell to the ground. He retrieved the beetle from the dirt. "Wow. He's a goner."

Good, thought Cass. She watched Geek's gloomy face as he inspected the wiggling legs of the dying bug. He was a nice guy, she thought. He knew computers, but he sure didn't know much about potatoes, or life for that matter. The fact was, some things had to die so that others could live, and the idea was to try to maximize your chances of staying on the living side for as long as you could. She wiped a leaf with her fingers, crushing a newly hatched clutch of feeding larva, then rubbed the orange smear on her jeans.

"What's amazing about the NuLife line," Will was explaining, "is that it manufactures its own insecticide. The idea is to cut back on the chemical applications we'd be using otherwise."

"When you say it makes its own insecticide, where does it do that exactly?"

"In the cells of the plant." Will spread his arm to encompass the hundred-acre field, a vast sea of green stretching out around him. "Every leaf and flower and stem . . ."

"In the roots?"

"You mean the potatoes? Sure."

"But we *eat* those."

"It's harmless to humans," Will said. "It's a bacterial toxin called Bt. It's used in organic farming. It works on the digestive tract of the insect. Turns it into pulp—"

"*Bacillus thuringiensis,*" Geek said. "Organic farmers use it topically, and very sparingly, and that's the point. These are very high concentrations you're talking about. Do we know what happens to people who ingest that much?"

Cass was watching Geek. Maybe he knew more about potatoes than she had thought. His forehead was sweating.

"Let me finish," Will said. "First of all, there's a big difference between the digestive system of a bug and a man. Second, Bt is a soil bacterium that's found in nature—"

"Sure it's found in nature," said Geek. "But not inside natural potatoes. And certainly not in concentrated doses inside every single cell of the potato. Organic farmers use it to control the worst of the infestations, but mostly they don't have to. They use other means, like rotating crops, planting different varieties of potatoes—"

"We rotate, too, you know."

"Yeah, but what's your schedule? A year? Two? Three? Not enough. And what about other beneficial insects? Like monarch butterflies that die eating Bt corn pollen?"

"Chemical pesticides kill off a lot more butterflies, believe me. It's a question of the lesser of two evils. Anyway, that was corn. We're talking potatoes."

"Okay, then what about the problem of resistance? What happens when your beetles become resistant?"

The two men faced each other over a leafy row. Cass could see Will's jaw tighten as he tried to control his temper.

"Then we'll just have to try something else," he said.

"It's the problem with the system," Geek said. "Monoculture is weak. You should know that. You're Irish."

"If you're talking about the Famine, it was caused by late blight. You're confusing blight with beetles. Monoculture is efficient. We got six billion humans on the earth, and a lot of them are starving."

"Oh, right," Geek said. "That's just corporate marketing. The masses aren't starving because there isn't enough food. There's a surplus—you know that! People are starving because that food isn't being distributed fairly, to those in need. The population explosion argument is the oldest spin in the books!"

Will turned and spat. Cass held her breath. "Look at the demographics. You want people not to have babies? You just try telling them they can't. Listen, I'm no lover of the corporations. As far as I'm concerned, our situation on the farm with agricultural chemicals isn't all that different from what happened to guys in Vietnam getting addicted to marijuana—"

"Aw, come on!" Geek said. "Marijuana's a plant. You can't compare it with chemical compounds like organophosphates and—"

"Fine. Heroin, then. Crack. Whatever. It's the system I'm talking about. The corporations are the pushers, the farmers are the users, and the fields are our bodies, mainlining the stuff in order to wake up in the springtime and keep ticking until fall."

Geek shrugged. "So just say no?"

"It's not that simple. Cold turkey would kill us, but at least we're trying to cut down. That's the whole point of this."

They both fell silent, looking out over the closing rows of NuLifes. Bees were moving heavily from flower to flower, and the air was filled with their buzzing.

"No wonder the beetles keep coming back," Geek said. "Reliable menu. Plenty of it. It's like a fast-food joint."

"Not now," said Will grimly. "Not anymore." They watched another beetle keel over and die.

"I don't know," said Geek. "Maybe now more than ever."

They moved off down the row. Cass hung back, watching a leaf where two beetles were copulating. The male had mounted the female, but when

Cass pushed at him with the tip of her finger, he fell off his mate and turned belly up, waving his legs weakly in the air. Poor thing, she thought. Just when he was getting lucky. She caught up with the men by the roadside and started back toward the house.

"Hey, Cass?" Geek said. "Before you go . . . ?"

She paused. They stood at the edge of the field.

Geek cleared his throat. He looked nervous now, standing there among the blossoms. "Well, I guess you know where we stand."

"I guess we do," Will said.

"It's nothing personal. It's just our position."

Will nodded.

"So," Geek said, "we wanted you to know that we're organizing a little event over at the Fullers' in a couple of weeks, on the Fourth of July weekend."

"What do you mean, an event?" asked Cass.

"Like a teach-in. To educate people about genetically engineered crops."

Will frowned. "Does Lloyd know about this?"

"He's being very supportive. He gave us his customer list. We're inviting the Power County community, too, and people from Pocatello and the university. And our friends. We're expecting a pretty wide range of folks. We thought you should know."

Will nodded, but he didn't look happy.

"If anything happens," Geek said, "we'll be responsible for it."

Cass looked up. "What's going to happen?"

"Probably nothing. All I'm saying is that *if* anything were to happen . . ." He gestured vaguely toward the field. "We'd compensate you for the damages, of course."

"Damages?" Will repeated. "Wait a minute. Are you saying you're planning to harm our NuLifes?"

"Not at all. I'm just saying, on the outside chance . . ."

On the way back to the house Will exploded. "I can't believe him! Criticizing the way I farm, then threatening my crops! If I catch those people anywhere near my fields, I'm calling the sheriff. No, that'll be too late. I'm calling Odell right now."

Cass placed her hand in the middle of her husband's back. He was perspiring, and his shirt felt hot against her palm.

"They haven't done anything."

"He threatened my crops. You heard him."

"It was hardly a threat," she said. "Anyway, what are you going to do? Have them all arrested?"

"Sure," he said. "Why not?"

"This is America, Will. You can't arrest people for their beliefs, remember?"

"Fine. I'll get a restraining order, then. Prevent them from assembling."

"It's private property. We don't own Fuller's house yet."

"Fuller!" Will said, shaking his head. "He's had some crazy ideas in the past, but this is too much. I know he's a sick old man and he probably isn't all there in the head anymore, but he shouldn't be encouraging them."

She tried to change the subject. "Is it true what he said about Bt concentrations?"

"Not you, too!" Will said, groaning. "How did this happen? And I'm supposed to sit by and let this . . . this *cult* take over the neighborhood?"

"They're not a cult, Will."

"I saw them doing something weird under that damn peach tree. They had Yummy's girl with them, singing and dancing and banging on drums like heathens."

"We sing hymns, too."

"It's not the same."

And so it went, all through dinner and up until bedtime. Will crawled under the covers still grumbling, but Cass had teased the worst of it out of him, so when she reached her arm across his stomach, he turned to face her.

"You want to try?" she whispered.

"Never hurts." But from the way he said it, she knew that sometimes it did hurt. As they made love, the image of the copulating beetles in the field kept flitting back into her mind. The doomed, futile mating distracted her, so that when she sensed that Will was close, she faked an orgasm and let him come, then held him until he fell asleep. But she felt restless and wide awake, so she lay there and watched him, checking his breathing from time to time, holding her finger below his nostrils to make sure he was still alive.

molt &

There were new deities on Duncan's desktop. Elliot glanced nervously at the pantheon as Duncan reached over and picked up a small bronze statue of a plump-bellied elephant wearing a diaper.

"Ganesh," Duncan said. "Remover of obstacles." He rubbed the little elephant's belly and handed him to Elliot.

Elliot looked down at the statue. The past couple of weeks had been filled with obstacles. Now he noticed that the incense in the room was different, too. Sweeter, and the scent unsettled him. He replaced the elephant and tried to pay attention.

"I felt myself moving away from Zen," Duncan was saying. "I was finding Buddhism somehow lacking—too spare for the new millennium. I was feeling that the times were calling for a more robust system of devotion, something more grounded in the body." Duncan picked up another deity. It was a flying monkey carrying a mountain on a platter. "Hanuman," he said. "Creativity. The power of persuasion. A lively mind. Renowned for his complete devotion to Vishnu, the Lord of all Creation." He gave Elliot a skewering look. "*He* can move mountains for his master."

Elliot braced himself. This new belief system did not bode well.

"Read an interesting article in the *Post*, Rhodes." It was always bad when Duncan used surnames. "Business section," he said, rotating the monkey slowly in his hands. He glanced up at Elliot and frowned. "By a female."

"Oh?" Elliot said. He felt he should attempt to participate in the conversation. He tried hard to look interested but not terribly concerned. "Yes?"

"Oh, yes." Duncan nodded slowly. "An article about the Cynaco Pie Incident. Which is not particularly noteworthy in itself, since *everyone* wrote about the Cynaco Pie Incident."

"The *Post?*" Elliot said, reminding himself to breathe. "I think I must have read that."

"You must have." Duncan placed Hanuman back down on the desk. "What made this woman's article particularly interesting to me was that she not only mentioned the name of Duncan & Wiley, she also mentioned you. Specifically." He sat back in his leather chair and brought his hands together in prayer position. "And do you know what I find *really* odd about this?"

Elliot really didn't want to know.

"You used to fuck her."

Elliot choked.

"Jillian Davies. You used to fuck her."

"Excuse me?" This was not what he'd imagined. It was worse.

"Yes. And now she's fucking you."

"I'm sorry, but . . . ?" He should have seen it coming.

"Don't apologize to me," Duncan said. "Save it for her."

"For Jillian?"

"Oh?" he asked, raising an eyebrow. "Are there others?" He opened a file on his desk and took out a newspaper clipping. He skimmed the article. "Ah, here we go. 'Elliot Rhodes, who coordinates Cynaco's strategic operations for the public relations firm of Duncan & Wiley, was in his Washington office when he received news of the pie-ing. "Tofu crème?" he responded limply.' "

He put the clipping back down on the desk. "I hate dangling adverbs." He cocked his head and fixed a sad gaze upon Elliot. "Was it a performance problem?"

"Performance?"

"Listen, I honestly don't care who you go to bed with, but if you're going to fuck the press, you've got to fuck them well. And thoroughly. No prickless little bumps in the night. Finesse, Elliot. Precision. You got her riled, so go out and placate her."

"Yes, of course. I'll take care of it."

"See that you do." Duncan picked up the elephant again and turned it over in his hand. "I want to stress that this Pie Incident was *highly* embarrassing, not to mention a deeply wounding experience for our client on a personal level. We're in the business of information. Why weren't we informed? These Seeds of Resistance were your people. You had a private investigator positioned to watch them. You had an informant on the inside sending you intelligence. What went wrong? Were you fucking *her*, too? What were you doing in Idaho all that time?"

"I'll take care of it," Elliot repeated. He couldn't think of anything new to say.

Duncan sighed. "I'm worried about you. Are you paying attention to your diet? Are you getting enough exercise? Are you unhappy?"

Elliot hesitated. It couldn't hurt to try. "Honestly, Duncan, I hate to bring it up, but it's . . . potatoes. I just don't feel I have a connection with them. Rice, yes, but—"

Duncan held up his hand. "Please. Not Tokyo again." He stood and walked over to the large tinted window that ran along the entire back wall of the office. "Japan is over, Elliot. Look at the markets." He gazed out over the government buildings. "The future lies in the Third World. In Mother India. That's where the starving populations are, who need our help. And now that you mention it, maybe we could move you over to Cynaco's rice division in Delhi once this potato situation is in hand."

"Actually," Elliot said, backpedaling now. "You know, I guess Idaho really isn't so bad. . . ." This was the problem with Duncan. Bad could quickly bypass worse and head directly toward debacle.

"In the meantime," Duncan was saying, "try some yoga. Maybe your *doshas* are out of balance. Book a consultation with my Ayurvedic doctor. Sedona will give you her number."

"Great," Elliot said. "You're absolutely right. I'll be more careful."

Duncan turned and examined Elliot's face as though searching for some evidence of candor and sincerity. Finding none, he prompted, "You'll be more careful of . . . ?"

Elliot hesitated. "Of my *doshas?*" he ventured.

"Precisely." Duncan turned back to the window.

It seemed he had finished, so Elliot stood to leave. He crossed the thick carpet. But just as he placed his hand on the brushed-chrome doorknob, Duncan spoke again.

"And who you choose to fuck. Don't be a slut, Elliot."

The skin on the back of Elliot's neck prickled as he slipped out the door.

Yummy's phone call provided a pathway to redemption.

"The whole thing seems ridiculous," she said. "They've gotten everyone all worked up—Phoenix thinks he's a young Che Guevara, and Lloyd's gotten this Terminator business mixed up with his right-to-life agenda, and he's all in a lather. They're planning two big demonstrations, one at the potato-processing plant in Pocatello and another in one of our old fields—Cassie's husband farms it now. He's growing some kind of genetically engineered potatoes, and they want to lead the whole group into the field and tear up the plants if they can get it televised. Will's threatened to call the sheriff, and after what happened with Phoenix, I'm worried."

"I'm sure it won't get out of hand," Elliot said. His heart was racing. "I'm so glad you called. It'll be great to see you. What else did they say?"

He brought it straight up to Duncan.

"Idaho Potato Party?" Duncan said, raising his eyebrows. "Pretty minor league, don't you think? I don't see why someone local can't handle this."

"According to my informant, they're trying for major media coverage."

"Trying for and getting are quite different. A pie in the face of one of America's most powerful CEOs at the Future of the World Forum in San Francisco is one thing. But some small farm town in Idaho? I think this is a molehill, Elliot. Not a mountain."

"They're planning to tear up a field of NuLifes."

"So? Let them. If it doesn't get covered, it doesn't exist." Duncan slid Elliot's report back across the desk. "I can see you're not convinced. Okay, what do you propose?"

Elliot took a deep breath. "Well, it occurred to me that it could be a good opportunity to implement some aggressive countertactics from the Proactive Management Strategy. We need victims on our side, and the guy who farms those fields is perfect. He's even a Vietnam vet, for chrissakes. I can see it playing as a story of domestic terrorism—honest American farmer, salt of the earth, his crops targeted by the antiprogress forces of the Luddite left sort of thing. A vicious attack on the American way of life. I happen to know that the Seeds of Resistance run a pornography Web site, and one source in the community tells me that we can count on church support."

Duncan nodded. "Interesting." He picked up the flying monkey and dangled it from his forefinger.

Elliot pressed his advantage. "It's an excellent opportunity for developing our affiliations with grassroots and local special-interest groups. I just have a hunch I should be there. In case an opportunity presents itself."

"A hunch." Duncan sighed. "Well, you might be right. Go, then. Fly away, Hanuman. Bring me back a mountain."

Elliot took his report and went. But when he reached the door, Duncan spoke again. "Just so we're clear, Rhodes. Whether this Potato Party of yours does indeed become a mountain or simply stays a molehill, I leave entirely up to you. Do as you see fit. But if you choose the mountain"— and here he made his hands into a steep peak, with the tips of his fingers touching in front of his forehead—"I want it to tower, as lofty and insurmountable as Everest. And if it stays a molehill, I want it to just go *poof* and vanish, silently. I do not want to see or hear anything more about it."

He let his hands part, drifting downward, and he made a broad, smoothing motion above the slick surface of his desk, as though calming turbulent waters.

After a storm.

It was a very good time to be out of the office, Elliot thought.

Once the plane had taken off, heading west, and he was able to sit back and enjoy the distance growing between himself and the ever mounting pressure at work, he felt an odd sensation, like the loosening of something hard and constricting, as though he were about to shed a skin. He took off his jacket and removed his tie, letting his mind travel on ahead, and that's when the thought of seeing Yummy again hit him full on. It washed over him, causing his chest to expand. He hadn't allowed himself to look forward to this, nor had he realized how much he'd missed her. This sense of loosening continued until touchdown in Pocatello, where he felt the first skin shed, shriveling upon contact with the dry desert air. A hot, dry wind blew it away.

He drove to Liberty Falls and checked into the Falls Motel. When he picked up the phone to call Yummy, the second skin started to loosen. An hour later, when he opened the door and saw her standing there, lean and golden, it dropped away, pooling around his ankles like a puddle.

The third skin she drew gently from his body. She pinned him naked to the pillow and looked at him intently, an entomologist studying his molt, tracking the instar, and observing the possible emergence of a fully developed organism. He could not get enough of her. This, too, took him by surprise. Their sex just kept going and going, each time rolling into the next with barely a beat in between, until he lay beside her exhausted and knew that the constriction he'd been feeling in D.C. was more than just a stagnant job or a stale lover.

He listened to her breathe for a while. "It's good to be here," he said. His sensors were awake from their lovemaking, attuned to dips in her temperature and flutters in her pulse, but he wasn't getting much of a reading now. "Even if I don't get a story out of it. I mean, I doubt this action will amount to much. Who in their right mind would come to Liberty Falls, right?"

He was simply chattering to fill the silence, but still she didn't answer. "Hey," he said, trying to be casual. "Did you miss me?"

She continued to gaze toward the ceiling, as though she were seeing far beyond the acoustic tiles, all the way to heaven, while his question remained earthbound, trapped in the small motel room, making nervous currents in the air. The question itself was familiar, but coming from him, it sounded strange. Then he identified the problem: He sounded like a woman.

He'd never seen what a brave little question it was, hanging there, edged with fearful expectation and banking stubbornly on hope. His response had always been to buy time with silence, but in the end he usually lied—*Sure I missed you. What did you think?*—and then gotten up to pee or changed the subject. He had sensed, but never before experienced, the shadow questions: *Do you love me? Is there any hope at all?*

She turned her head. Her eyes were unreadable. "Sure," she said. "I missed you."

He felt such relief. Another skin dropped away, and the air that washed over him felt fresh and charged. It wasn't love per se, but rather a trick of the pores, opening to release their little dew of sweat and then closing again while the body thrilled to the cool release of tension. But his heart marveled nonetheless.

Then she laughed. "But that was twenty-five years ago. I know better now."

pre-potato ℬↄ

During the weeks leading up to July Fourth and the great Idaho Potato Party, I was treated like a pariah, denounced by my parents and my offspring for my lack of proper revolutionary zeal. Every time I expressed my concerns, I felt like I was committing thought crimes. Elliot was the only ally I had, and I took his interest in the action as a measure of his feelings for me. It never occurred to me that he might have other motives.

I was excited to see him, standing in the doorway of the tawdry motel room. But then we made love, and while the sex was good, something was starting to change. I felt myself becoming remote, moving further and further away until my perspective was like that of a celestial body. I was seeing more, and he was becoming less. He had always been the distant one, which of course had been terribly attractive. Now his new postcoital manner was fraught with an eagerness that made me feel nervous and mean. I thought I would explode if I stayed in that motel room for another second. I rolled out of bed and got dressed. I gave him a brisk kiss on the forehead to make me feel less guilty, then careened out the door. Once in the car I floored it, happy just to be outside in the warm summer night air, happy to be driving home with the windows wide open. I still had not gotten used to his cologne.

The house lights were blazing when I pulled in, and I could see the shadowy stage by the barn and the poles set up on either side where a banner would be hung. The sweet scent of baking cookies drifted from the kitchen. The Seeds had colonized the entire downstairs, and by the time I had skulked out of the house that evening, the party was in full swing and they barely noticed I was leaving. They had established work stations— food preparation, banner painting, and information assembly—and had tacked up huge sheets of paper on the walls, covering them with schedules and maps and assignments. The phone was ringing constantly, and they'd bought a fax machine. A computer was set up on Lloyd's desk, and they were uploading information about the action to their network of friends and the press contacts who were expected to show up. They seemed to share a grand vision, which I couldn't imagine, yet which filled me with dread, including as it did the rental of several hundred folding chairs, the small breakdown stage, half a dozen PortaPotties that were due to arrive the following day, and the services of a health-food restaurant in Oregon, whose catering truck was crossing the Cascade Mountains loaded with organic food and a couple of cooks.

I had stayed safely out of it all, except to take Geek aside at one point and question him about the extent of Lloyd's involvement. The two of them had been sitting side by side, heads bent cozily over a speech that

Lloyd was writing. I could see that Geek was feeding him information, and I wanted to know what else was being traded. I called him out to the porch and demanded to know if Lloyd was funding the event. Geek sighed and shook his head.

"We're not extortionists."

"I don't know what you are. But somebody's paying. I want to know who."

"We are. We've got sources of income."

"What, dealing drugs? Selling pot? Distributing pornography?"

He looked hurt. "I told you we closed the Garden. And we promised not to bring pot onto your parents' property."

"You also promised not to engage in any political agitation within Power County limits. Excuse me if I'm finding it a little hard to trust you."

Geek nodded. He could see my point. "I was hoping you could get behind this."

"What my mother and father chose to get behind is their business. But I swear, if you get Phoenix or Ocean involved in any illegal shit . . ." I turned away and left the thought hanging—there was nowhere for it to go.

❧

Now I picked my way across the porch, avoiding the boxes and crates and bins, then stood at the door and looked in through the screen. I could see Charmey and Ocean by the stove, surrounded by cookie sheets and mixing bowls. At the kitchen table Lilith and Phoenix were working on the banner that would hang over the stage. Heads together, they were concentrating on erasing an E that had found its way onto the end of POTATO.

"*Ce n'est pas vrai?*" Charmey asked. She had lettered the banner and had drawn smiley potato heads on either end. "I thought certainly there was the E." She was wearing an apron above her bulging stomach and held a big wooden spoon, sticky with cookie dough. Geek walked in just then and overheard her.

"It's okay, Charmey," he said. "You can't help it. You're French." She brandished the spoon at him, and he leaned over and licked it. "Mmm. Chocolate chip."

"Carob chip," she said. "And I am Québécoise."

"Tastes good anyway, and that's still a good excuse."

I opened the screen door and stepped into the kitchen. Geek fell silent.

The others all looked up, and then, as though on cue, they looked away again, concentrating on their tasks. I could see Phoenix's cheeks redden, and I wondered if he guessed where I'd been. I hadn't told anyone that Elliot was coming, though. Nobody seemed to have much to say, so I started to walk on through, when Ocean skipped up with a cookie in hand, waving it in front of my face.

"Look!" she said. "You can eat one, but you have to pay."

"Okay. How much?"

"You pay what you can. It's by donation."

"How about a nickel?" I said, fishing in my jeans pocket.

She frowned. "It's *carob chip,* Mom. It's even better than chocolate chip, plus it's got nuts, plus it's got oatmeal and fiber, plus it's organic."

"How about a dollar?" I felt guilty, buying my daughter's love, but I was pretty desperate.

"Really?" she said, impressed. She was still at an age where a dollar seemed like a fortune. You could buy a lot of her love for a buck.

"Sure. It sounds like it's worth it." I handed her the bill and took the cookie. "Mmm," I said, taking a bite. It had the consistency of adobe and tasted like barely sweetened cardboard. "This is delicious." The chips were okay.

Ocean looked at the dollar bill, then danced over to Charmey. "Look!" she said. "I made a sale! A dollar!"

"You paid way too much," Geek said. "The recommended donation was a quarter. Fifty cents max."

"It's for a good cause." I offered him the rest of the cookie.

"No thanks," he said. "Do you mean that?"

"If you say so."

"Okay, I'll eat the rest of that for you." He took the cookie and popped the whole thing in his mouth and started chewing. Ocean was loudly counting all the cookies and calculating their profits at a dollar per.

"Eleven dollars, twelve dollars . . ."

I watched Geek chew for a while. "So I got you some more press coverage," I told him. He raised his eyebrows, still unable to speak, so I continued. "Elliot Rhodes. From Washington. Remember?"

He seemed to be having a difficult time with the cookie.

"I called and told him what you all were doing. He's here. He came for the action. He's going to try to write something about it."

Geek made a choking sound.

"You want a glass of milk?"

He shook his head. Finally he swallowed and could speak again. "That's great, Yumi. Thanks." But he sounded distracted, like he was already thinking about something else.

I didn't pursue it. It was enough that I had done something to help, and it was nice to be a part of things again. With the smell of baking and all the bustle of craft activity, it felt like Christmas Eve in the house, the way the holiday ought to feel but never had in our small, quiet family when I was growing up. I'd always wanted to belong to a big, happy family that felt like this, and maybe the sudden coziness led me to overlook my apprehensions. I went into the living room. Momoko, Lloyd, and Frankie were sitting around a folding bridge table, funneling poppy seeds into little packages.

"Can I help?" I asked, sitting down next to Momoko.

Lloyd looked up. "Why, thank you, Yumi," he said, and when our eyes met, he seemed as startled as I was. As I scooped up the tiny seeds in a spoon and let them roll into the mouth of the envelope, I was aware that my heart still thumped like a bunny with the pleasure of pleasing Daddy.

liberty rises ᗒ

On the second of July people started showing up. Lloyd was sitting on the porch in his rocking chair when the first vehicle arrived. He'd seen it coming from a ways off, lumbering slowly along the dirt road, kicking up dust. He felt a bit of a shock when it slowed, then pulled into his driveway. He didn't know what to make of it.

It was an old school bus, the top half of which had been replaced with wooden walls and a roof made of hand-split cedar shingles. A narrow deck with driftwood railings ran around the sides and back, and the entire exterior of the structure was covered with a web of hooks and nets and rigging into which were woven pots and pans, brooms and buckets, a winch and a come-along, some bicycles with miscellaneous spokes and wheels, and the day's laundry, hung out to dry. The vehicle had Oregon license plates. It pulled right up to the porch and cut its engine. The driver stepped down and threw his arms around Melvin, who was there to greet him. Lloyd could see the man's eyes gleaming under thick, shaggy brows. A dark beard covered the rest of his face. He wore a crocheted cap in rainbow colors and brown corduroy trousers that were sizes too big, held up by a pair of suspenders. He didn't have a shirt on.

The man's name was Cedar. His companion was a woman named Aloe, and they had a little boy named Bean. Where do they get these names? Lloyd wondered when Melvin brought them to the porch to introduce them.

A Volkswagen bus was the next to arrive, followed by a ratty parade of small, fuel-efficient cars from Japan. Battered and splotchy with rust. Patched with putty, and painted. Covered with bumper stickers. SAVE THE WHALES. HUG A TREE. LOVE OUR MOTHER. NO JOBS ON A DEAD PLANET. DON'T PANIC, EAT ORGANIC.

As he watched the vehicles congregate in his yard, a feeling of dread grew in Lloyd's heart. He pictured them driving through the center of Liberty Falls, maybe even stopping for gas at Mr. Petrol's Pantry. This was not the event he'd imagined. It wasn't his reputation in town that concerned him—he'd pretty much given up on that—but he simply couldn't countenance the way these kids were dressed. Undressed, more like it. The afternoon was hot, and the boys were all shirtless, their hair tied up in bandannas. The girls had on long skirts, which they gathered around their waists, baring their thighs. On top they wore skimpy scraps of fabric attached with straps, no thicker than baling twine and not half so sturdy. Most of them weren't wearing anything else underneath. It made Lloyd very nervous every time one of them raised her arms to hug a friend or ran too quickly across the yard.

He looked around for Yumi, realizing he hadn't seen her all day. Her kids were over with Melvin and Lilith, helping to set up chairs. He started rocking harder. Never thought he'd see the day when he'd look to Yumi for propriety. At least you could count on her to keep most of her clothes on in public.

The first rust-free vehicle to arrive was an Airstream Land Yacht motor home with Nebraska plates. Lloyd eased himself down the steps and into the yard to intercept it. The occupants made no attempt to exit. They sat behind the large tinted windshield with the engine running, staring around at the milling crowd. Lloyd slowly crossed the yard with his walker, then stopped in front of the bus and gave a wave. They raised their hands and waved back, and from where he stood, looking up at the windshield, their arms looked like the wipers, moving in unison. Then the man stood and opened the door.

"Didn't know if we had the right place," he shouted from the top of the steps. He wore plaid shorts and a pink golf shirt. "Things sure have changed a bit around here."

"Still the same," said Lloyd. "Still the same. Wife's in the garden. She'll be glad to see you."

Lloyd peered up at the woman, who hadn't moved from her seat. Outside the Land Yacht, a group of young men with bold tattooed designs on their naked torsos had formed a loose circle and were kicking a small crocheted ball up in the air with their bare feet. Sweat put a sheen on their golden skin.

"Howdy, Martha," Lloyd called up. "How's the garden?"

"Hard time to leave, Lloyd," she said, not taking her eyes off the circle. "Right during bean season."

"Appreciate you coming," said Lloyd. "We're expecting a few more of our customers. You won't be the only ones."

"Glad to hear it, Lloyd," she said.

They watched the tattooed men leap and twist, chasing the little ball. They wore kerchiefs on their heads. They wore necklaces with leather pouches.

"Hey," one of them shouted at the Land Yacht. "Turn off the engine! You're wasting fossil fuels."

"Don't mind them kids," Lloyd said. "They seem odder than they are."

"It's an interesting look," the man offered, making no move toward the ignition.

"We've got a bunch of 'em helping out. They're pretty good gardeners. We're having a productive season, in spite of my heart." Lloyd cleared his throat and spat.

"We were real sorry to hear about that," the man said.

"Guess it's just that time of life. Time to downsize, you know?"

"Early retirement, eh?"

"Can't keep on going forever. Let me call the wife."

Lloyd hobbled his walker around so that it pointed at the garden. He scanned the rows, then spotted Momoko bent over in a bed of melons. He raised his arm and tried to shout to her, but he started coughing and had to lean over to catch his balance. Martha honked the Land Yacht's horn, then turned off the engine as an afterthought. Momoko looked up. She waved and started walking toward them. Lloyd shuffled back.

"Hard to tell how much she's following these days," he said. "Appreciate it if you wouldn't mention downsizing to her. She's real worried about her seeds."

"Not a problem, Lloyd."

Momoko made her way through the circle of half-naked ballplayers. A tattoo caught her eye, and she stopped to inspect it—a bold black Japanese character in the small of a young man's back. She tapped him on the arm and looked up at his face as he turned, shielding her eyes against the sun with her hand.

"You know what means that one?" she asked, pointing to the large tattoo.

The young man twisted around and nodded. "Yeah," he said. "It's the Japanese word for happiness."

"Nope," she said, shaking her head. "It is not mean happiness. It mean stupid."

"No way!" the kid protested, twisting and peeking over his shoulder, as though the tattoo might have changed shape when he wasn't looking.

"So sorry," she said and started to walk away, but then she stopped. "Hey," she called back to him. "You a happy guy?"

"Yeah," the kid said, looking a lot less happy than he had before.

"But stupid, too. Stupid to put such big happiness in back of you." She turned and walked up to the Land Yacht.

"Hello, Mr. Jack!" she said. "Howdy Mrs. Martha! How is your bush bean growing?"

ॐ

The rally officially started on the morning of Saturday, the third. By ten o'clock there were approximately 120 registered participants, which would grow to twice that number by the end of the day. By the following afternoon, the Fourth of July, just over 400 people had stopped by. This number included customers of the Fullers, comrades of the Seeds, and citizens and supporters from neighboring cities and towns. It included poets from Pocatello, students from the university, and Shoshone representatives from the local tribes, as well as journalists from all the local papers, a couple of freelance photographers, and a camera crew from the network affiliate. The figure also included unregistered participants: a few fertilizer salesmen and other representatives from the agrochemical industry; locals who stopped by to gawk; a busload of interfaith, antipornography activists; and the police, who arrived on the second day to arrest the Seeds and shut the party down.

But that was day two.

On day one Cass got there just before ten. Frankie was testing the PA system, tapping the mike and causing an electronic squeal to rip through the mounting heat of the morning. People winced and laughed and clapped. Stragglers moved closer. The great painted banner that hung above the stage proclaimed WELCOME TO THE IDAHO POTATO PARTY! Pictures of smiling potato heads beamed down upon the crowd.

Cass found Yummy and Poo at the edge of the crowd of hippies who were gathering in front of the stage. They looked so colorful with all their exotic clothes and beads and hair done up in strange ways.

"It's like a rock concert or something," Cass said to Yummy, holding her arms out for the baby. She had come over as soon as she could, after Will had left for the fields. To keep an eye on things, she told him. But she liked the excitement that was filling the air. She stood on her tiptoes to see the stage. She lifted Poo up to her shoulders so he could see, too. He clung onto her hair with his fingers, then started to drum on her head.

"I'll take him if he gets too much," Yummy said.

Cass rotated her body in a way that meant no, but that also felt a bit like dancing. She loved the bouncy weight of the baby on her shoulders and the warmth of his ankle in her hand, sturdy and plump. She kissed his bare foot. She held on tight.

She could see Lloyd and Momoko sitting in the very front row. Lloyd looked anxious, but Momoko sat perfectly still, hands folded, waiting. Their seed customers and friends sat in a tight cluster around them, balancing coffees and napkins and doughnuts on their knees. They seemed nervously aware of the young people who eddied about them, as though they were afraid of being swallowed up, and for good reason, because the young people were like a great massing body of bare flesh and flashing colors and bells and musty smells of incense and sweat.

Yummy was scanning the crowd looking for someone, and then Cass caught sight of Elliot Rhodes. He raised his arm and waved, and Yummy waved back.

"Oh, Yummy," Cass said. "You didn't invite him, did you?"

Yummy had the grace to look embarrassed. "I wanted to help," she said. "The Seeds were trying to get more press to come. He's going to write an article."

Cass bounced Poo a little more. "They're not really going to damage Will's crop, are they? He's still real upset about that. Threatened to call the sheriff again this morning, but I made him hold off."

"They better not. I warned them."

Frank had come back out onstage with Melvin. They each were carrying a long pole, connected by a swath of dark brown fabric, which they laid on the ground, then raised and lowered, making waves that rippled across the cloth as though the earth itself were moving. A gentle drumming sound grew, low and insistent, as people filled in the back of the stage, carrying bongos and bells and gourds with beads. Then the drumming stopped and the cloth settled, revealing a small bump in the middle of the fabric. A clear, high bell sounded, and a little boy with matted blond hair came out on the stage, carrying an enormous watering can. He was wearing tattered overalls and a big straw hat, chewing on a long piece of grass. He stood next to Frankie on the edge of the brown fabric, shading his eyes as though surveying a vast acreage.

"He's adorable!" whispered Cass.

"His name is Bean," Yummy said. "Makes my kids' names sound almost normal."

Lilith stepped onto the stage holding a mike. "It starts with the earth," she intoned.

The drumming resumed, and Frankie gave Bean a shove. The little boy stumbled forward, then walked over the bump and held the can above it.

"For thousands of years farmers have been cultivating this earth and nurturing their seed."

Bean leaned down and gave the bump a hard swat on the behind. Frankie and Melvin slowly pulled the slithery fabric back to reveal the bump in a burlap sack.

"Now, imagine you are that seed, tucked deep within the earth. Slowly the sun warms you, tickles you awake—"

The bump started to writhe like a sackful of cats.

289

"Oh, so tentatively you send out a threadlike root—"

The bump stuck one leg out of the sack, and then another.

"While overhead, your pale shoot slowly pushes up—"

The bump got to its feet and waved an arm overhead, wiggling its fingers.

"Nudging your tendril toward the warmth of the sunny sun sun."

The drum rhythms started to build. The bump doubled over as though seized by a stomach cramp, then, at the crash of a cymbal, it straightened, and out of the burlap burst Ocean.

She was dressed as a sunflower in a green leotard, a little tutu of leaves, and a big yellow ruff of petals around her neck. Her cheeks and forehead were painted with brown spots. She glided over to Bean, who sat dumbstruck on the edge of the stage, hauled him to his feet, and started swinging his arms up and down and dragging him in a circle.

"We are here this weekend to affirm this sacred dance of life that has sustained us for millennia in harmony with our planet."

The drums gave a final flourish. Ocean and Bean abruptly stopped circling and stood in the middle of the stage panting and holding hands. After it was all done, Ocean came running over.

"You were great!" Yummy said, giving her a hug. "Such a pretty little bump."

"I wasn't a *bump*. I was a *seed*."

"Of course you were," said Cass. "A seed that turned into a beautiful flower."

"Yeah?" Ocean's little flower face was smeared with brown, and her petals were wilting. "They wanted to make me a potato at first, but I said I couldn't make up as good a dance as a potato."

"Really?" said Cass.

"I mean, a potato just rolls around on the floor, right? That's not a sacred dance of life."

"No," said Cass. "There's a limit to potatoes."

"Yeah," said Ocean. "They're okay. But sunflowers are prettier."

"I don't know," Yummy interrupted. "I'm sure you could do very creative and beautiful things with a potato."

"Mom," Ocean said, rolling her eyes, "you have *no* idea."

"That's right," said Cass. "She has no idea."

By noon the rally was in full swing. There were information tables set up all around the perimeter of the farmyard where you could learn about worm composting and gene splicing, the secret to effective protest letters and the ethics of patenting life, the latest in biotech research and European boycotts of American GMOs.

There were workshops, too. "A New Niche Market—Unprecedented Profits in Organic Potatoes" had attracted a few of the local farmers' wives. Others were taking garden tours with Momoko and Lloyd and learning their seed-saving techniques. Charmey was offering "The Art of the Sprout," a cooking workshop using sprouted seeds. At three there would be a performance of *The Tragedy of Cynaco the Evil Cyclops: A Morality Play in Three Acts*. In the meantime the painted backdrop of the Cyclops had been turned into a pitching concession—a hardball in his eye won you a tofu crème pie.

Frankie was making seed bombs at the "Guerrilla Gardening" workshop when Geek caught up with him. They were planning to bomb the chemical fertilizer plant just outside of Pocatello at the protest march the next day. Geek watched as Frankie spooned some Showy Larkspur seeds in the middle of his large mud pie.

"He's here," Geek said. "Erodes."

"Who?" Frankie asked, adding some Yellow Monkey-flower seeds. He looked up at Geek's glum face. "Oh, you mean Yummy's boyfriend?"

Geek nodded. "I need you to keep an eye on him. I want to know why he's here."

"That's obvious," Frankie said. "Yummy invited him."

"She thinks he's a reporter," Geek said. "She was just trying to be helpful."

"Dude," Frankie said, "she just wants to get laid."

"Whatever. Just keep an eye out for him. And anybody else acting weird."

"Can I make one more of these first?" Frankie asked, eyeing the mud bucket and a jar of Rosy Everlasting.

"Sure." Geek sighed. "Glad to see you're enjoying gardening."

Duncan had been right, Elliot thought. He needn't have come. An event like this did not require his personal attention, and there was no way they were going to get any significant media coverage. But as the morning wore on, he began to reconsider. It was an interesting mix. At first glance all you noticed were the kids, the usual collection of activists and hippies who showed up at any protest, but there were others here, too, a few farmers by the looks of it, local businesspeople, and a large number of just plain folks. Where did they come from? Elliot wondered. Just plain folks didn't usually attend events like this. It was worth a look around. He had spotted Yummy during the opening performance. He caught her eye over the heads of the crowd and waved, then, remembering that her father might be watching, wished he hadn't. He smiled. The thought of hiding from someone's father made him feel ridiculously young, and after all, the chances of the old man's recognizing him after twenty-five years were pretty slim.

A little after noon he realized he was being watched. The kid from the Mexican restaurant, the one with the pregnant girlfriend, was tagging him, keeping his distance but keeping him in sight. How amusing, Elliot thought as he approached the kid.

"Take me to your leader."

"Huh?"

The kid's eyes were a pale slate gray, with flecks of yellow just beneath the surface, like stones under water. Empty. Unwavering. Where did he pick that up? Elliot wondered. Duncan had it, too. A gaze like that was worth a lot, one of those tricks that life teaches you early on, or it doesn't and you have to learn to fake it. Elliot had acquired his later in life, and he knew it lacked conviction. He always felt self-conscious, whereas you could tell that this kid never did. He was the real thing: a loser with nothing to lose.

"I'm a journalist," Elliot said, averting his eyes to look for a business card. "Friend of the Fullers. Is there someone I could talk to about what's going on here?"

The kid shrugged. "Yeah." He turned away, and Elliot followed.

Geek was at the registration table, talking to a middle-aged couple with a terrier on a leash. "Today's mainly an information-sharing day," he was saying. "Tomorrow's the day for putting what we learn into action."

"We're customers of Fullers' Seeds," the man ventured.

"Right," said Geek. "We're leading tours of the Fullers' garden every hour—I'll be doing the next one, starting in a few minutes—and then we have a seed-saving workshop right afterward with Momoko and Lloyd."

Elliot moved in closer to listen. Geek ignored him. "They'll be giving away free seeds at the workshop as a protest against capitalism and the privatization of food production by greedy multinational agribusiness corporations, if you're interested."

"We'd love some more of the cucurbits," the woman said. "The Fullers always had the finest cucurbits."

"I'm sure that would be fine," Geek said. "I know they'll be very happy to see you. Please take a look around before the garden tour. There's some very interesting information on our government's failure to enact labeling laws that would help protect citizens and consumers from the hazards of genetically engineered foods."

"Oh, my goodness," the woman said. "That sounds very interesting." The couple and the dog moved on.

Geek turned toward Elliot. "So what could I possibly help you with?"

"It certainly does sound interesting," Elliot said. "And you know what? I agree with you completely. GE foods should have been labeled from the get-go."

"You don't mean that."

"Sure I do. Full disclosure. It's the only way." He held out a business card. "Elliot Rhodes. Journalist."

Geek took the card, looked at it, then handed it back. "Don't bullshit me."

"No bullshit. I said I agree with you, and I do. Where we disagree is about the effect labeling would have. You think the public will choose not to buy the stuff, and I say consumers are idiots. Give them the choice and they'll buy it anyway, regardless of any label you might put on it."

"Like cigarettes," Geek said.

"Exactly. Consumers are dangerous only when they think they've been cheated of their right to exercise free will."

"This being America and all."

"Exactly. Or when they think they've been duped."

"Right," said Geek. "You would know." He straightened the papers on the table. "I'm surprised to see you here. At a small local event like this. We're honored to have you, of course. I assume you'll be attending the entirely nonviolent protests tomorrow?"

"As a member of the press, I wouldn't miss it. Will there be other press members there?"

"I have to go lead a garden tour now," Geek said. He came out from behind the table and stood directly in front of Elliot. "Listen, Mr. E. Rhodes. This is not a big press event. I wish it were. This is a small educational get-together. One reason we're doing it is to help the Fuller family. The parents are old. They're going to die, and they're worried about the future of their seeds. That's all we're trying to do here. Help the family by getting more people interested in taking on the seeds."

A cheer went up from the pitching concession, where someone had nailed the cyclops in the eye. They both looked up to see Yummy heading toward them. She was wearing a loose white muumuu with a ruffle around the neck. She looked stunning.

Geek lowered his voice. "If you're really a friend of Yumi's, you won't interfere." He walked away, passing her and exchanging a few words before he cut over toward the garden.

And then she was standing in front of him. "Hi," she said. He realized he was staring at her. Embarrassed, he looked down at the ground. She was wearing Japanese sandals on her tanned feet. She had silver polish on her toenails and dust between her toes. She was wearing a toe ring.

"You look nice," Elliot said. "Very Hawaiian."

"It's hot," she said.

"Yes. It is."

They stood there, not looking at each other. He didn't know quite where to take the conversation. He had vowed he would not make a fool of himself, but he just couldn't help himself.

"That was nice last night," he said.

"Will this make an interesting article?" she asked at exactly the same time.

They both stopped abruptly, and he laughed. "Yes," he said. "I think it might." Again he paused. "Of course, it's just a part of a larger story."

Yummy nodded. He watched her scan the crowd for her children. They were taking turns at the pitching booth. She waved to Cass, who had the baby. Poo was toddling around on little bowed legs, hanging on to her hands. He squatted and picked up a fistful of dirt and put it in his mouth. Cass leaned over and made him spit it out.

Yummy frowned. "He eats dirt," she said.

"I've heard some babies do that."

"Cass likes looking after him."

"She seems to."

"She never had kids."

"Neither did I," he said and was startled to hear how plaintive he sounded.

"I guess you think this is all kind of silly," she said, looking around the farmyard. "But it's sort of fun, too, don't you think? It feels like an auction or a county fair. I just hope nothing goes wrong."

He couldn't quite see what was fun, but he understood that she wanted it to be, and that was enough. Duncan had been right after all. This homespun event was a molehill, and he would let it remain as such. Relieved, he decided to forget about work, to relax and just get into the swing of things for her sake. She looked so lovely.

"What could possibly go wrong?" he asked.

She didn't answer. Just then her daughter came running up.

"Did you see?" Ocean asked breathlessly. "Phoenix nailed Cynaco right in the eye!"

Elliot felt his chest constrict. Forgetting about work wasn't going to be that easy.

It was just after two when he spotted the Pinkerton leaning on a fence rail and headed over to talk to him. Yummy had gone in to put Poo down for a nap, and there was a lull in the events after lunch. Rodney was wearing a cap pulled down low over his face. He was watching Lilith get the children ready for the play. A pair of mirrored aviator glasses hid his eyes.

Lilith was painting the face of a little earthworm, holding the child between her legs. She was wearing a halter top, which bared her back, and a tattoo of a serpent coiled up her spine. She was explaining to the children, "You're all going to play soil organisms!"

"What's that?" one of them asked.

"Good things. Worms and bacteria. Beetles and moles. Stuff like that."

"Those are *pests*." The girl shook her head. "I don't want to be a pest!"

"How about a monarch butterfly, then? That's a big role. The Terminator kills you and you get to die."

"I don't want to die!"

They settled on a ladybug. Lilith picked up a paintbrush and hitched up her skirt, spreading her knees so she could draw the girl in close.

Elliot approached the investigator from behind. "She's even better in real life," he said.

Rodney showed no sign of surprise. He barely bothered to shrug, as though he'd been expecting Elliot to show up with a comment like this, and it simply wasn't worth an answer.

"Too bad about the Web site," Elliot said, leaning on the fence rail. "Wonder why they decided to shut it down. Was that your doing, too?"

Rodney didn't answer for a while. Then he said, "Lucky for them they did."

"You didn't like it?"

"I got grandkids."

"Of course," Elliot said.

They watched Lilith in silence. At one point she looked in their direction, and Elliot flashed her a smile, but her glance drifted past him to Rodney's cap. It was a promotional item from Cynaco's GroundUp™ Plant Protection Systems. On the front it read TOTAL CROP CARE, FROM THE GROUNDUP!"

"They're gonna demonstrate at a potato field tomorrow," Rodney said. "At oh-nine-hundred. Then they're planning to march on the fertilizer plant in the afternoon, but I don't think they'll get that far."

"What do you mean?"

"I've alerted the sheriff's office. They'll be here first thing in the morning." He turned to Elliot and fixed him with a mirrored gaze.

"You did what?" Elliot could see himself, tiny and furious, reflected in the flat planes of Rodney's glasses.

Rodney spoke slowly, as though explaining the rules to a slow child. "They're planning on tearing up the field, Mr. Rhodes. That's trespassing for starters. Destroying crops is criminal mischief and malicious damage to private property, not to mention un-American. Could be grand larceny, but they gotta take the plants out of the field first—"

"That's not the point! I don't want them arrested. I just wanted them watched!"

"You don't live here," Rodney replied, as though that were an answer, then turned his attention back to Lilith's thigh. Her ankle bracelet tinkled as her naked heel shifted in the dust. Elliot tried changing tactics.

"That's exactly what they want," he said. "These kids know how to play the cops and the press like a fucking Nintendo. It'll be all over the papers."

"Good," Rodney said. "People should know. Not that everyone don't already. They even told the farmer whose field they're tearing up. Lousy idea from a tactical standpoint. Besides, the sheriff's had his eye on them, too, long before you got involved. Said he had cause to interrogate Fuller's daughter on a couple of occasions, once when that punk kid of hers got caught bringing a knife to school. My grandson's in his class."

Lilith's ankle tinkled again as she jumped to her feet, hoisting the ladybug up by her arms. From the corner of his eye Elliot thought he saw her look in their direction again, but when he turned, she was spinning the ladybug in a circle to make her fly. The ladybug's laugh rang out loud and shrill, like a scream.

"Sheriff said he used to know Fuller's daughter," Rodney said. "Said he thought he remembered you, too."

Lloyd had noticed the man Yumi was talking to, thought he looked familiar but couldn't place him. He wasn't from Liberty Falls, that much Lloyd was sure of. Pocatello? At any rate he was a city man. Lloyd thought he might ask Yumi later on, but then he noticed how pretty she looked in her white dress, and after that, Melvin came to tell him that the garden tours were starting, and by the end of the long, exhausting, exhilarating day, he'd forgotten all about it.

So many of their old customers had come, some bringing children and even grandchildren. He hadn't expected that. He was worried, wondering how they would take to the Seeds and their crowd, but by and large, folks seemed tolerant and polite.

"She's adorable," said Martha from Nebraska after the morning performance.

"She's my granddaughter," Lloyd said, and he was amazed at the size of his pride. Then Martha asked her name.

"Ocean," he mumbled.

"What an unusual name!" she said. "My daughter named her youngest 'Moonflower.'"

"She goes for the plants," her husband said. "She called the boy Juniper.

297

I told her I didn't like it, but it was better than Sneezewood or Sandwort or Bladderpod."

"They like to be different these days," Martha said. "Don't you find?"

He must have answered hundreds of questions and held more conversations than in the last several decades of his life. By the time he retired upstairs that night, most of the participants had left for the day or bedded down in their campers and tents, and the campfires were dwindling into ash and ember. All he could hear from the bathroom window was the faint sound of the young people drumming softly in the night.

He left the bathroom and made his way down the hall, past Yumi's bedroom door. It was open, and he looked in. Yumi was lying on her back on the bed. He would have thought she was asleep, but her eyes were open, and she was staring up at the ceiling. He cleared his throat.

"Good night, then," he said.

She blinked, then turned her head.

"Oh," she said. "Good night, Daddy."

She spoke so simply. There were none of the usual currents in her voice, no hesitations or resentments or feelings withheld. Just the words themselves, sweetly said. She hadn't called him Daddy like that for as long as he could remember.

"Good night, Yumi," he repeated, because he wanted to say something else but couldn't think of what.

She smiled. "Sleep tight. Don't let the bedbugs bite."

That was it. That was what he should have said. What he used to say when he tucked her in every night, and gave her a kiss, and nibbled her nose, pretending to be the bedbug biting.

But she had already turned her head away and was looking back up at the ceiling. He knew he ought to go, but suddenly he thought of something else he wanted to say. "Oh, Yumi!" Breathless, he hesitated, holding on to the doorjamb for support. "It's so much fun to be alive!"

His eyes filled with tears then, and this surprised him, but he didn't mind. He was just happy he'd expressed his feeling. She looked alarmed, but he gave her a smile to reassure her. As he headed down the hall, he kept one hand on the wall. He would be fine as long as the wall was there, to steady him.

That's when it hit me for the first time, that when Lloyd died, I was going to be sorry. His words knocked all those intervening years of attitude right out of me. As he shuffled away, I listened to the frail grit of his slippers on the floorboards and the sound of his fingers as they brushed along the wall.

I had been waiting until everyone was in bed before going out to see Elliot, but now I went down to the kitchen and phoned his motel room instead. I stood in the darkened kitchen leaning against the wall and cupping the receiver.

"I have to see you," Elliot said. His voice was urgent, pressing me. "There's something I have to tell you."

"I can't," I told him. "Tell me tomorrow."

I slept badly that night and woke late the next morning, filled with dread. I got dressed quickly and checked Lloyd's room. His door was open, and the bed was empty. I collected Poo and continued my search.

The bathroom had been used. I smelled his aftershave, and the scent knocked me back through the years. Old Spice. It was only for special occasions.

Downstairs, breakfast was over and the kitchen was empty. Someone was testing the PA system, and the wail of electronic feedback cut through the stillness of the morning. From the window I could see the stage area where Ocean and Phoenix were playing. Ocean had let Chicken Little out of her coop, and now they were trying to catch her. Ocean was screeching, "The sky is falling! The sky is falling!" Her wild voice sent shivers up my back. I walked out to the porch. Lloyd was sitting in his rocking chair, leaning forward and gripping a sheet of paper in his hands. His lips were moving. He heard me and looked up.

"What's that?" I asked, shifting Poo on my hip. He was chewing on my hair. He wanted his breakfast.

Lloyd ducked his head, sheepish.

"It's my speech," he said, but his throat was so congested with spittle and fear he could barely get the words out.

"Oh, Dad! I wish you wouldn't . . ." My voice, too, had curdled into a petulant whine. He stiffened.

"I'll be fine," he said, speaking more clearly now, and there was enough reproach in his tone to get my hackles up.

"Fine," I echoed. "Whatever."

I clattered back through the kitchen door and dropped Poo in his high chair, wondering what just happened—how it was that in a matter of minutes my heart could harden so completely.

Still, when Lloyd stepped onto the stage later that morning, I held Poo so tightly he howled in protest. Cass reached out, happy for the excuse to take him. I handed him over and squeezed her arm.

"Lloyd will be fine," she whispered.

"Look at him," I said. "He's too sick. This is crazy."

He stood there, so tall and frail, holding the microphone and the piece of paper with his speech on it. He opened his mouth to speak, and the PA system gave an earsplitting squawk. He looked around, holding the mike away from him, not knowing what to do. The audience shifted, and someone laughed. It serves him right, I thought, furious with him, with everyone. I wanted to put a stop to this, to rescue him and drag him offstage, but I couldn't move. Then Geek came over and took the mike from him, tapped it, tested it, made sure it was safe and all was well, then handed it back. So calm and reassuring. Lloyd looked at Geek with bewildered gratitude.

Why couldn't I have done that?

The paper trembled in my father's hand. "My friends," he began, but even with the microphone working, you could barely hear him.

"Speak up, Lloyd!" someone yelled.

"My friends!" he repeated, loudly this time. "Mrs. Fuller and I welcome you."

Momoko was sitting just offstage in a folding chair. Someone in the crowd started to clap, and then a few more joined in. Lloyd waited until the clapping stopped, then raised his paper.

"Now, I'm not a minister," he read, and he broke off to look out over the audience. "I gotta say that," he explained, "seeing as it's Sunday and Reverend Glass is over there, and I don't want him thinking I'm stealing his show. . . ."

He nodded to the pastor, who held up his palm as in a blessing. They were old friends, and the audience laughed.

"Where was I? Oh, yes. Now, I'm not a minister, and thank God I'm not a politician either, but today is Sunday, and it's Independence Day, too, so I would like to take this time to reflect together on the place of faith, and government, and our Maker's design."

His reading voice was stilted and dry. I noticed a few of the young people rolling their eyes. Lloyd hesitated as though he had lost his place again, but instead of trying to find it, he just let the paper drop. The silence lengthened, and his head sank toward his chest like he was praying or falling asleep. Get him off, I thought, but the next moment he looked up again, straight out over the crowd. His eyes were clear, and when he spoke, his voice was strong.

"Mrs. Fuller and I have always assumed that whatever base corruptions man has inflicted upon nature, there were certain of our Maker's laws, sacred and inviolable, that even man could not breach. In this assumption we have been sadly mistaken."

I hadn't seen him like this since I was a kid and he was giving a talk to the Young Potato Growers, or to the congregation at a church function, or to the Rotary Club. He used to be a part of things, an important man, and one of the most powerful in Power County. And now he had it back. His sentences began to unfurl, tracing the peaks and valleys of his conviction, and his sudden confidence was like the scent of his aftershave, bracing to my pride. I took a deep breath, remembering the feeling. Nothing could go wrong now, because Lloyd Fuller was my daddy, and I could rest secure in the fullness of his authority.

"It has come to my attention that in 1998 the U.S. Department of Agriculture and the Delta & Pine Land Company, which is the largest cottonseed company in the world, announced that they had developed and received a patent for a new agricultural biotechnology that quite literally takes the breath of life right out of a seed. This patent permits its owners to create a sterile seed by cleverly programming a plant's DNA to kill its own embryos. This technology, nicknamed the Terminator, can be applied to plants and seeds of all species, including food crops, thereby, and in one ungodly stroke, breaking the sacred cycle of life itself."

Lloyd paused here and looked around. Everyone, young and old, was listening. "What good does this serve?" he asked the crowd. "To make a seed sterile? The answer is, no good whatsoever. Honest farmers, robbed

301

of their God-given right to save their seed, will be forced to purchase these new, blasphemous contraptions every year from corporations that claim to control the patent on life."

His voice tightened. "Corporations have words to make this sacrilege sound legitimate. They call it a 'Technology Protection System.' They claim it is necessary to protect their 'investments,' their 'intellectual property rights,' and their novel seed patents."

He raised his hand in the air. "Mrs. Fuller and I say this: *God holds the only patent!* He is the Engineer Supreme! And He has given up His seeds into the public domain!"

He brought his fist down as though banging a gavel. The gesture was too much for him, and he tottered. When he regained his balance, he turned and called to Momoko, who shuffled forward to stand next to him. He took her hand, and they faced the crowd, and when he spoke again, his voice was gentle and matter-of-fact.

"Mrs. Fuller and I sell only open-pollinated seeds, which you can save and plant as you choose. You may think that this doesn't make good 'business sense'—that it would be better to force our customers to buy new seeds from us each year—and you'd be right. That's the way of the corporations. But we're not concerned with that."

He swallowed, and I could see his bony Adam's apple leap up his neck. He looked down at the top of Momoko's head. "Our seeds contain our beliefs. That's why we urge you to continue to save them and propagate them and pass them on to others to do the same, in accordance with God's plan. In this way we chose to praise our Lord and to fulfill His design—of which mankind is just one small part."

He bowed his head.

"Amen."

He stood there gripping Momoko's shoulder. People rose to their feet and started to clap. The applause went on and on. Geek walked over and stood beside them. He took the mike and held up his hand for silence.

"As Lloyd has reminded us, today is the Fourth of July—Independence Day—and we are assembled here to declare independence from the corporate hegemony that is seeking to gain total control over global food supplies. In the spirit of America, in the spirit of our forefathers and foremothers, who fought for independence from economic slavery and colonialist oppression, in the spirit of the Boston Tea Party, we hereby declare this the Idaho Potato Party!"

What happened next I will never remember clearly, although later I would go over it again and again in my mind, trying to sort it all out. All I could recall was a series of impressions:

Lloyd standing onstage with a foolish smile, clutching Momoko's hand.

Geek raising his fist like a commander calling his troops to arms.

A television cameraman from the local news training his lens on them.

Frankie and Lilith and Melvin clambering onto the stage, wearing white protective suits and gloves and gas masks.

Ocean and Phoenix standing in the wings next to Lloyd's empty wheelchair. Ocean was jumping up and down, and Phoenix was holding on to her.

Then Geek had a megaphone and was instructing the crowd to move toward the potato fields, toward Fuller West Four, just beyond the poplars. The TV crew followed, staying close to the white-suited Seeds.

Cass handed Poo back to me and took off running.

And that's when I finally caught sight of Elliot. He stood to one side of the crowd, talking to a cop in uniform. When the cop moved off, I saw it was Billy Odell. Then I noticed the cruisers parked out along the road. Their lights were flashing.

I started toward Elliot, who was yelling at a man in mirrored sunglasses. Poo started to wail and wanted to get down. I held him tight and cut across the surge of the crowd. Dust hung thick in the air from all the feet. The man with the sunglasses turned his back, and Elliot saw me coming. He froze.

"Hi, Yummy." His voice was oddly cheerful, but his eyes were like empty holes.

"What's going on? What was the sheriff—"

But Elliot's cell phone was ringing, and he held out his hand in front like a cop holding up traffic. "Hang on." He flipped open the receiver to take the call. I heard him say, "A little bigger than I anticipated."

Then he said, "The sheriff called in the state troopers. They're standing by to—"

Then, "Well, we've got a citizen's group. A busload of church people. The contact assures me they'll speak on family values. I'm working on the farmer—"

And finally, "Of course, Duncan. But I'm just not comfortable—"

He listened for a while, staring but not seeing me at all, and then he snapped the phone shut. I watched as his eyes adjusted and I came back into focus.

"Yummy, I'm sorry," he said. "Come to the motel tonight."

"Elliot, what the fuck . . . ?"

"Please. It's important. I want to explain." He looked at me, and for a moment there was a door in his eyes that opened, leading back into a darkness that receded like a tunnel or a cave, but before I could see what was at the end, the door slammed shut and I heard his voice, faint now, coming from the other side.

"I'm sorry, Yumi," he said. He pronounced my name correctly, and I thought that was strange. "I didn't mean for things to turn out this way."

Everything was happening in slow motion, like a careful dance or a ritual war or a nightmare. Several hundred people were filtering through the poplar windbreaks and milling around on the far side along the dirt road, where the state troopers were waiting. Their squad cars formed a road block around the edge of Fuller West Four, which belonged to Will Quinn now. I was running, trying to push through the crowd, but I didn't know where I was going or why, certain of one thing only—that if there was going to be trouble, my kids would find the center of it.

A yellow school bus was parked just outside the police cordon. On one side hung a hand-painted banner, which read TRI-COUNTY INTERFAITH LEAGUE OF FAMILY VALUES. The man with the sunglasses was leaning against the bus, arms folded and watching. A picket line was starting to form, and placards were passed out to people as they got off the bus. I thought I recognized faces I had grown up with, members of the church and kids from my school. They were carrying signs: CLEAN UP LIBERTY FALLS! STOMP OUT PORNOGRAPHY! PROTECT OUR CHILDREN! THUS SAITH THE LORD . . .

I hugged Poo and pushed on, arriving at the edge of the field just in time to see Lloyd approach the sheriff. Lloyd was in a wheelchair, pushed by Melvin—or at least I thought it was Melvin, but it was hard to tell under the white suit and the gas mask. Phoenix and Ocean were tagging along.

"Billy Odell," I heard Lloyd say, "you're trespassing. I'm ordering you off my property."

And just then Will Quinn stepped up beside Billy.

"I'm sorry, Lloyd," he said. "This is my property now. Mine and Cassie's. You've got no right to allow these people to damage my crop."

"Let us through, Will," Lloyd said. "We have an agreement, remember? I'm entitled to use this land while I'm still living."

"Five acres of it. You're off the edge right now."

"Will Quinn, I sold you this land in good faith."

"And we've been good neighbors for years, Lloyd. Don't let these people make you forget that."

But it was too late, because the Seeds, dressed in their white suits and led by Geek, had stepped between the patrol cars and onto the field. They were making their way down the rows, parting the leaves as they tore the NuLifes from the ground. The tubers were still tiny, dangling from thick stems. The Seeds held the plants over their heads and shook them, and the dirt rained down over their white protective garments. I heard Lilith's shrill voice cry out.

"Liberate the farmers! Liberate the fields!"

Others picked up the chant, and a few dozen more people pressed forward.

"Liberty rises in Liberty Falls!"

The sheriff walked over with the chief of the state troopers.

"Well? What do you say, Will? They're trespassing now. If we're going to move, I'd say we do it soon, before they do too much more damage."

Will didn't answer. He watched the next wave of people move forward, uprooting plants as they went.

"This hurts me to see," he said, sounding puzzled, but speaking to no one in particular. Cass stood next to him, staring at the destruction.

"We can't let them get away with this," said the sheriff. "We'll have anarchy on our hands."

"Oh, for goodness' sake, Billy," said Cass. "Relax, will you?"

The sheriff stiffened. "Pardon me, Cass, but this isn't just about your crop. They're breaking the law, and I don't want precedents like this being set in my county."

"They said they'd reimburse us," Cass said. "It's not like we're going to be losing—"

The state trooper cut in. "That's not the point, ma'am. We've got intelligence that they're planning to move on the fertilizer plant in town later on, and I've got orders to treat this as an act of terrorism. We've got to send a message, loud and clear, or these punks will think they can get away with this kind of crap all over the state." He turned to Will. "We're going to have to move without you."

Will nodded, then looked at his wife. "What they're doing is wrong, Cass." He shook his head. "I thought I'd feel angry, but it just hurts me to see. How can they be so disrespectful of all those plants?"

And while everyone pondered the answer to that question, my father made a break for it.

Melvin had eased Lloyd past the sheriff and had gone to join his comrades in the field, turning the wheelchair over to Phoenix, who stood at attention behind his grandfather, with Ocean by his side. Now Lloyd urged them forward. Phoenix threw his scrawny weight behind the chair and gave it a mighty push, sending it careening down the embankment into the soft dirt at the edge of the field. The wheels sank and embedded, refusing to budge, but Phoenix came around one side and Ocean came around the other, and together they pulled Lloyd out of the chair and onto his feet. He stood on the spongy ground, tottering, his balance uncertain at first, and then he took a step. The children braced him. The Seeds saw him and cheered. A TV cameraman spun around and dropped to his knees, filming Lloyd as he reached down and uprooted a NuLife, holding it in his fist, high in the air above his head.

He stared straight into the lens of the camera. "Liberate the farmers," he croaked.

$\mathcal{BS}$

He looked unbelievable on the evening news that night. Standing there in the vast field with his fist raised against the blue sky, he shook the uprooted plant like a severed head, while his two grandchildren stood at his side.

"Tutu Lloyd, you're awesome!" Phoenix said, eyes glued to the TV.

"Look!" Ocean cried. "There we are!"

"Shhh," I said, trying to hear. The kids were ignoring me. Lloyd inched his wheelchair forward toward the television screen. I turned up the volume and listened.

"This land used to be mine," Lloyd was proclaiming. "I would never have planted these ungodly abominations on my land."

"You mean the potatoes?" the reporter asked.

"You can't call them potatoes, because they aren't," Lloyd replied. "Government has them registered as pesticides. Hell, I don't know what to call them. But I'll tell you one thing: I pray to God my grandkids won't have to grow up eating them!"

They showed a close-up of the potato plant and then a shot of Phoenix and Ocean helping Lloyd into the field.

Now, in the living room, Phoenix high-fived his grandpa.

"Yeah!" he said. "You tell 'em, Tutu man!"

Lloyd raised his palm to meet his grandson's. He was clearly pleased, but his face looked gaunt and exhausted. I had tried to get him to go to bed earlier, promising to videotape the news for him, but he insisted on staying up to see it for himself.

On the screen Will was standing next to Cass with the potato fields stretching out behind them. The caption at the bottom of the screen read WILL QUINN, LIBERTY FALLS POTATO FARMER, FIELD OWNER.

"I believe in freedom of speech and the right to protest as much as any American," Will was saying. "But this field is private property, and they got no right to trespass and undo all our hard work and interfere with my family's livelihood."

"His field. Ha!" Lloyd said. He sat back in his wheelchair. His color was rising. I looked at my watch.

"Dad? Don't you want to lie down?"

He flapped his hand at me. I was an annoying fly, and all my concern for him was just so much buzzing.

On the television the police moved into the field to arrest the protesters, who resisted, letting their bodies go limp and falling to the ground. The police dragged them out through the dirt. I watched them cuff Geek's hands behind him, throw Melvin up against the side of a squad car, and stuff Lilith into the back of the paddy wagon. Momoko had joined Lloyd in the field by then. One of the sheriff's men stood there cajoling them, but they refused to move. Charmey was the only one of the Seeds who was not wearing protective gear. Instead she wore a pretty sundress. She looked fragile and very pregnant, dragged by the armpits between a burly pair of cops.

And where had I been during all of this?

Scared witless, I'd entered the field, grabbed Phoenix and Ocean, and tried to haul them back to safety. It's that old fear of the cops. Hang back. Stay clear. Disappear. Clutch Poo and swear to the others that if they dare to leave my side again, I will lock them in the root cellar for life. But of course they wouldn't come. They were mortified—here it is, their moment of glory, and Mommy shows up. Panicking, I looked around for help. I saw Will talking to Odell. They were watching me and the kids. Odell shrugged, and Will spoke to Cass, then started toward us. He ignored me and addressed Phoenix. "You've made your point, son," he said, taking hold of his arm. "Now come along." In the face of that much authority, Phoenix's determination wavered, and Will led us all back across the road, behind the cordon.

Now, in the living room, watching the replay of the arrests on TV, Phoenix glared at me. "I shoulda stayed with the Seeds," he said. "I shoulda gotten arrested, too. Jail's not so bad."

Far better to be in jail than in the same house with your mother.

Just then Elliot's face appeared on the screen.

"Shhh," I said without meaning to, and the room fell silent.

"—like a modern-day witch hunt," he was saying with a smooth and pleasant smile. "Hysterical muckraking and fear-mongering by people who don't understand the careful science behind these technologies. These new crops are designed to minimize the environmental impact of some of the older farming methods, and as for the issue of human health, there's absolutely no evidence to substantiate accusations that—"

Lloyd sat upright and waved a trembling finger at the set. "Who's that?" His agitation was extreme. I jumped up and started looking for his nitroglycerin tablets.

"I recognize him," Lloyd said. "I saw him yesterday."

A caption scrolled across the screen, below Elliot's face: ELLIOT RHODES— CYNACO CORPORATION.

"No way!" Phoenix said. He turned and stared at me.

"What?" Ocean cried, tugging at her brother's shirt. "I don't get it. What does it mean?"

But Lloyd got it. He twisted in his chair and stared at me. His eyes were bloodshot. His hands gripped the padded arms. Behind him, on the television, the reporter had moved on to an interview with a spokesman from the interfaith group, who was demanding that the children of Power County be protected from pornographers.

I stood there holding out Lloyd's bottle of pills. Offering.

"Daddy?"

The word sounded like a question, and his answer was clear. As the high color drained from his face, he clutched his chest. Then he slumped forward, senseless, and toppled from his chair.

sixth

CRESS

I love everybody! I love everything!

—Luther Burbank,
sermon at San Francisco's First Congregational Church

visitations ℬ

Cass studied Elliot as he talked. He sat at their kitchen table, leaning forward, and he moved his hands a lot, something she remembered from when he was her teacher and would get excited about something he was saying.

"Frankly, Will," Elliot was saying, tapping the table, "I don't understand your reluctance. The Potato Promotions Council is on board with this. Damage was clearly done. We just want to see you recoup your losses, and in return we're asking you to help farmers everywhere by taking a stand to ensure that others in your position aren't victimized by this type of criminal mischief in the future."

Will wasn't saying much. "If they told you they'd reimburse you," Elliot said, "they were lying. These kids don't have two cents to their name. We're going to provide you with counsel and cover any court costs that the suit might incur. Of course we'd rather none of this had happened. We'd rather just ignore it, but that's not possible now. It's too . . . conspicuous. Too much press. Really, they brought it on themselves."

He turned his palms upward. His hands were clean, and his nails were buffed. Will's hands in comparison were big and hard, and now he was rubbing his face with them, up and down, like he was splashing on cold water. "What do you say, Cass?"

She thought for a while. Elliot was drumming on the table again. There was an underlying impatience in his manner that he was trying to hide, but she recognized it. She'd watched him pace back and forth in the dank room at the top of the stairs, waiting for poor Yummy to get her insides scraped out. It seemed to take forever, and he didn't say a word for the longest time, just walked back and forth, stopping occasionally at the window to stare down over the train yard, and maybe he felt the accusation in her eyes, because finally he turned and spoke to her. "I'm really bummed about this, too, you know. I wish none of this had ever happened, but it did. I'm just trying to help out, is all."

It was the same tone she was hearing now, bullying, ingratiating, and a little defensive, only he'd gotten better at smoothing it out.

"What's your role in all this?" she asked. "Are you a lawyer?"

Elliot smiled, but it was more for Will's benefit than for hers. "I work for a public relations firm that represents Cynaco," he said. His voice was careful and good humored, like he was trying to show Will what a nice, patient guy he was to indulge the wife's questions. "Normally I wouldn't be involved on this level, but since this case involves old friends . . ."

"We're not your friends," she said.

His smile wavered. "Well, I couldn't say. But Yummy is. She's been keeping an eye on that gang for me."

"She has?"

"In a manner of speaking. I was worried about her. You saw the way they moved in on the family, exploiting her father's illness."

"No," Cass said. "They weren't exploiting. They were helping."

"They got him all riled up, and he had a heart attack. That wasn't much help."

"He had the heart attack when he saw you on the news. The children said he keeled right over."

His face reddened. "I don't think—"

Will broke in then. "Cass, that's hearsay. And besides, it's not the point."

"Yes," said Elliot.

"No," Cass said. "It's totally the point. He doesn't care about Yummy or Lloyd. He never did. You weren't here before, Will. You don't know what happened."

"Cassie, the question is what to do now."

Cass turned back to Elliot. "Why do you need us? You've got the police and witnesses. All those church people on the bus."

"The damages occurred on your property. The DA wouldn't mind making an example of these kids, but he's not eager to move forward unless you're on board."

"Well, then I don't think we should press charges, Will. Our damages were so small, whether they pay us back or not, and I don't want to have anything more to do with this business than we can help."

She looked at Elliot critically. "I remember your history class, you know. You were an okay teacher."

"Thanks."

"It's a shame you turned out like this."

"Like what?"

"Lying to your friends. Doing whatever it is you do for that company."

"Cynaco's not a monster," he said, giving Will another long-suffering smile. "Neither am I. There are millions of starving people out there. We're just trying to feed the world."

Will nodded. "Those plants were our private property," he said. "It was wrong to destroy them."

Lilith telephoned the next day from the jail where the Seeds were being held. She sounded terse and upset.

"We heard you're pressing charges. I wouldn't have called you, except nobody's answering at the Fullers'."

She went on to explain. Charmey was having cramps. She was nauseated, and her lower back hurt. She'd had some bloody discharge over the night. Lilith was afraid she might be going into labor prematurely.

"I told her we had to tell someone," Lilith said. "She wanted you."

"Hold on," Cass said. "I'll be right there."

It took the rest of the day, but by the late afternoon Charmey had been transferred to the hospital and the doctor had given her a steroid and something to relax her and make her sleep. Cass stood by her bedside talking on the phone.

"Well, make it your jurisdiction," she said into the receiver. "Do what you have to do, Billy, because when the doctor releases her, I'm taking her home with me."

She hung up the phone and looked at Charmey. The girl's face was pale, her wild mop of black hair flattened against the pillow. Cass pulled the curtain shut around her, then left the room and took the elevator to Intensive Care.

She found Lloyd in one of the cubicles that faced onto the nurses' station. He lay there, eyes closed, arms straight at his sides. A web of tubing fed into his limbs, and a heart monitor beeped weakly above his head. On the oscilloscope screen a thin green line peaked and dipped, scrolling out the reading of his life.

Cass stood at the foot of the bed. Behind her she could hear the hospital sounds—footsteps, phones ringing, voices—but in front of her everything was still, except for the thin green beeping of the EKG. She heard Poo's voice cry out, "Caaa, caaa!" and she turned to see Yummy hurrying past the nurses' station with the baby clamped to her hip. He had spotted Cass and was squirming, reaching for her. Cass held out her arms.

"Thanks," Yummy said, handing him over. "He's sick of me carrying him, but I can't let him loose around here." She turned toward her father, and her shoulders slumped.

"How's he doing?" Cass asked.

"He's stable now, but his heart was fibrillating again last night. He's delusional. The doctor said his brain isn't getting enough oxygen. He keeps moaning on about seeds, how he's got to save them, but I don't know whether he's talking about his and Momoko's seeds or Melvin and the others. He knows they're in jail." Her voice was flat and monotonous. "The doctor's moving him to the cardiology unit. I guess they'll just monitor him and see what happens."

They stood side by side at the entrance to the cubicle and watched Lloyd breathe. His body looked so frail beneath the sheet. His gown had fallen open, and they could see the electrodes that were taped to his papery skin. Even those looked painful.

"The doctor says his heart has been severely compromised," she said. "It makes it sound like it's someone's fault, doesn't it? Maybe mine. . . ."

"No," said Cass. "It's not your fault."

"A compromised heart," she said. "Kind of poetic, isn't it?"

That night Cass started to clear out the spare room. It had been her room as a child, and when she and Will moved into her parents' bedroom, she had started getting it ready for a baby. She had painted the walls yellow, a cheerful color that would do for a girl or a boy, and made new curtains for the windows and even refinished the dresser. But over the years the empty room got tired of waiting. The walls dulled, and slowly things began to accumulate: canning jars, a broken toaster oven, a box of clothes for the Salvation Army, Will's college textbooks, back issues of *Spudman,* empty computer boxes with their molded foam inserts. At one point they had talked of converting the room into the office, but Cass couldn't bear it, so they built the addition instead. Somewhere along the line they'd stopped calling it the baby's room and started calling it the spare room instead.

Now she hauled all the old junk out to the car and brought it to the dump. Once the area was cleared, she saw that the walls were stained, so she went out and chose some new paint, a pale violet this time, and when the walls were done, she bought curtains and a bedspread and a rug to cover the cracked linoleum. She even bought a crib. It was sturdy and plain but would convert to a junior-size bed as the baby grew. She knew she was being stupid. The bed would never fit into the Winnebago.

Will didn't say a word. He didn't offer to help either.

"She's coming to stay with us," she had told him, standing in the doorway to the office. He just nodded. He'd been opening the mail, slitting the envelopes with his penknife.

"I stopped in on Lloyd," she said. "They're moving him out of Intensive Care, but he's not looking good."

"It's a shame," he said, glancing over a glossy fertilizer pamphlet before chucking it into the trash. "Those people really took advantage—"

"No. Lloyd knew what he was doing. Yummy says he's worried sick over them."

He swiveled his chair around toward the computer. She felt her face redden as she addressed his back. "Don't go pretending you care about him, Will. If you did, you'd drop the charges and get them out of jail."

ฟ๖

She stopped by the hospital every day to check up on Charmey, afraid that the sheriff would steal her away, but the girl was there and feeling better.

"Oooh," she said when Cass came in at lunchtime. "Look at it! They call this food! *Ce n'est pas possible!* I cannot feed my baby this crap!"

The lunch tray contained a bowl of tomato soup, a package of saltines, and a processed turkey sandwich on white bread. Charmey pushed it away. She was refusing the sleeping pills and the steroids, too, but her pregnancy had stabilized, and the doctor said he would release her by the end of the week.

"And Frankie must be released quickly, too," Charmey said. "Don't you think? There are so many things we must do to prepare for the baby."

Up in Cardiology, Lloyd was refusing food as well, but his condition was not improving. Yummy was cooking his favorite dishes at home, trying to tempt him, but he wouldn't eat.

"Ugh," he said, screwing up his face after a spoonful of her applesauce. "It's awful!"

Her split-pea soup was too thick and salty. Her oatmeal tasted like paste. Yummy left the room, and Cass found her in the courtyard smoking.

"He's impossible!" Yummy said. Her hand shook as she held the cigarette, and her eyes were bloodshot. The glare of the sunlight reflected off the concrete walls, and when she exhaled and squinted, Cass saw fine wrinkles lining the skin. "He's got water in his lungs. They drain it, but it keeps filling up again. They say only a small fraction of his heart is still alive, but I don't understand that. What does that mean?"

Cass shook her head.

"I wish they'd be specific," Yummy said, stubbing out the butt. "A quarter? An eighth? How much heart does a person need?"

chicken ✍

"There's no escape," Y said, inhaling deeply through his nose. "The physical body is a prison."

"They can't do this!" Frankie said, bouncing off the bars. "I mean, *terrorism?* What the fuck!"

"They're afraid we'll jump bail. Split the state." Y closed his eyes. "The only true freedom is in your mind."

Terrorism, pornography, obscenity, interstate trafficking, sedition. "Fucking right I'll jump if they charge us with all that." Frankie struck his forehead against the cinder-block wall. He wheeled around. "Oh, shit, do they have firing squads in Idaho?"

"Release the thought," Y said, exhaling. "They're just messing with your mind."

But Frankie was sensitive to lockups. Closed-in places made him tense—closets, classrooms, wards, and cells. He had a problem with authority, and when he was confronted with it, a shitty little sneer rose up inside him like sap in a young tree in springtime. It curled his lip like a leaf and narrowed his eyes. A long line of foster fathers had failed to wipe it off his face. He knew he had a bad attitude, but he couldn't control it.

ॐ

"What are you laughing at?"

Frank redirected his gaze at the concrete floor. Just him and three guards in a long, empty hallway.

"What's your name, boy?" said the guard who was doing the talking.

Frankie stared at the scuffed cinder-block wall. He tried to remember Charmey's coaching. *Think calm thoughts,* she said. *Think of funny things. When you laugh, they cannot make you angry. Breathe.*

"Speak up," the guard said. "I can't hear you." He rocked back on his heels, prodding the air with his lower jaw. The skin on his cheeks looked like a fat plucked broiler. When he elbowed his friends, his arms were like chicken wings flapping.

"Frank," Frankie said.

"Frank what?" He had wattles that wriggled. The other two were chuckling behind him, and it sounded like the clucking of excited fowl, filling the empty concrete spaces. "What's your last name, boy?"

"Perdue," Frank said, and now the clucking was getting louder. The long corridor echoed like a ghostly battery.

"What's that?" the guard squawked. "I didn't hear you!"

"*Frank Perdue!*" Frankie said, real loud and clear, but by now the three guards were crowing. They knew his name. They didn't need to hear it. They hooked their thumbs in their armpits and flapped their wings. They were having a good time.

Frank sighed, massaging his wrists, which were cuffed behind him. In his mind he was already launching himself headfirst into the bulging gut of the nearest guard, and he could almost feel the release that the pain would bring as the guard's fist made contact with his nose. He could see himself lying there in his own blood, gazing up at the bright, caged ceiling fixtures, debeaked and bathed in swimming lights.

Cock-a-doodle-doo.

His body tensed like a rocket yearning for takeoff, but he didn't move. Didn't head-butt the guard. Didn't even talk back. Instead he took a deep breath and got very still inside and allowed the three men to crow and flap and shove him around.

"What's wrong, boy? Are you *chicken?*"

Then, when the big guard collared him, he allowed his body to go limp. His cheek came into contact with the edge of the man's boot, but still he didn't resist, didn't even sneer. He just lay on the cold concrete, keeping his eyes closed and his mind focused inward on Charmey and the baby, and made the first of the compromises required of a father—that he be relatively intact, present, and alive.

traitor ✍

"It's all your fault!" Ocean yelled, throwing down her fork. She hadn't touched her food, and it was getting cold.

"It's true!" Phoenix said. "Nobody else wanted him here. If you hadn't invited him, he wouldn't have come, and Tutu Lloyd wouldn't have had a heart attack, and the Seeds wouldn't be in jail either!"

"That's ridiculous." I gave Poo another macaroni to chew on. Macaroni and cheese, and the cheese was congealing. "Geek said they wanted journalists and people from the press, so I—"

"Well, he *wasn't* a journalist, was he?" Phoenix said, driving his fork into a clump of noodles. "He lied to you, and you believed him. So that makes you an idiot *and* a traitor—"

"I was trying to help."

"—*and* a whore." He knew he had gone too far, but he couldn't stop. "The kids at school were right. All you care about is getting laid."

I didn't hit him hard. It felt like my body was obeying some hidden set of instructions and rose of its own accord, and my arm reached out and slapped him across the face. It wasn't hard enough to do much more than redden his cheek, but it was harder than I'd ever hit anyone. Phoenix sat back in his chair. Stunned, he looked at me, then quickly turned away, the way you might turn if you caught sight of a stranger doing something disgusting.

Ocean, on the other hand, just stared. "You hit him!" she said.

Poo tossed his macaroni onto the floor and started to cry.

Phoenix didn't say a word. He just pushed away from the table and walked out the door.

"Wait!" Ocean cried. "I'm coming, too!" She leveled a furious gaze at me. "We hate you!" she said, and took off after her brother.

I sat there for a while, watching Poo wail and hurl his noodles as the cheese continued to harden on my older children's plates, and then I went to the door. I saw them in the distance, walking down the road toward Cassie's house. Phoenix had a stick, and he was whipping the ground with it. I phoned Cass.

"Just intercept them, will you? Maybe you can let them play computer games for a while. They'd probably feel a lot better if they could blow something up."

"Sure thing, Yummy. What's going on?"

"Nothing." I thought about that. It didn't sound quite right. "Phoenix made a very mean crack, so I hit him." A long silence followed. "I've never hit him before," I added. There was more silence. I realized she could probably hear Poo, who was wailing behind me. "For God's sake, Cass. I'm not like your father. I don't beat my children as a matter of course. Phoenix was really rude. It just happened. Once."

Finally she spoke. "I know."

"I shouldn't have. I feel terrible. I'm just exhausted is all. It's no excuse."

"Listen, I see them outside. I've got to go."

I hung up and looked out into the garden. Momoko was standing by the fence looking down the road after the kids. She had stopped eating meals with us ever since Lloyd had gone to the hospital and the Seeds had been taken to jail. Instead she brought a small Tupperware container of food outside with her and ate it with chopsticks under the peach tree. I didn't know what would happen to her when winter came.

Winter. The word felt like lead. I could not imagine another winter here. But nothing had changed. My father was in the hospital again, in Cardiology, right back where we started seven months ago, when I first came home to say good-bye.

By the time Cass came over with the kids, Momoko had gone to bed and I was sitting in Lloyd's big armchair staring at the blank TV screen and drinking whiskey. The ashtray on the side table next to the armchair was full. Lloyd used to keep his reading glasses on that table, and a section of the evening paper. A letter opener and a cup of coffee.

The kids walked by me silently. Whiskey brave, I reached out and caught Phoenix's sleeve. He tried to pull away, then let his arm go limp.

"I'm sorry, Phoenix. I was wrong to hit you."

He ducked his head, which I took for an acknowledgment, and I hung on, hoping for more. "Yeah," he muttered. "I'm sorry I said that stuff about you, too, all right?" I let go. I knew I was not going to get a hug this time.

Ocean watched. Her brother headed up the stairs, but she lingered. She was still a little kid, needing a full reconciliation with her mommy, so I held out my arms and she sidled into them. I wrapped her up, folded her in. She was such pure solace, and I blessed her silently, appreciating every last sweet bit of her while I still had access. Eventually I had to let her go, and she gave me a nice big smack on the lips and ran upstairs.

I turned to Cass. "Wanna drink?"

She shook her head, but I led her back into the kitchen anyway. The half-emptied whiskey bottle was sitting on the kitchen table. I topped up my glass and sat down.

"Well?" she asked.

I explained what had happened. "It's Elliot. They blame him for everything—Lloyd's heart attack, the Seeds' arrest. He phoned the night of the action, just after I'd left with the ambulance. Phoenix answered. Called him a scumbag and a murderer."

"Good for Phoenix. Did you ever call him back?"

"No," I said, rubbing my temples. "I didn't know about it until tonight. Apparently he's called a couple of times, but the kids never told me. That's what started this whole thing—he called again tonight during dinner. Phoenix answered the phone, and I heard him saying something like 'Stay away from her or I'll kill you, you motherfucker.' I thought it must be those classmates of his, that maybe they were threatening Ocean, so I kept at him until he told me the whole story. I was sort of touched at his gallantry until he called me a whore."

I expected Cass to rise to my defense, but she just sat there, lips pursed, frowning and eyeing the level of my whiskey. I raised my glass in a toast to her.

"So are you going to call him?" she asked.

322

"I don't know. Do you think I should?"

"No. You know, he came by our house after the action to talk Will into pressing charges against the Seeds. I had a chance to look at him for the first time since . . . well, you know. He's a liar, Yummy, but it's worse than that, because he doesn't even know he's lying. He manipulates people. He was using you to get information about the Seeds. Now he's trying to use us. I just hate seeing Will fall for it, but he doesn't know any better. You do."

I felt my face go hot, and I took another swig. The disgust in her voice unnerved me. "Of course I know better," I said haughtily. "I'm just curious to hear what he has to say for himself, that's all. And while we're at it, what about Geek? I mean, talk about manipulating us!"

Cass shook her head. "At least Geek has an honest belief. I don't see Elliot believing in much of anything, except maybe himself."

"Maybe that's true, but at least Elliot's not turning my kids into young anarchists."

"No," Cass said. "You're doing a fine job of that all by yourself." She stood up, took the whiskey bottle from the table, and put it away on the top shelf of the cabinet.

"Hey . . ." I said. "Give me that!"

She turned around and glared. "You know what, Yummy? Sometimes I think you don't deserve those kids of yours. Sometimes I just want to snatch them away."

I glared back at her. I don't know how long we would have stayed there, glaring at each other like that, but just then the phone rang. We'd been talking in a hush, trying to keep our voices quiet, and now the ringer on the old wall phone made such a clamor that we both jumped, and somehow this struck us as funny.

"What if it's Elliot?" I whispered. "I don't want to talk to him now! You answer."

"I don't want to talk to him!"

"Quick before it rings again and wakes everybody up. It might be the hospital about Lloyd. Please, Cassie!"

So she picked up the receiver. "Fuller residence," she said. She listened for a while, then made a face at me. "Just a minute. I'll see."

She held her hand over the mouthpiece. "It's some woman journalist," she said. "Jill something or other. From Washington, D.C."

kali, the destroyer ∂

She had four arms and three eyes, and her tongue was snakelike and red. In one left hand she held a bloody scimitar, and in the other a severed head, but both her right hands were extended, palms up, as though offering benedictions. Around her neck she wore a garland strung with more human heads, and the belt that encircled her waist looked like a grass hula skirt made of hundreds of dangling arms, dismembered at the shoulder. Her skin was blue. She stood on the chest of a supine white man.

"Kali," Duncan said. "Goddess of Destruction. Quite something, isn't she?"

Elliot shuddered. He folded up the wrapping paper that had contained the small statuette. "Thank you, Duncan."

Duncan laughed. "I can tell you're not quite sure about her. I can read it in your eyes."

"No . . ." Elliot started to protest, and then he looked at her again. "Well, she is a bit terrifying, you have to admit."

Duncan leaned back in his oversize leather chair. "To the Western mind, hopelessly caught in the dualities of illusion, she would appear to be so. But Kali transcends paradox. She represents death and birth, because one cannot exist without the other. She represents the destruction of the ego, the liberation from the concerns that bind us to this plane of life and keep us from reaching enlightenment. She is violence, and she is compassion. Sybaritic and nurturing, cruel and benign, kind mother and vengeful whore . . ."

Sensing a shift in his employer's tone, Elliot looked up from the severed head.

Duncan was contemplating him. "Speaking of which, I got a call from Legal, Rhodes. About that friend of yours. Jillian. She's turning up with disturbing frequency in the oddest places. Legal ran a check on her and got the confirmation today. She's doing a piece on strategic litigation. Unearthed every SLAPP that Cynaco's got going."

"What?"

Duncan nodded. "Part of a series on corporate imaging. She's featuring the seed copyright infringement lawsuits that Cynaco has pending against farmers, as well as some rather confidential details from the Proactive Management Strategy."

"She got hold of the PMS?"

"Apparently." Next to the pantheon of gods on Duncan's vast desktop was a single folder, which he now drew in front of him. "She's leading off with your Idaho Potato Party and the subsequent case against the Seeds of Resistance. Which, let me remind you, I went along with as a means of proactive neutralization of a hostile cell, and you assured me the press would see it that way. But this?" He opened the folder and held up a batch of clippings, then started to read: "'Potato Party Protesters Liberate Cynaco Spuds.' 'NuLife Grower Powerless in Power County.' 'Farmer says, This Spud's a Dud.'" He replaced the clippings in the folder.

Elliot spoke up quickly. "I'm not worried about any of that," he said, looking Duncan straight in the eye and flapping his hand. "Those are just a few local papers. By the time this goes national, we'll have the whole thing turned around. The farmer I told you about is bringing the suit, and he's going to play even better than I thought. Salt of the earth, humble, and injured. We've got the church people out there in full force, picketing in front of the courthouse every day. We've got the Potato Promotions—"

But Duncan shook his head. "No, Elliot. You're not hearing me. Your friend Jillian has taken this to a whole different level."

He reached out his hand for the Kali statue, and Elliot passed it to him. He turned it over in his palm. "She is all women, all nature, the dark secret of the Universe." He pointed to the supine man, under her feet. "This is Shiva, by the way. Kali's consort. You know why he's lying here? To placate her. Story goes that she went on a killing spree, got drunk on all the blood and power, and started destroying everything in sight. To calm her, Shiva lay down and let her dance on top of him. It worked. Put an end to her rampage."

He handed back the statue. "The Hindu pantheon has some truly remarkable lessons, Elliot."

᠔᠊

By the time Jillian returned his call, three days later, the first of her series of articles had run. He had attempted to get the piece quashed, but she'd gotten to his other contacts at the paper first, so that when he called, he could sense their bemused smiles over the phone as they assured him they would do what they could do. Of course they didn't. As a former journalist and fallen member of their ranks, Elliot knew that any further persistence on his part would only confirm the truth of her assertions and make the situation worse.

What he needed was leverage. He couldn't go back to Duncan yet. Idaho was bad, and Delhi was worse, but there were still other possibilities that made Elliot wince. "Oh, Elliot, we're having a little image problem with that pipeline up in Umiat, Alaska." So instead he waited.

The article astonished him. It was entitled, "The Idaho Potato Party: A New American Revolution?" and it focused on the lawsuit brought by Will, Cynaco, and the state of Idaho against the Seeds of Resistance. She had described in detail the Independence Day action in the potato field, and in the process she had dug up everything else: Cynaco's use of private investigators to spy on farmers and infiltrate activist groups, lawsuits against farmers charging them with patent and copyright infringement for planting unlicensed seeds, and libel cases against activists and reporters for criticizing food and agricultural products.

She had spelled out the meaning of SLAPP—Strategic Litigation Against Public Participation—and delicately lambasted Cynaco and other corporations for using the American justice system as a censorship tool to undermine the First Amendment and to squash criticism of their products and practices.

Somehow she'd even managed to imply that Lloyd Fuller's heart attack was caused by Cynaco's harassment.

It was a compelling, if somewhat audacious, piece of investigative journalism, and there was a time when Elliot might have felt proud of her spunk. He didn't know she had it in her. Though, on second thought, maybe she didn't. Maybe her spunk was simply rage at him, for being such a prickless little fuck. At least that's what he surmised, talking to her on the phone when she finally called him back.

The ringing woke him from a deep, dreamless sleep. The machine picked up.

"Wake up, Elliot, if you want to talk to me."

He grabbed the receiver. "Aw, Jillie . . ." he groaned, rolling over. "Why'd you have to go and write that?"

"It's my job. Let's just say I got real interested in the thoroughness with which certain PR operatives infiltrate their sources."

"Huh?"

"You used to fuck her, Elliot."

He choked. "Excuse me?"

"Yummy Fuller. I always knew you were a dick, Elliot, but she was fourteen years old! You were her goddamned history teacher!"

Elliot sank back against the pillows and closed his eyes. Her voice had the effect of a wood rasp on the soft tissue of his brain. He didn't know that he could feel pain there. He held the receiver away from his ear, let it rest on the pillow beside him. Her voice was tinny now.

"And twenty-five years later you screw her some more? What were you thinking?"

He pondered her question but couldn't come up with an answer. He picked up the receiver again and put it to his ear.

"Why'd you do it, Jillie?"

He heard her sigh. "You really don't get it, do you? At first I was just curious. I wanted to find out why you were so preoccupied with Liberty Falls. But after talking to her—"

"To Yummy?"

She paused. "How could you have sex with someone named Yummy?"

"That's not her real name."

"Whatever. Yes. I talked to her. She wasn't terribly helpful, but her son certainly was. As was Cass Quinn, and the local sheriff, and the lawyer representing the Seeds of Resistance, who are languishing in jail. And after hearing about the way you treated all of them, I just decided to fuck you. Interpenetration, Elliot. For the way you screwed us all."

"For chrissakes, Jillie," he said huffily, starting to defend himself. "I didn't *screw* anybody." But then he remembered Shiva and backed down. "At least I didn't mean to. Was I so bad? I thought we had a good time. I thought that's what you wanted—"

"What I *wanted!*"

So much for placating. He held the receiver away again, shrinking from her rampage.

"I'm thirty-four years old, Elliot! I'm not part of your free-love generation, remember? That was just a lousy exploitative concept you hippie dickheads came up with to get fourteen-year-old chicks into bed."

No, he thought mournfully. You don't understand. It wasn't just that. Free love was so wonderful. So . . . free.

"Love is not free, Elliot. It costs. And you're just a fucking stingy bastard who's too cheap to pay."

327

He tried Yummy later that day. As usual, the kid answered.

"I told you to stay away from my mother, you scumbag!"

He sighed. He was really beginning to hate the telephone. He stared at the statue of Kali that sat on the far edge of his cluttered desktop. "Don't talk to me that way," he said listlessly.

He heard the click of an extension picking up, then, finally, Yummy's voice.

"Phoenix, get off the phone, please."

"It's a wrong number, Mom."

Elliot broke in. "Yummy, it's me."

"I know," she said. He heard the sound of a receiver clatter to the floor, followed by the boy's footsteps.

"Just a moment," she said, then muffled the phone. He waited, straining to hear what she said to her rude brat of a son, but he couldn't make out the words.

"Hi," she said. "Sorry about that." She sounded very composed.

"Hi." He sounded less so. His heart was pounding. He tried for levity. "Your secretary does a good job screening your calls. I've been trying to reach you for weeks."

"He's very protective." She paused. "I haven't been home much."

"Yes, I gather." He paused, listening to the silence that was opening between them. Now that he finally had her on the line, he couldn't think of what to say. He scanned the heaps of paper and junk on his desk, looking for a clue. He wasn't even sure why he was calling, except that she was one more urgent item on an urgent list of things to do, calls to make, business yet unfinished, crises ready to break.

He knew he had lots of things to tell her.

"So?" she asked.

"I'm sorry about your father," he said weakly.

"He's not dead yet."

"It must be hard."

Another long silence, and then she spoke. "Yes. There's no one left here to help."

"I've been trying to call. Did your son give you any of the messages?"

"I heard."

328

"I don't think Phoenix likes me much."

"No. He sort of picked up on the general Elliot-bashing vibe. He blames you."

He felt his heart constrict. "For what?"

"Well, a lot of things. You got his friends thrown in jail, for one."

"I didn't make them go into that potato field."

"Then your girlfriend called and talked to him. By the way, she seemed shocked to hear that you'd had sex with me when you were my teacher. I didn't think people in Washington, D.C., got shocked about that kind of thing."

"She's not my girlfriend."

"But mainly Phoenix blames you for his grandpa's heart attack."

"Me?"

"Sure." He heard the ratchet of her lighter as she lit up a cigarette. "Lloyd has hallucinations about you. He calls you the Terminator."

"Why me?"

"Well, aren't you?"

He could almost hear the subdued rattle of her scimitar, the build of her rage. He knew he was making a tactical error, but he was tired of getting stepped on. "Listen. I didn't start this. I wasn't the one exploiting a sick old man to further some political agenda."

She exhaled sharply. "No. You exploited me instead. And now you're exploiting Cass and Will. You lied to me about being a reporter. Why didn't you just tell me? I wouldn't have cared."

"I never said I was still a reporter. I said I was working on a story. Which was true."

"Oh, right! Your girlfriend told me all about the slimy way you operate. Phoenix is right. You are a scumbag—and a murderer."

He could picture it perfectly, the old man's panic, the pain as he gripped his heart.

"No," he told her. "I *saved* your father's life."

"What?"

"That night in Liberty Falls. When you ran away."

It was time to lie down under her feet. Time for full disclosure. He started talking. The words came, fast and urgent, and he hoped that when he finished, her manifestation would be merciful and compassionate.

"That night, after the abortion, when I drove you home, I knew I had to break it off. I'd made a terrible mistake, Yummy, and I didn't want to hurt you any more than I already had. When I told you, you didn't seem at all sorry or surprised, and I figured you were sick of me. I didn't know you had run away until later.

"I was asleep. There was a pounding at the door, and I got up to answer, thinking it was you. The wind rushed in. It was freezing outside. Your father was standing there. I could barely see his face, but I knew who he was. He had a rifle hugged to his chest. He demanded to know where you were. He raised the rifle like he was going to shoot me, but instead he pushed me out of the way with the barrel and came into the house. He was clumsy and half crazed, knocking over chairs and the table, slamming doors and smashing holes in the drywall with the butt of his gun, just tearing the house apart.

"I stayed out of his way. I managed to find some clothes and put them on. I had my car keys in my hand and was looking for my shoes, about to make a run for it, when it got real quiet. I heard a strangling noise coming from the bedroom. I went in. Your old man was kneeling on the floor next to the mattress, rocking back and forth. He was holding a small knitted thing. A sweater you'd left behind. He was twisting it in his hands and saying, 'Where is she? Where is she?' like he could wring you out of the fabric. He was sweating, then this gurgling sound came from his throat, and his body went rigid. His hands curled into fists, like mallets, and he struck his chest, once, twice, hard, then he doubled over and started gagging. I went over to him, asked him what was wrong, but he couldn't talk.

"Somehow I got him on his feet and out the door. It was icy, and I could barely support his weight and keep from slipping in the driveway. I didn't call 911. Maybe he didn't want me to. He was so big I could barely manage to fold him into the Volkswagen. He didn't say a thing for the whole ride in, just sat there gasping and clutching your sweater, but as we approached the emergency room, he started to speak. He told me one of your neighbors was going to report me to the sheriff and have me arrested for statutory rape. As the orderlies were taking him away, he grabbed my sleeve. 'Go!' he said. 'Find her. . . .' There were nurses and people watching, so I guess I promised. He let go, and they wheeled him off. I went back to my house and packed and left that night. I wasn't going to wait around for the sheriff or a lynch mob from the PTA."

He paused. Full disclosure, he reminded himself.

"Your father survived, so you see? I saved his life. But I didn't try to find you. I had no idea where you might have gone. I figured if you had run away, it was just some attention-getting stunt, that you'd come home on your own. Kids do it all the time, and you were pretty precocious. Right then I just needed to get out of Idaho before the cops showed up. I had friends in New York, so I drove east. You know the rest. I wasn't proud of what had happened, and I guess I just forced myself to forget all about you."

He took a deep breath, waited, and then he spoke again into the deadening silence of the long years and miles that lay between them.

"Yummy, you've got to believe me when I tell you how deeply I regret all this now."

full circles &

I replaced the receiver into the cradle and stared at the phone. It was the living room phone, made of thick black plastic, and, like the phone in the kitchen, it had a real metal bell inside that rang loudly whenever a call came in. These old phones are cumbersome to operate, and the higher the number, the farther your finger has to travel around the dial. I stuck my finger in the zero hole and rotated until it hit the crescent-shaped steel stop, and then I pulled it out again and watched the dial revolve slowly backward. Zero has the longest arc—the wheel has to come full circle.

Momoko was weeding by moonlight. I walked out onto the porch with a glass of ice water and watched for a while, then threaded through the maze of beds to join her. The moon was almost full again, and my mother's garden glimmered. She didn't hear me coming, but I could hear her. Amid the night cries of insects, she muttered and sang. Cajoled her seedlings. *"Gambatte ne, tané-chan. . . ."*

Be strong, little seed.

It was a sound that moved me like a heartbeat. I walked along the dirt paths to the bed of bunching onions where she worked. The smell of onion was sweet in the air.

"They're not *tané,* not seeds anymore," I said, squatting down next to her. "They're full-grown plants."

331

She looked up and blinked. The moon cast a silvery light across the planes of her face. "No," she said. "Grown-up plant is seed, too. Like those ones." She pointed to a cluster of tall purple flower balls, perfectly round and globelike on their thick stems. "Those ones are only flowers now, but they gonna be seeds." She stretched her arms to accommodate the whole garden. "Everyone gonna be seeds."

The onion flowers looked comical. They oscillated like Styrofoam balls on the ends of car antennae. I pulled one close to my face and studied the little florets. The smell was stronger. Momoko went back to her weeding. I released the flower and watched her for a while longer, drinking my water until the ice rattled against the plastic in the bottom of the tumbler. It was tricky, talking to her. Her memory waxed and waned, returning in phases only to disappear into darkness again. These days she usually remembered she had a daughter and that daughter had run away, but only rarely did she connect that girl with me.

"Mom? When did Lloyd have his first heart attack?"

She jabbed at the earth with a trowel. "I don't remember."

"Was it the night I ran away?"

She nodded. "That's right."

"I didn't know that." I dug a small hole in the earth and planted an ice cube, then covered it up again. Maybe tonight was a good night. I took a deep breath. "Was it my fault?"

She shook her head. "No. It was his heart. His fault." She jabbed the ground vigorously, over and over. His heart. His fault. I watched the chrome tip of the trowel sink into the loam.

"Why didn't he ever come after me? You know, after he got better."

She looked up, bewildered, and nudged her glasses with the back of her hand. No, she was too far gone for this conversation. She couldn't possibly remember, but still I pushed on. "The least he could have done was write. He never answered a single one of my letters!" It sounded like whining, but I couldn't stop.

She bent over and teased out another weed, then sat up again on her heels. She wiped her hair off her forehead with the back of her sleeve. In the moonlight she looked young as she gazed off toward the potato fields.

"He never saw letters," she said.

Her words were slow to sink in. "Never saw them?"

She looked down at her hands. "He was too sick. He almost dying. Doctor said I must not make any upset for him. Upset will kill him."

She was talking to herself now, and her voice sounded far away. "Yumi's letter is so full of upset, I think maybe it gonna kill him. Even if she is so mad at him, I know she don't want to kill her daddy. She is not that kinda girl."

"He never knew about them?"

"Oh, no. I tell him. I tell him about Yumi, how good she is doing."

"But he never asked to see them?"

She shook her head. "He is too scared of her. He is too much coward."

"Dad?"

She nodded. "His heart attack make him like that, cut him down like a big tree. Before that he was so proud man! He make big money that year. He was real big shot around town, let me tell you. All puffed up. He got lotsa land and lotsa potatoes. Nine-Dollar Potatoes."

Momoko smiled, remembering, and so did I. "What happened?" I asked. "What changed him?"

"First she run away from him. Then his heart go against him, too. After that he is always scared. Doc say when the man cannot trust his heart no more, maybe he gonna go a little crazy, too."

Momoko was stabbing the earth and pulling up clumps, tossing them onto a wilting heap. I watched her, then noticed she wasn't pulling up weeds but the onion plants themselves. My own heart was beating fast.

"Mom?"

Mechanical. Plant after plant.

"Didn't you worry about me?"

Yanking the stems. Head bowed to the task. "She write me lotsa letters. I know she is strong girl. *Shikkari shiteru*, you know? Like me. I send her all my seed money."

I reached out and put my hand on her wrist. "Those are the plants, Mom. Not weeds. You don't want to be pulling those up."

She looked up, and her eyes were wide and confused as she searched my face.

"Yumi chan?"

My heart leaped. It had been weeks since she'd called me by my name.

"Yes, Mom." I knelt in the dirt in front of her and put my hands on her shoulders, facing her squarely, the way I faced Ocean when I wanted her to understand how seriously she was loved. I pulled her toward me and hugged her. She was as small as my child, and I felt her frail bones next to my breast and her heartbeat against mine. She clung to my waist like a vine, and I wanted to whisper to her, *Gambatte ne!* I watched the moon over the top of her silvery head.

Small explanations, pulled like pebbles from the ebbing tide of her mind. But they helped to fill me up, so I didn't feel so hollow.

"Come on," I said, releasing her. "Let's get some sleep now."

She nodded obediently and looked around to collect her tools. "I'll come back for them," I told her. "I'll pick them up later."

I helped her to her feet, steadying her as she navigated the crumbling earth. I led her by the hand, out of the onion patch and back up to the house. After she was tucked into bed, I crept up the attic steps. Phoenix was asleep, the blankets and bedclothes all tangled around his skinny limbs. I wanted to go and straighten them out and smooth down his covers, but instead I just stood in the doorway and listened to him breathe.

birth ❧

When Charmey was hungry, Cass felt the pangs. When the baby kicked and fluttered, burped and hiccupped, these mundane signs of life made Cass stop what she was doing and catch her breath. Charmey sensed the pull, and she shared the baby's gestation, drawing Cass's hand to her abdomen and pressing it against the swell until Cass could tell the difference between a punch and a roll, a poke in the cervix and a kick in the ribs. Together they played Name That Bump, gently pressing Charmey's belly to identify the baby's body parts—the rebounding head, the soft bottom, the bundle of extremities opposite the smooth arc of the spine. Charmey was not shy with her body. She shared her most intimate indications: the thin leak of colostrum from her breasts and all her various discharges. Cass spent hours rubbing oil into the girl's tight, itching skin while Charmey described the details of this miracle of birth.

"Oh! *C'est terrible,* these . . . how do you say? These diarrheas, *les hemorrhoids!*"

They were like mother and daughter, Cass thought as she calculated their ages. It was not a stretch. Charmey was nineteen, the age Cass had been when she miscarried her first child. That child would be Charmey's age now. The thought excited her, and she felt fiercely maternal as she coached Charmey with her breathing exercises, puffing along, or peeked into her room at night to watch the girl sleep.

Then she realized that if she were Charmey's mother, she was about to be a grandmother. This was not so exciting, and she shook off thoughts like these. They confused her, made her angry, as though the whole middle section of her life—the part where she was supposed to grow to adulthood, bear children, be a young mother, and watch her children grow—had simply been elided. Slurred over. She felt, at once, far too old and impossibly young, and there was a great gap in the middle, like a section of her torso had gone missing. Sometimes in dreams she lived in these gaps, where small false starts came to naught, and sparks of life shriveled or spiraled up like burning ash only to turn to powder on her fingertips when she tried to catch them in the air.

Will would shake her awake, woken himself by her twitches and groans.

"Cass," he said, his hand firm on her arm. "Cass."

It was the only time she still felt close to him, in these half-dream states in the middle of the night. He had bad dreams, too, and over the years she had woken him often enough, sweating and shaking, to feel grateful when he reciprocated.

The two of us! she'd think, watching him crawl back into consciousness and shiver off the nightmare.

The two of us. Will had first used the phrase one night before they were married. How it had thrilled her seventeen-year-old heart! It was a grim little phrase, and hardly as grand as other declarations he might have made, but the sense of bonding it conveyed made Cass feel safe for the first time in her life. They were survivors. They belonged together. Running beneath the words was a feeling of awe at the luck of their union. It meant far more than "I love you."

Daily living had eroded much of the awe, but the phrase had endured. It continued to comfort her even while its meaning changed, growing tougher with every year as it mocked their childless number.

When Will had decided to go forward with the lawsuit, Cass felt a huge rift splitting the two of them apart. And maybe the rift had started earlier, since the arrival of the Seeds, or since Yummy had come back to Liberty Falls—Cass couldn't quite locate the onset, but she had felt herself drifting away from Will.

"I'm not testifying against them," Cass told him. "I don't want any part of this."

Will stuck to his guns, even though she could sense that he was not convinced by Elliot's fast talking. "It's the principle of the thing," he insisted. "They can't just go around violating other people's rights."

"People's rights? What about Frankie's? You don't think he has a right to be here when his baby's born?"

"Not to mention the fact of them bringing that pornography into the town."

She exploded at that one. "Oh, like no one in Liberty Falls ever bought a dirty magazine at the gas station! That's just hypocritical, Will, and you know it. You never even looked at the Web site."

"I don't need to." Will shook his head. "I just don't approve of them, is all."

Conversations always ended something like this, and Will spent a lot of time out in the fields or in his office. He stayed clear of the spare room. Meanwhile, down at the courthouse, the Tri-County Interfaith League of Family Values was holding a daily vigil, picketing outside with signs that read TERMINATE THE DEMON SEED! and PORNOGRAPHY IS TERRORISM OF THE SOUL! and RID US NOW OF THE SEEDS OF TEMPTATION!

Cass had to pass by this gauntlet on her way to the jail next door, where the Seeds were being held. People recognized her as Will's wife and cheered whenever she passed by. She knew some of the local folks, but others were strangers to her, clearly from out of town. She wondered why they were there and where they had come from. They had crazy petitions for passersby to sign, demanding that the Seeds be brought to trial for felony offenses including terrorism and even treason. Of course they all assumed that Cass was supporting her husband and their cause. What they didn't know was that she was harboring a demon seed in her spare room and conveying updates to another one in lockup.

"Charmey's fine, Frank," she told the boy. "The doctor just wants her to stay lying down. That's why she can't come to see you."

He didn't look so fine. He had a fresh cut on his chin, and a bruise healing on his cheekbone. He beat on the bars with his fist. The guard glanced up, but Cass shook her head, and he went back to his magazine. It was the local jail, and the guard was the son of someone she knew.

"I can't believe this shit!" Frankie said. "That's my fucking kid getting born. I gotta be there!" He bowed his head and ran his hands over his scalp and stayed like that for a while. Outside, the protesters had started to chant something, but she couldn't really hear what they were saying.

"Listen," Frankie said, raising his head. "Tell Charmey to hang in there, okay? Tell her to stay chill and keep on breathing like we practiced. Tell her . . . I don't know what the fuck to tell her."

"What happened to your face?"

He ducked his head again. "I fell." Then he looked up quickly. "Hey, don't tell her that, all right? Tell her everything's cool. Tell her I love her and I didn't hit back."

Cass delivered the message, but as the days wore on, the girl was starting to fret. She drew her lips together in a little pout of worry. *"Ce n'est pas possible,* do you think? That the baby will arrive before they are liberated?"

Given the severity of her preterm labor symptoms and the stubbornness of the judge, Cass thought it quite possible. She tried to encourage Charmey to prepare herself for a hospital birth, but Charmey just shook her head—Frankie and Lilith would be liberated, and they would give birth in the Spudnik as planned. So Cass contacted the hospital behind the girl's back and made arrangements for a delivery room. She packed a suitcase, but she assembled a collection of clean towels, antiseptics, shower curtains, and a dishpan, just in case Charmey was right.

"He will be here," the girl said.

Groans in the night. Yelps of pain. Unquiet repose. Common sounds in the Quinn household, which was why, one night in early August when Cass woke to the sound of whimpers coming out of the dark, she rolled over to rouse her husband from his dream only to find him wide awake and staring at her. They both sat up in bed. The noises were coming from the spare room.

They worked quickly, snapping back into orbit with an efficiency you learn on a farm. Will called the hospital and the sheriff's office while Cass sat with Charmey timing her contractions, which were coming fast and strong. Charmey was moaning and calling out Frankie's name as Will carried her out to the Suburban. He placed her in the backseat, and Cass climbed in after, with the pillows and blankets and the suitcase she'd packed in advance. Will gunned the engine.

"Ready?"

Cass nodded, and they took off. The potato fields were lush and gleaming on either side of the dirt road. A streak of moonlight rippled along the massy surface of the leaves, moving along with the car. Charmey let out a long howl that ended in a sob. "Frankie . . . *please!*"

Cass glanced up at the back of Will's neck as she drew the girl toward her, cradling her head and wiping the damp hair from her brow.

"Oh . . . *je crève!*" Charmey moaned, arching her back and twisting as the contraction wracked her. "I'm dying!"

Cass held her down, pressing her shoulders. "Charmey, listen to me! You're not dying. You're having the baby."

"Please . . ." Charmey's eyes were dark, and tears glistened on her lashes.

"Just breathe. Come on. You know how to do it." Cass started panting the short rhythmic breaths. Ahead she could see the red and blue lights from the sheriff's SUV, waiting for them at the entrance to the highway. Will honked and flashed his headlights, and the SUV pulled out in front of them. Charmey started to moan again as the two vehicles spiraled up the tight ramp.

The sheriff's siren wailed as they merged onto the highway.

"Frankie!" Charmey howled, and Will floored it.

Cass knew hospitals, and her associations had nothing to do with the joyful emergence of a new life. Sweat and antiseptics. Anesthetized fears. Exactly what the girl wanted to avoid. The obstetrician arrived. He palpated Charmey's hard belly and checked her dilation. "Prep her," he barked to the nurse. "Don't let her push." He looked at Charmey's white face. "Did you hear that"—he glanced down at her chart—"Charlene? Hang in there, but no pushing." Then he turned to Cass. "Follow me."

"Charmey," Cass said. "Her name is Charmey."

The doctor led her to a prep room, where a nurse handed her a surgical gown and mask and pointed her toward the sink. "The baby's a breech," he said, slipping on his gown. "We're going to stand by to do a cesarean if we can't get it out." He scrubbed his hands. "You say there were preterm complications?"

Cass explained.

"She should have been monitored constantly," the doctor said, holding his hands in the air while he backed through the swinging doors that led into the delivery room. "In this day and age! With all the technology of modern medicine . . ."

"She wanted to deliver at home," Cass said.

The doctor snorted. "Medieval. There's no excuse."

ॐ

Later on, after hearing the details of his daughter's birth, Frankie would proudly announce, "Ass backward! That's how my daughter came into the world."

But at the time, on the delivery table, it seemed like a long shot that the baby would voluntarily enter the world at all. She was a frank breech, folded in the uterus, her legs pressed flat up against her face and her buttocks presenting. A perfect pike position. For a gymnast.

"Paschimottanasana," Y would say. "Forward bend."

"Can you believe they call it a frank breech!" Frankie would muse. "Isn't that wild? She musta been thinking of me."

"A posture of surrender," Y said. "A pose of release."

"Fuck that," said Frank. "She wasn't surrendering to nobody." He slammed the heel of his hand against the frame of the bunk. "Shit, dude, I shoulda been there!"

But he wasn't.

In the waiting room Will paced like an expectant father, stopping in his tracks every time a nurse or a doctor or member of the hospital staff passed by. There was one other man in the room, a farmer by the looks of him, watching an infomercial on the television.

A nurse poked her head in the door. Will paused and waited, but the nurse left.

"Must be your first," the farmer said to Will. "First one's always tough."

Will was about to explain, but instead he found himself nodding.

"They say it's easier if you get in there and watch," the farmer said. "Give 'em a hand, you know? But my wife says she'd be embarrassed to have me

339

there, and frankly, I get queasy looking at all that blood. I've done my share of calving, so I know what I'm talking about, but it's different when it's your wife, you know? I figure I done my part, and this part of the business is up to her. I'll just sit out here and watch TV, thank you."

Will sat down in an adjacent chair. He wanted to explain that the baby wasn't his, that he wasn't the father, that the father would have been right there pitching in and helping out, only he couldn't because he was in jail. And that was Will's fault. He sighed. "You farm?" he asked, changing the subject.

"Dairy," the guy said. "Just a small operation. Used to grow potatoes, but we got out of it. Margins just got too tight."

Will nodded. "I know what you mean."

"Thought you was a spudman," the guy said. "You look beat."

A nurse poked her head around the corner. "Mr. Lauterbach?"

The farmer sat bolt upright, like he'd been poked in the chest with a prod. He opened his mouth, but no words came out. The nurse smiled.

"Mrs. Lauterbach is fine. She did a great job. And the baby's fine, too. Come on, see for yourself."

Lauterbach gripped the arms of the chair and got to his feet. Will did likewise. He held out his hand to the farmer, who took it and clasped it hard.

"It's a boy!" Lauterbach said. "We knew that part beforehand." He pumped Will's hand up and down. "Whoa, Nellie! I got myself a son!"

"Congratulations," Will said.

"Hey," Lauterbach called over his shoulder. "Good luck!"

Will sat back down and aligned his arms along the armrests. He looked back up at the television. The infomercial host was leaning forward in his chair, holding up a box containing a digestive aid, labeled SPIRULENA PLATENSIS, THE HAWAIIAN SUPERFOOD.

"Grown organically at the Aloha Aina Algae Farm," the host was saying. "*Aloha aina* means 'love of the land.' Isn't that just what it's all about, folks?" The studio audience broke into ragged applause.

The door opened. It was Cass.

Will jumped to his feet and went to her and wrapped his arms around her. Her body swayed as though her knees were about to give out. "Do you want to sit down?"

She shook her head. "She's fine," she said, but her words were so muffled he could barely hear. He took her by the arms and held her away from his chest. "Charmey's fine," she repeated. He led her to the chair and sat her down, then squatted in front of her, holding on to her hands.

"The baby?"

"She's fine, too."

Will exhaled. He stood and walked across the room, then came back again.

Cass looked up. "It was hell," she said. "It was amazing." There were tears in her eyes, and her face was pale.

"You okay?"

She nodded, and then her face lit up. "You want to see her?"

He followed her down the hallway to the nursery. There, behind a plate-glass window, was a double row of cribs filled with babies. Cass clutched Will's arm and pointed to one of them. She was lying on her back, bright red and naked except for a diaper. Will could tell she was a girl by the pink bow on the crib. A nurse came by to collect her and caught sight of Cass. She pointed toward the baby and made a cradling motion with her arms. Cass gripped Will's arm harder and nodded. The nurse met them at the nursery door, carrying the baby wrapped in a blanket.

"I was just taking her back to see her mommy," the nurse said. "But I guess it's okay if you hold her for a bit. You certainly did your share of the work in there."

She placed the baby in Cass's arms. Will watched the way his wife held the infant, as though she could absorb it into her body. He heard the humming sound she made. The baby moved her wrinkled hands weakly, batting the blanket like a blind worm. He reached out his fingertip and touched the tiny palm. The baby grasped it. Innate. Reflexive. Fingers gripping. Cass looked up at him and smiled with such infatuated delight he couldn't bear to look anymore. He withdrew his fingertip.

"Cass, I'm sorry—"

"Don't," she said. Warning him. Don't say something you don't mean.

He paused, wanting to apologize some more, but not knowing for what.

"The boy should have been here," he said finally, choosing the simplest of his regrets. "He shouldn't have missed this."

terminated 🐚

The call came in during the middle of Shavasana, the Corpse pose. Duncan had hired an instructor to teach a yoga class during lunch hours in the conference room, and Elliot had quickly signed up. He was trying to be a team player, and it really wasn't bad. He liked the way the yoga made his body feel, but more than that he liked the way his colleagues looked dressed in leggings and tank tops. He had positioned his mat behind a young woman from Personnel and had spent the class contemplating the illusory nature of perception—how it was that you could see a person every day for months, or even years, and not really perceive her virtues until they were clad in spandex.

He had his cell phone set on the vibrate mode, which was part of the yogic code of conduct. Turning phones off entirely was preferable, but the instructor was willing to make allowances. When his waistband started to pulse, he sat up and slipped out the door. An Idaho number. Rodney. Calling from the courthouse. Elliot listened, then wheeled across the corridor and hammered his fist against the wall.

"What do you mean, dropped out?" he yelled. The door to the conference room was closed, but he could see the yoga instructor frowning at him through the glass. He lowered his voice. "He can't just drop out."

"Well, he did," Rodney said. "Told the DA he didn't want to be a part of it and refused to testify. DA's dropping the whole thing."

Elliot ground his teeth.

"Judge is letting them out of jail," Rodney continued. "Big mistake. There's some folks who are pretty hopping mad."

Oh, yes, Elliot thought. Here, too.

"Of course, the courts is just one way to go. . . ."

"Huh?" He was trying to think of his next move, but the yoga had emptied his mind.

"Don't you worry, Mr. Rhodes."

Dimly, Elliot registered what he was hearing. "Wait a minute. What did you say? Listen, I don't want you harassing them, you hear? That would look bad. I want you to leave them alone. Call off those family values people and pack up the sideshow."

The connection was breaking up. Then the phone went dead. Elliot tried punching in the callback code to retrieve the number, but it came up listed as unknown. The class had chanted its final *om,* and his colleagues were switching on their cell phones and pushing past him through the door. Elliot grabbed his gear and hurried back to his office. He dialed Rodney's office number, but got a message saying that the number was no longer in service. He slammed down the receiver. This was bad. Extremely bad. The man was a loose cannon. Elliot had never trusted him. He never liked using outside operatives in the first place. If you wanted to do something right, you had to do it yourself.

His mind flipped back to the bigger problem. It was time for damage control. He could feel the wheel of his fortunes at Duncan & Wiley grinding in a most inauspicious direction, but he was still hoping to avert the inevitable. He stared at the Kali statue on his desk, meeting her inscrutable, sloe-eyed gaze. The cruel, curved blade of her scimitar was painted with a wisdom eye. The blade dripped blood, as did the severed head she held up by the hair. Then the phone rang. It was Duncan's assistant, summoning him.

Duncan got right to the point.

"I had a long consultation with Cynaco, Rhodes. They're very upset about the dropped lawsuit, especially coming so soon after the *Post* fiasco. Something like this really erodes consumer confidence. It's the worst kind of publicity."

Elliot shook off the last of his yoga trance. "Not necessarily," he said. "The way I see it is—"

But Duncan held up his hand. "I haven't finished. Several of Cynaco's top french-fry and snack-food processors both here and in Canada are buckling under the pressure from the anti-GMO forces and are insisting on nonmodified, identity-protected products. My point is this—and it is highly confidential—Cynaco is planning to terminate its NuLife potato line."

Elliot felt a wave of relief wash over him. This was good news after all! Duncan wouldn't be telling him this if he were getting ready to fire him, would he? Duncan picked up his elephant statue, and Elliot racked his brain for the significance of the little diapered deity.

Duncan continued. "Frankly, they're mystified at the resistance to their product and see the fault lying in an unduly aggressive sell, especially overseas, where they are perceived as being excessively American and arrogant. They want to take a step back and retool their entire presentation, targeting it to Asia and the Third World."

Elliot's heart sank. Delhi.

"I've suggested 'Enlightened Compassion' as the motivating theme to drive the new campaign, which will focus exclusively on the human health benefits of GE crops, like Golden Rice and the other pharmaceutically enhanced lines. Of course, knowing your fondness for things Asian, I immediately thought of you."

Still, Delhi was better than Alaska. Better than no job at all. Elliot did his best to look compassionate and enlightened.

"But unfortunately, after this most recent Potato Party debacle, our partners at Cynaco have expressed concern about working with you. In fact, they think of you as something of an impediment to their future with D&W."

It was a blow to his ego, but according to Duncan, even that could be a good thing. He took it in stride. Maybe Duncan would move him back to tobacco. He lowered his eyes, striving to appear humble, and watched his boss's long, slender fingers fondle the elephant. Then he remembered. Ganesh. Remover of obstacles. His heart started to thump.

"Think of it as an opportunity for change," Duncan was saying. "Life is change. Death is rebirth. Destruction is redemption. This is a marvelous opportunity for a new beginning, Elliot. You know, in a way, I almost envy you."

"Duncan, I'm not quite following. Does this mean . . . ?"

"I'm afraid you've been terminated, Elliot."

tibet ℬↄ

Charmey sat up in bed in the pale violet room, holding the baby to her breast. Frankie lay next to her, watching the efficient way she pinched her nipple, tilting it upward and brushing it against the infant's cheek. His brand-new daughter knew exactly what to do. She opened and closed her miniature lips, then fastened her pink gums around the nipple, tugging at the darkened skin of the areola, dimpled now and swollen. The tiny fingertips clutched at the heavy, low-slung flesh with a perfect sense of entitlement.

The shape of the breast was still fine, Frankie noticed, more awesome than ever, but now blue veins filigreed the alabaster skin, turning it into something . . . well, more like an organ. Like a stomach sac, for example. With a function and a purpose other than his pleasure. In fact, Frank realized with a flicker of panic, his pleasure was just a by-product—entirely beside the point. The breast, now devoted exclusively to feeding his daughter, had nothing to do with him. He struggled to stay focused on the beauty here—his woman, his suckling child, his contribution to the future—but his appreciation was undermined by a niggling sense of being gypped. He'd been to jail. He'd been persecuted for his beliefs. Throughout his incarceration he'd been looking forward to curling up with Charmey, stroking her soft body, making love. He was only just learning the joys of the breast himself, and now to have it all snatched away by a blind, pouting dwarf who'd snuck onto the scene behind his back. Granted, it was *his* blind, pouting dwarf, but it was not something he'd ever thought to want, necessarily. All in all, he was not ready to find this situation entirely beautiful. Not by a long shot.

But still, it was complicated. When Charmey tucked her chin and gazed at the infant, her whole face took on a dewy glow, as soft as a flower opening at dawn. Watching her, Frankie experienced a funny rush of understanding—*So this is what a family feels like*—which was at once detached, amused, and, fuck yes, profound. He was happy that Charmey was so happy. He felt proud of himself. He smiled, and some of the tension left his body.

The baby drifted off to sleep. Gently, Charmey pressed on her breast to break the suction, then disengaged the tiny mouth from her nipple. She lowered the baby, laying her across her belly. She held out her arm to Frankie, who scooted up the bed beside her. Her nipple was still wet, still secreting moisture. More than anything, Frankie wanted to take it into his mouth and suck it as his daughter had, but he held back. He had taken care of dozens of babies in his various placements—that's what foster kids were good for—but he knew very little of the intimate business of mothers and infants, what was appropriate, what was not. So he just gazed at the nipple. But Charmey took his hand and cupped it around the soft weight of her breast.

"Go on," she said. "Try it."

"Really?" He looked up at her, doubting and amazed. He slowly brought his mouth to the nipple and gave it a tentative lick, then brought his lips around the nub of flesh. There was a mild but unexpected sweetness, like it had been dipped in sugar water, and as he started to suck, it became sweeter still.

Charmey giggled. "How is it?"

He tried to think of what the thin liquid tasted like. He wanted to say something nice, but all he could think of was lukewarm milk at the bottom of a bowl of Frosted Flakes.

"It's good," he said, releasing the nipple. He ran his hand along the side of her body, resting it on her hip, careful not to wake the baby.

Charmey sighed.

He took his hand away.

She shifted the baby off to the far side of the bed, cradling her in pillows. Then she took his hand and brought it back against her stomach.

"*C'est bon*," she said.

He ran his hand in circles around her navel, small at first, then widening. Her skin felt soft and flaccid, puddling in the basin between her pelvic bones. It was not the taut, boyish abdomen he'd first known, but he didn't mind. He let his head rest next to her hip. He kissed her hipbone. He felt his body relax a little more. Prison was exhausting. So much had changed, he thought, drifting off. He felt her hand rest lightly on his face, fingering a newly healed scar.

"I want to name her for you," she whispered.

"For me?" He struggled to breach the surface of sleep. Frank was a terrible name.

"Well, not only for you. But for orphans. For people who have lost their homeland."

Perdue? That was even worse. You couldn't call a little girl Perdue. He rolled over, ready to argue, but she was looking down at him with a totally blissed-out smile.

"I want to call her Tibet," she said.

Tibet.

He nodded. He didn't quite get the connection—he was never very good at geography—but he liked the way it sounded. He leaned across Charmey's legs so that his face hovered just above the baby's. She was all red and

346

squashed. She had a wispy ridge of hair, which stood up along the center of her head like a Mohawk, and a cluster of tiny white pimples across the bump of her nose. Her eyes were blue and still unseeing, but that would change in time. He scooped her carefully off the bed and sat up, cradling her in his arms. She was not beautiful, but he didn't care. He wasn't beautiful either. He supported her neck. He kissed her foot.

"Hi," he whispered. "Hello, Tibet."

the d word 🐚

Buddhists teach that there are only two things in life you can ever be sure of: the first is that you will die; the second is that you won't know when.

"Is this it? Is it happening now?"

The pulmonary edema is critical. He's jaundiced. His blood pressure is down.

"Why won't they say it? Why won't they tell me?"

He's listless. Incoherent. In imminent danger of cardiogenic shock.

Cass held my hand. She patted my arm. We stood outside Lloyd's room in the hallway, waiting for the doctor to finish the examination. "They probably just don't know," she said.

Geek was leaning against the opposite wall. The Seeds had been released two days earlier, and they had descended onto the Cardiology Unit, establishing a base camp in the waiting room. They took turns visiting Lloyd, and sometimes I found it a relief to have them back, but other times it was just an annoyance. Now Geek, eager for a chance to console, offered up the teaching. "Buddhists say . . ."

"That's bullshit!" I said. "They're fucking doctors. They must know. They see this all the time. They just won't say it. It's the D word. They won't say the D word. It makes them look bad, like they've failed or something."

The doctor emerged from behind the curtain. Melvin followed close behind. The doctor was showing him a notation on my father's chart. Melvin had cut off his dreadlocks in prison and removed most of his earrings. Now, except for the perforated earlobes, he looked almost normal. He was wearing a crew-collar shirt. He and the doctor conferred.

End-stage congestive heart failure.

347

A terminal situation.

"Just say it," I interrupted. "Just say it. He's dying, right?"

They looked up, surprised, like they'd just discovered a gauche or fee-bleminded child. A foreigner who didn't know the rules.

"Right," Melvin agreed.

What good did that do? I slumped against the wall. Cass put a hand on my shoulder.

"We want to move him to Palliative," the doctor said.

"What's that?"

"Hospice care," Melvin explained. "They'll be able to make him comfortable. Manage his pain."

"Hospice?" I turned to the doctor. "You're giving up on him?"

"Suspending life-prolonging measures . . ."

"Letting him die." It was like we were playing some kind of strange word game.

"We think it's time to move him," the doctor continued after a discreet pause. "But we'll need him to agree to a DNR status."

"DNR?"

"Do Not Resuscitate."

I sank slowly down the wall and hugged my knees like Ocean.

"Wait a minute. I don't get it. Are you saying he's got to *agree* to die?" I realized how dumb I sounded, but I couldn't help it. I'd always thought it was straightforward. Life or death. Black or white. I didn't realize there were so many shades of dying. So many different levels. "Does he know?"

The doctor shook his head.

"Well, then, good luck. Last I heard, he likes being alive, and he's planning on continuing awhile longer." I was beginning to catch on. It was all a matter of intention. The doctors' intentions. Lloyd's. God's. And whoever else wanted to weigh in on the matter. Death would come when everyone agreed and arrived at a consensus.

"If you could talk to him," the doctor suggested gently. "Help him to understand, to accept—"

"Me!" I cowered against the wall, holding up my hands to fend him off. "Whoa! That's your job, isn't it? You're the expert."

"You're his daughter."

A simple statement of fact. But so misguided.

"You're telling me *I'm* supposed to convince him?" I crouched there, staring at this man in disbelief. I wasn't even sure who this doctor was, there had been so many. I started to laugh. I threw back my head and howled with laughter. The nurses at the station looked up, alarmed, but I didn't care. I was a lunatic. Fine.

"Maybe ask him about his wishes," the doctor suggested.

"His wishes? Oh, wow! You really don't get it." I stopped laughing abruptly and swallowed. "My father and I don't exactly see eye to eye when it comes to making life-and-death decisions." I let my head fall once more to my arms and rocked back and forth like a catatonic child. "Melvin will talk to him. He'll be real good at this."

The doctor and Melvin conferred again. Geek walked over and joined them. Good. Let the men sort it out.

"He's a farmer," I heard Melvin explain. "He's suffering from a paranoid delusion about his seeds—"

Cass hunkered down next to me. "A word from our resident psych nurse," I muttered. "Pretty profound, huh?"

"Yummy," she said, "you need to talk to Lloyd."

They were all waiting. I held up my hands and surrendered. "All right! You move him. I'll talk to him. After I have a smoke."

∂⊃

I guess cowardice just runs in our family. I sat outside for an hour or two, smoking one cigarette after another, getting up occasionally to walk around the block, then returning, trying to think of what to say. When I finally went back in, they had transferred him to Palliative Care. The high-tech computerized paraphernalia of the Cardiology Unit was conspicuously absent here. No more chrome and latex. There were soft pastel colors on the walls. Potted plants lined the windowsills. A pair of harpists were setting up their instruments in the hallway.

Melvin and Lilith sat on either side of Lloyd's bed. Melvin was cradling Lloyd's head while Lilith fed him tiny spoonfuls of vanilla ice cream. He opened his mouth to the spoon like a fledgling bird, but his mouth was blue. Blue lips. Sluggish blue tongue. Charmey was sitting on the foot of the bed nursing Tibet. Lloyd watched her, smacked his lips, opened his mouth for more.

He gurgled every time he took a breath.

I threw myself into the chair by the window and planted my boot heels on the radiator. I stared out at an adjacent wing of the hospital, identical in architecture to the wing I was in. With one big difference. There, lives were being saved. Here, in Palliative, they were ending. I closed my eyes. Behind me, soft harp music wafted from the hallway. I sighed and swung my legs around. Lloyd's wishes. I glanced across the room. Melvin looked up.

"Ready?" he asked.

I nodded. They moved slowly so as not to jostle Lloyd or startle him. Lilith took the spoon from his lips. Melvin eased him back against the pillows and raised up the bed to relieve his sodden lungs. My father looked stricken. He sensed that something was up.

"We have to go now," Melvin said. "Yummy wants to talk to you. But we'll be back."

"We'll bring you more ice cream," Lilith whispered, stroking his sunken cheek. "Chocolate next time."

Charmey held up Tibet in front of him, so he could see. The baby gurgled at Lloyd. Lloyd gurgled back at the baby.

They trooped out of the room. A band of anarchists. A caravan of gypsies. A posse of saints. It was so easy for them to offer comfort, to tap compassion. He wasn't their father. Silently I cursed them.

"Dad?" I said.

The whites of his eyes had yellowed, and his nostrils flared with each breath. The tip of his nose had turned bluish, too. His extremities were dying. His gaze settled on me, and he gave me the sweetest smile.

"So good . . ." He sighed.

"What's good, Daddy?" My heart was pounding.

"Ice cream. Most delicious thing . . . I ever tasted."

Ice cream. Why hadn't I thought of that? It was hopeless. I would never please him, and I might as well accept it. Really, it was a relief. I felt efficient. A bit brutal even.

"Dad, I have to talk to you."

His eyes fluttered open.

"Do you know where you are?"

"Of course," he said. His voice sounded perfectly normal, and for a moment I almost believed that everything was fine, that my father would be back on his feet in no time, and I would be free to run away again. Leave Liberty Falls. I wanted to dash to the parking lot, gun the Pontiac toward home, and get the kids packed for the trip back to Pahoa. Then he spoke again, breathless and gasping. "I'm in the damn hospital. They're killing me! Get me out of here!"

My heart sank. Not this time.

"Dad, the doctor told me—"

His hand twitched impatiently against his thigh. "Doctors . . ." he said.

"I'm supposed to ask your wishes."

"Wishes?"

I was doing it all wrong. He didn't know what I was talking about. But I couldn't bring myself to say it. Not the D word. Not to Daddy.

He giggled, and the sound unnerved me. "If wishes were fishes . . ."

It was the morphine talking. The doctor had warned me. His mouth opened and closed. A salty tear leaked from the corner of his eye. "Take me home," he pleaded, and now his voice was so weak and sad that, in spite of myself, I reached out and touched his forearm.

"I can't, Daddy. You need to be here. They can take care of you better. They can help you." I really wanted him to understand, but he closed his eyes.

"Melvin will take me home," he said. "I love Melvin."

"That's good," I said, accepting this information and withdrawing my hand.

"I love Lilith, too," he confided.

"That's just great." Still I waited, but it seemed like that was all he had to say to me. It made what I had to say a whole lot easier. "Dad, you're dying."

The minute the words left my mouth, I wanted to snatch them back out of the air. "I'm sorry," I added.

He opened his eyes wide and stared at me, and then suddenly his body went stiff. I reached for the call button to summon help, but he clutched my arm. "He's coming," he gasped, looking wildly around. "My seeds. I have to save them!"

"Who's coming, Dad?"

He was panting hard, gaping at something that loomed over my shoulder. "Him! The Terminator! . . . I have to save them!"

"Dad, your seeds are fine. . . ."

The delirium subsided, and he fell back. "It's too late," he whispered. "Too late." His eyelids fluttered shut again, and for a while he just lay there letting the breath shudder through him. When he finally spoke again, his voice was so low I had to lean way down to hear.

"I don't want . . ." he said, but his mouth was dry and gummy, and the words got stuck. He reached out a trembling finger toward the water jug on the side table. I supported his head, held the cup to his lips. The back of his neck was as hot as a child's. He took a sip.

"I don't want . . ." he repeated, but still the words wouldn't come. It was horrible to see him struggle. Of course he didn't want to die. He couldn't say the word either.

"I know, Dad," I whispered, stroking his hand. "It's okay. You don't have to tell me. I know."

He pulled away and shook his head. He opened his mouth, and his wish leaked from his lips like air from a punctured tire. "No . . ." he said. Then, "I don't want . . . to be a vegetable. . . ."

I looked at him, deflated and waxy against the pillow.

A vegetable?

I might have laughed if I hadn't been crying.

garden, reborn &

The Spudnik was trashed. The sheriff's department had ransacked it several times, then the state prosecutor's office, possibly even the FBI.

"They just kept coming," Phoenix said. "I didn't know who they were. I don't think they found anything."

"That's because there was nothing to find," Geek said. He was lying on his back by the Winnebago, trying to track down the damage to the propane line. "Thanks for keeping an eye on them."

Phoenix shrugged. "I tried. Mostly they told me to get lost. There was one guy who came back a couple of times, who talked to me sometimes."

"What were they thinking?" Geek said. "That we had heroin stashed in the propane tanks?"

"I believe it was the plastique, dude," Y said. "The TNT. The blasting powder."

Lilith giggled. "No, it was the manifestos."

"The one guy, he kept asking me about dirty pictures," Phoenix said. "That's what he wanted. And the computer. They all wanted your computer."

"Fucking cops," Lilith said.

"I don't think this guy was a cop. He seemed kind of old. He was wearing those sunglasses with mirrors, but he didn't have a uniform or anything."

"Mirrored sunglasses?" Lilith frowned.

"Well, he didn't find anything," Geek said. "Since there was nothing to find. But they sure managed to screw things up."

"We gonna have heat for the winter?" Y asked.

"You could come back to Hawaii with us," Phoenix said. "You don't need heat there. Mom's taking us back there as soon as . . . you know . . ."

He kicked at the dirt, sending a spray of gravel toward Geek, who was still lying on his back. "Hey!"

"Sorry."

"You sad about your grandpa?" Lilith asked.

Phoenix nodded. "He's all freaked out about his seeds. Mom's all freaked out about him."

Geek sat up and looked at the boy. "I know," he said. "We're working on it."

Throughout their incarceration the computer had stayed hidden deep inside a small lava tube on the back acres of the land where the foothills started to crumble. Wrapped in layers of plastic, then packed carefully in a high-impact, shock-resistant, waterproof case, the top-of-the-line Macintosh PowerBook had frustrated searches by the various engines of the law.

As soon as they were released, Geek went for a long nighttime walk through the potato fields and liberated the computer from its rocky nest. He brought it back, hooked it up, and got to work. A few days later he walked next door to the Quinns' place with the PowerBook under his arm and confronted Will. The two men sat down together in Will's office.

"Listen," Geek said, "I want you to know that we appreciate you dropping the lawsuit. We know you don't agree with what we did, and we can respect that. We don't even mind the time in jail, because we ended up getting some good publicity out of it."

Will sat back in his chair. "I dropped the charges out of consideration for my wife. Now, what's your point?"

"We're hoping we can put all that aside and do something for Lloyd."

Will frowned. "You got him pretty upset with all that Terminator nonsense. He thinks it's real."

"I know," Geek said. "Ironic, isn't it?" But he didn't say anything else, and Will continued.

"Just wish we could do something about the old man's seeds. Normally there's an offspring who takes over the operation, but, hell, that Yummy—"

Geek leaned forward. "There is something we can do." He turned on the PowerBook and started to explain the idea. Will listened, nodding every now and again and asking a few questions.

"It's kind of a long shot," Geek concluded. "But when you think about it, the Internet is a perfect vehicle for dissemination. All I need from you is some desk space and access to your high-speed line. Once the site is up, and the initial distributions are made, it'll be easy to maintain. We can do most of it remotely."

"It's nuts," Will said. "But if it'll set the old man's mind at ease, it's worth a try."

"Excellent," said Geek, beaming.

Geek moved his base of operations to the Quinns' office, and by the end of the week the New Garden of Earthly Delights was up and running and open for business. This time there were no nude pictures of Lilith. There were no sex acts or mudwomen against swags of burgundy velvet, no pagan feminist texts or shamanic discursions or anything that the Tri-County Interfaith League of Family Values could find even remotely offensive. But there were still zucchinis. There were cucurbits and lots of squash.

perpetuity of life &

It was like a party in Palliative Care, with my dying father as the centerpiece, lying in bed like a long white cake. Geek was leaning over him, doing something with a laptop computer, which sat on the tray table where dinner would have been had Lloyd been eating. Momoko stood next to his pillow, and all the rest of the Seeds were crowded around. Frankie and Charmey were sitting on the end of the bed with their baby. Will and Cass were there, too.

We were the last to arrive, which was Ocean's fault. Ever since Cass had told her that Chicken Little was old enough to start laying, she had been driving me nuts. She'd gotten it into her head to take an egg to her grandpa—maybe she thought it would cure him or something—and she was practically living in the greenhouse. She followed the hen around, picking her up from time to time and flipping her over to inspect her underneath.

"Wanna see her vent?" she asked anyone who ventured in, brandishing the upside-down chicken. "That's where the egg's gonna come from."

Somehow, despite these levels of surveillance and harassment, the little hen hunkered down just before we were about to leave for the hospital that afternoon, and there was no prying Ocean away.

"She's doing it!"

"Ocean, come on!" Phoenix shouted. "Geek said we don't have a lot of time. He's going to tell us something important."

"Wait! I want to bring Grandpa the egg."

"If he dies before we get there, it'll be all your fault."

Mercifully, a few minutes later the unflappable chicken rose to her feet and hopped off her nest box to resume her pecking and scratching, and we were able to reach the hospital in time to save Ocean from a lifetime of guilt and recrimination from her brother. Now the two of them ran up to their grandfather and kissed him.

"We're late," Ocean announced. "Because of this!" She reached into her pocket and, with greatly exaggerated care, drew out a very small egg. "It's from Chicken Little. I brought it for you, Grandpa. It's her first one ever!" She took his hand and opened it, then slipped the little brown egg onto his hardened palm, curling his stiff fingers around it.

He brought the thing up close to his face and studied it, blinking his watery eyes like he'd never seen such a marvelous egg before.

"My!" he whispered. Then he looked at his granddaughter like he'd never seen such a marvelous child before either. "Thank you, Ocean." He held the egg in one hand and reached with the other toward her face. You could see how much effort the gesture cost him, he was so weak. His hand shook. He touched her cheek, patting her as gently as if she were an eggshell.

I felt a quick, sharp pang as I watched my daughter squirm with delight under my father's approbation. Poo was squirming, too, so I put him down on the floor. He promptly crawled under the bed and started reaching for the various tubes that were conveying fluids in and out of my father. Cass retrieved him, and he seemed perfectly happy to let her bounce him for a while.

"Ocean, take that egg and put it away before Grandpa breaks it."

She shot me a wounded glance.

Geek and Will were fiddling with the computer, their heads bent together. "Okay," Geek announced, "we're up and running." He swung the tray table closer to Lloyd and adjusted the angle of the screen while Will cranked up the bed.

Cass stood next to me. "They've been working really hard," she said.

Lilith helped Lloyd with his glasses. Geek glanced at me and seemed nervous, even a little shy. He started to speak.

"Welcome to the New Garden of Earthly Delights," he said, clicking and opening the home page. Everyone crowded around to see the computer screen. I held back. Apparently it looked good, because the kids started to clap. Lloyd just looked confused. He was peering at the liquid crystal screen through his reading glasses, which Lilith had positioned crookedly on his nose.

"Basically the site is the computerized seed-library database," Geek said. "The one we've been working on with Momoko and Lloyd. It contains every single variety of Fullers' Seeds, all arranged by genus and species and cross-referenced with the plant names in both Latin and common English."

He paused, waiting for Lloyd to take in the information. "The idea is to invite growers across the country to become members of the virtual Garden. They'll register with the Web site, adopt whatever seeds they're interested in, then grow them out and offer them back to other Garden members through the online catalog."

Lloyd's glasses slipped down his nose. He pushed them up again and moved his head closer to the dim screen, trying to see what was on it.

"Other members can contact growers by e-mail and request seeds. It's awesomely simple, because it will take care of itself—it really takes advantage of the nonhierarchical networking potential of the Web. We sent out a huge mailing to your entire customer list and all our friends and contacts, directing them to the site."

Lloyd shook his head. It was clear to me that he wasn't following. He wasn't about to understand the Internet, never mind appreciate the awesomeness of its networking potential—there was just not enough oxygen getting to his brain—but Geek was prepared. He reached into the battered knapsack at his feet and brought out a sheaf of printed pages. Hard copies.

"Look." He removed the computer and placed the sheaf carefully on Lloyd's lap. "They're from your customers across the country."

My father picked up a sheet of paper. It trembled in his hand. He brought it close to his face, then held it away and shook his head.

"It's blurry."

So Melvin read it to him. It was a Grower's Pledge. In exchange for receiving seeds for free, the growers promised to propagate them organically, to save seeds from the plants they grew, and to make these new seeds available to other members, also free of charge. Melvin read slowly and carefully. When he finished, he riffled through the stack of pages.

"There's over forty people right here," he said. He placed Lloyd's hand on top of the thick pile. "And more people are sending in pledges every day."

The small hospital room fell silent. Lloyd looked at the pile of paper in his lap, then looked up at the people assembled there. In a weak voice he whispered, "You're giving away my seeds?"

In a way I felt sorry for Geek and the rest of them, but it served them right. They didn't know Lloyd like I did. Didn't know how stubborn he was, or how controlling. The last thing he'd want was someone else getting fancy ideas about how to run his operation.

Geek looked stricken. He shook his head. "We're not giving them away, Lloyd. People are offering to adopt them. It's different." But the confidence had ebbed from his voice, and he did not sound convincing.

Nobody knew what to say. Finally Phoenix spoke up. "Grandpa, it's so the Terminator won't get them."

Lloyd closed his eyes for a long time. Then he sighed. "Momoko?" he said, sounding worn down and defeated.

Everyone turned to look at her.

"She's asleep," I said. She was napping in the reclining chair, and I was perched on its arm.

"Wake her up," Geek said.

So I nudged her. "Mom?" I called into her ear. "Hey, Mom, wake up." She didn't move. I looked over at Geek and shrugged. I mean, personally I didn't care one way or the other, but what was he hoping to accomplish

357

here? If Lloyd couldn't follow all this, how could she? The part of me that wasn't feeling sorry for him was feeling pretty smug. See? And you thought you knew them so well. . . .

Then Momoko's eyes blinked open.

"Grandma," Phoenix asked, "did you hear Geek's idea?"

Momoko nodded. "Yes. I like. It's very nice idea."

I looked up at the group. "She was sound asleep. She didn't hear a word."

But they waited, because at least she was agreeing, and that might be enough to convince Lloyd.

"Very nice idea," Momoko repeated. "I think so."

Lloyd roused himself. "Momoko, they want to give away all our seeds!"

She stood then. Scooting herself to the edge of the chair, she got to her feet and shuffled over to Lloyd's bed. She held on to the metal safety bars and looked down at his unhappy face.

"It is good way."

"But they're ours. We have to keep them safe!"

She shook her head. "No. Keeping is not safe. Keeping is danger. Only safe way is letting go. Giving everything away. Freely. Freely."

She made a gesture with her hands, like she was shooing small children out the door to play, and then she patted his arm. Lloyd closed his eyes and rested his hand on the stack of pledges. The room was still. Then his lips moved. I thought I saw them form the words *Pray take these seeds*— but it might have been my imagination. When he opened his eyes again and blinked, it was like a long pain was finally breaking, and a clarity suffused his face that made him seem translucent. He looked up at Momoko, then at Geek, then at Melvin, and then slowly his gaze traveled around the room to take in the rest of us.

"Well!" He sighed, and it sounded like a chuckle. "My, my, my . . . !"

I made my exit then, at that tender moment when the perpetuity of life itself was being affirmed. I could feel my face burning. Maybe it was the way Lloyd gazed at the Seeds, so pleased with them, that made me feel so excluded. Or the fatuous expression on Geek's moon face as he looked to me for my approval. Maybe it was the way Melvin and Lilith hovered fondly beside my parents, smiling like proud parents themselves, or the adoring looks my children cast upon all their planetary heroes. Or maybe it was just the way that Cass cuddled Poo, my baby—proprietary and always ready to help. I don't know why. All I knew was that I couldn't stand it in that pastel room for another cozy second. My brain had started to tighten, squeezing like an empty fist, and I was flushed with an old, creepy, drugged-out need to claw the skin from my bones.

I stood up and edged toward the door, then slipped from the room, walking quickly down the hallway. A Christian folk trio had replaced the harpists that day, and I shoved my way through the middle of the group as they made their rounds, serenading the dying. I caught the refrain, spiritual and uplifting, as the elevator descended. I didn't really intend to leave the building, but I didn't stop until I hit the air outside. Then I paused. No one had noticed me leaving, except maybe Cass, and either way I knew she would figure it out and make sure the kids were okay. I could always count on her for that. I headed for the car park, where I spiraled up and down until I found the Pontiac.

So many fucking levels.

I hit the first liquor store on the way out of Pocatello.

Tucked the bottle in my bag, opened a new pack of cigarettes, and headed for the Falls.

falls ℬ

In a place like Liberty Falls it wasn't hard to track a person down. Cass spotted Lloyd's Pontiac on the way home from the hospital, sitting in the parking lot of the Falls Motel, in full view of the road. With the kids in the back of the Suburban, she wasn't about to stop. She had told them that Yummy had errands to do, but she could see that Phoenix didn't believe it. She was glad he hadn't seen the car in the motel lot. She drove them home, got them fed and settled for the night. When the Seeds returned, she asked Lilith to keep an eye on things, and then she drove back into town.

Downtown Liberty Falls never had much of a nightlife, even back when she was growing up, but these days after sunset it was deserted. The only thing that moved on Main Street was the revolving sign above the storefront of the Falls Mortuary—a place Cass passed almost every day of her life and somehow managed not to see. Tonight, though, the radiant plastic caught her eye with its eternal rotations. She wondered what Yummy would want for Lloyd. He'd been a well-respected farmer, and people would want to show up. She could imagine Yummy's reaction—*I have to plan a what?* Cass sighed. She knew the funeral director. She would give him a call in the morning.

Cass parked next to the Pontiac. There was a DO NOT DISTURB sign hanging on the door in front. She could hear the sound of a television coming from the room. She knocked, but there was no answer. She crossed the parking lot to the motel office. A little bell tinkled when she pushed open the door. The office hadn't changed much since the Olsens had retired and the new owners had taken over. They were Indians, from India. The Olsens had been from Twin Falls. There was a sign on the front desk that read SE HABLA ESPAÑOL.

A woman appeared from the back apartment and stood behind the desk. She was short, compact, and plump, with dark skin and long black hair, coiled into a bun at the nape of her neck.

"I'm looking for my friend," Cass explained. "Her father is in the hospital, and I have to find her."

The woman tilted her head to one side. Cass could hear the TV in the background. Cartoons. The woman must have children.

"Her name is Fuller. Yummy Fuller." Cass pointed. "That's her car."

The woman looked down at her register. A little girl emerged from the back and slipped behind her mother, holding on to her legs.

"Room Four," the woman said. "Fuller. Yes?"

"I'll need a key," Cass said, smiling at the little girl. The girl giggled. The woman said something in a language Cass couldn't understand. It wasn't Spanish, and the tone was sharp. The little girl shrank into the background. The woman hesitated, holding on to the key.

"I can call someone from the sheriff's office to come over—"

The woman slid the key across the counter.

The TV was still on inside Room 4. Cass jiggled the key until she felt the catch give way. The room was dim and close. A thick haze of cigarette smoke hung in the air, lit by the blue flicker from the television. Yummy was lying faceup and motionless across the bed, her tangled hair spread out across the pillow.

Cass felt her heart pound once, a singular thud, and then she ran to the bedside. She didn't know what she expected to find. Maybe blood on the

360

sheets or an empty bottle of pills. But there was only a whiskey bottle and a glass and a smoldering ashtray. A melting bucket of ice cubes sat in a wet spot on the carpeted floor. The remote control lay on the bedspread, where it had slipped from Yummy's hand. Cass pushed the mute button, and in the sudden silence she could hear Yummy breathing. She laid a hand across her friend's forehead. Yummy groaned but didn't wake. Her skin was damp with sweat. Cass went to the bathroom to wet a washcloth, which she pressed over Yummy's eyes.

She took off her coat. She helped herself to a cigarette from the pack on the table, then drank the inch of whiskey left in the glass. She felt all shaky inside, a little scared still, though relieved, of course. But there was something else, another feeling. She poured an inch more whiskey and added an ice cube. She thought back to what had just happened, how she'd stood in the doorway and seen Yummy lying there, and how her heart had leaped to her throat in fear, thinking her friend was dead, but how the very next moment, her thoughts had flown to Poo, and then to Phoenix and Ocean, and what would happen to them—and for a split second she'd felt the quick certainty and stunning joy of knowing they'd be hers. It was so clear and simple. So obvious.

But of course it wasn't. Yummy was fine—she was just drunk—and now Cass realized that what she'd felt was disappointment. There was no point denying it. She bent over and covered her face with her hands, horrified. She was a sick, loathsome person who had once tried to steal a child and was gladdened by the thought of her best friend's death. The only time she'd ever felt this much revulsion was when the cancer was diagnosed and she wanted to crawl out of her body, but this was almost worse, because you couldn't just cut away the bad parts.

After a while she sat up and looked over her shoulder, then crawled up the bed and sat cross-legged next to her friend. "Yum?" she said, but there was still no answer. In sleep Yummy looked ridiculously young. Her eyes were swollen from tears, and the rims of her nostrils were red. Seeing her passed out like this, Cass felt a sudden icy sense of what it must have been like for her in San Francisco. Taking drugs until you passed out. Probably shacking up in seedy motels like this with God knows what kind of man, because how else do you get by with no money? It was awful to think about. Cass reached out and stroked her friend's forehead.

Yummy made a little moaning sound and shifted onto her side. Cass set

361

the alarm on her watch, then turned off the light and stretched out on her back, but when Yummy moaned again, like she was having a bad dream, Cass rolled over.

"Shhh," she said, putting her arm around Yummy's waist and holding her, lightly at first, and then snugly, the way she held Will, to anchor her and keep her safe.

When her watch alarm sounded in the early morning, she ran a shower and got Yummy to her feet and into the bathroom. She called the hospital and went out for coffee. When she returned, Yummy was seated on the side of the bed, dressed and cradling her head. She jumped at the noise of the door slamming. She squinted into the light.

"What happened?"

"Nothing. Here, drink this."

She took a sip of the coffee and winced. "How did you find me?"

"I saw the Pontiac in the parking lot on the way home with the kids."

She looked up quickly. "Where are they?"

"They're fine. Lilith is looking after them."

"Oh." She relaxed, took another sip of the coffee. "Did you stay here all night with me?"

"Yes."

"I was passed right out, huh?"

Cass didn't answer.

Yummy sighed. "Thank you."

"You're welcome."

She yawned and kneaded her temples. "God, I feel like shit!"

"I'll bet," Cass said. "Come on. I'll take you to the hospital."

Yummy laughed. "I'm not that sick—" Then she stopped.

"Your father," Cass said.

"Right." Yummy closed her eyes and let her head drop.

"I just phoned the hospital. He's unconscious. They said you should come."

ॐ

She was silent in the car, bracing her head against the headrest. Cold air from the window hit her face. Her lips were pressed tightly shut, and she frowned, trying not to throw up. Cass offered to pull over, but she shook her head.

"Just drive."

At the hospital Yummy led the way up to the ward, but at the entrance to his room she paused and slumped.

"I can't."

The strains of harp music wafted from the hall.

"Fucking harps," she said. "Come on."

He lay there on his back, propped on all sides by pillows. His breathing was spasmodic. Each gasp convulsed his chest, followed by a terrible silence that threatened to last forever, but then the next breath would rattle up from somewhere deep in his lungs. Yummy groped for Cass's hand.

"Oh, shit. This is it, isn't it?"

Cass squeezed as the doctor came in.

"Good," he said. "You're here."

He shuffled through a batch of papers attached to his clipboard, then handed one to Yummy.

"What is it?" she asked, staring at the paper.

"It's the DNR order. It states that he doesn't want any heroic measures taken to keep him alive."

"Heroic measures," she repeated. "He signed this?"

He pointed to the bottom. "Last night. After everyone had left. He had the night nurse witness."

Yummy passed it quickly to Cass. It was clear how hard it must have been for Lloyd to hold the pen and sign his name. The letters were faint and wobbly, and the signature tilted to one side like it was going to slide off the edge of the form.

"He designated you as his proxy," the doctor told Yummy. "Which means he wants you to execute his wishes and make decisions for him should he become incapable of doing so."

"Me!"

"Well, it's usual to designate a son or daughter."

The doctor waited for her to take in this information, and then he continued. "You're going to have to make a decision now about a feeding tube."

Yummy looked down at her father. "Is he conscious?"

"Hard to say."

"Is the tube painful?"

"Well, it's not pleasant. It's inserted down the throat, you know. Into the stomach . . ."

"Oh, God," she choked, holding up her hand and swallowing hard. "I'm not feeling well. I'm going to be sick."

"Sit," said Cass, leading her to the armchair. "Put your head down." She cupped the back of Yummy's head and pushed it in between her legs. "Breathe."

"I'll let you think about the tube, then," the doctor said, backing out of the room.

"Wait," Yummy called. "Without a tube what happens?"

"No tube means no food or liquids, and when you withhold hydration and nutrition . . ."

"He starves to death?" She raised her head and looked at him.

"It's not exactly like that."

"What else is it? Forget it. I'm not starving my father to death."

The doctor hesitated. "It's really more about his wishes, you know."

"I know that. Do the tube."

"Why don't you take some time before you decide? Let me know."

"No." She dropped her head between her legs. "Do the tube."

The doctor frowned and made a notation on the chart. "If she changes her mind, tell the nurse," he said to Cass, and slipped out the door.

Cass got a plastic basin from the bathroom and slid it under Yummy's head. She kneaded the back of her neck and listened to the sounds of breathing, Lloyd gurgling and Yummy gulping for air. After a while Yummy lifted her head and sat up in the chair, then pushed herself to her feet and went to stand by her father's side.

"Lloyd?" she said, peering into his face. "Dad?"

There was no response, just the rhythmic wheeze and rattle. Cass came over to stand beside her. When Yummy spoke, her voice was hushed. "It's hard work, dying. I never realized."

Cass nodded.

"Did you go through this with your parents?"

"More or less. I think it's always different."

"Do you think I'm doing the right thing?"

"It's really about what he'd want," Cass said. "That's what's important."

"You know how he feels about life! What am I supposed to do?"

"I know he hated all the fussing and hospital procedure," Cass said. "You remember last time how much he wanted to come home? You gave him that. He got to be home for the best part of a year because of you. He got to meet his grandkids. He got to be a prophet of the revolution. But this time is different."

Yummy thought for a while. "He told me he didn't want to be a vegetable."

Cass nodded. "Well, I don't blame him." She gave Yummy a little shove. "You have no idea. . . ."

"Right," Yummy said. "But you do."

"I can imagine."

"So no tube, then?"

Cass shrugged. "If you can live with it."

Yummy returned to the chair. "You can go now. I mean, I'm not going to throw up or anything. I'll just sit here. Maybe he'll wake up, and I can ask him what he wants."

"You sure?"

"Yeah. I'm fine."

"I'll go get Momoko." Cass picked up her bag and turned on her cell phone. "Call if you need me." She headed toward the door.

"Cass?" Yummy called. "Thanks."

"Sure."

Yummy sat there bent over her knees, her face in her hands. "I know you think I'm losing it."

"Just don't drink so much," Cass said. "You'll feel better."

the beginning &

Imagine the worst hangover you've ever had. The kind you loathe yourself for incurring, where even the slightest movement or sound or wafting scent or change in the quality of light makes your world keel onto its side. The kind where you've smoked so many cigarettes that your lungs ache and your head feels like it's been skewered with a red-hot metal rod between your eyes, and the slightest movement, or sound, or wafting scent . . .

That was my hangover on the day my dad died, but I was there by his side nonetheless when he made his last appearance.

After Cass left, I watched him labor, too sick to move.

"Lloyd?" I said. "Do you want a feeding tube?"

I watched him for a sign, expecting little, but slowly losing even what hope I had. I dragged the chair closer to his bedside.

"I'm here if you change your mind." My stomach was starting to churn again. I leaned my head back in the chair and closed my eyes. That was when he rallied.

"Oh—" he whispered. "Oh, my . . . !"

I barely heard him at first. Then I sat up, reeling and dizzy. His eyes were shut, but when I leaned over, bracing myself against the bed, they opened. Milky and startled, they were brimming with tears.

"Dad?"

The blue eyes focused briefly on me before swimming away again, chasing something.

"I . . . I had . . ."

"What is it, Dad?"

He coughed, bringing air up from his waterlogged lungs. "I had . . . the most wonderful dream!"

I held a tissue to his mouth so he could spit. "What did you dream?" His lips worked, pushing out a gummy white mucus. I used the little sponge on a stick the way I'd seen Lilith do, dipping it in water and swabbing his tongue. He sucked gratefully. When I withdrew the sponge, he closed his eyes.

"I was there." He sighed. His eyelids twitched as he watched dream images play across them, spinning and shifting.

"Where, Dad?"

He paused, searching for the answer. He was as frail as a newborn.

"At the beginning . . ."

"The beginning of what?"

He fell silent. Maybe he was sleeping again. I watched him for a while, and then I closed my eyes, too, because his face was too exposed, too fragile to bear. I drifted, still whiskey drunk, so that when he spoke again, his voice was far away and it felt as if I were dreaming, too.

"Everything," he whispered. "Of life . . ." His words were like faint puffs of a breeze stirring. "So beautiful! Everyone I love . . . was there. Momoko. My father, mother. All my seeds. My potatoes . . ."

By now I was sitting up, gripping the edge of his sheet, and my heart was pounding. I knew the danger in the question I was about to ask. My throat closed. I felt like I was going to retch if I spoke, or if I didn't. He closed his eyes. He was slipping away fast.

"Daddy!" My voice was too loud, and I could feel my face flushing, but I needed to know. "Wait! Am I there? Am I in your dream?"

I held my breath. Miraculously, his eyes opened once more, peering out at me, watery blue and blinded. He opened his mouth and closed it, and I was afraid he would die before he could answer.

"Why, Yumi," he said at last, as though it were so apparent to him, the most obvious thing in the world. "Of course you are." His words were no louder than air.

I crumpled then, bending and gripping his cold wrist. "I love you, Daddy," I sobbed into his palm. "You're with me, too."

"My . . . !" He sighed, drifting. I felt his thick, swollen fingers move a little against my eyelids, which was all the comfort he was capable of offering me now. His voice was whisper thin and barely audible. "My, my, my . . ."

seventh

Science, unlike theology, never leads to insanity.

—Luther Burbank,
from "Why I Am an Infidel," published in *Little Blue Book #1020*

rogue &

My father died without a feeding tube on the first Sunday of September. It happened several hours after he spoke his last words, and he dissolved so quietly out of life that Momoko and I missed the moment of transition. We were by his bedside, but we had both dozed off, and maybe he was waiting for us to do so. It's hard to check out when your loved ones are watching.

That same Sunday, September 5, the *New York Times* ran an article entitled "Hidden Traps in Fooling Mother Nature," which outlined in some detail the potential environmental hazards that could result from genetic engineering and the biotechnologies. Geek downloaded the article from the *Times*'s Web site, and the Seeds rejoiced, and they decided Lloyd was rejoicing with them, wherever he was.

On that same morning when Lloyd's heart gave its final palpitation, the first frost of autumn settled on the fields, freezing the potato vines and signaling the start of harvest. Will and his crew would spend the next few days beating the plants. Some of the farmers used chemical desiccants like diquat, paraquat, Enquik, and Endothall. Others used sulfuric acid. But, as Will carefully pointed out to Geek, whenever it was possible, he preferred to kill mechanically what the frost left standing. After the plants were dead, he would wait for three weeks, leaving the potatoes in the ground so their skins could thicken, and then came the real race   to dig the tubers out of the ground before the hard frosts set. That was where a little rotten luck could do you in.

So it was a busy time of year for all of Idaho's farmers, but this didn't keep the people of Liberty Falls from gathering at the Falls Mortuary to pay their final respects. Geek had sent out notices for the memorial service, and many of my parents' longtime customers had come, as had some of the Seeds' friends. Everyone packed into the chapel for the service, which was led by Reverend Glass. The old minister looked around at the variegated congregation, at the local folks and out-of-towners, the gardeners and hippies, the pornographers and members of the Tri-County Interfaith League of Family Values, and he read to us from Paul's letter to the Corinthians. "'Thou fool, that which thou sowest is not quickened, except it die. . . .'"

ॐ

We followed the casket to the cemetery. The grass was as green as the town golf course, and the newly dug grave was raw and shocking, a perfect gaping rectangle of naked earth, just the size for a flower bed. Reverend Glass said a few last words as the coffin was lowered into the ground. Earth to earth and dust to dust. Being mostly farmers and gardeners, the people who'd come to watch understood this, and they stayed until the very end, because you would never walk away from a seed half planted. Then, when the last few shovelfuls were placed, people stepped forward and took turns planting a few seeds of their own in the newly turned soil. It was primarily a symbolic act. Only some of the seeds would overwinter, to germinate in the spring, but nobody seemed to mind. They planted and spoke.

"I'm Ellen Anderson. I've been a customer of Fullers' Seeds for about twenty-two years now. I met Mr. and Mrs. Fuller one time on vacation with my husband, God rest his soul. We saw the sign for Fullers' Seeds on the roadside, and we stopped and bought some melon seeds. Hearts of Gold and Mr. Uglys. My husband loved those melons, and I've kept them going in his memory, and I'll continue for Mr. Fuller, too, but I'm seventy-three years old, and I only got a backyard garden plot, and you know how melons like to spread. I'd appreciate some help from some of you young people here."

"I'm Joe Delaney. I live just west of here, over in Idaho Falls, but I was born here in Liberty Falls, and . . . well, I've known Lloyd since we was boys. Used to farm potatoes, too, but couldn't keep up. Well, I live with my son and his wife now. They both got jobs with computers and such, but they got a nice place with a garden, and they've signed on to keep a couple of the beans going. We always liked Lloyd's beans."

"My name's Edith McCann, and I'm sure going to miss Lloyd's newsletters. I subscribe to several magazines, but I always read Lloyd's newsletter first. I'm cultivating three of Momoko's squashes, and I just hope I can keep them growing true, but if anybody gets any strange crosses from my seeds, you be sure to let me know."

"I'm Will Quinn. My wife and I live next door to the Fullers, and I've been farming Lloyd's acreage for the past twenty or so years now. I guess we're going to take on some of his peas and whatever else gets left over. Lloyd was a good farmer and a good neighbor."

"I'm Cass Quinn. I've lived next to Lloyd and Momoko all my life. I'm going to miss Lloyd. He was a good man."

"My name is Ocean Fuller, and Lloyd is my *kupuna*, and I was scared of him at first, but now I just love him a lot. I didn't bring a seed, but I brought an egg from Chicken Little instead, and I *know* they don't grow this way, but Grandpa likes eggs, so I'm gonna plant it anyway."

"I'm Phoenix. Lloyd was my grandfather, too. We only met him this year for the first time. I wish we'd known him for longer. He was totally awesome. He was a prophet of the Revolution."

And on it went. Momoko didn't speak, and neither did I. We just stood side by side, and we listened. Geek spoke for the Seeds of Resistance. He told how they'd come to Liberty Falls, what they'd learned from Lloyd and Momoko, and how much Lloyd's support had meant to their cause. "He was a man of vision. Don't let his dying nightmare become our living reality!" Geek was never one to pass up an opportunity to spread the word.

Elliot didn't speak, because, really, what could he have said? It was hard to believe he had come at all. Phoenix was standing next to me, glaring murderously. Lilith was doing likewise. Will barely acknowledged him with a nod, and Cass ignored him completely. Elliot stayed in the background and tried to catch my eye, and when the graveside ceremony drew to a close and the mourners dispersed, he intercepted me. Poo was getting heavy, so I set him down on the sod. Elliot took my hands.

"I'm sorry about your father," he said.

I pulled away. I didn't want to be standing there by Lloyd's newly dug grave holding hands with Elliot.

"Yummy, I know this is a hard time, but we have to talk."

"Now . . . ?" I could see Cass looking over at us with her arms folded. The kids were already in the car.

"No. I'm at the motel. I'll call you. Or just come."

"Please don't call. It'll only upset Phoenix. He's furious that you're here."

"I know. I'm sorry. Listen, Yummy, I have to tell you. I've . . . left my job."

I didn't know quite what to say. "That's good, I guess. Is it?" I looked around for Poo.

"It's amazing. I feel, I don't know, reborn or something." He took a deep breath. "Yummy, a lot has gone wrong between us, but it's time for a fresh start. Will you come tonight? So we can talk?"

Poo had crawled back over to the edge of the grave. His fists were deep in the freshly dug dirt, and his face was smeared. I knelt down next to him and pulled his hands away, scooping around inside his mouth with my finger and bringing out clots of grass and mud. I wiped his face with the sleeve of my coat, and he began to whimper. Elliot was standing above me.

"Why did you come?" I asked.

"I needed to apologize to your father. I want to make amends to you."

He stood there at the gravesite, looking eager and contrite. "Please," he said. "Yummy. Yumi . . ."

"All right," I said.

Oh, God, how nice it would be if the story could just end here! With Lloyd's earthly body dead and buried in the ground and his heavenly body in transit to the hereafter. With his seeds safely disseminated, his wife wading in shallows of forgetfulness, and his daughter poised on the threshold of reconciliation with her onetime rapist. I could turn over the farmhouse to the Quinns and take Momoko and the kids back to Hawaii. Elliot could join us, and Phoenix would learn to tolerate his new stepdad, or he wouldn't. Cass and Will could get back to their business of growing potatoes, a little lonelier—no, a lot lonelier—than before, and the Seeds of Resistance could pack up the Spudnik and move along down the road, sowing their message and saving the world.

How nice it would be. . . .

Wouldn't it?

Impossible to say, because something went suddenly and terribly wrong in the story. It may simply have been an accident, random and tragic, a bit of very bad luck. Or it may have been something far more sinister—a rogue element set loose in Liberty Falls, who knew about Lloyd's passing and when the funeral was scheduled to start. Maybe he watched us leave the farmhouse that morning, all dressed in black, crammed into the Pontiac and the Quinns' Suburban. Maybe he parked on the side of the road and slipped down the driveway, knowing no one would be there. I can imagine him, shadowlike, skirting the barn and moving toward the parked Winnebago. Maybe he'd been inside before.

Geek would say that when you release an agent, randomly and carelessly, into an environment, it follows that all hell breaks loose, but even Geek was blindsided. "I expected a fallout," he said, broken and bewildered. "Just not like this."

The mourners brought casseroles and salads and roasts and gratins. They brought brownies and cookies and pies. Following the service, they reconvened at our house for a supper, which had been precisely coordinated by the members of the Ladies' Aid Society. They had preassigned the courses in order to avoid an insufficiency of meats or an overabundance of side dishes. They brought the floral arrangements from the funeral home and placed them in the parlor. They greeted the guests and took their coats, steering them past the flowers toward the food, which they had set up buffet style in the kitchen.

Reverend Glass was one of the first to arrive, accompanied by members of the congregation. The president of the Chamber of Commerce was next, then the veterans from the local VFW, who had fought alongside both Lloyd and Will in their respective wars. Sheriff Odell brought his wife. The men from the Potato Growers Association arrived with their families, looking stiff and uncertain about mingling with the gardeners and the hippies. They greeted Momoko, then stood apart and admired the floral wreaths. The wives sneaked sidelong glances at me. They helped themselves to potato salad. They ate ham.

It is said that the brain retains the moments that precede a disaster with preternatural clarity. Time slows—or so it seems—and images linger, imprinted on the memory like shadows on a retina, bloated with light. I had put Poo down for his nap in my bedroom, then changed out of the black dress I'd borrowed from Cass for the funeral and put on something loose and yellow and, by Liberty Falls standards, entirely outlandish. Downstairs, amid all the somber funereal garb, I felt like a dislocated sun on an overcast day. Geek had brought a bottle of rum from the greenhouse and stashed it in the kitchen, and I drifted through the roomful of my parents' friends drinking a heavily spiked Coke. Little groups of ladies eddied around me, patting my arm and telling me over and over what a good man my father had been until I wanted to scream. *Yes!* He was a good man, and a lot of other things, too, but I didn't say anything. I just wanted them all to finish up and leave. I was half thinking about Elliot, wondering what he had to say and if I even cared anymore. I spotted Ocean and called to her. She threaded her way toward me through the forest of legs.

"Geek's taking us out to the Spudnik, Mom," Ocean said. "This scene is a drag."

I agreed. I gave her a polite smile and a little pat, something I'd picked up from the ladies. She looked at me like I was weird, then headed over to where Geek was standing with Phoenix at the edge of the crowded room. I caught his eye.

"Thanks." I mouthed the word, pointing to my children. He held up his fingers in a peace sign. He was trying to help. Things had been strained between us. A lot had happened since we'd shared blue drinks in the hammock.

I was dying to slip away, too, but I didn't want to leave Momoko. She was doing a pretty good job pretending to recognize all the people who approached her, but I didn't know how much longer she could keep it up. I watched as she straightened a lampshade and noticed that one of Lloyd's labels was attached to it. The label said LAMPSHADE. It was the last normal thing I recall.

inferno ౨ఎ

Cass was slicing ham when the first explosion occurred. She and Charmey had been organizing the donations of food, but Charmey still got tired easily, and after sorting out a few vegan dishes for herself and the Seeds, she had told Cass that she wanted to lie down. She took Tibet to the Spudnik, and Frankie went with her. He came back to the kitchen awhile later, bouncing the baby up and down in his arms.

"She nursed, but she wouldn't go to sleep," he explained to Cass. "She likes it here with all the people. She likes to party. Don't you, babe?"

Cass worried about the way the boy handled his daughter, but Tibet just gurgled and wiggled her fingers at Frankie. He bent his head and nuzzled her belly. She patted him on the head.

Geek, Y, and Lilith came tromping into the kitchen, followed by Phoenix and Ocean. They all headed toward the door.

"Hey," Geek said. "We're gonna split. We'll be in the Spudnik."

"Wait up," Frank said. "Charmey's out there. She's trying to take a nap. You mind hanging out here awhile longer?"

They all stopped and did an about-face. "Well?" Geek said.

"We could go up to the attic," Phoenix said. "We could play Monopoly."

"A brainwashing tool to indoctrinate youth into the values of the capitalist hegemony," Geek said happily. "Sure."

"I hate Monopoly," said Ocean. "Phoenix cheats. He changes the rules."

"That's what happens in a patriarchy," Lilith said. "Men make the rules. But I'll tell you what. We'll form an anarcho-feminist collective. We'll organize and overthrow the system."

Cass was just starting to slice the ham when Frankie sidled over. He cradled Tibet against his shoulder and snagged a thick slab with his fingers, tearing off a bite.

"Ooooh, look!" Ocean cried. "Frankie's eating meat! I'm telling Charmey. She'll be mad at you!"

Frankie dropped the rest of the ham into his mouth, spit out a clove, then sucked his fingers clean. "Ocean's a snitch," he said to Lilith. "I wouldn't trust her."

"I'm not a snitch. I'm a narco-feminist, and eating meat means *you're* a traitor."

"It's not meat," he said. "It's fruit." He peeled a round slice of soggy pineapple from the top of the ham, wiggled it over Ocean's head, and pretended to drop it.

"Oooh, gross!" Ocean cried, and twisted away.

He licked the sweet, sticky rind. He took a big bite, and that's when it happened.

Cass felt it an instant before she heard it. She felt it in her feet and legs, a jolt followed by a violent tremor, and then the sound reached them—a deafening clap and boom of thunder, only she knew it couldn't be thunder, because it was far too loud and besides, it had been a beautiful day. Everyone froze, and Cass would never forget the look on Frankie's face, caught there with his daughter in one hand and a limp slice of pineapple in the other.

"Charmey!" he said. He dropped the fruit back onto the platter and passed Tibet over to Cass. A split second later he was through the screen door. He moved so quickly it was like he left a hole behind him, which the others soon filled, but by the time they caught up, following him out the door and onto the porch, he was already down by the barn, a small figure silhouetted against the inferno that was now the Spudnik. Whorls of flame rocketed up into the darkness with each new explosion as, one by one, the tanks blew. First the propane. Then the methane. Then the biodiesel. The smell of burning french fries filled the air.

People came streaming out of the house. Y and Geek ran after Frankie. He was dancing at the edge of the flames, screaming Charmey's name. He covered his head with his jacket, bent low, and charged, again and again, trying to breach the wall of fire, but it kept spitting him out. They grabbed him and tried to hold him back, but he fought them off, flailing and kicking. On the porch Cass clutched Tibet and watched the howling shadows of the boys against the bonfire. It looked like they were dancing. She shielded the baby against her chest. She saw Yummy, frantic, searching for Phoenix and Ocean, then spotting them on the porch as they were about to follow Frank into the yard. Cass heard her scream, *Do not leave this porch!* Phoenix shot her an anguished look, but he obeyed.

Someone phoned the fire department, but it was a volunteer department, and half the firemen were here already, and they had no truck. Yummy ran down to help Will direct them, locating buckets and irrigation supplies, whatever they could find. They formed a bucket brigade, heaving containers of water from one to the next, knowing all the while that it was too late.

Hours later, when the ambulance pulled away from the driveway, it was empty. There was nothing left of Charmey to find or remove. Frankie had been standing quietly off to one side while the sheriff and the paramedics searched, but when he saw the empty stretcher carried out, he snapped. He plunged back into the charred shell, kicking and ripping away at the buckled metal. Will and Billy Odell went after him, lifting him by the armpits and dragging him up to the porch. Frankie fought them, but when he caught sight of Cass standing there with Tibet, he stopped. Stricken, he held out his hands, burned and bloodied and caked with soot. Cass hesitated, then handed him the baby. He sank down onto the top step and curled his body around his tiny daughter. Tibet started to cry.

"Shhh, baby, please," Frank said, but her crying just got louder. He looked up at Cass. "Oh, fuck," he said. "I think she's hungry."

The mourners left as soon as the fire was out. They had come to grieve for Lloyd. They didn't even know who Charmey was, and what are you supposed to do when someone gets blown to pieces at somebody else's funeral? Even the Ladies' Aid Society was at a loss for what to do. The fire truck had finally arrived, and in the stillness that settled, the lights swirled red against the wreck of the Spudnik, making it throb in and out of darkness, like a skeleton breathing. The firemen were packing things in, getting ready to go.

The baby had worn herself out crying and gone off to sleep. Cass brought her inside, and when she came back out again, Billy Odell was taking statements. The Seeds were there, and so was Yummy. They were all watching Geek, who was sitting on the bottom step of the porch pounding his forehead against the newel post. His glasses were broken. "It's my fault," he was saying, only he wasn't talking so much as intoning the words. Over and over.

Odell stood next to him with his notebook in hand. "What's your fault, boy?"

Geek's face was smeared with soot. The emergency lights were flashing red in his busted glasses.

"The propane tanks. Something was wrong. I was trying to fix them—"

"For God's sake, Billy!" Cass said, cutting him off. "Don't write that down. He's in shock. He doesn't know what he's saying." She went over and stood beside Yummy, who reached over and squeezed her arm.

The sheriff said, "A statement's a statement."

"You want a statement, I'll give you a statement," Lilith said. "You're the one responsible. Your guys were screwing around with the Spudnik when we were in jail. They busted the propane line."

"That's right," Y said. "Geek was just trying to fix it. This is a fucking setup."

Geek just sat there, slowly banging his head.

"Surely it was just an accident," Yummy said.

Lilith looked at her like she wanted to spit. "*Just* an accident? Ask your son." She turned to Odell. "Phoenix was here. He witnessed what went down."

Odell looked around.

"Phoenix didn't witness anything," Yummy said. "Anyway, he's in bed."

"No I'm not." The door slammed, and Phoenix sauntered out onto the porch. He was wearing his surf jams and a T-shirt. His feet were bare.

Odell looked him over. "You ever seen someone tampering with that vehicle, son?"

"Sure," Phoenix said, going to stand next to Lilith. "Lots of people. You should know. You were one of them."

Odell's face turned red. "Don't get wise with me. That was part of a crime investigation."

The boy shrugged. "Whatever."

"Tell him about the other guy," Lilith said. "The one with the sunglasses who kept coming back."

Phoenix frowned. "He wasn't wearing a uniform or anything, just these sunglasses with mirrors. He had a real old car, and he looked kind of gnarly."

"Gnarly?"

"Yeah. You know. Skanky."

"He was a spy!" Lilith said. "I remember him from the action. He was wearing a cap with a GroundUp logo." She spun around and pointed at Yummy. Her eyes were dark and accusing. "He worked for her friend, the PR fuck. I saw them talking."

"Oh, please," Yummy said. "That's insane."

"Sure is," Odell said. "This is farm country. You know how many guys around here got caps like that?"

"Exactly," Yummy said, nodding at the sheriff.

Phoenix stood beside Lilith, looking as dark and bruised as she did. He glowered at his mother.

"No!" Lilith said. "I'll tell you what's insane. Every time her old Cynaco fuck buddy shows up around here, some evil shit goes down! First it's letters threatening to burn us down and kill us with swords. Now our trailer gets bombed, and Charmey is murdered. It's not a coincidence. It's conspiracy and terrorism, and her friend is behind all of this."

"That's ridiculous," Yummy said. She turned to Phoenix. "Elliot Rhodes isn't a terrorist, and he wasn't hiring spies to bomb us. Besides, he quit his job. He has nothing to do with this or Cynaco or anything else, so don't look at me that way."

"God!" Lilith said. "You really are an idiot."

The sheriff interrupted. "This is all beside the point," he said, snapping his notebook shut. "We got a confession right here." He pointed the edge of the book at Geek. "That's good enough for me."

Will stepped forward from out of the darkness. "Leave it, Odell," he said. "Just walk away." He had been helping get the fire truck ready to leave, and now it had turned off its emergency lights and was backing out of the drive. "You can't even search that wreck properly until it cools down."

Everyone got real quiet. Then Odell raised his hands in exasperation. "I don't get you, Will Quinn. This is the scum that tore up your field."

"Go home, Billy. We'll deal with it in the morning."

"He might flee our jurisdiction," the sheriff said.

"My husband and I will vouch for him," Cass said, placing a hand on Geek's shoulder. "He's not fleeing anywhere."

The moon was high in the sky as the sheriff's truck drove away. Will came over and helped Geek to his feet. "I'll take him on home, then," he told Cass.

She watched as her husband put his arm around Geek and slowly walked him away. You could always count on Will. When they passed Yummy, Cass saw her reach out to Geek, to touch him perhaps, or offer him some comfort, but he flinched and pulled back as though she'd slapped him.

Y and Lilith collected Frankie.

Cass headed inside to get Tibet. "We'll find room for them all at our place," she told Yummy. "They shouldn't stay here."

The baby was sleeping in a corner of the sofa, barricaded with pillows and blankets. Yummy followed Cass into the living room and sank into Lloyd's recliner.

"Oh, God!" She rubbed her face and looked at her watch. "It's only nine o'clock. It feels so late."

Cass looked down at the baby. A lot had happened.

"I don't suppose you could take the kids, too?"

"Sure," Cass said. "If you think it's better for them not to stay here."

"Just for a couple of hours. I'll pick them up on my way back."

Cass gasped. "Oh, no you're not! Not tonight!" She watched the color in Yummy's face rise.

"I won't be long."

Cass looked away and reached for the phone. "I'll call Will," she said. "I'll stay here until you get back."

The screen door slammed. "You don't have to," said Phoenix. "My mom's not going anywhere." He stood there in his surfing jams, silhouetted in the doorway.

"Phoenix . . ." Yummy said. There was a warning in her voice.

He wouldn't meet her eye. "My mom's staying here."

"Phoenix!"

But he wasn't listening, he was talking right over her. "My mom's not going off to a sleazy motel to get fucked by some fucking PR scumbag murderer."

"Damn it, Phoenix! Don't you talk to me like that!"

"I'm not talking to you. There's no point." He wouldn't even look in her direction. "You can go home now, Cass." He climbed the stairs. "We'll be okay."

Cass looked at Yummy.

"Fine," Yummy said, clenching her jaw. "I'll stay."

aftermath ⌘

I knew that Cass was thinking I might go after my son with a horsewhip or something. "Don't worry," I told her. Not that I wouldn't have liked to.

When she left, I poured some of Geek's rum into a large glass and added some Coke, then went upstairs. I could hear Phoenix in the attic, but I wasn't going up there. Poo and Ocean were both asleep, but Ocean stirred when I pulled up her covers.

"Mommy?" she said. Her voice was fuzzy. I sat down next to her and rubbed her hot back. How could I feel so tender toward one child and so hard toward another? I watched the sleep clear from her face, and then the awful moment when she remembered and her face crumpled and she started to cry. Poor little thing. She couldn't understand how all these people she loved so much could just vanish, one after another, like bubbles bursting. "Where do they go?" she sobbed.

I wished I could give her some simple comfort, offer her God's heaven or some other divine and beneficent plan to make sense of all these earthly misfirings, but I couldn't. I did my best.

"They go back to the beginning, Puddle."

"Beginning of what?"

"Of everything. Of life. Where things start."

"What things?"

"Well, people, for one. And seeds. And potatoes. That's what Tutu Lloyd told me just before he died."

She looked up at me with those clear blue Fuller eyes. Tears clung to her lashes. Her gaze flickered past me to the ceiling and the stars. I remembered the light in my father's ruined old face when he told me his dream, and I lay down next to Ocean so she wouldn't see that I was crying, too. I hugged her for a while until my voice started working again, and then I whispered in her ear.

"Grandpa told me that the beginning was very beautiful, and everything he loved was there. Can you imagine a place like that?"

"No," she said, still sniffling.

"Sure you can. Let's try, okay? Close your eyes. Tell me something you love."

She shut her eyes, took a deep breath, and promptly said, "Mommy," which was exactly the right answer, so I gave her a big kiss on the forehead to reward her for her vast intelligence.

"And Phoenix and Poo," she said. "And Grandma and Grandpa. And Geek and Chicken Little and all the Seeds. The flowers and potatoes and the big sky . . ."

"What about things in Hawaii?" I asked her. "The mangoes and frangipani . . ."

"And yummy pineapples . . ."

"And the ocean and the black sand beaches . . ."

We took turns listing until she fell asleep. Then I finished my drink and watched her for a bit longer, feeling thankful that I had a child who still trusted me enough to be bamboozled with a story. Poo was sleeping soundly. His cheeks were smudged with dirt and sticky glaze from the ham. I licked my thumb and tried to rub some of it off, then stopped when he began to grunt. I let him be. Ocean. Poo. Two out of three. I thought of Phoenix, lying awake in the darkened attic, listening, and I felt my face flush with anger.

I went back down to the kitchen and poured more rum, then stared out the window. The carcass of the Spudnik was still smoldering in the dark, but I could make out only the faintest outline. I thought about calling Elliot. He couldn't be responsible for this. I turned away. My eyes were still burning from the smoke, and sleep was out of the question. I got the broom and started sweeping the house, not caring how much noise I made. Ocean and Poo would sleep through it. The floor was streaked with mud and cinders, so I started in with the mop. I mopped and drank and smoked one cigarette after the other until the place was spotless and the rum and cigarettes were gone. I ate some leftover potato salad, then dug into the ashtray and smoked the last few butts. I still wasn't ready for bed. There was a twenty-four-hour gas station with a convenience store up at the entrance to the freeway. I lifted my car keys off the hook in the kitchen. My footsteps crunched in the gravel. When the Pontiac engine roared to life, I looked up at the house. I kept my eye on the rearview mirror as I bounced down the driveway, waiting for the light to go on in the attic window, but it never did.

To get to the gas station I had to drive by the motel. The low cinder-block building hunkered down in the shadows. The parking lot was full, and the neon sign said NO VACANCY, which surprised me, until I remembered all the funeral guests. I gunned the engine. I'd come out to buy cigarettes, not to go visiting. The convenience store shone brightly on the hill, looking over the dark town. I made the U-turn too fast and left skid marks on the pavement.

Number 6 was unlocked. The room was dark, but that didn't stop me. I knew the layout of the Falls Motel quite well by now, knew how many steps from door to bed, from bed to bathroom. I crossed the room and sat down hard on the edge of the mattress. I started shedding my clothing. I pried off a boot.

"Yummy?"

384

The boot went flying into the television set.

Elliot sat up. He sounded alarmed now. "Is that you?"

"Sure. You expecting someone else?" The other boot took off after the first one.

"That's not what I meant."

I pulled off my jeans, crawled across the bed, and straddled him. "I never know what you mean, Elliot. Let's fuck."

"Yummy, wait." He peered at me. "Are you okay?"

"Fine." I pushed him down against the pillow. I didn't want him in my face. "Listen, I don't have a whole lot of time. I gotta get back before the kids wake up. They'll kill me if they find out I'm here."

"What are you talking about?" He sounded confused. Poor man. I ran my hand down his front, kneading his balls, then leaned over and nuzzled his ear.

"My kids?" I said. "You know I have kids, right? The ones that hate you? At least the two big ones do. The baby doesn't know how yet, but maybe he'll learn."

"Stop that, will you?" He took me by the wrist, pried my hand away from his crotch. "I'm sorry to hear it."

"Why?" I asked.

"Why am I sorry?"

"No. I can imagine why you'd be sorry. I mean why should I stop? You want to fuck me, right? C'mon, let's go." I peeled off my shirt.

"Yummy, I want to talk to you."

All the hard, twangy, boozy energy was coming to a head now, and I twisted my hand from his grip and pushed him back down. Then I started shoving him, sort of bouncing him into the springy mattress. "Well, that's just tough, Elliot. Because I don't want to listen." I could hear my voice getting loud, and before I knew it, I was punching and slapping him, too. "I don't want to listen, because nothing you say is true, and you're a lying piece of shit and I hate you!"

He held up his hands to shield his face. He was bigger and stronger, and he could have stopped me, but he didn't. He let me go on and on, pummeling and pounding him with the pent-up force of twenty-five years, and when I was finally done, I felt strangely calm. I gave him one last shove and let my hands drop. I was still very drunk, but the fervor was gone. I looked at my watch. It was time to go home. I slid toward the edge of the bed and felt around for my jeans. They were somewhere on the floor, with my boots.

"Yummy? Can we talk now?"

I got down on my hands and knees to look for my pants. "Not a good time for talking, Elliot." I located the jeans and pulled them over my feet. The legs got all tangled up, so I rolled onto my back and tried to kick them straight. "Bad time for talking."

He turned on the bedside light. I was lying on the floor with my pants half on and my legs in the air.

"Turn off that fucking light!" I yelled.

But he left the light on and came to sit beside me on the floor. He gathered me into his arms. "Poor Yumi," he murmured into the top of my head. "Yumi. You. Me . . ."

He was rocking me back and forth, and I started to relax in spite of myself, to soften into the familiar warmth of his chest. I was worn out from all that punching.

"Are you too drunk to hear me?"

I nodded.

"Try," he whispered. "We need to talk. About us . . ."

I opened my eyes, but the idea failed to register.

"About the future," he said, looking down at me. "Our future. Together."

His face was too close, and his eyes started to drift, moving apart so that at first there were four eyes, then merging again until there was only one. I shook my head to clear it. I hated being this drunk. He was still talking. I stared into the one eye in the middle of his forehead and concentrated on not getting sick. The potato salad had been a mistake. One mistake. Of many.

"I've been doing a lot of thinking," he was saying. "About what happened back then. What we did. We took a life, Yumi. From the universe. And the way I figure it, we owe one back. You and me. Life is sacred. I want to make amends."

"Huh?" I struggled to sit up.

"I thought we could get married first. . . ."

The meaning of his words began to penetrate the rum fog in my brain. "What?"

"Then I want us to have a child."

I pulled away and stared at him. At a distance his eyes held still. "Oh, my God. You're serious!"

"Perfectly." He stood up and went to his bedside table. When he returned, he took my hand and placed something in the center of my palm. I looked down. It was a ring. He was on his knees now, in front of me.

"Yumi. My life has been . . . well, I won't say it hasn't been fun, but being with you after all these years, and seeing you with your kids, I had this feeling—" He stopped. "I don't know how to put it. . . ."

I held my breath.

"Like I may have missed something."

That was it. Granted I was very drunk, but this struck me as hilariously funny and I started to laugh. I doubled over, clutching my stomach, and gasped for breath. "I think I'm going to be sick," I said, and toppled onto my side like a roly-poly fetus. Finally, when the laughter subsided, I wiped my eyes.

"You're a fucking piece of work," I said. "You know that, Elliot?"

"Yeah?" he said. His face lit up as he cocked his head hopefully.

But the laughter had sobered me up. I pulled my jeans on the rest of the way, then buttoned them. I found my boot and stuck my foot in it.

"So," he said. "What do you think?"

The truly bizarre thing was that I could actually picture it. Through my alcoholic haze I could see the two of us, what? Returning to Pahoa? Moving to San Francisco? We could buy an old Victorian and paint it pretty pastel colors. Pastels were big out there, layers of peeling pinks and tawdry blues.

Maybe he felt my hesitation. Recalling it afterward, I think he probably did. I hope he did. I hope he believed, for one wild moment, that I would agree, that our two hearts would align with a click and we would live happily ever after. It was a moment of delicate equilibrium. His hopes had finally caught up with the ones I'd discarded some twenty-five years earlier.

I looked into his face, searching for a trace—but it was all gone. He was just an aging businessman, out of a job, and for the first time in my life I felt sorry for Elliot Rhodes. I didn't care if he had used me or lied to me. I didn't want to know. I rocked forward and stood, straightening my knees and tugging on my jeans. He looked up at me, still grinning, still believing.

"Well?"

"Forget it, Elliot. Not in a million years." I looked down at the top of his head and briefly rested my fingertips there. "You had your chance," I said, giving his brainpan a hard little tap. "You blew it."

His grin, the last remnant of his confidence, lingered on his face. I walked to the door and was just about to sweep through it, when a vertiginous upswell of remembering stopped me dead. It's terrifying how that happens, how you can completely blank out on something so big and awful, and when you recall it, you feel like the solid earth has vanished from under your feet. There was only one thing he could tell me that I truly did want to know. I turned back and took a deep breath.

"Elliot, you didn't by any chance hire someone to spy on the Seeds and plant a bomb in their Winnebago and blow it up and kill Charmey, did you?"

"*What?*" He looked at me, aghast.

"Because that's what happened. She's dead."

For the first time ever, Elliot was struck dumb. That was enough for me, at least for the moment.

"No," I said. "I knew you were a creep, but I didn't think you'd do something like that."

choices

The phone rang once.

"Cass?" His voice was thin and distant in the dark.

"Who is this?" Cass struggled to sit up. "Phoenix?" She held the receiver and turned her back to Will, whispering so as not to wake him. It was cold. She shivered and brought the covers up. She listened, then asked, "Where's Yummy?" And then, "I'll be right there."

She slipped back the covers and fumbled for her clothes. Will rolled over and flicked on the bedside light.

"Thanks," she said. She stepped into a pair of sweatpants.

"Who was that?"

"Phoenix." She pulled on one of Will's sweatshirts. Wearing his clothes made her feel strong. "Poo is throwing up. Phoenix thinks he ate something. I'm going over."

"Where's Yummy?"

Cass grimaced. "Don't ask." She sat on the edge of the bed and tied her sneakers.

"You want me to come?"

"I'll take the cell phone. I'll call if I need you."

He nodded. "She doesn't deserve to have those kids. She's an unfit mother." Somehow he managed to sound both angry and wistful.

Cass leaned over and gave him a kiss on the forehead, and then she ran out the door.

The Pontiac was parked in the lot of the Falls Motel. She spotted it on the way to the hospital, but she didn't stop. At the emergency room there was a slight delay in admitting Poo because she wasn't his mother. Finally the doctor pumped him out, extracting a frothy soup of curdled earth and grass, chunks of ham and pineapple and stomach acids. A kind of thin adobe gruel. Termites could build nests with it.

"He eats dirt," Cass explained weakly.

"Geophagy," said the doctor. "I see."

"What's that?"

"What you said. Eating earth. There's nothing wrong with it. It's basically what you get when you take an antacid formula."

"Antacid?"

"Sure. Kaolin. Or calcium carbonate. Accounts for that chalky taste. We've been practicing geophagy for as long as we've been human. It's the earth that isn't what it used to be. Dirt isn't clean these days. Where did he eat this, do you know?"

Cass shook her head. "Could be anywhere. No, wait. There was grass? Then it was probably up at the cemetery. He was playing on a grave."

The doctor raised his eyebrows. "That's not good."

"We buried his grandpa," Cass explained, but the look on his face stopped her short. "Oh, no! You mean, because there's *dead* people in it?"

The doctor gave a grim little smile. "Decomposing bodies are the least of the problem. I'm talking about the lawn."

"But it's a nice lawn."

"And it takes a lot of nice lawn chemicals to keep it that way. Don't get me wrong, it's not a problem unless you ingest it. Or feed it to a baby."

Poo was sleeping, spread-eagled on his back, draped in a white sheet. His dark cheeks were tear streaked and smeared with dirt.

"Is he going to be okay?" Cass asked.

"He's going to be fine. I'm going to let you take him home, but I want you to keep a close eye on him." He paused. "Oh, right," he said. "You're not the mother."

∽

"What kind of a mother *are* you?" Cass said. She wasn't yelling. Phoenix and Ocean were in bed, and Poo was asleep in the living room, so she was being careful not to raise her voice. In fact, she was whispering. But the effect was the same as if she'd been yelling at the top of her lungs. She watched Yummy flinch.

"I just went out for cigarettes . . ."

"That's a lie!" Cass said. "I saw the Pontiac in the motel parking lot."

"I didn't mean to go there. It just sort of happened. I didn't stay long."

"I know. I called the motel from the hospital. They wouldn't let me admit Poo because I wasn't his mother. I talked to that creep, and he said you'd gone. At least if you'd still been there, you could have come."

Yummy shrugged. "Damned if I do and damned if I don't." She stood up and went to the fridge. "I need a beer. Want one?"

"You do not!" Cass said, surprised at her own vehemence. "It's morning. You don't need a beer at this hour. You drink way too much and . . . well, I think you've just got to stop."

Yummy stopped. Her hand was on the refrigerator door. "Excuse me? I don't think you have any right to tell me what I should or shouldn't do."

"I have every right. As a human being concerned for the welfare of your children, but even more as your friend."

Yummy didn't say anything. Cass waited, but Yummy just stood there watching, and her eyes were so expressionless they made Cass shiver. Her stomach felt suddenly hollow, as if it had been pumped out, too.

"Fine," she said. "Maybe we're not friends. I always thought we were, but maybe we're not. That's beside the point. What's important is your kids, and I just think you're being a really lousy mother to them right now. The way you've been carrying on, it's like you forget they even exist. You don't know how lucky you are, and I just can't stand to watch you treat such a blessing with such . . . such carelessness."

She tried to continue, but her voice was choking, so she stopped.

Yummy left the refrigerator door closed and came back to the table. "Oh, please," she said. "Don't start crying, okay? I'm sorry."

"I'm not crying," Cass said stiffly. "I'm angry."

"Oh. Well, good."

"I mean, how could you go running off like that? Tonight! Of all nights!"

"I know. I know. And you know what? You're right."

"Of course I'm right."

"I've been out of control lately. I'm not usually like this. Something about coming back here, just being in this house . . ."

"I know," Cass said. "You've told me many times."

"The minute I got back here, it all just came flooding back, all the acting out and the anger at Lloyd. . . ."

And hearing this set Cass off again. "For God's sake, Yummy, just drop it, will you? Lloyd's dead. It's over. You can't blame everything on him. Not anymore."

It came out harsher than she meant it to.

Yummy sat back in her chair as though she'd been shoved. "Wow." She closed her eyes and didn't speak for a long time.

"I'm sorry. I didn't mean . . ."

"No. You're right." She covered her face with her hands, and her body started to shake. "It's really over, isn't it?"

She was laughing, Cass thought, or maybe she was crying. It was hard to tell, and it didn't much matter. Cass looked at her, disgusted. "You're still drunk," she said. She picked up her jacket and stood to go.

"No, wait," Yummy said. She looked up, and Cass saw there were tears in her eyes. "I'm not drunk. I'm serious." She wiped her eyes with the heel of her hand. "It's so hard to remember that I loved him; I'm so used to calling it something else, you know?"

She got up and went to the sink to fill the coffeepot. Cass watched her spoon coffee into the filter and realized she had stopped being angry. Now she just felt drained and a little bit lonely, too. "Do you know what you're going to do next?" she asked.

Yummy turned and leaned against the counter, aligning her feet over the two worn spots on the floor in front of the sink. She hugged herself. "Getting the hell out of here for starters. I'm taking the kids back to Pahoa."

Cass felt her heart sink. "What about your mom?" She could just picture the next few years, hauling casseroles up and down the road.

"I was thinking of trying to bring her back, too. You think she'd be up for it?"

"She can't stay here on her own."

Yummy nodded. "She can have a garden. Things grow like stink in Hawaii. I thought if she likes it there, we'll forfeit the life-estate clause, and you and Will can move into this house. I certainly don't want it, and you own it, so you might as well live in it."

They would finally have enough room, Cass thought, but she felt oddly disappointed. She'd always wanted to live in the Fullers' place, ever since she was a little girl. Of course, she'd wanted to live here with the Fullers. She'd wanted the house and the family, too.

"That's good, right?" Yummy said. "You guys want to move in?" She brought the coffeepot over to the table. She poured two cups and sat down across from Cass and shared the cream and sugar.

Cass stirred her coffee and felt the loneliness grow. "I'm going to miss you," she said suddenly. "I said it was beside the point, but it's not. I thought we were friends."

Yummy looked surprised. "Of course we're friends," she said. "We've always been friends. We grew up together."

But it wasn't the same thing, Cass was thinking. It was just what happened with country kids. People's houses were so far apart you didn't really choose your friends, you just ended up living next to a person. When they moved, you grew apart.

"Cass?" Yummy said. "You okay? You're real quiet."

"I'm fine," Cass said. "Really. Just fine."

Yummy reached out across the table and took hold of her hand. "Thanks," she said. "For everything. For giving a shit."

Cass nodded. "Well," she said, "I guess that's what friends are for."

It had been a long night. It was still dark outside, but from the kitchen window she could just make out the horizon line, where the sky met the potato fields and was starting to brighten. Now that the vines had wilted and died, the fields looked like the aftermath of a battle, but underneath the earth the tubers were hardening off and soon would be ready for harvest. Will would be up and outside already. It was a busy time of year, but after this it would be winter and things would settle down. She brought her coffee cup to the sink, said good-bye to Yummy, and pulled on her jacket to go.

Outside, the smell of burning hung in the chill air, but it was not autumnal. It wasn't leaves. It was the acrid stench of scorched rubber and battery acid and diesel oil. It was french-fried potatoes. She looked down from the porch into the yard at the skeleton of the Spudnik, crouching in the dim light.

She crossed the porch and picked her way through the muddy yard, looking toward the wreckage. A few birds, muted and irresolute, chirped in the overcast morning, but their cries were swallowed by the silence that the explosion had left in its wake. Cass shivered and turned away, but as she headed down the drive toward her car, she heard a noise. She stopped, then heard it again, a low groan that sent shivers across her skin. She approached the wreck and stood at the edge, straining to see into the twisted shadows. A large black scar marked the ground, and the torqued metal seemed to remember the force of the explosion that had melted it down. The ground was littered with bits of shattered glass and bubbled plastic. Cass stared into the darkness. How could a person just vanish like that? An entire girl, plump with milk, brimming with life. Where does she go? Does she just get reabsorbed into the air?

She heard a rustle, the sound of a boot scraping, then a sigh. Her heart leaped, fully expecting in that moment to see Charmey reappear, soot smudged and disheveled, poking her head out from behind a pile of rubble. *Ooh la la!* And if not Charmey herself, then at least her ghost or spirit, some residue or trace of her to ease the transition that the living hadn't yet had time to make.

But it wasn't Charmey. It was Frankie, hunkered down on the ground, rocking on his heels and waiting.

"Hi," Cass said. Her breath came out like smoke in the chilly morning air.

"Hi."

"What are you doing?"

"Nothing." He shrugged. "I just thought . . ."

She waited for him to continue.

"I don't know," he said. "Maybe she was still here? Maybe she'd come back? It's stupid."

"I was thinking that, too."

"Yeah?" He looked up quickly, then dropped his head and let it hang. "Well, she isn't here," he informed her. "So I guess she's pretty much split for good."

He hugged his knees and nodded to himself. The sky was growing brighter now, and Cass could hear the low drone of a harvester starting up in a distant field. She squatted beside him and put a hand on his back. She could feel his ribs under the T-shirt.

She started to talk. She told him about the weeks leading up to Tibet's birth, and all about the birth itself, and how difficult it was and painful, and how brave Charmey had been. "She didn't think she was going to make it. All she wanted was to see the baby just once."

"Yeah," he muttered. "It was always about the baby."

"No. When things were really bad, you're the one she called for. She squeezed my hand so hard I thought the bones would break. She said, 'Tell Frankie I love him.'"

"Yeah?" He looked up.

"She was in more pain than I've ever seen a person bear, but she made me promise to tell you. I didn't before, because she made it through just fine. But I'm telling you now."

He dropped his head again and butted up against her chest, and it was like holding a calf or a goat kid, the way he bleated and breathed so rapidly. And just as she would calm a scared animal, she rubbed his back in long, even strokes and restrained him gently while he cried.

checking out ℬ

Later that morning, around eight o'clock, the sheriff came back out to the house to question Phoenix about the man with the mirrored sunglasses and the GroundUp cap. Someone had phoned in an anonymous tip, he told us. Phoenix repeated his story, and Lilith confirmed it. She had seen the man talking to Elliot at the action. Everyone fell silent, and Phoenix stared at me until I volunteered the information that Elliot was in Room 6 at the Falls Motel. I also told them about Elliot's reaction when I'd asked him about the explosion. Odell immediately sent a pair of officers around to the motel, but they found the room empty. It was the second time that Elliot Rhodes had checked out of Liberty Falls just before the police could talk to him.

Billy was disappointed. He came back several times to grill me about the events of that night and my relationship with Elliot. He seemed to think that I was withholding information as to his whereabouts. He was all puffed up and secretive about the anonymous tip, and for a while it seemed he was looking to implicate us all in a Washington-based conspiracy, but in the end he concluded that Elliot's sudden departure was consistent with that of any spurned lover and had nothing to do with the explosion. Besides, Billy informed me, Elliot had been fired from his job at Duncan & Wiley, so he no longer had any motive to harass the Seeds.

In the course of the investigation they turned up bits of Charmey. Unrecognizable pieces. A section of her skull, I heard them say. A bit of blackened heel that looked like a charred potato. I told Cass, and together we kept everyone else away. Frankie. Geek. My own kids, who were still in shock. Momoko was there, though. We held hands and edged toward the police line and peered at the evidence bags that the forensics men were filling.

Why did I let Momoko watch?

How could I have watched without her?

She knew the old ways. She knew how to identify remains. In Japan bodies are ritually cremated, and afterward the relatives use chopsticks to pick through the bones, identifying this bit and that. Momoko stood next to me and said nothing as we watched the forensics men work. She squeezed my hand, hard, but when the bags were removed, I felt that we had witnessed Charmey's earthly body passing.

Odell turned his attention to Geek's confession, but Will stuck by. He made sure Geek didn't say anything to implicate himself further. It was a horrible and tragic accident, Will insisted, and when Geek had claimed responsibility that night, he hadn't been in his right mind. When the results of the fire department's investigation failed to produce any evidence to support charges of arson, terrorism, or even criminal negligence, the sheriff gave up. Happenstance prevailed as an explanation.

On his way back from the Quinns' one day, Odell stopped by to thank me for the way I'd handled the information about his son's bringing the handgun to school. He said that after Will had spoken to him, he'd confronted his son and gotten him to admit to it and to say he was sorry.

"Phoenix might like to hear that, too. He was the one with the gun in his mouth."

Billy nodded. "Of course. I'll bring him by." He was standing at the bottom of the porch steps, and he turned to go, but then he paused. "The gun wasn't loaded. I don't keep loaded weapons in the house."

"That makes me feel a lot better."

Odell did track down and question Rodney Skeele, retired private investigator and a founding member of the Tri-County Interfaith League of Family Values. He denied any knowledge of the explosion but freely admitted he had done patent-infringement work for Cynaco in the past. With Elliot checked out, however, any further connection to Cynaco ended with the logo on his cap. Lilith fumed. She muttered dire prophecies of corporate conspiracy into my son's ear. I found it worrisome, but Phoenix didn't seem to mind. More troubling to me was the thought that by banishing Elliot I had blown the only chance we had of ever finding out what really happened.

🕭

"What did Elliot want that night?" Cass asked a few weeks later.

I was packing up by then, sorting out the winter stuff I'd bought for myself and the kids at Wal-Mart—all the snowsuits and mittens, the parkas and muffs and thermal socks—to donate to the Salvation Army. I hoped I would never need them again.

"He asked me to marry him."

"No! He didn't!"

"Had a ring and everything. I told him to fuck off."

"Good for you."

"I'm sure he didn't mean it. He lied about everything else. He even lied about being fired. He told me he'd quit. Like I would have cared?"

"It was just habit with him." She saw me toss a knit shawl into the discard pile. "Hey, I'll take that. It's nice and soft." She folded the shawl and placed it in the bag that she'd been filling. "He was a fucker, Yummy."

"Cass!" I was shocked. I'd never heard her swear before.

She made a face at me. "I've been wanting to say that since we were fourteen."

"How does it feel?"

"Great," she said grimly. She sat there and fingered the shawl and thought for a while. "You think he had anything to do with it?"

"You mean the explosion?" I sat on the side of the bed. "Oh, God, Cass,

I don't know. What if he did? Maybe I shouldn't have sent him away like that—"

But Cass cut me off. "No, you did the right thing. He was in public relations, for goodness' sake. PR people don't just go around blowing things up!"

"Yeah." I nodded. "I guess that's what I think, too."

"He was a fucker and a liar, but I don't think he was a murderer, in spite of what Lilith says. You know, the way that girl carries on, you'd think you could actually *kill* someone with public relations. . . ."

ℬↄ

Maybe you can.

After she left, he'd sat there for a while longer staring at the phone, then he reached for his pants. He dressed quickly and started throwing stuff into his suitcase. He grabbed his toilet kit from the bathroom, put on his coat, and left the key to the room on the dresser along with a dollar for the maid. He felt remarkably calm. He carried his suitcase to the doorway and took a last look around. When he was sure he hadn't forgotten anything, he closed the door behind him.

It was still dark in the parking lot. He loaded his suitcase into the trunk, got into the car, and started the ignition. Then it hit him. He had no plans, nowhere to go. He drove toward the interstate and stopped at the twenty-four-hour gas station up on the hill. As he filled the tank, he knew he had to decide. East or west. The East Coast filled him with dread. He couldn't see going back, tail between his legs, to scrape up another PR job at a lesser firm. It was too depressing. But the West Coast—now, that had some appeal. He thought about San Francisco. About Berkeley in the sixties. Maybe he could find a job on a newspaper somewhere and get back to writing. He went inside to pay for the gas and asked the attendant for a map of the western United States.

"Taking a trip?" the guy asked.

Elliot nodded. He started to spread out the map on the counter, then changed his mind when the guy started getting nosy. "Where you heading?"

"North," Elliot lied. "Up to Canada." He handed back the map. "Wrong one. Hey, listen, you got a pay phone?"

It was just before sunrise when he called in the anonymous tip to the Power County sheriff's office. He gave the officer on duty Rodney's name and suggested they question him in conjunction with a vehicular explosion that morning at Fullers' Farm. Then he got back into his car and pulled onto the interstate, satisfied that he'd done what he could to make things right. He headed west on 84, past Massacre Rocks. When he passed the sign marking the Liberty Falls town limits and watched it disappear in the rearview mirror, he felt glad to be putting all this behind him—it was terrible about the girl that died, and the propane tanks probably leaked, but if not, if Rodney had taken it on himself to go solo and had done something crazy, it wasn't his business anymore. It was already the past, and there was his entire future to think about.

He reached into his jacket pocket and pulled out the statue of Kali. He set it on the dashboard, but after a few miles he started to worry. The statue sat there, centered in the windshield, holding her severed head like a pocketbook. He used to like the way she looked at him, dusky and ever so faintly cross-eyed, but now it struck him that in all likelihood it was inauspicious to travel with the deity of destruction on one's dashboard.

Just then the sun broke over the rimrock. The glare reflected in his rearview mirror, blinding him, so he changed into his sunglasses. The light chased him, bright and hard, across the desert. It was a good day for driving. He would have to ditch the rental car along the way, but he could buy a secondhand beater to get him out to the coast. Maybe an old VW. He switched on the radio, scanning the airwaves for classic rock, then laughed as he recognized the lyric.

"You are the crown of creation . . ." Gracie sang, *"and you got no place to go. . . ."*

The little goddess on the dashboard was sticking her tongue out at him. He rolled down the window and chucked her out the window.

With no place to go, he felt like he was going back to the beginning.

small victories ℬↄ

In early October the *New York Times* ran an article with the news that Cynaco's main rival in the life-sciences industry had decided not to sell seeds sterilized with Terminator technology. The CEO had written an open letter stating that his corporation was committed "not to commercialize gene-protection systems that render seed sterile." Geek printed out the article, and the Seeds gathered around the computer and surfed the Net for reactions. The alternative presses were declaring it a victory. TERMINATOR TERMINATED! read more than one banner headline, but Geek shook his head.

"It's a total lie. A PR maneuver. The Terminator issue is too hot right now. They're just distancing themselves from it. Going underground."

"But it sounds so positive," Lilith said.

Geek shook his head. "It's completely meaningless. Sterilization technologies are years away from commercialization. They'll just quietly continue with the R&D, and when it's ready to take to market, they'll announce they've changed their minds again. Terminator will be back, I guarantee."

Y finished reading the article. "Hey, it's a start," he said, handing it back. "Geek, man, you gotta snap out of it. I mean, you're probably right and all, but the little victories count."

Geek shut off the printer. "Not when you've lost the war, dude. It's over."

"What's over?" Frankie asked.

"Nature."

⬧

They were planning to leave after harvest. They were helping Will get the potatoes out of the ground, and he was paying them for their labor, after deducting the costs of his damaged crops.

"We said we'd pay you back for the potatoes we destroyed, and we will," Geek told him. "But we're not harvesting the NuLifes."

"You were perfectly willing to harvest them awhile ago," Will pointed out, but in the end he agreed.

They were pooling their wages to buy a used Winnebago, which they'd found in Idaho Falls. They would have to run it off fossil fuels until Geek had time to convert it to biodiesel, but the engine was solid. They were planning to drive it down to Frisco for the winter, after making a detour to Seattle, where there was a huge demonstration building.

"It's gonna be massive," Y told Frankie. "Global. The whole concept of the nation-state is an anachronistic fiction, a comforting smoke screen for the multinationals. The WTO is the throbbing heart of the new world order. It's a new millennium, dude."

They would make a stop in Eugene, Oregon, to rally and to organize. "It's a radical scene," Lilith said. "You'll totally dig it."

They were in Will's office before supper, waiting for Geek to finish inputting Will's harvest data so they could use the computer to surf the Net. Tibet was lying on her back on the meeting table, watching Frankie play with her toes. Lilith was practicing mudras with her fingers, and Phoenix slouched next to her staring at a chart of potato diseases on the wall.

"You should come with us," Lilith said to Phoenix.

Phoenix shoved his hands into his pockets and slumped deeper into his chair. "Yeah," he said. "Pahoa's lame. It's, like, totally cut off from reality."

Lilith held up her hand. "Pahoa's cool, too. You just gotta choose your choice, you know? Go with the flow."

Frankie snorted. "That's a pile of hippified crap." He let Tibet grab hold of his fingers and pulled her up by the arms. "Look at how strong she is! She's gonna be a real fighter. Look at her punch. Pow, pow . . ." The baby was flailing her arms and legs. "You wanna come? Come," he said to Phoenix. "We're gonna kick some ass."

Tibet started to fuss, so Frankie picked her up. He looked over at the kid, sitting there with a dark scowl on his face. "But you should tell your mom," Frankie said, walking Tibet around the room.

"Huh?" Phoenix looked at him like he was nuts.

"Let her know you're coming so she doesn't worry," Frankie said. Recently stuff like this was popping out of his mouth, and it surprised him, but it almost felt like the words were Charmey's, and she would have said them if she were here, so he thought what the fuck, and let it happen.

Phoenix made a face. "No way, man. You got it all wrong. She doesn't worry. She doesn't give a shit about me. She's totally whacked."

"Gotta tell her anyway," said Frankie, patting his daughter's back. "I'll bet she worries plenty."

reap in joy ℬↄ

Harvest had been going full guns for several weeks, and once the Seeds had gotten the hang of it, they were doing eighteen-hour days alongside the Mexicans.

"It's good for them," Will told Cass in bed at night. "They need hard work and lots of it. We all do."

Cass and Lilith took turns driving trucks, cooking for the crew, and taking care of Tibet. Every time they turned around, it was like they could see the empty place where Charmey should have been. The two women worked side by side, but they didn't talk much. Cass sensed that Lilith resented her for taking Charmey to a hospital and for coaching her during the birth. That was to have been Lilith's role, but Cass shuddered to think of the two girls going at it alone in the trailer.

As the harvest wound down, Cass always felt a sense of completion. The windrowers made their final pass through the fields and retired, and the trucks trundled the last of the potatoes into the clodhoppers. When the tubers were tumbled and sorted, spud from stone, and conveyored into the storage cellars, then they could all rest and overwinter. But this year felt different. There was no completion, only a tugging sense of loss. Charmey was gone. The Seeds would be leaving, and Yummy, too, taking all the life with them. Cass couldn't bear to contemplate the winter.

On the last night of harvest they gathered in Cass's small kitchen waiting for Will, who was paying off the last of the Mexicans. The Seeds were sitting around the kitchen table, and the table was set. Supper was mostly ready, but Cass was still fussing at the stove. She had been feeling anxious all day. She wanted to make them a nice meal to celebrate their hard work.

Frankie was cradling Tibet in the crook of his arm and feeding her from a bottle. Eyes squeezed shut, she was intent on her sucking, and Frankie was bending over, watching her. When Will walked through the door, Frankie sat up a little straighter. Will washed his hands, popped open a beer, and raised it.

"To a successful harvest," he said.

Frankie cleared his throat. "Uh, before we do all that, can I say something?"

He sounded very nervous. Cass turned down the heat on her spaghetti sauce and wiped her hands on a dish towel. She glanced over at Will, who shrugged.

"Okay," Frankie said. "So I just gotta tell you, this is what I decided. This is how I want it to be."

He paused. No one spoke, although Lilith looked like she very much wanted to. Frankie looked around the group.

"Shit, this is hard," he said, moving his shoulders up and down, like he was loosening up tight muscles. He took a deep breath and started again. "Okay. So this one time Charmey told me that you guys were trying to have a kid and it wasn't going so good, so what I want to say is, like, that if it's cool with you, I think you guys should take Tibet."

It felt to Cass as if her heart had stopped beating. He was looking directly at her with his clear gray eyes like stones underwater. She stared back at him, speechless, then dropped her eyes and blushed. She couldn't bear for him to see her face. She was so ashamed, because of course this idea was not new to her. How could it be? It was the single hope she had been struggling to overcome since the night of the explosion, when Frankie handed her the baby and ran out the door. She had despised herself for feeling it then, and she continued to feel sick with guilt every time she fed the baby or bathed her or sang her to sleep. Now, hearing it spoken out loud, she was horrified. He knew.

Lilith clearly felt likewise. "You can't do that," she cried, glaring at Cass. "You can't just give Tibet away! Charmey would have hated that!"

Cass found herself nodding. She felt her hope start to die then, and it was a relief. She had worn it out at last.

"We can take care of her," Lilith was saying. "We'll be back on the road soon. We'll parent her collectively."

But Frankie shrugged. "I think Charmey would have wanted it this way."

Lilith was furious. "I disagree. Besides, you can't let her grow up here! This place sucks! I think we should decide this together. She's our baby, too, you know. Charmey was our family, dude. You just showed up."

Y stood and went to stand behind her. He put his hands on her shoulders. "He showed up at just the right time, Lil."

Lilith looked around the table, appealing to Geek, who nodded. "It's Frankie's call. He's her dad."

"But he's just a dumb-ass kid. He doesn't know shit."

"I know a kid needs a mom and a dad," Frankie said. "And I know it sucks getting moved around from one place to another. Besides, Charmey liked it here. She liked living on a farm, and she really liked Cass a lot. She told me she trusted her because she's old—I mean, like, she's a grown-up and all."

Lilith fell silent, and for a while all they could hear were the tiny sounds of Tibet, sucking. Cass was wringing the dish towel in her lap. She was afraid to speak, afraid that a wrong word might break the spell, and Frank would laugh and say he was just kidding. When nobody said anything more, he spoke again.

"Cool," he said. "So that's basically it. If you want her . . ."

Cass felt Will's eyes on her. She bit her lip and nodded quickly.

"Yes," Will said, but he sounded worried. "Of course. We want her, but—"

"Excellent," Frank said. "Now, the only thing is, I want this to be legit. It can't be a foster-care situation. I want you to adopt her and make it totally legal. Forever, you know?"

"Forever," Will said. "Got it."

Cass was barely breathing. She felt the blood pushing up into her face, and she was afraid she was going to cry. She couldn't cry. She had to be a grown-up.

Frankie was clearly relieved and speaking freely now. "I want her to know me, too," he was saying. "I'll write to her and come see her, and I'll tell her about Charmey so she knows about her birth mom. That part is important. My mom dumped me before I even knew who she was, and I don't want Tibet to ever feel like that. But don't get me wrong. She's your kid. It's just that she's got this extra dad who loves her and a birth mom who died and everything but who loved her, too."

"Of course," Will said.

"Cool," said Frankie. "Because I do totally love her, you know. It's just that I'm only seventeen, and that's way too young to be somebody's full-time dad. Not by myself anyway. I'd blow it big time. Right, baby?"

Tibet had stopped suckling. Frankie shifted his position and eased the rubber nipple from her lips. He leaned over and blew softly into her face, and she waved her hand, batting him on the nose. He flipped a tea towel across his shoulder and held her up against his chest, then rubbed his hand in circles on her back. "So are we cool, then?" he asked, getting up and walking around the table.

"We're cool," Will said.

Frank stopped in front of Cass. "Hey, Tibet. Here's your mom." He turned the baby around and held her out.

Cass reached up and took her. For a moment she did not believe that the tiny body was still real, the insignificant weight, the slight bones, the doll-like legs and arms. But the baby's heat was undeniable. Cass brought her to her chest and held her there, whereupon Tibet promptly burped up her dinner on the front of Cass's sweatshirt.

"Well, that settles it," Frankie said, tossing Cass the towel. "You're official now."

Cass wiped the thin, milky drool off Tibet's chin. She looked into the baby's face and took a deep breath.

"Oh, yeah," Frankie said. "There's one more thing I almost forgot. It's about her food. I know it's a pain in the ass, and it's not like I care that much, but could you try to feed Tibet the organic stuff? Charmey would have wanted it that way."

Cass looked up at Will. He nodded. "Sure."

"Awesome," Frankie said.

"Awesome," Cass echoed.

waking up ∂⟩

My son rarely deigned to come home for meals during those last few weeks in Idaho. When he did appear, slouching through the door into the kitchen, he sat with his shoulders hunched to his ears and his elbows on the table, propping up his head like something badly taxidermied and left on a shelf. I wanted to breathe vitality and humidity back into him. As the temperature dropped in Liberty Falls, I babbled on about beaches, about surfing and warmth and rainbows and aloha, avoiding the tarnished glassy eyes that stared lifelessly at me. We'll be going home soon, son. Everything will be fine in Pahoa.

Or so I believed, until he told me he was running away.

"What?"

"I'm staying," he said. "I'm not going home."

Of course, staying is not the same as running away, but this was just semantics.

"Here? In Liberty Falls?"

"No!" he said, with contempt that would have outdone mine at his age. "No, I'm going to Seattle with the Seeds."

And while it doesn't quite count when your runaway informs you beforehand, wasn't it crueler this way? Wouldn't it have been more considerate of him to slip off silently into the night? Like I'd done. I stared at him, my sullen boy, as he shape-shifted before my eyes. Time plays tricks on mothers. It teases you with breaks and brief caesuras, only to skip wildly forward, bringing breathtaking changes to your baby's body. Only he wasn't a baby anymore, and how often did I have to learn that? The lessons were painful. Like that time when I inhaled, expecting his sweet scent, and got the first fetid whiff of adult decay. He must have been six or seven, and how I grieved for his infant perfection! Soon after, I reached for him, still full of confidence and maternal entitlement, and I felt him stiffen and pull away.

Now time's arrhythmia had tripped me again, catching me off guard and holding my breath. I stared at him, then exhaled. My heart beat like it would crack my rib cage.

"Thank you for telling me."

He looked up at me, surprised. "You mean you're going to let me go?"

NO! I wanted to scream, but I didn't. "I don't think I can stop you, can I?"

He shook his head. He waited.

So I kept talking. "Listen. I don't want you to go. I want you to come home with me and Ocean and Poo. I think you're too young to go off on your own."

"I'm almost fifteen," he said with exquisite condescension, causing me a small spasm of acute tachycardia.

I said, "Your wanting to leave, does it have to do with me or just with you?"

He thought about this for a moment. "Both."

"Okay, well, the you part of it is up to you. I can't do anything about that. But the me part—just hear me out, and you can think it over." Now what? I had to think fast. "I've never been very good at doing the mom thing, and I'm sorry about that."

Impatient now, he shook off my apology.

"I also know that I've been even less mommylike recently and I'm sorry about that, too. I know it's been stressful for you. I've been preoccupied . . . no, what am I saying? Honestly, Phoenix, what with Grandpa and coming back here and all, I just lost it. But that's over now. I'm on track. I promise."

He was balancing on the rear legs of his chair and rocking to and fro, something every mother hates, but I refused to be distracted.

"How do I know that?" he asked.

"Well, you don't. It's one of those times where you just have to trust a person. And look at the history you have together."

I watched his face for clues. "I've never let you down real bad, have I? I've always been there for you."

He was guarded, but still listening. "Yeah," he conceded. "I guess."

I wished I could just stop there, but I couldn't. So I continued. "About Elliot . . ."

His face darkened like he'd tasted something foul.

"That night, before he left, he asked me to marry him."

The chair legs hit the floor with a thump. He braced his hands against the edge of the table.

"I told him no, Phoenix."

He was looking from me to the door and back again, contemplating his options. His face was blank. "Really?"

"I just thought you should know."

He kicked at the leg of the chair, taking time now to ponder the situation. "Are you sorry?"

I took a deep breath and tried to decide how to answer his question. "I'm not sorry I said no."

"Charmey didn't deserve to die," he said.

"No."

"And he *was* responsible."

"Perhaps. We don't know."

He jiggled his foot some more, and in that gap, while time unfolded and I waited, I was overwhelmed by what seemed to me like a miracle, in all its humdrum banality: There he was, my son, sitting in front of me contemplating fate and making decisions about his very own life. It brought tears to my eyes.

"Okay," he said. "I'll think about it. I'll let you know."

"Thanks, son."

He frowned at me, alert for irony, but I was not kidding around. The appellation had just slipped out. I was dead serious.

"I didn't say I was coming with you," he said. "I just said I'd think about it."

I nodded. I didn't trust myself to speak. Everything I wanted to tell him at that moment would just embarrass him, so I took it all outside, into the cold autumn night. Flushed with unspoken feelings, I craved the bite of frost on my skin. Mostly I felt overwhelmed with gratitude. How had this happened, that I had raised up a son into this world who could actually *think* about his decisions before he made them? No matter what Phoenix decided to do, I felt consoled knowing that while he might still break my heart, he wouldn't do it carelessly. Ocean was another matter. She was my little *pakiki*-head, stubborn and wild, but I figured we still had a couple of good years before she started to reject me. If I tried real hard, maybe I could grow up a little more before then, so it wouldn't hurt so much. Maybe, but I doubted it.

I cut across the garden. The greenhouse glowed like a large lantern, but tonight the luminosity seemed nervous, with a rhythmic flicker, like the flutter of an old film projector. As I approached, I saw it was the turning blades of the overhead fans, agitating the light and casting shadows on the drying racks of seeds below.

Geek's silhouette moved against the glass, a hulking alchemist bending over his benches, practicing his arts. He had moved back into the greenhouse, and ever since the potato harvest ended, he'd been spending all his time trying to organize the last of Lloyd and Momoko's seeds, getting them dried and processed, logged on to the Garden Web site, and packed for storage or distribution. Many seeds from the year's crop had been lost. Momoko had done what she could, and everyone had helped, but there had just been too much disruption. The Potato Party, the lawsuits, the time spent in jail, the birth and deaths and the bombing of the Spudnik—all these had taken up too much time, and the seed crop had suffered. Some seeds had rotted. Others had succumbed to fungal infections and molds or had been damaged by heat. Bacterial cankers afflicted the tomatoes. Downy mildew spoiled the spinaches. Farming requires a kind of stability that is incompatible with revolution, but even knowing this, Geek worked alone after everyone had gone to bed, pulping and washing, winnowing and separating seed from chaff. Saving what he could.

I opened the door and was greeted by the sweet smell of pot carried on the breezes stirring up inside. Geek looked up, startled. Then, seeing me, he looked away.

He was standing at a worktable shelling a large heap of beans, crushing the brittle pods between his fingers, and letting the chaff fall away as the beans dropped into an aluminum bowl below. They made little pinging sounds as they hit the metal. Every so often he would stop and inspect a few beans in the palm of his hand. Finally he held some out to show me. Small holes marred the surfaces of the seed coats.

"Weevils," he said bitterly. He broke one open with his thumbnail. The tip of the bean was hollow, and curled inside was a tiny grub. "The whole crop is infested. I'm going to try freezing them, but I don't think they're dry enough yet." He mashed the grub between his fingers. "These should have been threshed and dried weeks ago. I fucked up."

He picked up half a joint that was sitting on the edge of the workbench. He lit it and toked, then offered me some, but I shook my head. He shrugged and ground it out. His hands were covered with small lacerations from the sharp, brittle pods. He scooped up another handful and started crushing.

"It's not really your fault," I said. "There hasn't been a lot of time. . . ."

His fists were like a threshing machine, grinding the pods. "Wrong," he said. "It is very much my fault. And we don't *have* a whole lot of time."

"Geek . . ." I touched his arm.

He pulled away and turned on me. "Listen, I accept my responsibility, okay? I accept that the explosion may have been my fault. Human error, right? Or maybe not. I accept that, too. I accept that I will never, ever know. Do you know how painful that is? And it *still* doesn't change anything. Charmey still didn't have nearly enough time. Neither did Lloyd. He was just starting to catch on and figure out how to do stuff differently and to teach the rest of us, but then he died. And Momoko's knowledge is as good as dead now, too. How the fuck are we supposed to *learn* anything? How are we supposed to make any progress?"

I should have known not to push it—he was too stoned and upset to be rational—but I was feeling just a little bit positive that night, for the first time in so many months or years, and I wanted to help. So I said the most real and banal thing I could think of. "Learning takes time. You have to be patient."

He brought his fists down hard on the wooden table, making all the beans jump, and now he was mad, but pleading with me, too, desperate to make me understand.

"You're not hearing what I'm saying! *We don't have time!* Don't you see? It's all moving too fast. Life itself is on the line here, and unless we can slow down the machine, none of this is going to survive!"

He spread his arms out to encompass the contents of the greenhouse with the racks upon racks of drying seeds. "This is the blueprint of your mother's garden, Yumi. Imagine it in bloom, in all its incredible beauty and diversity and rich profusion, and now . . . *zap!* Picture it gone. Now picture the whole planet as a garden, teeming with millions upon millions of flowers and trees and fruits and vegetables and insects and birds and animals and weevils and us. And then, instead of all that magnificent, chaotic profusion, picture a few thousand genetically mutated, impoverished, barren, patented forms of corporately controlled germplasm."

He held out his hand, as though he were offering me a peach or a tennis ball, then shook it in front of my face. "*This* is how diminished, how pathetic the planet has become, that you can picture it like a cute little blue-green orb cupped in the palm of your hand. Like a logo or a fucking brand! Is this progress? I don't think so. It's bullshit, but that's all we hear— the same old stories, justifying the same old bad, exploitative, greedy, fucked-up behaviors. The same old excuses about why it's okay—no, it's economically beneficial—to raze the land and destroy animal habitat and exploit people and drive honking big SUVs to go shopping at the fucking mall. Nothing changes."

I backed away from him. "We do what we can—"

"Do we? Really?" He was bearing down on me, eyes bloodshot from the pot. "Well, that's funny, because I don't see that. I don't see you doing much of anything. Look at you, all wrapped up in your neat little stories, blaming your daddy and refusing to take responsibility for your life, spinning all these super justifications for your addictions and the crappy way you treat your kids and bombs that go off in the night—spending all your time feeling cynical and sorry for yourself while the whole fucking world is going to hell in a handbasket!"

"Listen," I said, getting angry now, "maybe that's so, but I don't go around exploiting people and using them to further my political agendas."

He stopped. He looked at me, aghast. "I use people?" he said. "Who?"

"Lloyd and Momoko for starters. And the kids. And me."

"I didn't *use* you!" he said. He bit off his words, and his shoulders slumped. "Forget it. This isn't about you or me. It isn't personal. It's much bigger."

"Geek . . ." I said.

"No," he said. "I'm stoned. Go away." He turned his back to me. His large shoulders started to twitch, and I realized he was crying.

"What is it?" I said, touching his arm.

He spun around, and his face was wet with tears behind his glasses. "I didn't use you! I *loved* you! All of you! I'm not like fucking Rhodes. For God's sake, Yumi, wake up! I'm not saying you needed to fall in love with me or anything, but can't you even tell the difference?"

I stood there and held his arm. I watched him cry. I didn't try to hug him or kiss his tears away because it wouldn't have been appropriate. Like he'd said, it wasn't personal. Somehow, though, I got it. The bigger picture.

Standing in my mother's greenhouse that night, surrounded by mounds of wormy seeds and chaff, I felt the brittle coat around my heart crack open at the hopeless beauty and fragility and loss of all that is precious on earth. He was right, we are responsible. Intimately connected, we're liable for it all. I had to take responsibility for myself and my kids, but also for Geek and Elliot, and for Charmey and Lloyd, too, and yet at the same time I realized I was powerless to forecast or control any of our outcomes.

But maybe that was the trick—to accept the responsibility and forgo the control? To love without expectation?

A paradox for sure, but such a relief.

toasted ℬ

You know how good-byes feel. How the air gets excited when all its ions and electrical charges are disrupted, first by the intent to leave and later by the leaving itself. Then, when the bodies move away through space, they create empty pockets where feelings get caught and eddy around in the vacuum, creating little vortices of relief or sadness or confusion. That's the way it felt on the day the Seeds left town.

We all turned out to say good-bye. Momoko was there, looking distraught and bewildered. For the last few days Geek had been helping her put the garden to bed, carefully digging under the rows and covering them with straw, while Frankie mulched the perennials and Lilith cut back the roses. Cass and Will would be moving into our house, but between the baby and the business of the farm, Cass wouldn't have time for much more than a small kitchen-garden plot with basic vegetables, and besides, she didn't have Momoko's green thumb. So putting the garden to bed was a sad business, knowing it would never wake up. Not fully. Not next spring. Not ever.

But there would be perennials. And volunteers. And the odd seeds, spit from the lips of children, or shit by birds or small animals, or blown by the wind.

Life is evanescent, but left to itself it rarely fails to offer some consolation.

Cass and Will had come to say good-bye. Of course they brought Tibet, who was far too young to understand that her father was leaving. After all, "father" was a concept that both she and Frankie were still too young to master. "Leaving," however, she got. The key event of her brief postpartum infant existence had been the abrupt departure of a pair of breasts and the steady heartbeat that defined the world. But there were other hearts and sources of sustenance, and true to her name, Tibet was a patient and long-suffering baby. She waved her hands in the air and fixed her gaze into some middle distance that was not quite Frankie. He didn't mind. He loved her even if she couldn't love him yet. Even if she couldn't quite focus on his not-quite-fatherly face. He'd be back in time. He'd teach her stuff to remember.

Will was talking with Geek, who was doing a last-minute check of the automotive fluids. Will was anticipating some problems selling off his NuLifes, Cass had told me. There were boycotts of genetically engineered products in Europe that were eroding the market, and prices were down. McCain, the largest Canadian potato processor, had decided to go GE free, and Frito-Lay had followed suit.

Will was saying to Geek, "I'm not going to plant them if people don't want to buy them."

He was ducking under the chassis with Geek. "Don't get me wrong, it's a solid potato, but I ran that data, and I can't see any appreciable gain in yields. I'm betting there won't be much savings in inputs either. Not in the end."

He was tailing Geek around the back of the Winnebago. "Heard there's an organic dairy moving in over by Idaho Falls that might mean a new market for hay. Thought I might check it out."

He was saying, "Philosophically speaking, I've got nothing against growing organic, you know. Problem is, you can't eat philosophy."

But Geek was running checks on all the systems of the Spudnik II and simply wasn't paying much attention.

411

So Will shrugged his shoulders and stated flat out, "It's not like any of us are in love with chemicals, but you can't operate three thousand acres any other way. If I had a choice, I'd farm without them."

Geek straightened his back and turned to face Will. "You got a choice, dude. We've all got choices. Lots of them. Every single second of the day we're making choices. You've just been making bad ones, is all."

What farmer wouldn't bristle? Cass was standing next to me holding Tibet, and I heard her draw in her breath. But Will held his tongue and just nodded. "Well," he said mildly, "we'll see."

Cass looked at me then, and her eyes widened.

I was hanging on to Poo and watching Phoenix and Ocean, running frequent checks on their whereabouts. I was looking for signs of imminent departure—a packed duffel bag, a furtive glance in my direction. But Phoenix was just hanging out with Frankie and Lilith, and then just with Lilith, kind of sidling up to her. With a shock I realized he was flirting. He had a crush. I held my breath and prayed.

May he abide in his righteous, childish scorn for members of the opposite sex . . .

No, it was too late for that.

May the son prove stronger than the mother.

Then I saw Lilith cock her head at Phoenix and say, "Well, are you coming?"

And, to my everlasting amazement, I watched my son shrug his boyish shoulders. "I can't leave my mom," he said. "She needs me."

Then Geek ambled over and gave me a powerful hug. "So maybe I'll see you in Pahoa," he said, and I really hoped he would.

Frankie took Tibet in his arms one last time before handing her back to Will, and his eyes got all red rimmed and his face so stricken with grief that everyone looked away and got real intent on saying good-byes, and there erupted a sudden confusion of kissing and hugging and handshakes that lasted until the Seeds piled into the Spudnik II. Then the doors closed, and the boxy, inelegant vessel of revolutionary zeal trundled out of the driveway and turned onto the road.

Phoenix stood next to me. I put my arm around his shoulder, and he let me.

"Thanks," I said. We watched the vehicle disappear behind the poplars, and then we went into the house to finish packing.

412

We left Liberty Falls in mid-November, a week or so before Thanksgiving. Cass asked us to stay. She wanted to make a big dinner and celebrate, but I found it a lot easier to be thankful outside of Liberty Falls and told her so. Cass hid her disappointment, as always, but I figured it was a lot easier now because she truly had so much to be thankful for. We would be staying in close touch, since, in a moment of weakness, I had volunteered to run the Garden of Earthly Delights Web site from Pahoa, and Cass would be distributing the seeds from Liberty Falls. We would all be meeting up in Hawaii come winter. Cass was delighted when I invited them. It would be the first trip she and Will had taken since their honeymoon, and they would need to buy new suitcases, she said.

"Geek might be there, too," I told her. We were having a pre-Thanksgiving dinner, with a turkey and vegetables from the garden and, at my insistence, a sampling of Momoko's many promiscuous squashes. "There's a spirulena algae farm over on the Kona side of the island that he's interested in visiting."

Will had been focused intently on his plate, scooping out the baked contents of something that was not quite Delicata, nor was it Sweetnut. Now he looked up. "The Hawaiian superfood," he said. "*Aloha Aina*. 'Love of the land,' right?"

I stared at him, astonished. "How do you know that?"

Will sat back, looking pleased with himself. "Just because I'm a spud farmer from Idaho doesn't mean I'm not interested in all that alternative . . . you know . . . stuff." He mashed a little of the squash with the back of his spoon and fed it to Tibet on the tip of his finger.

"Honey," Cass said, "she's not ready for solid food yet."

But Tibet smacked her lips and waved her arms enthusiastically.

"She likes it," Will said, beaming and feeding her some more. "Don't worry, Cassie. It's organic."

Momoko and I spent the last few days closing up the house.

"Just leave it," Cass said. "We'll take care of it. Just pack what Momoko needs. If you forget anything, I'll send it."

But Momoko didn't seem to need much at all. She put a few things in a small bag—a pair of pajamas and a toothbrush, a change of clothes and underwear, a bathing suit and a bathing cap, and the framed photograph of Lloyd standing next to a tiny Indian princess whose feather barely reached his belt buckle. And that was that.

"How about some of your favorite seeds?" I asked her. "Geek packed some up for you."

But Momoko shook her head. "Plenty of seeds in Hawaii," she said. "Lotsa nice plants already growing there."

"Well, what about your gardening tools and all your stuff?"

"Too hard work," she said. "I don't need to make garden in Hawaii. Everywhere is garden. It is enough."

So we left the house exactly as it was. I told Cass that if Momoko didn't want her things by the end of the year, she and Will could just throw out what they couldn't use, and when the time came to go, we just walked away, leaving everything, even all of Lloyd's handwritten labels, in place.

Well, almost all of the labels. The last thing Momoko did was to take a piece of packing tape and a label that said TOASTER and stick it to the back of Phoenix's jacket when he wasn't looking. Ocean started to giggle, but Momoko shut her up, and nobody else said anything either. We rode in the Quinns' Suburban to the airport, where we said good-bye to Cass and Will, and then we transferred to three different planes. We made it all the way to the Big Island before Phoenix even noticed.

"Cute," he said, peeling it off in the baggage claim at the Hilo airport. "I'm not a toaster."

And you know what Geek would have said to that—in this day and age, without a label, how can you tell?

414

epilogue: daddy's letter 𝒟

Seattle, November 30, 1999

Hey Tibet,

How ya doing, baby? So, we made it to Seattle, and the scene here is totally radical. I mean this thing is huge, and there's all these people who've taken to the streets to protest this fucked-up thing called the WTO, which you don't know about yet, but unfortunately you probably will. And what's cool is that there's workers and environmentalists and anarchists and direct action factions, all pulling together to take back the power. I'll write you more about this shit, but before that, I want to tell you about how we got here.

At first it was just more flat farmland, and, I mean, look around you. Boring, right? But then we headed north and suddenly we were on this totally gnarly road with curves that wound up and up into the Cascade Mountains. It had just snowed, all white against the blue sky, and there were these crazy trees that were the hugest living things I've ever seen.

We got to a rest stop—it was like a campground in the middle of a park with bathrooms—and I was pretty ragged out from being in the vehicle, so I took my board and skated around, and the next thing, I'm standing on this beach next to the most awesome lake, plunked right down there in the middle of the mountains. And it was so pretty and sparkly, and the water was an intense blue-green color—Geek said it came from glaciers—and I'll tell you, there was absolutely nothing around it. I mean, there were trees and stuff, but nothing *human* at all.

415

And this next part that happened was probably on account of the dube we'd been smoking, but I was just sitting there next to the lake with my hands in this freezing water, and I started thinking about how Charmey would have totally gotten off on how pretty it was, and I started bawling like a baby—no offense—just missing her and wishing she could be there with me to see it.

Of course, it's a personal thing—Charmey was really into nature, and I prefer asphalt—but suddenly I understood why I'm doing all these political actions. It's because I gotta make sure there's still some nature around for you when you grow up, in case you decide you dig it, too. Geek took a picture of the lake, and I promise one of these days I'll take you back there so you can see for yourself, and we'll camp on the bank and look at all that sparkly water together.

For now, I'm just stoked to be back in the city, cruising around. The shit is going down in Seattle for real. I'm sending you a badass picture of me that was taken yesterday, on the first day of the Revolution. I hope you like it. And that's the report from the front. It's a class war, Tibet, and we're fighting for the planet, and your daddy's gotta go kick some ass. I'll write more later. Sayonara, baby. I love you.

    Frank

Cass folded the letter and slipped it back into the envelope. Frankie's daughter was lying on a blanket in the middle of the floor, playing with her toes and watching Cass intently.

"You like it when I read his letters, don't you?" Cass said.

In the envelope were two photographs. Cass took them out. One was a snapshot of a glacial lake, azure and sparkling, set high up in the mountains. The other was a picture of Frankie in Seattle. He was standing on his skateboard, dressed all in black and carrying a placard. The lower part of his face was hidden by a gas mask, but from his eyes you could tell he was smiling. Looking more closely, Cass could read the slogan, drawn in black spray paint on the sign:

**RESISTANCE
IS
FERTILE!**

She held the picture up in front of the baby's face. "Look, Betty," she said. "It's Daddy Frank."

Betty flailed her arms and legs. Her tiny fist closed around the edge of the photo, and she waved it back and forth for a while, then she put a corner into her mouth.

"That's right," Cass said, gently prying the picture away from her and replacing it with a pacifier. "Daddy's going to save the world."

Acknowledgments ✑

I would like to thank the potato farmers, the potato breeders, the plant pathologists, the seed savers, the wild potato collectors, the newspapermen, the molecular biologists, the agricultural extension agents and the environmental activists who took time to answer my amateur's questions. I am grateful for the wealth of information these kind people so generously provided, and assert that if mistakes were made in this book, they are entirely my own.

Many thanks to Dan Jason, Jack Kloppenburg, Sascha Scatter, Sara and Jane Schultz, and John Stauber for their wise advice and wonderful stories.

I am especially indebted to J. L. Hudson, Seedsman, whose annual ethnobotanical catalogue sows a wealth of inspiration, as well as to Michael Pollan, whose article "Playing God in the Garden" in the *New York Times* planted the particular idea that germinated into these pages.

Thanks to Molly Friedrich for her sustaining faith in the seed of this book. Thanks to Susan Petersen Kennedy for casting her light upon it and causing it to grow. Thanks to Karen Murphy for her careful weeding and pruning. And special, heartfelt thanks to Carole DeSanti. A few words at the back of a book can never express how deeply I appreciate her skill as an editor, her insight as a colleague, and her generosity as a friend. Without her, there would be far less joy in these acts of cultivation.

Thanks to all my friends who read early drafts and offered invaluable critique, and in particular to Marina Zurkow for being near and dear.

Thanks to my parents for loving and supporting me and for being in every way different from the parents I invented for this story. And finally, thanks to Oliver Kellhammer for exemplifying the extreme patience and love required of a gardener and a husband.

Thanks to all who save and plant. May your gardens grow.